I0838298

# THE VEILED HEIR

# THE VEILED HEIR

S.T. FERNANDEZ

This is a work of fiction. Names, characters, places, and incidents either are the product of the author's imagination or are used fictitiously. Any resemblance to actual persons, living or dead, events, or locales is entirely coincidental.

Copyright © 2024 by S.T. Fernandez

All rights reserved. No part of this book may be reproduced or used in any manner without written permission of the copyright owner except for the use of quotations in a book review.
For more information, address:
stfernandezwrites@gmail.com.

Published by Azalea Press

First paperback edition July 2024

Book design by Krafigs Design
Map by Samantha Gase
Taíno Language Citation: The Modern Taíno Dictionary from Jatibonicu Taino Tribal Nation | Higuayahua: Taíno of the Caribbean
Edited by Ramona Mihaj
Formatting by S.T. Fernandez

ISBN 979-8-9886397-4-9 (paperback)
ISBN 979-8-9886397-3-2 (ebook)
ISBN 979-8-9886397-5-6 (hardcover)

www.stfernandez.com

For my Dad. I hope you're having a blast beyond the Veil...

# **TRIGGER/CONTENT WARNINGS**
### (THIS BOOK IS INTENDED FOR READERS 18 AND OLDER)

Attempted Murder
Bullying
Death
Decapitation
Depression
Gore
Grief (Parent, Spouse)
Human Exploitation by Fae
Kidnapping
Murder
Physical Abuse
Profanity
Sexual Assault
Sexually Explicit Scenes
Torture
Violence

PLEASE READ WITH CARE

# PRONUNCIATION GUIDE

**Airelandia**: eye-reh-LAHN-dee-uh
**Akani**: Ah-KAH-nee
**Anacaona**: Ah-nah-cah-OH-nah
**Atlantis**: at-LAN-tis
**Baba**: bah-BAH
**Bibi**: bee-BEE
**Borike'n**: Boh-REE-keh-en
**Calichi**: kah-LEE-chee
**Cibao**: SEE-bow
**Cobo**: KOH-boh
**Corenathia**: Kor-reh-NAH-thee-uh
**Earthos**: ER-thohs
**Fotuto**: Foh-TOO-toh
**Guake'te**: gooah-KEH-teh:
**Guali**: GOOAH-lee
**Guaraguao**: gooah-rah-gooah-OW
**Hekiti**: heh-KEE-tee
**Jimagua**: Hee-MAH-gooah
**Jujo**: JOO-joh
**Lomeage**: low-meh-AUJ
**Maboya**: mah-BOY-yah
**Nanichi**: nah-NEE-chee
**Sabana**: Sah-BAH-nah
**Shingu**: Sheen-goo
**Wylemei**: WHEYE-leh-may

# CHARACTER NAME PRONUNCIATION GUIDE

**Asherah Delmar**: ah-SHER-uh   del-MAR
**Atabey**: ah-tah-BAY
**Aurelio Martenos Anthysius**: Ahoo-REH-lee-oh   MAR-teh-nohs   an-THEE-see-uhs
**Asu**: ah-SOO
**Ayi Jiba**: ah-YEE   HEE-bah
**Behuko Delmar**: beh-HOO-koh
**Braeliah Morvyn**: bray-LEE-uh   MOR-vin
**Cathan Rosahan Delmar**: Kay-thuhn   ROH-sah-hahn   del-MAR
**Chrissy Baker**: KRIS-see   BAY-ker
**Dax Lumeya**: daks   loo-MAY-uh
**Draevyn Eliron**: DRAY-vin   el-er-RON
**Ezra**: ez-ruh
**Fynlor Velafyn**: FIN-lor VEH-luh-fin
**John Adams**: jon   AH-duhms
**Kane Ruema**: kayn   roo-EH-muh
**Laenah Karaya**: LAY-nuh   kuh-REYE-uh
**Loma**: LOH-mah
**Lux Zarlonia Nacan**: luhks   zar-LOH-nee-uh   Nuh-CAHN
**Mayana Yaralyn**: mah-YAH-nuh   YAH-rah-lin
**Melysah Velafyn**: meh-LIS-uh   VEH-luh-fin
**Myles Anthysius**: Mahyels   an-THEE-see-uhs
**Neleah Delmar**: neh-LEH-uh   del-MAR
**Reneah Diaz**: reh-NEH-uh   DEE-ahz
**Roarvyn Syles**: ROR-vin   Seye-els
**Samani Eliron**: sah-MAH-nee   el-er-RON
**Sessi Nacan**: SEH-see   Nuh-CAHN
**Shaegana**: shay-GAH-nuh
**Silas**: SEE-lahs
**Zoriato Eliron**: zoh-ree-AH-toh   el-er-RON

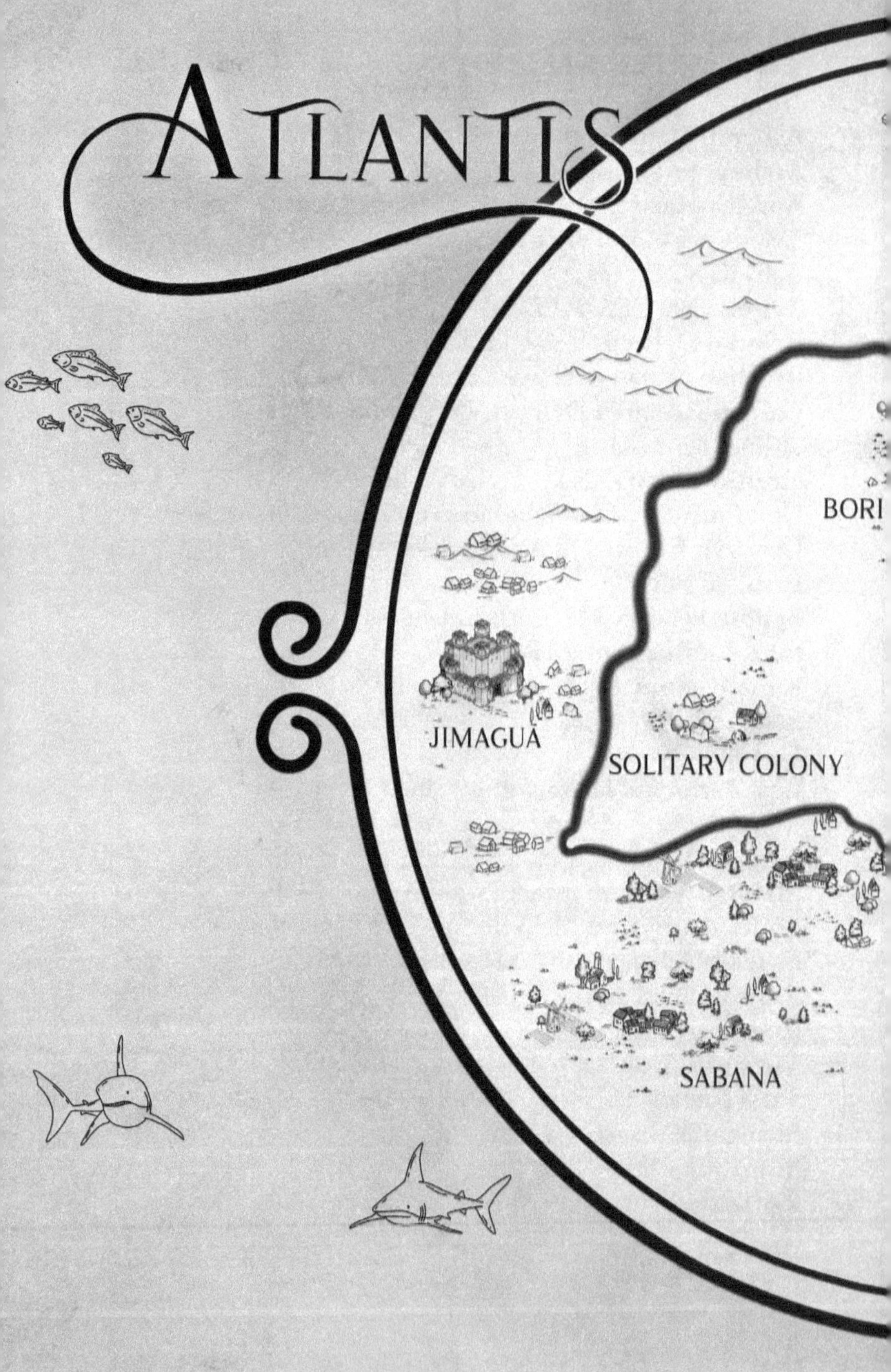

ATLANTIS
BORI
JIMAGUA
SOLITARY COLONY
SABANA

HI
CIBOA
UNIVERSITY
PALACE
PALACE
GARDENS
PLE PARK
GUARDIAN
TRAINING
FACILITY
GATES
OF ATLANTIS
LE OF ATABEY
OTUTO
DRAEVYN'S
CAVERN

# Chapter 1

Trying to calm my mind in the brutal Florida heat was like trying to read a book with someone banging on a drum next to my head. I tipped my head back, my lids closing against the sun's rays that scorched my tanned skin as I bobbed on the water—my abdomen tightening with the effort to keep steady. The warm summer breeze crested across the waters of the Atlantic, whipping my long, black hair behind my shoulders. Gentle waves pressed against my board as the palm trees hissed with the winds of change that had inevitably arrived, change that was now neatly packed into twenty-three boxes, one suitcase, and a toiletry bag that would be ready by morning.

The high-pitched squeal of children's laughter interrupted my moment of zen, and my eyes snapped open—my gaze landing on the group of people snorkeling a few paces away.

Not just any people.

Tourists.

Lots of them.

While they'd mostly followed the instructions I'd bellowed over the deafening roar of the boat's engine, it was clear most of them hadn't paid attention. Water periodically shot from their snorkel tubes like whales breaching the ocean's surface. It was difficult for them to keep their heads down long enough to catch the various fish species that populated the John Pennekamp Coral Reef State Park in Key Largo. No matter. I won't have to bellow any more instructions after today.

I reached down to cup the warm water and splashed it over my arms to cool my skin. Just thirteen more minutes, according to my Garmin; probably eleven since I'd checked about two minutes ago. The back of my neck prickled with awareness, prompting me to swivel around—my gaze catching on John Adams, the captain of our snorkel excursion tour boat. Deeply tinted aviator glasses rested upon the arrogant blade of his nose. His dark brown close-cropped hair remained flawless, and dark stubble shadowed his shapely jaw. The chiseled lines of his alluring mouth—one that had me desperate to move out of the friend zone this summer—formed a grin.

"Asshole," I murmured.

I could see John's shoulders shake with laughter even from this distance—quite the mouth reader, that one.

*Watch the tourists*, he said. *It will be fun*, he said. I resisted the urge to roll my eyes. The only reason John insisted I be the one who monitored our well-meaning customers was because I was a freak of nature. At least that's what I'd always called myself. My co-workers called me their good luck charm. The social media followers across Snorkida Shore Excursions' pages called me a viral sensation.

I'd rather do my job and be none of those things.

With my feet dangling in the water, I watched the man from Wisconsin barrel around again, attempting to right himself. Wisconsin's son popped his head out of the water and waved his hands in the air. "Chriiiiiiiiiiiiiis! I found one! I found one! Come quick!" he yelled.

In all her long-legged swimmer glory, Chrissy leapt from the boat's stern and gracefully swam the distance with minimal effort. Her Snorkida one-piece clung to her torso like a second skin as her body disappeared momentarily below. Despite the snorkel gear in hand, her muscular arms peeled through the water with natural strokes. The four years on the University of Miami swim team were precisely why I'd recommended her in the first place. While Chrissy Baker didn't have a marine biologist bone in her body, her bubbly personality played right into the hands of Snorkida's customers.

"What did you find, Sam?"

"The brightly colored one," he replied with an adolescent croak in his voice, his arms working feverishly to hold his body afloat.

Chrissy laughed. "They're all brightly colored, silly."

I could see the color bloom on the young man's pale cheeks from where I floated. "Right. Well. Um. The blue and yellow one."

"Ah, you're talking about a Blue Tang. The one with the yellow stripe?"

Sam pointed at her. "Yup, that's the one."

She put on one of her signature Chrissy smiles that had the hearts of men, both young and old, desperate to know her. "Then let's see if we can find it again, shall we?"

*Damn, she really knows how to work 'em. That's another five-star review on TripAdvisor.*

Chrissy fastened the snorkel gear skillfully over her ash-blond hair and dipped below water, searching for the fish she'd challenged the customers to find. She was notorious for claiming these fish were rare, but they were everywhere in these waters. "It's an attempt to make their experience special," she'd say, and judging by the number of people joining our excursion on any given day, I had no doubt that it was indeed working.

"Ash!"

I twisted around to John. A crease dipped below the top of his aviators as he pointed behind me. I wheeled back around, blocking out the sun with a raised hand. A hint of a fin slowly cut through the water a couple of dozen yards away.

It was heading in the direction of the tourists.

Without a second thought, I paddled feverishly for the boundary of the snorkel area—my board gliding on top of the surface. The muscles at my shoulders and biceps burned with each stroke. I instantly regretted packing those last few boxes before my shift. I'd have packed tomorrow before breakfast with my parents, but my driving desire for preparedness won over.

As I reached the perimeter, I bolted upright, willing air into my lungs. The fin slowed, slinking lazily back and forth in front of me.

*Come on. Prove them wrong. Come at me.*

But the shark did no such thing.

It transversed back and forth within ten yards from where I perched, my toned legs dangling below the water's surface in a tempting invitation.

*So, we're going to do this dance again, are we?*

Just when I thought this stand-off would last well after my shift was over, water splashed across my face, causing me to flinch. The shark retreated like it was being chased. I let out a long sigh. "They always do that," I muttered to myself. I allowed one final scan of my surroundings before paddling back to the boat.

The final guest climbed the ladder that dipped into the water at the stern. As I grabbed a rung, Chrissy stood above me with her hands on her hips, smirking. "Way to save the day, Aquawoman."

I huffed a laugh as I climbed. "How fitting."

"You've certainly earned your happy hour slash celebratory farewell beer." Chrissy pulled me over the final rung of the ladder, and we began gathering the fins, goggles, and vests that littered the floor. My mind raced—as always—desperately trying to make sense of what happened as the engine roared to life.

*Perhaps the little sharky was just used to humans?*

It was a lie I greatly wanted my pulsing heart to believe.

With the equipment safely tucked away and Chrissy off to entertain the guests, I stomped up the stairwell to the top deck and slid into my usual seat beside John—his rough hands held firmly on the wheel. He spared a glance at me, and the corner of his mouth twisted into a smirk.

"Don't say it."

"I haven't said anything," John said with mock innocence dripping in his tone. When he bit his lower lip, I swatted his upper arm. He broke out in hysterical laughter that drifted over the sound of the engine. "I'm sorry. I'm sorry. It's just so weird."

I shook my head. "Don't remind me."

"But really cool at the same time, Ash." He gazed blankly into the distance, as if replaying the incident in his mind. "Every. Single. Time."

I shifted in my seat. I should have felt flattered by the awe in his voice, but confusion harbored that space. All my life, the most dangerous ocean predators seemed to avoid me. An unspeakable kinship had become the motivation to major in marine biology. Perhaps it was a kinship I'd been imagining, but as a semi-pro surfer, I'd witnessed firsthand the behavior of sea creatures when I was in their presence. I'd never revealed my obsession to anyone, but the 'why' of it all held my fascination in a death grip. Testing my limits always gave me an adrenaline rush. And I'd become addicted to it.

An old college memory came to mind.

My classmates and I had been invited to participate in a dive. There had been no shortage of sharks in the water that day, which was perfect for what I'd been eager to test. I recalled my classmate's ashen face and could still hear her screaming in the water around her mouthpiece.

I tested the limits with a raw piece of meat that I had stealthily brought into the water. I can still see the crimson blood drifting into the water from the bait that was gripped tightly in my hand. I remembered the great white shark that had emerged from the shadows. It had circled me a few times, making no move to eat the meat...or my arm. And I could still feel my heart nearly coming out of my chest. After a several-minute standoff between us, I abandoned the meat and swam for the surface, but not before I witnessed the shark return to devour the bait I'd left behind. After that, most of my classmates thought I was some sort of shark whisperer.

To myself, I would always be Asherah Rey Delmar, a freak of nature. To my classmates, surf pros, and co-workers, I'd been nicknamed the queen of the sea creatures. And I'd made it my life's mission to find out why.

# Chapter 2

I smoothed out my baby-blue Instant *Mermaid Just Add Water* tank that fluttered over my light denim shorts. Since the boat docked a little later than usual, leaving me with little time to get ready, the damp strands of my hair dried in long black waves down my back. I had just enough time for a quick in-and-out shower and a final check of my suitcase, and I was off to my favorite dive.

The music blared within The Blue Fin and carried over the crunch of gravel under my flip-flops. Tucked away from The Overseas Highway, the local joint was a cherished spot for the residents of Key Largo to catch a cheap bite to eat and a cool drink after a long day at sea, one I was surely going to miss. The wooden steps protested with every upward move I made, their familiar creaks echoing as I climbed towards the entrance. Wide-open doors and windows invited in the breeze, causing the triangular beer flags to dance on lines above. To my delight, only a few people milled about the space—my crew included. The low hum of conversation met my ears, along with the clink of pool balls and the chirp coming from the electronic dartboards. The scores of locals and brave tourists who frequented the dive were blissfully missing. This worked in my favor since I didn't care for large crowds, preferring to avoid them whenever possible. One of the benefits of working in the tourism industry? Most of the business occurs on the weekends, leaving places like grocery stores and shopping plazas less crowded during the week. It was my favorite time to venture into town.

Glancing in the corner by the electronic dart boards, I counted a couple of pitchers of beer already flowing at the table my co-workers occupied. As I approached the bar, my gaze snagged on two men with dark gray hoodies hanging off their broad shoulders, their heads hanging low. It was unusual for anyone to wear a sweatshirt in the Florida summer heat, but perhaps they didn't want to be bothered, something I deeply empathized with.

I leaned on the bar, a smile spreading on my face as I beheld Bobby. He was the best bartender on this side of The Keys; his bright yellow *Salty Beach* cut-off shirt said everything you needed to know about the man. He looked up from the glass he'd been drying, the corner of his mouth hidden behind a sandy blond mustache lifting in return. "Decided to grace us with your presence, Your Highness?"

From my periphery, I saw the two men drag their gazes up from their frosted pints—their dark brows dipping as they gazed upon me from beneath their hoods.

*Weird.*

"Only on the slow nights, my valiant drink maker," I answered.

Bobby let out a hearty laugh with a shake of his head—the tips of his sandy blond hair falling just past his bushy brow. With his peppered five o'clock shadow, he was irresistible to the local ladies who loved to show appreciation for a good-looking older man. It was precisely why his tip jar stayed full to the brim even during the week. "Will you be partaking in the pitcher ritual, or shall I make you something special to drink this evening?" he asked.

I glanced behind and squinted. The pale-yellow line of the beer dipped to the bottom of the last pitcher on the table. "Pitcher ritual. Better hook me up with another round and a cup. It seems they're pretty thirsty tonight."

"Coming right up." He reached for a clean pitcher on the shelf just beside the tap and began filling it with my favorite local microbrew.

I perched on the weathered wooden barstool before me and chanced a glance at the two men again. Their gazes were still cast in my direction. The hairs on the back of my neck began to rise. Pushing off the footrest, I scooted back on the stool and leaned forward, placing my elbow on the bar top. My chin came to rest in the center of my palm as I glared right back at them. "Like what you see?"

Even with his face covered in shadow, the man closest to me gave a faint quirk of the lips, his pearly white teeth gleaming against the neon signs on the wall. I narrowed my eyes.

"Everything okay, Ash?"

My body nearly jumped off my barstool. I swiveled around to John, who glared at the men with equal interest—his arm came to rest on my shoulder.

The men turned their attention to each other. They polished off the remaining beer in their pints and dropped a crumpled twenty on the bar. I lifted a brow as they headed for the exit; I could have sworn I caught a faint sooty smell. Unlike an aggressive tobacco aroma, it resembled the scent of a fierce forest fire.

John's eyes bore into their backs till the darkness of the parking lot enveloped them. "Who the hell wears a hoodie in the middle of summer?"

A small wave of beer splashed over the side of the pitcher Bobby placed before us. "You're asking that question while you live and breathe alongside the crazies in Florida?" he quipped as he deftly wiped the spilled contents and added a frosty pint glass at its side.

John nodded. "Fair point." He carefully reached for the pitcher. "Put this one on my tab, Bobby."

"I got it." I grabbed my pint glass and hopped off my stool.

"I insist." John's panty-melting smile emerged. "My lucky charm doesn't pay for the drinks." I froze as he leaned down softly, pressing a smooth-lipped kiss on my cheek. I could feel the blood rise to meet the stubble that gently brushed against my skin.

*There he goes again, toeing that line.*

John pulled back, his gunmetal eyes glinting mischievously as a soft flutter of butterflies erupted in my stomach. For all the years we'd known each other, he'd never verbalized his feelings to me, something I'd often pondered. Beyond the obvious attraction, I wasn't sure about my feelings toward him either. I simply chucked it up to his flirtatious nature and nothing more, neither of us wanting to ruin a friendship that had been going on for more than two decades. We'd been childhood friends since before we took our first steps. His parents had lovingly welcomed me into their home to play, have dinner, or watch movies on multiple occasions.

My parents?

Not so much.

"The dart board awaits you, my talented dart queen," he said, holding out his arm for me.

"Great, maybe you'll manage to beat me this time." Giving John a warm smile, I looped my arm through his awaiting elbow.

My thoughts drifted back to my parents as we glided to the dartboards, John skillfully keeping every drop of beer in the pitcher gripped in his hand. Cathan and Neleah Delmar were never cruel to John. They were just very cautious with him. After a few awkward hangouts at my house during our teenage years, we decided to walk the few blocks in the other direction to hang out at John's house more often than not. It was almost like my parents didn't want to lead John on, or encourage him to think he was good enough for their daughter. They'd all but said that to me, which I'd never repeat to my friend. And while my parents never asked me how I felt about John, I assumed they could guess my affections. I'd bet my bottom dollar they were banking on my blossoming feelings for John fizzling out when I left for college. For the most part, they did. I'd given up hope that John would cross the line long ago. Perhaps some semblance of those feelings remained, even though it wasn't entirely fair to him with the next chapter of my life about to begin. I'd wasted little time replying to the offer letter for an entry-level marine biologist position in San Diego. It was my dream job, after all. I cared enough for John not to foster my affections, but the wall I'd been trying to erect all summer was crumbling under the weight of my curiosity about his feelings for me.

As we approached, I noticed Chrissy's baby-blue eyes momentarily catching on our linked arms. It was over in a second as she recovered and smiled brightly. "Finally here to show me up?"

I let my arm fall away from John's as he carefully set the pitcher on the table. "Of course. Hopefully, you've been kicking everyone's ass," I said, giving her a quick hug.

Chrissy snorted. "Hardly, but now that you're here, you can be my partner and make me look good."

Chrissy and I teamed up against John and his best friend Ralph, who—per usual—avoided eye contact with me and provided clipped one-word answers when I tried to engage in conversation with him. For the life of me, I couldn't figure out why Ralph acted like this. I realized long ago that it was best to ignore him since everyone else seemed to like me just fine.

The rounds of darts grew, and the beers flowed as the night peeled on. It wasn't until a little after midnight that I took a break at one of the empty high-top tables. My anxiety hummed at a simmering boil, but the crowd of people trickling into the bar hadn't escaped my notice. Clusters of people snatched the remaining tables around us. Unfortunately, no amount of alcohol could keep the rising tension from my body. I couldn't recall a time when this exact reaction hadn't occurred. Perhaps it was why I preferred sea creatures to people.

My gaze snagged on Chrissy sitting across the way. As usual, Chrissy chatted it up with everyone around them. I'd always admired her ability to make friends with complete strangers. When she dragged me to college parties, I'd always take my usual position by a wall and watch on as Chrissy fluttered her way through every social group in the room. But she'd never forget to flutter over to me and spend some quality time people-watching with her bestie. It had always brought a smile to my face, just as it did now. One couldn't help but love her. It was why, when Chrissy voiced that she needed an after-college break, I suggested she join me in The Keys instead of returning home to Minnesota. We found a granny flat for her to rent that same day.

My observations continued as Chrissy hopped off her stool and settled between John's open legs, her arm resting across his shoulder. She was well on her way to being drunk, as evidenced by the octave at which she spoke. But I froze when John's arm came around Chrissy's waist, pulling her into him. I couldn't take my eyes off the gesture. One moment, they threw their heads back in laughter. And the next moment, John's lips were on Chrissy's. My mouth fell open as whistles and catcalls sounded from the neighboring table.

"Ring the bell, Bobby! Ring the damn bell!" Ralph called.

Bobby chuckled and gave the bell on the side of a bar a few good tugs, the ding peeling through the room. Everyone roared with more cheers and whistles as John and Chrissy smiled into their kiss.

"Finally!" Ralph exclaimed. He spared a glance in my direction with something resembling pity, which I didn't care for. I snapped my jaw shut and quickly plastered on a smile. Internally, though, the numbness settled like a door slammed in my face. Perhaps it just had. But an entirely different awareness began to fill the numb space.

Relief.

I'd be mulling over 'the why' behind that particular feeling on my walk home.

Ready to make my break away, I hopped off my stool

and quietly gathered my keys and wristlet from the group table.

"You out of here?" John asked from behind me.

*Do not show your emotions.* I spun on my heels with a smile. "Yeah, you know crowds aren't my thing."

"You okay?" he asked, a worried expression marring his face.

It was unclear whether he was asking because of the growing crowd and my rising anxiety or the public display of affection between him and Chrissy. If I were being honest, I might've noticed the signs of something budding between the two of them these past few weeks. Perhaps I let my own unrequited feelings get in the way. "Yeah, yeah. I'm good. Don't worry about me." I thumbed over my shoulder. "I'm going to walk home. Get some fresh air and calm my nerves."

"Let her get home before she has a nervous break-down, John," Ralph said from behind him, darts in hand for their next game. Chrissy swatted him on the arm as I lifted a brow at him.

John leaned into my ear. "No. I meant…are you okay…with me and Chrissy?"

He and Chrissy. Okay. He wanted to talk about this like…right now. I nodded. "Sure. Of course. You two look great together."

He scrunched his nose. "We look great together?"

"Yeeeaaah," I replied, ending the word in a drag. "Is there something wrong with looking great together?"

"No. But. It's just—"

"It's okay, John. Truly. I'm not sure why you need it, but you have my approval if that's what you're looking for." My shoulder rose in a half-shrug. "You two are my best friends. I care for both of you, and you both de-serve to be happy. Besides, it's kinda nice knowing you'll be caring for one another while I'm in California. And look at the bright side; two-for-one video chats save me a bunch of time and effort repeating myself."

He glanced at his shoes briefly before the corner of his mouth quirked. "You'll always be my lucky charm, you know that?"

I rolled my eyes. "Yes, yes. But you pay me to be your lucky charm, so there is that. And your lucky charm may ask for a raise next summer if you're not careful."

John raised his palms in the air. "Duly noted. On that note, have a good night, Ash."

"Night, John."

I glanced behind him, and a panicked expression flittered across Chrissy's beautiful features. I blew her kisses with a wave. She beamed with delight and what looked like a dash of relief. That's the thing about keeping your secret feelings for someone under lock and key, even from your best friend. The denials slip off the tongue so easily after a while that it's not Chrissy's fault she believed mine when she had asked about my feelings for John. In fairness, there's no way she truly could have known how I felt about him. There was a more in-depth conversation that would happen between us at some point, but my growing anxiety put that on hold. I had to get out of there.

I gave the group one last wave before forcing myself through the growing crowd, bodies pushing and jostling my much smaller form. The anxiety had my lungs in a vice. As I finally reached the exit, my shoulders sagged with relief; the long breath I'd held blew from my lips.

I should have expected it: John and Chrissy.

Chrissy had a natural femininity about her, while I was a tomboy of sorts. Add to it that I was laser-focused on my studies, future career, surfing, and not much else;

it was a recipe for relationship disaster. The fact that I was an introvert didn't help either. John told me once that my quietness came across as snobbery, but I didn't know how to fix it.

A motorcycle roared to life as I stepped gingerly through the gravel parking lot, careful not to get pieces stuck between my feet and my flip-flops. Once I was safely on the sidewalk, I shook my leg to dispel a few pieces. The cooler yet humid night air entered my lungs on an inhale, and a sense of peace settled with each step I took toward home—tumultuous thoughts fading in my head like wisps of mist lost to the night.

A rustling to the right captured my attention. A shadow emerged just beyond the car in the driveway of the house I'd just passed, and the memory of the two hooded men came to mind. Strange people weren't new in Florida. They were the State mascot, after all. But something about those men felt…off.

When another shadow appeared beside the other, every muscle in my body went rigid. I recognized them immediately. It was as if my thoughts had summoned them.

The two men strolled nonchalantly in my direction, eyeing me from underneath their hoods like a pair of cats catching a mouse. I nearly choked on a gasp when a sound pitched from my pocket. I quickly reached for my phone, accepting the call without taking my eyes off the two men.

"Hello?" I answered. There was no hiding the shake in my voice. The men had stopped in their tracks as I answered the call.

"Asherah. Darling. Where are you? We've been calling you for hours," my mother asked.

"Hey, Mom. I was at The Blue Fin with my co-workers. The music must have drowned out my ringtone. I'm a few houses down."

"She says she's a few houses down," my mother said in a hushed whisper. I heard my father's murmur in the background, and my brow reached for my hairline.

"I thought you weren't coming home till tomorrow?" I asked as the men began to move.

*Don't just stand there, you idiot!* I stepped backward on unsteady feet, my eyes glued on them.

"Change of plans. Sweetie, your father's walking down the street to meet you." The sound of the front door slamming against the frame carried through the phone.

Usually, I'd protest. I was a twenty-three-year-old grown woman in between living arrangements, but since these strange men were closing in on me, I welcomed the rescue. "Sounds good, Mom." I desperately tried to hide the trembling from my voice but failed miserably.

"Are you okay, my love?" *Damn, her motherly intuition is good.* The men edged toward the bottom of the closest driveway, now only a few yards away. My backward steps quickened, and I prayed that nothing in the walkway would cause me to fall.

"Sher!" My head twisted at the sound of my father's voice. Cathan Delmar careened down the sidewalk at breakneck speed, his muscular arms pumping. He slowed when he reached my side and bent at the waist, his dark hair falling to his brow as his chest rose and fell with hasty breaths. "Everything…" *Huff. Huff.* "Okay?" More huffing. Big inhale.

My shoulders sagged with relief as I patted his back. "Still got it, old man."

"I am…" slower huff, "not…" deep inhale, "old." He rose, resting his hands on his hips. "I just haven't full-out sprinted like that since—"

"The 90s?" I supplied.

Dad's lips pursed. "Very funny, daughter of mine." His gaze traveled behind me. His nostrils flared on an inhale, and his expression slid into a frown. I could have sworn I heard a growl rise from his throat. I wheeled around, and my mouth slackened. There was not a soul to be found behind us. The street was entirely empty.

"There were two men just there," I breathed, pointing to the driveway. "Some weirdos that were at the bar."

Dad squinted at the darkness beyond the streetlight's warm glow, then placed an arm around my shoulder. "Come on. Let's get back to the house."

For the first time since I was a child, I welcomed the refuge of my father's arms, but couldn't shake the feeling that we were still being watched.

# Chapter 3

My feet marched over the gravel of our front drive leading up to our two-story home. The first level—reserved for cars and storm surges—remained quiet in the dead of night. The house was likened to a beacon, with its white paneled exterior reflecting the moonlight. I could make out the kitchen light in the second-story window toward the back of the home, and I briefly caught Dad's worried expression as we ascended the stairs. My growing sense of unease climbed. I had an inkling that this was beyond the men who followed me home from the bar, as was evident by how he entered the house in a sort of panic.

"It's all right, Dad. I'm home in one piece," I reassured him. Shutting the front door behind me, I followed him down the hall, but a strange feeling had me twisting around. Something invisible to the eye but detectable to my senses cascaded down from the ceiling to the baseboard. I blinked a few times and looked around but came back with nothing. Without any further hesitation, I hurried after him.

Dad sighed. "It's not all right, Sher."

My jaw opened to protest, but went slack when I saw who was in the living room. "Myles?"

Myles Anthysius, my mother's long-time assistant, drew his gaze from her, his expression morphing from anxious to warm. "Hello, Asherah. It's a pleasure to see you again."

I couldn't recall the last time I'd seen him, but his perfectly combed, peppered brown hair, sculpted dark brows, rich brown eyes, and impeccable dress still all looked the same. He reminded me of a butler, only hotter. I could swear he didn't age, but it was hard to tell since I didn't encounter him often. Myles preferred to draw a firm line between business and personal. I'd seen him in passing on occasion after school when work carried over into family time.

Whenever we had family time, that is.

Mom didn't look up at us. It was as if we hadn't entered the room. She just continued to pace back and forth in front of my father's favorite gray sectional, the fluorescent light emanating from the kitchen revealing the dark circles under her eyes and the crease between her brows. Her long legs stepped with effortless grace, and her long, black hair flowed behind her. She looked oddly out of place with her black pencil skirt and pearly white blouse amongst all the nautical decor of their home.

I couldn't help but take a moment to admire her beauty. Neleah Delmar was a successful businesswoman who was constantly absent from my life for weeks at a time, leaving Dad the task of raising me. While she was there during the most important times of my life—when a girl needed her mother the most—I couldn't help but feel her absence growing up. The effort she made to call every evening before bed just to let me know how much she loved me was always appreciated. I tried desperately not to hold it against her, but truth be told, I missed having my mother present for my day-to-day life.

I stepped into her peripheral, and Mom's emerald green eyes shifted to me, her shoulders sagging. "Asherah. Darling. I was so worried." She wrapped me in a tight embrace. "Those men didn't do anything to you, did they? Did they approach you?"

I froze. "How did you know about the men at the bar?"

She slowly pulled out of our embrace, her face turning serious. "I'm afraid that is a longer story, one you deserve to hear. But there is no time. We need to leave."

I lifted my palms in the air. "Wait. Wait. What?" I whipped my head around to Dad. "What's going on?"

"Cathan, there is no time for this," Mom cut in.

"Madam, I must insist we go. Your guard will only be able to distract them for so long," Myles carefully insisted as he rose from the dining table.

My breathing began to accelerate. "What the heck? You have bodyguards now?" I squealed.

Mom's hands flexed at her side. "Asherah, do you trust me?"

I rubbed my temples. "What kind of a stupid question is that? You're my mother. Of course, I trust you. Oh, God—"

"Goddess," murmured Myles.

"Please tell me you haven't switched careers into drug trafficking or something."

Her mouth twitched slightly. "Goodness no. My life isn't that interesting."

"I beg to differ," Myles murmured again.

She cupped my face, her eyes pleading. "Please, do as I say. Save the questions for later. I promise to answer all of them. We need to leave."

"But what about my job?" I questioned. "I leave for California tomorrow."

"Asherah Ray Delmar. This situation is bigger than your job. It is bigger than us."

A sudden sense of dread rose from my gut. Dad put a gentle hand on my shoulder. "Sher, we have to go. I'll be right by your side the entire time."

"But when will we be back?"

A knock sounded on the front door. Everyone in the room tensed.

"Dax?" Myles asked.

"Possibly," Dad replied. "I'll go check." He dashed from the room while Mom and Myles gathered the suitcase I'd packed earlier. I'd open my mouth to ask why they were in my room when a looming presence at my back captured my attention. I turned, my eyes going wide. An imposing Viking-like man filled the hallway. The muscles of his arms, stacked and ripped, were on full display. His light grey tunic and black trousers looked like something from a Renaissance festival. Dirty blond hair reached to his shoulders, and he had a chin that begged to be sculpted in stone. He was—in short—godlike.

The man's cobalt blue eyes landed on me, and his jaw fell open. My lifted brow seemed to jolt him out of his shock. He shook his head and bowed to Mom. "Your Maj—"

"Dax, I don't believe you've ever met our daughter," Dad said, pulling him upright by the shirt. "Asherah, this is Dax, a long-time friend of the family."

I tilted my head as I inspected Dax from his head to his toes. "Looks pretty young to be a long-time friend."

Dax beamed, seemingly taking my comment as a compliment.

Dad cleared his throat. "Dax, this is our daughter, Ash."

Dax's forehead creased. "Ash?"

"Is there something wrong with Ash?" I questioned.

He blinked repeatedly. "Well, no, Princess. But—"

My body jerked back. "Princess?"

Dax grimaced. "My apologies."

"It's alright, Dax," Mom interjected, glaring at the newcomer. "But we need to save the…formalities for later. Those men could still be out there."

Dax straightened with a nod. "I searched the perimeter. The other men have searched the surrounding areas. It appears they have fled."

"For now," Myles said with a sigh. "I'm assuming the other guards are preparing for departure?"

"Yes, sir. All is prepared. We wait for orders." Dax glanced at my mother.

"We are ready." She placed a hand on my back. "This way."

Mom's tone left no room for argument. The five of us fled out the sliding glass door at the back of the house and down the stairs to the small yacht tied to our dock. It bobbed back and forth as we silently boarded, Dad leading us toward the interior cabin.

As we stepped inside, I found Dax curiously observing every detail of the room—his brow furrowing at one of the decorative sconces on the wall. His head jerked back as it lit. "Fascinating." He continued his assessment, moving around the length of the room.

I quietly padded behind him. "First time on a yacht?"

He glanced at me, a wry smile on his lips. "First time above water in a while."

"Above water?" The yacht gave a violent jerk, and my arms flung out to steady myself.

"Best get settled, Sher bear. The water will be a bit choppy," Dad said as he strolled into the room.

I sat on the white leather bench that lined the room with the strangest feeling that my whole life was about to get choppy.

The yacht rocked steadily over the water, the black outline of the shore disappearing in the darkness and the evening sky swallowing the distant specks of lights. The walls of the yacht were covered in a luxurious, white wallpaper with floral accents that exhibited a sparkling, barely discernible pattern in the moving light. The living room was luxurious, with comfy leather couches at its center on top of plush white carpeting that had been vacuumed obsessively, as evidenced by the lines still marring the floor. There was still a hint of lemon-scented cleaner in the air. Floor-to-ceiling windows showcased the open ocean, now dark with night. I stared blankly out of them, my arms wrapped tightly around my knees as I watched Dad, Mom, and the wall of muscle, otherwise known as Dax, chatting among themselves in hushed whispers from where they stood on the other side of the room. I couldn't make out what they were saying, but the occasional glances my way left no doubt that this was about me. By the twelfth glance, I'd had just about enough.

"Can someone please tell me what in the world is

going on?" I bellowed. Their heads turned collectively in my direction, a palpable look of concern etched on their faces. However, it was Dax's persistent expression of anger, worn since the beginning of their conversation, that left me perplexed.

Mom wrung her hands. "Yes, dear. Of course. I suppose…well, we're just trying to figure out the best way to tell you."

"Seems like that should've been taken care of twenty-three years ago," Dax said.

Dad pointed a finger at him. "She was just a child at the time. Beyond "mamá" and "dada," there wasn't much comprehending."

"But surely you could have let her know when she was older. Shown her something." Dax motioned at me. "Look at her. She's so…" His face went askew.

I gave him an incredulous look. "I'm so what?"

"Human."

"That's quite enough out of you, Dax," Mom reprimanded.

Dax bowed slightly. "My apologies. I meant no disrespect, my Queen."

"My…my *what*?" I jumped from the bench. "What did you just call her?"

Dad rubbed his hands down his face, letting loose a long sigh. "This is going terribly."

I came to stand in front of them, my back ramrod straight. "Someone better start being honest about what's going on. Don't just ask me to trust you. I need more than that. I deserve more than that. You all took me from my home in the middle of the night, telling me that we needed to leave, and now, we're in the middle of the ocean with some mountain of muscle telling me that I'm so "human" and calling my mother a "Queen.""

Would someone care to explain what the heck is going on?"

Mom sighed, grabbing my hands and squeezing them gently. "My dear, I'm afraid the truth will be a bit of a shock."

"How shocking," I quipped.

"I understand you're frustrated, but try to curb your tone. I understand you're a young woman now, but I will always be your mother." She inhaled deeply, seeming to work up the nerve to reveal whatever secret they held from me. "Asherah, there's a reason why I'm gone all the time, and it's beyond my role as the CEO of a company. I'm afraid that's a lie we had to tell you to keep the truth hidden, at least until you were old enough for us to reveal it."

"And I'm guessing you feel I'm old enough now?" I tried but failed to keep the anger from rising in my tone.

"Yes, darling. You are." She glanced at Dad, who nodded to her in encouragement. "The reason I'm gone frequently is because I'm greatly needed in my homeland, now more than ever. And I…" She paused to clear her throat. "I am the Queen of Atlantis."

The waves lapping against the yacht were the only sound in the room for a long minute. "The Queen of Atlantis? Do you mean the resort in the Bahamas? Like, their CEO or something?"

"No, honey. Atlantis, as in the lost city of Atlantis."

I felt my eyes widen and then busted out laughing. "You're kidding me, right? Is this some sort of prank?"

"This is no prank."

I stopped laughing. "No, seriously."

"We are serious," Dad confirmed.

I dragged a hand down my face. "This is bullshit."

"Language, Asherah," Mom scolded.

"Perhaps it would be better if you just showed her, my love?" Dad suggested.

"Show me what? Atlantis? Are you going to throw me to the bottom of the ocean?"

"If you keep speaking to our Queen that way, you may very well find yourself there quicker than you think," Dax threatened, his eyes narrowing.

"Not helping," Dad said, glaring at him. "Neleah, show her."

She nodded, and her gaze landed back on me. I placed my hands on my hips, waiting in anticipation. Suddenly, my breath caught in my throat. Her hair began to shine, her skin took on a bluish tint, and her eyes gleamed blue like the depths of the ocean. Pointed tips materialized on her ears. The lines creasing her eyes and forehead vanished instantly, revealing a woman who could easily be mistaken for my sister. I couldn't reconcile just how young her face had become in just a matter of seconds. But what had my heart kicking out of my chest were the bluish-green fishlike scales that flowed down to her wrists from underneath her elbow-length sleeve.

Every inch of her body was rich with indescribable vibrancy, from the color of her hair to the tint of her scales to the color of her eyes. Tiny stars began blanketing my vision.

"We're going to lose her," Dax cautioned. He lunged to my side, his arm pressing into the small of my back.

Panic clawed at my throat as my eyelids began to flutter. "Who are you?"

My mother's spine straightened. "I am, first and foremost, your mother. That will never change. But I am also the Queen of Atlantis, ruler of the Water Fae. And you, my darling daughter, are my Heir."

The roar of a distant engine grew louder by the second. Mom, Dad, and Dax looked at each other, their eyes going impossibly wide. The quick tap of footsteps raced down the stairway of the cockpit, a panicked Myles meeting the alarmed gazes of the room. "They found us."

A chill crawled down my spine. "Who are *they*?"

"Myles, I need you to prepare Asherah and Cathan for their arrival in Atlantis," she instructed as her trembling hands reached to cup my face. "There's no time to explain. I need you to listen to me and listen to me carefully. Whatever happens, I need you to stay with your father and Myles."

"I'm not leaving you," Dad pleaded.

She straightened to her full height. "You can and you must. One of us must see her safely to Atlantis, and it can not be me. Dax will be with me. I trust him implicitly and have my whole life. Besides, I will do what I must to resolve this diplomatically."

Something terrifying began to consume me as I watched my father's face fall. "Neleah, you know the Fire Fae are not here for diplomacy."

"We must not be the aggressor. It would drag our people into a war they didn't ask for. I will not allow it."

"Cathan, I will protect her with my life," Dax swore.

"Then I risk losing my mate and my best friend in one night," Dad wrung his hand through his hair. "This is insanity. I can't do this. I cannot leave you all."

The rumbling from the approaching boat vibrated through the cabin. Mom closed her eyes, a tear escaping down her cheek. "We knew this might happen. Please. Please do not make this any harder. For Asherah's sake. You need to be there for her if something happens to me."

"But we can all leave together. Now."

"I have made my decision," she said, her voice leaving no room for argument. "You are to bring Asherah to the gates and wait for me there."

Dad stiffened, his hands dropping to his sides with clenched fists. "Is that a command?"

"Yes." Her lips trembled, the tears flowing freely now.

A sigh escaped his lips as his hair began to shine unnaturally. His skin transformed into scales stopping below his collarbone, just like my mother's. His deep brown eyes glowed amber and pointed tips appeared atop his ears. A youth he didn't hold a minute earlier graced his features from head to toe. He bent at the waist. "As you wish, my Queen." Dad flicked his head toward me. "Unbind her."

Mom reached forward, her arms wrapping tightly around him. As she pulled back, she kissed him fiercely before twisting to me and placing her hand on the crown of my head. A thick liquid trickling energy traveled from her palm over my entire body, causing me to draw a sharp breath. The strands of my hair gleamed, and the tips of my ears itched. The energy moved like a slow drip over my collarbone, breasts, and hips. It continued down my legs until my feet felt too tight in my shoes. I swiveled to my reflection in the window illuminated by the soft glow of the cabin lights, and my breath snagged. "I have scales," I breathed.

"Dearest goddess," Dax whispered. His eyes were firmly on me in his reflection in the darkened window, his own ears peeking through the curtain of shining blond hair. "There is no mistaking the likeness."

I frowned as the scales disappeared, my own skin appearing again.

"Shit. She's not holding them," Dad said in a panic.

"We knew this might happen," she warned. "I'll have to compel her. Swim with her to the gates as fast as you can. There's no telling if the Akani are with this lot."

My father's fingers dug into my shoulder. "We need to go."

I shifted my gaze to my mother, and my vision blurred. "Mom?"

Her arms came around me in a tight hug. "You are the best thing to ever happen to me," she whispered. "My greatest achievement above all else. I love you. Always." She pulled back, the tears welling in her firm gaze. "Listen to your father." Heavy thuds sounded from above, quickening in our direction. Her lips wobbled as she placed her hands on top of my head. "Sleep."

And the world went dark.

# Draevyn

# Chapter 4

My limbs remained frozen, the soles of my webbed feet rooted in the sand beneath me. The Heir lay in my King's lap, completely immobile—her long dark hair soaked and spilling on the ground. Her human clothing hung from her shoulders and stuck to her slender frame. Her lovely muscular legs draped over Cathan without a single scale in sight. The exposure of so much skin made my heart race. She was so very humanlike.

Yet, so perfect.

"Commander Eliron, we need you to head to the Above World immediately. I fear there may be more than just the two Fire Fae that tracked Asherah to her home," I heard Myles say, but I couldn't bring myself to take my eyes off of the Heir, and I desperately needed to remember who I was and what I had been called to do.

I cleared my throat. "It will be done." Myles—with a face that reflected the seriousness of the situation—fled toward the palace. I turned to my regimen. Their widened eyes and faces full of confusion wouldn't be the last in Atlantis. Dax was the only other Guardian who had any knowledge of the Heir's existence, and even Dax was unaware that I knew of her despite being my mentor and friend. It was a secret I guarded with my life and grasped close to my heart. No one could know of the Heir. I'd made sure of it. "Guards, our Queen has summoned us to the Above World. Her life is in peril. We must hurry. There's no telling how many there are or if this is the work of the Fire Fae, the Akani, or both."

"And what of the Heir?" I heard one of the males toward the back ask. "Who is to stay here and guard her?"

"I will," Mayana said, sliding through the crowd of Guardians.

My brow lifted. "Major Yaralyn, I'm surprised. You want to miss a good fight?"

Mayana flung the hair of her midnight-black braid behind her back. The nostrils of her broad nose flared, and her charcoal eyes scanned me from head to toe with offense. "I know this may come as a surprise to you, Commander, but if the Akani have made their move on our Queen, the Heir will need protection here in Atlantis. I do not trust anyone else to guard her, not with those rebellious assholes on the loose. So, it would be my duty and my honor to protect her."

I should've chastised her for speaking to me in such a condescending manner, but that was never my style. Mayana Yaralyn was one of my most trusted Guardians. I'd never seen anyone, male or female, work as hard as she did—something I appreciated since my work ethic matched hers in kind. Mayana was an elite warrior. The thought of her protecting the Heir brought me a sense of relief I wasn't permitted to verbalize or show.

I nodded. "Very well. The rest of you, we head out."

One by one, the guards with tridents gripped tightly in hand marched through the golden gates of Atlantis, piercing the wall of water that led into the ocean. The force of the intrusion caused it to ripple in their wake. My cautious steps took me forward to Cathan and the Heir. "Your Highness?"

The King lifted his head. I didn't think the red rim of his eyes was due to any saltwater; the despair on his face all but confirmed it. This was the look of a man who had his world ripped from him, a world I knew he and our Queen worked tirelessly to hide. "Please, Draevyn. Please, go save them."

I noted the lack of formality; my first name was called in a plead from my King. As a sign of my eternal reverence, I placed my trident across my chest. "I promise to do everything in my power to bring them home."

A tingling sensation began in my chest, and my gaze shifted back to the Heir. The most beautiful aquamarine eyes peered up at me, staring right into my soul.

"She wakes."

# Chapter 5

A DOME OF WATER ROSE HIGH ABOVE MY head. I blinked to make sure I was seeing correctly. It was as if I was underwater in an enormous, giant bubble that seemed to hold out the sea around it. The top of the dome wall faded into a brightening morning sky—nearly transparent, puffy white clouds slowly drifting across pale orange hues. My gaze shifted to the tall, glowing golden gates above my head that arched to a point, then to the hoards of scaled warrior-like beings charging down a beautiful stone pathway and plunging into a massive wall of water. Naturally, this should have held my attention from where I lay.

But none of those things did.

The exquisite Caribbean green eyes of the massive man standing over me caused the hair on my body to rise. My gaze traveled over the bluish tint of his scales, which lent to the vibrancy of his olive skin. Scales and skin met on a well-defined lower abdomen. My gaze drifted further up his torso to his rock-hard chest, the statuesque lines of his jaw, full succulent lips, and sculpted nose. His long, dark brown hair flowed like a curtain around his beautiful face. He was the most breathtaking man I'd ever seen.

"She wakes," he announced with a deep masculine voice.

A voice that made my stomach churn.

No, wait. That was…

I turned my head and began heaving. Dad rubbed my back in gentle circles. "That's it, Sher. Get it all out."

"I will leave you," I heard the stunning man say. Pretty sure I left quite an impression on that one, with my retching up seawater and all.

When I turned back in my father's lap, his lips quirked solemnly. "You okay?"

"I'll be fine," I croaked. Well, as fine as I could be considering. I wouldn't voice that to him, though. Not with his barely maintained panic bubbling on the surface.

I wiped my mouth with the back of my hand. "Nothing's ever going to be the same, is it?" I asked.

His gaze lifted to the top of the golden gates. "I'm afraid not. Your mother and I had the best intentions. I swear it. We truly thought we could…"

"You thought what, Dad?"

He let out a heavy sigh and shifted my body to the sandy ground, helping me sit upright. "We just thought we could do things differently. Live differently. I'm afraid our choices are coming back to bite us in the ass," he fretted, rubbing his chin. "But that's to be expected.

Your mother and I are nothing but unconventional to the people of Atlantis." The concern grew on his face as I listened. "Your life *will* change, but my hope, your mother's hope, is that what we did will be for the better. It will all make sense in time, and your mother will do her best to teach you the ways of our people, our traditions, and our culture." Darkness crossed his eyes. "But she'll also teach you all the painful parts of our history, the things we fight for, and what we stand for. And what we stand against. Those will be the most important."

He exuded a confidence I didn't quite feel concerning my mother's life, which lived in limbo as we spoke. It dared me to hope—hope that I knew was dangerous to entertain. "And what of my friends? Are they just going to think I died?"

Dad pinched the bridge of his nose. "Please don't be mad. Myles sent a text to John already. He's under the impression that you had to leave early and couldn't wait. The job was starting sooner than expected."

"Guess that solves that problem," I muttered. Even though I'd only left The Blue Fin a few hours ago, it felt like an eternity—discovering John and Chrissy's relationship paled in comparison to my current situation. "And Mom? You sound so sure that she will be okay."

Dad smoothed his hand over my head. "Let's not give up hope yet. The Guardians are some of the best in the realms. I trust Draevyn implicitly."

Draevyn.

That was his name.

Myles dashed past a tall woman standing with a trident at the top of a pathway just beyond the gates, his face tight with panic. Gone were the suit and tie he'd always worn. The scales that donned his skin rose to form a stand collar and traveled to his wrists. He looked formal even in his Water Fae form. "Your Highness. The council has called an emergency meeting. They've asked for you to bring Asherah." He glanced at me with a wince.

"It's too much, Myles."

"I'm afraid there's little choice in the matter. Melysah left no room for debate."

"Of course, she didn't." Dad rushed to his feet, pulling me up with him. He swiveled toward me and held his palm in front of my face. A tickling sensation broke across my skin, and my eyes went wide when all the water that had soaked me from head to toe formed into a perfect sphere floating in the air before us. *Instant Mermaid Just Add Water* tank, jeans shorts, hair, and every inch of my body was now flawlessly dry. With a flick of the hand, he cast the ball into the wall of water. "Do me a favor and stay quiet. Only a select few in Atlantis knew of your existence, and even fewer knew exactly where you were hidden. The council has been demanding your presence for years, and they can be very overbearing. They'll likely be upset you were right under their noses the whole time. Try not to take offense."

"Princess Asherah, this is your guard, Mayana," Myles advised, motioning to the woman behind him. "She's been assigned to protect you."

Mayana brought her trident across her muscular body and bowed. "It is an honor to serve you, Your Highness."

"I'm afraid we need to keep the introductions short. This way," Myles called as he advanced up the pathway.

I drew a long breath, the trepidation building within, and took my first step through the gates of Atlantis.

The early light peeked over a towering dome, its summit obscured by the vastness of its height. It revealed the evenly arranged large white stones lining the path ahead, guiding us toward a black metal portcullis. As we walked beneath it, the portcullis ascended to an astonishing height. The hallway was flanked by colossal stone bricks, crowned with a barbican. At both ends of the palace, imposing circular towers stood at six to seven stories, each adorned with rows of arrow slits. The Guardians gaped at us as we passed the guardhouse, but I paid them no attention. I was too busy admiring the highest tower that rose above them all, its dark castle turret pointing high to the top of the dome with a glowing blue light at its tip. Three other circular towers—all equally as charming—hugged the larger one around its perimeter. More Guardians paced the length of the battlements surrounding the sandy bailey, the workers pausing to stare at us as we followed Myles. It was an underwater fairy tale castle, and despite the dire circumstances plaguing my thoughts, I couldn't help but be mesmerized.

"This is unreal," I breathed.

Dad smiled warmly. "This is your home."

That stopped me in my tracks. "I'm sorry?"

He placed a hand on my upper back, guiding me forward. "It's your home. Well, our home. I wish there were enough time for a tour, but I'm afraid it'll have to wait. This way."

We quickened our pace, passing through another hallway that ran through the largest tower. A circular two-story building stood at the end of the hallway. The open doors revealed a long wooden table at its center with around twenty sets of eyes appraising us. My heart rate began to beat erratically.

"Greetings to you all," Myles said, bowing to the

group as we entered. He directed me to a chair near the head of the table, facing a wall of arched windows beginning to emit the light of day. A woman with a severe expression—hair pale blonde and tied back at the nape of her neck—stood before her chair at my side. Her pale blue eyes bore into me as I sat on the wooden high-back chair. She held a certain youthfulness that made her appear to be in her late twenties, but it seemed foolish to guess since the Fae could be any age.

Mayana came to stand at the wall behind my chair as Myles departed on swift feet, the doors closing behind him with a loud click that echoed across the room. Dad sat at the head of the table beside an elaborate chair with intricate wood carvings and golden accents that could only be reserved for royalty—a place for my mother.

*Please be okay.*

"I think it best if we put the pleasantries aside," the woman suggested in a condescending tone.

"Yes, by all means, Melysah. Let's be vastly unpleasant," the male across from me chided. His full lips quirked as a gray eye gave me a wink. His face held a handsome ruggedness, his long brown hair carrying just past his medium-built shoulders. "Welcome to Atlantis, Asherah."

"Yes, indeed. Welcome. We've been anxiously awaiting your arrival for some time," Melysah sneered.

"That's enough, Melysah," Dad scolded. "My daughter has been through a lot in the past twenty-four hours. She's only just found out who her mother is. About Atlantis. And may I remind you that she is the Heir, and you will remember your place."

Melysah gave a curt nod. "As will you, my King. You and the Queen owe the council answers."

"And you will have them. But right now, your Queen

is in peril in the Above World, and you are wasting our precious time acting as if you have the authority to reprimand my daughter or me. I can assure you that you do not. I understand it's been a long time since I've sat at this table—"

"Too long—"

"But I still know the rules. So if they've changed, and the council—with Neleah's approval—granted you more authority I'm unaware of, then by all means, let me know."

The room grew deathly silent, Melysah's lips pursing so tight wrinkles formed around her thin lips.

"Well, that escalated quickly," murmured the ruggedly handsome man. He shifted his gaze my way. "Roarvyn Syles, if you're wondering, my sweet."

Dad cleared his throat and cocked a dark brow at him, causing Roarvyn to squirm in his seat. Melysah glared between the both of them before rolling her eyes. "Are the two of you done with the male posturing?"

"Depends on Romeo over there," Dad quipped.

"Your Highness," a woman from the other side of the table intervened, "can you please advise the council regarding the heir and where she has been hidden all these years?" The rest of the table nodded politely at Dad.

"Thank you, Shaegana. Since before Asherah's birth, we've been living in Key Largo, Florida, in the United States. It was a very peaceful life amongst the humans, allowing Asherah to grow up without any expectations or interference. Asherah didn't know she was a Water Fae, nor did she have any knowledge of Atlantis or her role in this queendom. Neleah glamoured her to protect her identity. It wasn't an easy decision, but it's one we made together as her parents."

"But why?" Shaegana asked, aghast. "Why would

you do that to our only heir?"

"As the future ambassador to the humans, we believed it was essential that Asherah live among them."

Melysah's dainty hands balled into fists from where they rested on the table. "At the sacrifice of our people."

"I hate to say it, but I agree with Melysah on this," Roarvyn commented. "How will she rule our people if she's unaware of our customs? Our very nature?"

"My daughter is incredibly smart. She will learn. I have faith in her."

Melysah's scaled arm cut through the air as she motioned at me. "Look at her! She wears human clothes, and there's not a single scale on her body. She doesn't even know how to morph! And you want her to lead our people?"

My arms wrapped around my middle as the blood rose to my cheeks, my humiliation making me feel like a child.

"I do," Dad seethed through clenched teeth.

Melysah scoffed. "You underestimate the time it will take to educate her, to prepare her to be queen. If something's happened to Neleah, the heir takes over the queendom."

"Do not put that energy out there," Dad growled. "Not when I just left our Queen in the Above World with goddess knows how many Akani."

"Agreed," Shaegana interjected. "We should pray to the goddess for her safe return to Atlantis," she affirmed and glared at Melysah, "where she has ruled for nearly a thousand years."

"A thousand years?" I squealed. They were the first words I'd spoken, defying my father's orders to stay quiet. All eyes in the room swiveled in my direction.

"She doesn't even know how long we live. Does

she, Cathan?" All the humor Roarvyn previously held was gone, his face held in arrested shock. "My goddess. You've handicapped her."

Melysah buried her face in her hands. "This is a disaster."

"Enough," Dad bellowed. His chair scraped across the floor and echoed off the walls as he rose. "It's past dawn, and we haven't slept. Asherah's life was uprooted; she's been stalked, our boat attacked, and my mate is in critical danger. We'll reconvene when we receive news of the Queen."

The chamber doors banged open against the wall, and a pale-faced Myles rushed in. I couldn't breathe, my body going cold. Myles scanned the room before setting his gaze on my father. "The Queen…"

"Is she alright? Where is she?" Dad pressed.

Myles swallowed hard. "I'm so sorry, Cathan. The Queen…she is dead."

# Chapter 6

Grief is heavy, like a solid weight on your chest that doesn't ease and feels never-ending. It's so potent you almost feel like you're drowning in it. It's like trying to breathe while covered in a soaking wet blanket, your lungs desperate for every breath but barely mustering the energy to take in what little air they can. Was it ever going to end? Would I ever feel the same? Or would this feeling accompany me for the rest of my life, in my dreams, as I woke and tried to go about this whole new world without my mother?

How strange that a person can be there one moment and gone the next. They were just here, sitting by your side, on the phone, a normal part of your daily routine, and then…just…gone. You count the hours. It'll be twenty-four hours since they passed soon. Then days. One week has passed. How can they be gone? You saw them in the flesh with your very own eyes. And now, all that occupies the space is this empty void that will never be filled. How does one fill a void so large? My heart would always have a hole where my mother's spirit would be.

On top of the grief sat the guilt—the guilt of ever thinking a bad thing about my mother, and there were many thoughts like that. One could chuck it up to petty feelings, but to me, it didn't matter. I felt guilty for ever raising my voice or getting mad—even though I was still mad. I was mad about not knowing about the strange new world I was expected to lead, mad that she raised me like a regular human child when I wasn't ordinary. I was a Water Fae.

Fae.

How in the world was I supposed to lead these people? I wasn't my mother.

My perfect mother.

The one that everyone looked up to. I would know. I stood in her shadow all of my life. Everything I loved—the surfing, the sports I played, the marine life I studied—was nothing compared to my mother's accomplishments. Looking back, all those things I loved were inconsequential. They did nothing to propel me forward or prepare me to be a queen. No wonder Mom tried so hard for me to study business or anything with some leadership skills. How stupid I was to rebel against her guidance.

What's worse? There was nowhere to go with my grief. I didn't have a familiar home to go to where I could wrap myself in Mom's favorite throw and sit in her favorite reading chair by the slider that overlooked the canal. I couldn't spray my mother's go-to perfume in the air just to remember how she smelled. I'd remember the musky sent anywhere, and I longed for it. I was desperate for just one hour to roam our home and feel close to her.

I didn't feel close to her here. Not in this place. It wasn't my home.

The grief and guilt wrapped tightly around the void in my heart, like her favorite throw blanket. I stared at the high ceiling of my room—my new room, one that was vastly unfamiliar and felt at odds with who I'd been my entire life. Aches and pains plagued my body, matching the feeling in my heart. Try as I might, sleep was impossible. Constant troublesome thoughts battled with each other. Did I even know Mom? Did she love me? Why didn't she leave the yacht? What if we stayed? What if I'd never gone to the bar to meet up with my crew? Would Mom still be here to help me in this new world I found myself in?

It was all pointless. None of those questions would ever bring Mom back to life—a life she lived for close to a thousand years, unbeknownst to her very own daughter. I was just a blip on the radar of my mother's life.

A soft mattress enveloped my body into a warm cocoon. A sea of plush velvet pillows and a cozy duvet anchored my body into a sense of false comfort. Fresh tears I didn't think I had trickled down my cheeks onto the awaiting pillow—my eyes red-rimmed from the endless tears that flowed throughout the days and nights as sleep eluded me. At least, it's what I believed to be afternoon. According to Mayana—who had been checking in on me constantly—the dome's magicked light brightens during the day and darkens during the evening, mimicking the Above World.

After Myles informed the council of my mother's passing, Dad ran from the room like a man possessed. I had trailed after him, my vision blurring as my feet dug into the sand at the front gates. He'd stopped mid-run when he realized I'd been following him and urged me to go with Mayana to my quarters. He didn't want me to see Mom in whatever condition she was in; he didn't want the last sight of her to be one of horror.

Because the Fire Fae had burned her face after they had turned her heart to ash.

I'd heard as much from the chambermaids who tended to my quarters in the middle of the day when they thought I was asleep—their horrified whispers from beyond the bedroom door carrying to my now pointed ears. I tried to extinguish the image of her body burned as they had described, but the visions relented, causing me to sob uncontrollably. The concern I held for Dad— who had seen her in that state—grated at me. A part of me wanted to console him. Another part wasn't able to, my own grief wildly debilitating.

There were moments of rage in which I longed to grab my board and surf the waves in what the Water Fae called the "Above World." My world. Or what I *thought* was my world. A deep sense of loneliness settled, causing my anxiety to spike. I was saved from diving too deep into the depression when someone knocked on my bedroom door. "Come in," I said, my voice raspy with exhaustion.

The drapes had been pulled across the windows to block out the light of the dome, but I could still make out Myles' silhouette in the doorway. I felt broken and didn't have the energy to care if anyone saw me this way.

Myles moved cautiously toward the bed and sank into the chair beside it. "I'd ask you how you're doing, but that doesn't seem like the proper question at such a time." He shook his head, his empty gaze traveling to his feet. "I both know and don't know how you're feeling."

I blinked to clear my vision. A tiny sliver of light from the side of the curtain reflected off Myles' face. He was always so impeccably dressed—his hair always perfectly set with a clean shave at all times. This Myles was entirely at odds with the Myles I was used to seeing. Deep dark grooves blanketed the area around his eyes; his hair was mused and untidy. I could make out the dark stubble growing on his well-defined chin. I realized then that I wasn't the only one feeling the loss of my mother. The rest of Atlantis grieved, possibly more than I had, because they knew her better than her own daughter. That thought was a kick in the gut.

I leaned up from the pillow to face him. "I don't know how to feel if I'm being completely honest. I'm filled with just as much grief and anger as I'm filled with confusion. All I keep asking myself since I found out about her murder is, did I even know her?" I confessed.

He looked at me with tears welling in his eyes. "Oh, Asherah. Please don't say such things."

"Do you understand why I would?"

"Of course. I suppose finding out your mother is the Queen of a mythical queendom you never knew existed until you were heaved into it would be the cause for some distress." He leaned forward, crossing one leg over the other. "I won't insult you by giving you fluffy words to settle an aching heart, or to make you feel better because grief tends to stamp out all other emotions. But I will tell you that your mother loved you dearly—so very dearly. She was most herself when she was around you. As Secretary to the Sovereign, I had the privilege of witnessing the Queen in all her forms. I saw her as the mother, the wonderful, loving mate she strived to be, and our Queen. Neleah was such a wonderful Fae who touched so many lives, but she cherished the role of being your mother the most. She wanted that experience so badly, and she was willing to separate you from the only world she knew so that she might raise you away from this, so that she might raise you as a young girl with a run-of-the-mill family in the Above World. And while she had been away frequently, making time for video chats and phone calls with you was the number one priority." He smiled warmly. "I know because I had to schedule all of her important meetings around your soccer, swimming, surfing, and whatever else you found yourself enjoying at the time. And let me tell you. It brought her such joy to know you were enjoying those things. Such immense joy." The smile faded from his face. "Neleah knew one day you would be here, because duty would demand it. But she just wanted a small sliver of normalcy for you. Just for a while." Myles reached forward, placing his hand upon mine. "So you see, you knew her best because she wanted you to know the real Neleah. The one that laughed and smiled and loved her family fiercely. Never question that. And if I have to remind you every day of it, so be it. I will."

I couldn't hold back the tears as I nodded. "How is Dad? I mean, I'm guessing he's not okay, but where is he?"

Myles sighed heavily. "He's at the infirmary with Dax. His burns are slowly healing. Cathan stayed there all day in lieu of sleeping in his quarters. I tried bringing him something to eat at midday. I hope he'll get some rest before your mother's Wylemei."

"Wylemei?"

"It's what the Atlantians call a funeral. Our ritual is a transition ceremony. We celebrate the soul rejoining our loved ones on the other side of the Veil." Myles' brow furrowed. "I must warn you because you are unfamiliar with our customs, but there will be a pyre. Your mother's body has been wrapped in traditional ceremonial cloth. The process may come as a shock to you—"

"Because I'm human."

The intensity of his gaze held me captive. "Raised human. You're very much a Water Fae. In the coming months, it will be hard to forget that fact. The council is clamoring to get your education and training started," he said bitterly. "Their lack of compassion makes me want to choke them all."

"Given their grand welcoming, I'd pay money to see that."

Myles laughed as he rose from the chair. "Well, I'm afraid after Neleah's Wylemei, life will take off at a million miles an hour. Rest assured. I'll be by your side the entire time. It may not save you from being over-whelmed, but I can be the shoulder for you to cry on when you need it. After all, it's what I'm best at—*years* of training with Neleah."

A slight grin lifted the corner of my lips. "Thank you."

"No need to thank me, but if you need me, my quarters are on the first floor. Ask any of the palace staff roaming around, and they'll direct you my way."

My bare feet met the cool stone floor. My favorite Hurley tee Myles had retrieved from the house gathered over my sleep shorts. I rejoiced in the small comfort. "Actually, I do need something."

"Anything."

"Can you show me where the infirmary is? I'd like to see Dad."

Myles bowed at the waist. I tensed slightly at the action, unused to the formality. "Of course. I'll give you a few minutes to get ready. Your chambermaids have filled your wardrobe with traditional Atlantian human attire until you learn how to morph."

My brows furrowed. "There are humans in Atlantis?"

Myles tilted his head. "Of course. This is where they've sought refuge during every Ice Age." He huffed out a breath. "There'll be more about all of that later. No need to overwhelm you." He pointed down to my feet. "You'll also find a few sets of silk slippers to wear. You won't need those once you morph either, on account that the bottoms of your feet are protected by the webbing there, but you'll have the slippers nonetheless until that day comes." He thumbed over his shoulder. "I'll be outside in the living area when you're ready." He pivoted, heading for the bedroom door.

"Myles?"

He paused and glanced back at me. "Yes, Your Highness?"

"She cared about you, too."

Fresh tears welled in his eyes as his bottom lip wobbled. "That is very kind of you to say. Thank you…for reminding me."

The infirmary was a short walk across the bailey. We arrived only minutes after we departed my quarters. Mayana kept a respectful distance behind us as she eyed everything and everyone in the vicinity.

I couldn't recall a single time when I'd witnessed Dad grieving. The occasional neighbor may have passed away here and there, but it was never someone near and dear to him, not until Mom. My nerves began building as I proceeded down the long corridor. The traditional Atlantian clothing I'd chosen wisped behind me. In truth, I'd never worn anything like it. The soft lilac silk wrapped around my torso, leaving the top of my breasts exposed, and the long pant legs cinched at the ankles and whispered against my skin. I felt a certain level of exquisiteness I wasn't used to. The lady's maids—as Myles called them—tied my hair back and softened it in a matter of minutes. It left me in awe. I let them know, too. They were beaming with smiles of pride.

Myles stopped before a large wooden door at the end of the hall and turned to face me. "He'll be right through here. I have a few things to tend to, but Mayana will stand guard until you're ready to return to your quarters. If you need me, she knows how to find me."

"Thanks, Myles."

He nodded and went on his way.

Mayana brought her back to the wall, her spine going impossibly straight as she kept a firm grip on her trident. She gave me a short nod before her gaze traveled down the hallway. In the short time I'd been around Mayana, I figured out she was always on guard. It brought me a little relief to know she had my back.

I inhaled deeply and clasped the steel handle, strolling into a deathly silent room. The dome light bathed the room in a soft white glow. Dax lay on a bed wrapped in blankets, his eyes closed. Spread out upon an armchair in the corner of the room, Dad slept with his arms and a leg splayed over the armrests, his other leg stretched out to the stone floor. The scales that blanketed his upper torso formed into a sleeveless tunic. The points of his ears and the youthfulness of his face were something I didn't think I'd ever get used to seeing. I glanced down at my arms, surveying the tanned skin, and wondered if I'd ever be able to don my scales.

I left Dad undisturbed and ambled to Dax's bedside. The damage Dax incurred became vastly evident as I crept closer. Deep red burns trailed up his bare arms and peppered his face. Half of his hair was singed off his scalp. My gaze caught on his chest. A hole the size of a fist sunk into his body, the charred skin beginning to flake. It rested right above his heart, and I guessed the same hole hit its mark on my mother's body.

"He'll be more disappointed by his hair than any other part of his body."

I wheeled around to Dad, his eyes barely open. "Will it grow back?" I queried.

"Most definitely. We rejuvenate quickly unless a Fae from a sister realm injures us," he explained. A darkness fell over his gaze. "This includes the Fire Fae that attacked them. They hailed from Corenathia, the realm of the Fire Fae. It will be a couple of weeks before his hair starts to grow back. He'll bitch about it the whole way through, but he'll live with it."

He stretched out fully, giving a few good stretches to his neck before rising to join me at Dax's side. He appraised me, a smile spreading across his face. "Your mother would have loved to see you in Atlantian garments. Goddess, you look so much like her." He swallowed hard. Much like they had with Myles, dark circles spread out toward his cheekbones, his exhaustion evident. "How are you doing, Sher Bear?"

"I should be asking you the same question."

He nodded solemnly. "I guess it's a stupid question. We're not good right now, are we?"

My vision blurred. I rushed forward, hugging Dad tightly, his arms squeezing me back as he rested a cheek upon my head. "I don't understand. Why? Why would anyone want to kill her?"

He sighed. "That is such a long and elaborate explanation. One that you deserve." He motioned to a bistro-style table next to the chair he'd been sleeping in. I went on my toes to reach the high chair and faced Dad.

"As you know, your mother is the…" he shook his head, "was…was the Queen of Atlantis. She ruled over this queendom from the age of one hundred and twenty-five when her mother—your grandmother—decided to step down and pass the torch to her daughter. To do so is incredibly rare. Throughout history, the queens of other queendoms reigned for thousands of years before dying on the throne. This is why heirs are incredibly rare and often protected. In some queendoms, they're imprisoned."

I jerked back. "Imprisoned? Their own children?"

He chuckled lightly. "I know. It's barbaric. Not to worry. In Atlantis, we practice the Ritual of Passage, which your great-great-grandmother enacted during her reign in order to keep her heirs from getting power-hungry. So far, it's worked." His eyes wandered. "Your mother planned on performing the Ritual of Passage with you much sooner than her predecessors. We had plans to…" He squeezed his eyes shut. "Well, I suppose it doesn't matter now, does it?"

I reached for his hand, squeezing it tightly. "Of course, it matters, Dad. I want to know. Why was she going to step down?" I questioned encouragingly.

"She felt that it was time, wanted to see the parts of the world that were still above water, felt in her heart that you were called to lead her people through the next Lomeage, what the humans call an Ice Age."

"Because Atlantis was around for the first one, if the

rumors are to be believed?" I didn't know much about the mythical Atlantis, but I'd watched a documentary or two about it, most of them calling its existence a bunch of hogwash.

"Correct. We were a beacon for the humans, a refuge of sorts. It's why Atlantians are known for coming to the aid of humanity. Some other realms aren't keen on helping the humans, which is why they were at odds with your mother. Prophecies have indicated that the next Ice Age is soon. They all have differing opinions about what to do with the humans."

My head tilted. "Do with them? What do you mean?"

"In some queendoms, they do not treat humans as anything more than cattle. It's something Atlantians frown upon." Dad's face grew angry. "It is something the Corenathians are constantly petitioning for. Evil demon spawns." The muscles of his jaw popped. "Your mother predicted something like this would happen, warned me of it even. I wouldn't listen, of course. I truly thought we'd live long enough to be there for you as you reigned over Atlantis. I realize now it was all wishful thinking. She was right. She was always right." The tears streamed down his cheeks. I felt my own cheeks dampen; the reality of the broken man sitting before me began to settle in. He lost his *mate*, a term I'd heard him use to refer to Mom both on the yacht and in the council room. While I didn't know much about mates, it seemed the connection went beyond the label of husband and wife.

My father's shoulders sagged, and my heart ached for him. "I'm so sorry, Dad."

He huffed. "Don't be, Sher. Your loss is no less than mine, and it comes with so much more weight because you've now been pulled into a world you don't know. You've given up a happy life for one you didn't ask for. I know this was our plan all along, and perhaps we should've been better prepared for this moment, but we just got so lost in the happiness of being a family that we kept kicking the can down the road." He regarded me with sorrowful eyes. "Your happiness was her absolute joy. She lived for it. Despite being gone with ambassadors of the other queendoms half the time and trying to save humanity the other half of the time, the only thing that mattered was your happiness."

I shook my head. "My happiness is her being back here. I don't care where we live or what we are. I want her back." The anger rose from deep within as I thought of the ones responsible for taking her. "And I want to hold those evil, fire fuckers accountable."

Dad smiled at that. "I won't even scold you for your language. Although, your mother most definitely would." He breathed deeply. "After your mother's Wylemei, we have to begin your studies."

"Myles mentioned that already."

He nodded. "Good man, Myles. He'll teach you what he knows. There's a lot for you to learn before your coronation."

I felt the blood drain from my face. "Coronation?"

"Yes. For the time being, I'll be your Regent. I don't trust the Council and didn't get the best feeling when we met with them. But I can't hold them off for long. Something tells me Melysah has plans of her own. I just don't know what."

"You can't rule over Atlantis?"

He looked at me with an incredulous expression. "Goddess, no. Why would I want to do that? That's a female's job." He shivered like the thought was appalling, making me smile. I glanced at the bed where Dax slept. "And Dax?"

"Dax will be under for a bit longer. The healers didn't want to wake him, so they prolonged his sleep. If he were awake, he'd be itching the piss out of his skin. Fire Fae burns are the worst. Plus, I don't know that he'll want to wake up to all this. He'll likely feel responsible once he discovers his queen is gone. For his sake, I hope he doesn't wake up soon." He rubbed a hand over his face.

"One step at a time, Dad."

He nodded, smiling at me. "One step at a time. You'll need to get ready for the Wylemei."

"If it's alright with you, I'd like to stay here a bit longer."

"Okay then. Just a bit longer."

We sat in companionable silence the rest of the afternoon, our grief a silent guest that loomed in the air around us.

# Chapter 7

Hundreds of Fae and humans lined the stone pathway that cut through the lush green park before the Temple of Atabey. The humans dressed in Atlantian-style pastel silks that drifted on a current of air as our procession passed them by. Mom's wrapped body lay upon a strong canvas material with its ends stitched around decorative steel poles, each held by four Guardians who dutifully carried her before us. I looked down at my own garments, still feeling uncomfortable, still feeling so human, feeling like the color didn't match the scene before me. When I asked why the humans weren't wearing black, Dad replied that the Atlantians didn't wear black for mourning. Tradition mandated that those who choose to wear clothing don our brightest colors to celebrate the soul's passing onto the

Veil, their term for heaven. I didn't bother arguing that the black would better reflect how I felt internally. Utterly hollow.

I cast a glance around the crowd, some of them looking upon Mom's body with tears in their eyes. Others stared at her wrapped body as if she were an apparition. All bowed slightly in reverence as her body passed them by. When I felt the weight of their gazes pressing down on me, I held tighter to my father's arm for support and stared blindly forward as if I weren't hyper-aware of everything happening around me.

The Temple of Atabey rose high above us with stone steps leading to an open-air entrance bracketed by rough stone pillars, and a large metal bowl hanging from linked brass chains above the entrance. Myles had informed me that the temple had been erected to honor the goddess, Atabey, who was responsible for carrying us beyond the Veil. The Bohiti—the spiritual leader who led the high priestesses and lived in the temple—stood beside the pyre that sat before the entrance. The Guardians ascended the temple steps on graceful webbed feet, laying her body gently upon it. It was then that I recognized two of them. The first was Mayana. But my attention was fixed on the second Guardian, Draevyn. As if summoned by thought, his Caribbean green eyes landed on me—the same intensity cutting through me and causing my heart to beat erratically. I gasped a breath as he broke the connection and took his place with the other guards on the right side of the temple steps. The rough stone pathway bit into my knee as everyone knelt in reverence to their fallen Queen, to my mother.

Dad had warned that this would be different. There were no eulogies to utter pretty words about the dead, no burial site to visit when I was missing her. The Atlantians didn't believe in that either, choosing instead to deposit the ashes of their dead into the ocean depths beyond the dome.

We bowed our heads, giving every living Fae and human a moment to reflect on our thoughts and memories. It was a designated time to have private conversations with the recently deceased. There were too many memories that flashed through my mind at once. Yet, I only thought of one thing I wanted to tell her. Please come back, Mom. *Please, please come back. This new world is so scary, and I'm trying to play it cool and keep it together for Dad's sake. I really am. But I'm terrified that I'm going to fuck it all up.* I glanced around at the crowd weeping over my mother, their Queen. *They will not love me as they love you. How am I ever going to do this? I just wanted to be a marine biologist, save sea animals, and be alone in a quiet life. I'm not you. These people will hate me, Mom. Come back. Please come back.*

But as I beheld the Bohiti carrying the torch and lighting the pyre, I knew there would be no answer from her. My father's muffled sobs heaved from behind the hands covering his face. Myles put an arm around his shoulder to console him, and I was grateful to him. I could offer him no comfort because I felt exactly the same—my own sobs threatening to tear from my throat as I gazed upon the dancing flames turning Mom's body to ash.

The whole crowd seemed to disappear around me. I didn't care about them, or my appearance with my puffy red eyes, or my face splotched and dampened with tears. All I cared about was anchoring myself to this moment and letting the grief consume me. It was precisely why I'd missed the man leaping from the crowd and running up the temple steps.

A giant ball of fire materialized from the pyre's flames, catching in my peripheral vision. My head snapped up, and I gaped at the Fae at the top of the stairs. I'd never seen such sheer determination and anger in anyone. This was not a friendly Fire Fae come to mourn the leader of Atlantis. No one had ever looked at me with such hate in their eyes as this Fae did. His arm pitched forward, casting that ball of flame right at me. I braced for it, knowing there was no escape, knowing I'd soon be joining Mom because I didn't yet know how to protect myself with my scales.

But the fireball never came.

The hissing sound of steam prompted me to cover my ears and squeeze my aching eyelids shut. The hissing continued for an eternity until, finally, it relented. I pried my eyes open, and my breath quickened at the sight above me. A small dome of water rose from the ground, encasing me in a half-sphere that appeared as solid as a wall. Ever so slowly, it lifted from the ground, and the erupting sounds of chaos instantly met my ears. Hoards of humans and Fae ran in every direction, seeking cover. Children wailed, and people yelled as they pushed each other to seek refuge in the village on the other side of the park.

"Long live the Akani! Death to the humans! And death to the Heir of Atlantis!" the attacker bellowed from underneath Mayana, whose trident pressed into the back of his neck as she pinned him to the ground. The other Guardians ran to her aid, but I held my watery gaze on the one before me, the being responsible for saving my life. Draevyn Eliron's upright palm navigated the small dome of water before him. It fell with a loud splash at his webbed feet. My chest worked with the effort to steady my breathing as Draevyn's pleading gaze met mine. I didn't know how I knew what he was asking, but I nodded, and his shoulders sagged in relief.

I flinched when a hand grabbed my upper arm. I spun around and found my father's face filled with panic. "We need to get to safety. Follow me." Without a second thought, I followed him and a large group of Guardians through the hoards of panicked Atlantians and toward the village. I twisted mid-run as pounding footsteps amplified behind us, and instant relief consumed me. Draevyn followed in our wake. With every step we took through the village's alleys and closer to safety, the inexplicable tether to my savior strengthened. The lingering glances we snuck each other as we hurried behind the various village shops, and finally, the safety of the castle confirmed that I wasn't the only one who felt it.

The chaos from the Wylamei carried into the council room, all twenty-one members talking over one another in hysterical and angry outbursts. Draevyn and Mayana stood in silence at the wall behind my chair, and I felt grateful to them for not contributing to the circus unraveling before us. My head swelled with the shouts reverberating off the chamber walls, the hours and days of endless tears contributing to the pounding ache at my temples. I stared mindlessly at the dark and light patterns of the deep mahogany table before me, the numbness settling in as the adrenaline drained out.

"How the hell did the Akani breach the city?" Roarvyn asked, his expression turbulent.

"An Elemental Appraiser would've approved his entry," said Shaegana. She was the only one who'd joined me at the table, the others too restless to sit. "All Fire Fae who have sought asylum here are heavily vetted and accounted for. The appraiser would've been the only way in."

"Someone go fetch the Elemental Appraiser who was on duty today. I want them brought in for questioning," Dad barked. Every strand of his dark hair was disheveled from repeatedly raking his fingers through it.

"I'll fetch him straight away," said Mayana. I heard the chamber doors lumber shut a moment later.

"My regimen has already begun questioning the Fire Fae who attempted to take the Princess' life," Draevyn informed the council, the deep baritone of his voice carrying across the room from behind me.

"By the goddess. Asherah could have been killed," Roarvyn fumed, dragging a palm down his face.

"Thank Atabey that she wasn't." Dad shot Draevyn a look full of gratitude. "I will never be able to thank you enough."

Draevyn's trident came across his chest in my periphery. "It is my honor."

"I hardly believe the honor is necessary, Draevyn. You were simply doing your duty. Besides, had the Regent and our former Queen taught the Heir even the barest of skills, she might have been able to protect herself," Melysah scolded, her arms crossed tightly over her middle. The minimal light that shined through the tall arched window by which she stood reflected the pert nose turned up at Dad, expressing clear impertinence.

My father's lips thinned. "Be that as it may, I am thankful to him regardless. Your Heir is alive because of his quick thinking. Perhaps you can save your bitchiness for a more appropriate time."

"Fighting each other doesn't help," Shaegana pleaded. "We must figure out who did this."

"The more important question is why the Akani did

it and why the Queen is dead," Melysah continued despite Shaegana's pleas. Her casual steps took her closer to the table as she glared at me. "And it is because of *you*."

I flinched, and I caught Draevyn's low growl behind me.

Barely contained fury simmered across my father's face, the muscles of his jaw ticking. "How dare you speak to our Heir that way? You will show some respect," he roared.

"Maybe we should be questioning where your loyalties lie with that kind of talk?" Roarvyn questioned.

"I'm only saying what every council member in this room is thinking." Melysah pointed a well-manicured finger at me, and I had the sudden urge to snap it. "She will be the downfall of Atlantis. You'll remember this moment when it happens. You've been warned."

"I think it best if you sit down, Melysah," Shaegana said, flicking a hand to Melysah's usual chair. "You make a fool of yourself speaking on behalf of everyone on this council."

Melysah ignored her, continuing with her righteous rant, "She knows nothing of our customs, nothing of our culture, and nothing of the other realms. She doesn't even know about herself! There are faelings who know more than her—some only a few years old. And you expect her to lead this queendom? It's ludicrous. Her knowledge of the humans is more extensive than that of the Atlantians."

"And that was our intention all along." Dad placed his rugged hands on the table, leaning toward her. "We wanted Asherah to learn about the humans, to learn about their ways, their countries, their conflicts. Who better to guide the humans into the next Lomeage than someone versed in their ways?"

"But at the sacrifice of ours!" Melysah cried out.

"I see some merit in our Queen and King's intention with this strategy," a male council member sitting at the far end of the table remarked. "If Asherah has created connections with and learned of the humans, she'll be better able to communicate with them. It is, after all, what the goddess would want."

Melysah arched a lean arm through the air. "Oh yes. Our wonderful, absent goddess."

"That is blasphemy!" Roarvyn admonished.

"Enough." Melysah strode to the head of the table, her hip brushing against Mom's chair. "I motion on a vote of no confidence in our Regent and the heir based on a severe lack of Atlantian knowledge and to protect our people."

The entire room went deathly silent, a few gasps echoing throughout the room.

Roarvyn was the first to speak, his grip tight on the back of his chair, "This was your plan all along, wasn't it? You were just waiting for the proper moment." His tone was heavy with accusation.

The corner of Melysah's mouth faintly twitched up. It could've been missed in the blink of an eye.

"Melysah, you cannot go against the goddess' blessing. Her element must be revealed. And going against the goddess' Mark has never been done," Shaegana breathed.

Melysah's head tilted. "And an heir has never been raised amongst the humans and away from this realm." She glanced around at the other council members. "All in favor?"

I could hardly breathe as the hands of several council members rose, and an evil smile spread across Melysah's face. "All opposed?"

An equal number of hands rose in the air save for one. A male with long black locks tied at the nape of his lean neck sat at the opposite end of the long table. He glared at Melysah, his deep brown eyes cold as ice, before shifting his gaze to Dad—his demeanor softening. "My King, I want you to know I don't fully disagree with what Melysah has said today. She is right. The people will likely challenge the authority of an heir who's never been educated and trained to lead our people. However, I do see the merit in raising her in the Above World." His flawless, fair-skinned aristocratic face held its neutrality as he addressed the room. "If Princess Asherah has experience as a human, I see no reason why we couldn't convince the Atlantians to accept her on the basis that she can help our cause," his head cut to Melysah, "to the goddesses' cause. We also owe it to our Heir to give her a chance. For this reason, I must abstain and put forth a new, more reasonable motion."

"Thank you, Silas," Dad said on an exhale, but I barely shared in his relief.

"I motion that the Regent rule for six months," Silas declared. "Should her Elemental Mark reveal what we expect since her lineage has revealed little else, the Regent and The Secretary shall educate her on our customs and traditions as well as the ways of the other realms."

I leaned in and whispered into my father's ear, "Elemental Mark?" But he gave a small shake of the head. Message received. Not now.

"I volunteer to assist in her education," Roarvyn interrupted. "She'll need to know the council laws that govern this chamber; no one knows them better than me." He gave a wink in my direction.

Silas' head dipped in a quick nod. "Very well. Roarvyn has volunteered to teach Princess Asherah council law.

For her protection, I request that the Commander train her in self-defense tactics." I stiffened at that suggestion. That meant spending time with Draevyn—one on one. My anxiety began building in the pit of my stomach. "No minute will be spared save for eating and sleeping while she prepares for the role of Queen. In six months to the day, we will reconvene and vote on the status of her coronation or present alternative options. All in favor?"

My breath caught in my throat. For the first time since arriving at the gates of Atlantis, I had an overwhelming feeling of want. I *wanted* to be the Queen of Atlantis. Even though she was no longer with us, I wanted to make my mother proud. I wanted to prove to the council members who'd raised their hands against my reign wrong. A small flame flickered from deep within. It was tiny, but it was there nonetheless. The desire to prove myself to the people—her people—burned like kindling in a newborn fire. As every council member save Melysah lifted a hand, I exhaled in relief. Roarvyn wiggled the fingers of his smooth hand at her with a Cheshire cat smile.

Melysah's face burned beet red. "So be it."

The council room doors flew open, and Myles rushed into the room with Mayana hot on his tail—his mouth set in a grim line while her eyes were impossibly wide. He placed his hands on his hips and tipped his head toward the high dome ceiling. "The Elemental Appraiser has been found dead."

# Chapter 8

Time unfolded like a leaf carried along the water's surface, with the dome light intermittently filtering through the dense, deep blue velvet curtains drawn tightly over each bedroom window. The plush duvet cover wrapped snugly around me, a constant companion as the hours drifted away. I only summoned the energy to eat or bathe. The pressures of this new world were pushing down on me, and the weight became unbearable. Friend or foe. Enemy or ally. I could hardly tell. Everything felt so...overwhelming. I decided it was best to hole myself up in my bedroom, with its high stone walls and ceiling, very ancient-looking tapestries I didn't dare touch for fear of ruining them. One day, I fixed my stare for hours on the ornately carved mahogany bed frame that gleamed like a brand-new copper coin. It complemented the blinding white rug spread across most of the large, comfortable room. Every evening, the dying embers in the double fireplace shared with the living room of my quarters winked like a dying star. Occasionally, I'd caught my reflection in the floor-length mirror in the corner of the room, but the woman—female, as the Fae called it—staring back at me was unfamiliar. So, I didn't bother studying her reflection there for long, but I committed everything else to memory every evening before sleep finally claimed me.

On the third day of my new sulking routine, I planned for another day of solitude despite the looming responsibilities carefully laid out by the council.

Unfortunately, Myles had other plans.

The faint sounds of male voices carried from the hallway outside my quarters. My attention was fixed on the door visible through the bedroom doorway, awaiting the unexpected interruption.

"My dear, please do not bother her," I heard Myles plead.

"She cannot possibly stay in that room one more day," said a concerned male voice that was both light and masculine simultaneously.

"And I do not intend for her to," Myles assured him. "She just lost everything. Her mother. Her life in the Above World—"

"And she's expected to be queen. She must be prepared, my love, or else that rigid wench with the unstyled hair and bland manicure will rip away what is rightfully hers. And no one should be ruling Atlantis with a bland manicure."

A knock sounded a second later, fierce and frantic. I slowly pulled myself upright, readjusting a pillow to lean back on. "Come in," I croaked, my voice crackling from lack of use.

The steel hinges of the front door creaked with the swing of the door. A male with a long, velvet red robe trimmed in golden filigree swept into the room—the golden bangles that adorned his wrists jingling with the determined swing of his arms. His perfectly cut, black hair rose an inch off the top of his head and was shorter on the sides. He pressed a slender yet well-manicured masculine hand to his throat as rich, amber eyes appraised me with a mix of concern and shock. "Oh, dear. It's far worse than I imagined."

Myles strode in behind him, wincing. His scales blanketed his broad form, something I was still unused to seeing, but he still managed to look clear-cut. "Do not be so dramatic."

"But…her hair."

I patted my hair down, my self-consciousness causing the heat to rise in my cheeks. Perhaps I overdid the whole recluse thing.

"It can be fixed. You are one of the best, after all."

The robed man bowed low, the bangles jingling again as his arm extended in a flourish. "Your Highness, it is an honor to serve you, however challenging it may be."

Myles smirked, shaking his head. "Asherah, this is my bondmate and the head of all things fashion and beauty for the Royal family, Aurelio Martenos Anthysius."

My attention traveled between them. "Pleased to meet you," I attempted to speak again, my voice still raspy with misuse. I cleared my throat before saying, "You never told me you were married, Myles."

A wonderfully proud smile emerged on his face. "Mated. It's a much stronger connection than a marriage. And I suppose if I had informed you, you would've asked too many questions. I felt it best to keep it professional at all times. Plus, Aurelio doesn't travel to the Above World very often."

"Just on festive occasions," Aurelio said, resting the outer part of his wrist on a narrow hip. "The Above World humans are a little stiff in this era. It's like they've forgotten how to have fun and invented new ways to judge, judge, judge. Atrocious," he scoffed. "They desperately need to remove the stick that's been firmly lodged up their—"

"Well then!" Myles interrupted with a clap. "Aurelio is here to prepare you for the Elemental Ceremony and the ball in celebration of your Elemental Mark."

Aurelio wagged perfectly sculpted brows, beaming.

My fingers picked at a stray thread of the intricate duvet stitching. "Elemental Mark. They mentioned that at the council meeting, but I didn't understand what that meant. And what is the Elemental Ceremony?"

Myles gazed softened. "It is our sacred ritual where your goddess-blessed element is revealed."

"We each have an Elemental Mark," Aurelio said, pulling up the sleeve of his left arm to reveal a mark resembling a tattoo on the cream-colored skin of his wrist. The midnight black ink resembled an incomplete circle, with its ends curving out in pointed loops. "They're our calling, our way to serve the goddess Atabey, the goddess of Fae and humans alike. Mine is the artist's symbol. Each Elemental Mark is different." His hand came to his elegant throat, and I could have sworn I saw a mist build in his eyes. "The entire family knew I would be blessed with it, given how much I've enjoyed drawing since I was a tiny Faeling."

"During Mabon, every Fae gets their mark at the Elemental Ceremony," Myles explained. "Some are blessed as dome lighters, healers, architects, water purifiers, appraisers. The goddess always gives us purpose to survive and provide in the realms."

My brow furrowed. "The Elemental Appraiser. The one who let in the Fire Fae? That's one of them?"

The corners of Myle's mouth dropped into a frown. "That's correct. He was from a long line of Elemental Appraisers, one that will be thoroughly vetted moving forward. Luckily for Atlantis, we have many more Elemental Appraisers. It's a crucial and prestigious role. They're responsible for all the citizens of other realms who travel in and out of Atlantis. As you found out, one slip-up can cause quite a stir."

"Yes, that's for sure." The image of the Fire Fae, his face distorted in such fury and anger, flashed through my mind. But it was quickly replaced by the arresting features of another face, one that had lived rent-free in my head. That curious tug I felt around him had been one of the many passing thoughts I'd had these past three days. My thoughts should have been occupied with grief for Mom, and yet I was busy fawning over a stranger. Granted, he saved my life, but it did nothing to ease the guilt I felt for feeling anything other than grief. Even happiness felt like a violation.

"Since you missed this year's Mabon ceremony, I took it upon myself to create a special event for you. It'll be a great way to get to know your people," Myles encouraged.

"And to set some boundaries so the rest of your council haters know not to mess with you," Aurelio added.

I tried to call to mind my mother's left wrist but came up blank. I didn't recall seeing any tattoos on my father's left wrist either. "My parents. They glamoured their Elemental Marks?"

"I'm afraid so," Myles confirmed. "For their protection and yours. Plus, there were fewer questions at parent-teacher meetings. Humans can be very closed-minded about body markings, unfortunately."

I nodded. "And what was Mom's sign?"

Myles straightened to full height. "It is the most prestigious of marks, Asherah. She bore the Royal Elemental Mark. Each family that presides over each queendom has one."

"Each queendom?"

"Oh yes, there are other queendoms," said Aurelio, a saucy smirk lifting his lips, "just not as fabulous as Atlantis. And their fashion tastes." He shivered. "Dreadful. Just dreadful."

"Now, now, dear. We mustn't insult the other queendoms in front of Atlantis's future ruler. She must learn to be diplomatic."

Aurelio glared at him. "Diplomatic? One of them just tried to take her out."

"We still don't know if it was Corenathia or the Akani…or both. But we must always strive to be better than them, in every way."

Aurelio huffed. "You're a better male than me, my love. I want to grab them by the—"

Myles cleared his throat, looking at him pointedly.

Aurelio sighed. "Very well then. Let's focus on getting you ready for the ball."

"You'll first be fitted for your gown," Myles informed.

My brows dipped. I didn't want to be the only one parading around in a gown when all the Fae were in their scales—scales I had yet to conjure. "Will I be the only one wearing a gown?"

"Despite the Water Fae proudly donning scales both

in the water and in Atlantis, the traditional balls are a time when even they embrace the human fashions."

"Some of them quite poorly," Aurelio murmured.

"So," Myles continued, "you'll feel right at home."

With the pleased look on Aurelio's face, I didn't have the heart to tell them that I detested anything that wasn't swimsuits, flip-flops, tanks, and shorts. So, I simply nodded in return.

"And a few outfits as well." Aurelio grinned, looking positively elated. "This is such a treat. A queen who wears human clothes. What a time to be alive!" he bellowed enthusiastically. Myles hid his laugh behind his hand, prompting Aurelio to reach out and pinch Myles' buttocks. Myles flinched, a deep red color rising on his cheeks. He gave Aurelio a look that promised retribution, and there was something so entertaining about seeing this side of Myles.

Before I could help it, I let out a small giggle. It was the first time in what felt like an eternity. But the guilt took over and stifled it, my mouth dropping into the straight line it had been in for days. I let out a heavy sigh. "So, what's next?"

A gleam sparkled in Aurelio's eyes. "If we're to make a Queen of you, you must look the part. I, for one, have been dreaming of this moment all my life. If we're to silence your haters, we'll do so with fashion. We're going to have heads turning and tongues wagging." He gave me a pointed look, his shoulders pulling back. "Rest assured, Princess Asherah. We'll give that wench of a female, Melysah, something to talk about. To think, she wants to erase a millennia of precedence."

"Yes, well, we're not going to let that happen," Myles said with assured confidence I didn't entirely feel. "I've had the privilege of watching Asherah grow into the young female she is today; I'm certain she's up for the challenge. Am I correct?" Despite my never-ending uncertainty about filling my mother's shoes, I dipped my head in a nod. "Splendid."

Aurelio's mischievous smirk appeared. "We will have them groveling at your feet. When you walk in that hall, every inch of you will scream of the Queen you are born to be."

"And trust, he knows queens," Myles teased.

Despite the endless days of grief and sadness that seemed to consume my days, a smile tugged at my lips. With Myles and Aurelio guiding me, I didn't feel so alone anymore. Perhaps Mom had sent them from heaven…beyond the Veil…or whatever they call it; my two fashionable guardian angels. "Okay, what first?"

"Shower," they said simultaneously.

I brought my nose to my armpit and sniffed. Okay, perhaps I'd been holed up in my room a little *too* long. Without another word, I hopped out of bed and shuffled to the adjacent bathroom.

My gaze traveled over my reflection in the floor-length mirror framed in decorative metal curls resembling ocean waves, hardly noticing the woman before me. Aurelio insisted on dragging the heavy mirror to the living room for more space, and who was I to argue with his genius?

All the muscles in my uplifted arms ached as Aurelio cinched the fabric on the side of my upper torso. Sweat beaded on my forehead with the effort to remain still. I'd already faced his scolding for flinching when he accidentally pricked me with a pin.

"There." He stepped back and gazed over my shoulder at my reflection, a smile dawning on his angelic face. "Absolutely stunning."

I could hardly disagree. Tiny diamonds traveled down the teal fabric and sparkled like a flowing river reflecting the golden rays of an afternoon sun. The mermaid-fit bodice clung to my body like a second skin, the top of the strapless dress cutting a dividing line down my breasts and exposing the bit of skin there. The soft silk material flowed to the floor and brushed the tips of my toes. I was all but guaranteed to trip and land on my face in front of everyone.

As if sensing my anxiety, Aurelio squatted and folded the hem of my dress an inch shorter. "There. That should do it," he said, inserting another pin to secure the length.

With the fabric just a bit shorter, exposing my bare feet, I looked even more like a mermaid. Fitting, I guess.

A knock echoed across the living room of my quarters, and Dad walked in a moment later. He scanned the room until his eyes landed on me in the corner, and his mouth dropped open. His eyes immediately glistened. "Oh, Sher bear. You look so beautiful."

My heart swelled at the sight of him. It had been some time since we'd seen each other, not since the Wylamei. The sense of loneliness from the past few days eased. "Thanks, Dad."

"And to think, Your Highness, this is without the art of her makeup," Aurelio raved as he adjusted a pin on my right side. "Just wait till you see what we have in store for her."

Dad flashed a huge grin at us. "I have no doubt whatever you have planned will be fit for a queen."

"Exactly," Aurelio beamed. "Now, let's get you out

of this dress."

Aurelio and I padded gingerly to the bathroom, carefully removing the exquisite dress. At the start of the fitting, Aurelio had advised that there was no reason to be shy about my nakedness around him since my breasts were dangling flesh ornaments with tips that did nothing for him. I didn't know whether to be offended or relieved by that.

Within a quarter hour, I was back in my soft, weathered jeans and my go-to *Hola Beachachos* flowy tank that warmed my soul with thoughts of home. Dad rested on the comfy white armchair in the center of the room, staring out the arched living room window. I leaned against the door frame, observing how he fashioned his scales—a tunic-like shape covering his upper torso and cutting off at his broad shoulders. The crow's feet around his eyes were no longer present due to the lack of his glamour, but the dark circles under his eyes seemed to be a permanent fixture. He never sported those before Mom's passing. And just as Myles had said, the inside of his left wrist was decorated with a tattoo-like symbol very different from the one on Aurelio's wrist. A triangle sat atop a decorative line, swirls resembling wings in the center.

As if sensing my appraisal, he rose from the chair. The smile that spread across his face felt so at odds with the man I'd just silently observed. Feeling the grief we shared, I rushed to him and wrapped my arms around him—resting my head against his chest like I'd done so many times as a child. The safety of his fatherly embrace would be something I'd never tire of, no matter what age I was. His cheek came to rest on the crown of my head. "I missed you, too." We stood there in silence, seeking refuge in familial comfort. Just a minute later, he pulled back. "Come, let's go walk the gardens. There's a lot we need to catch up on."

I followed him out of my quarters and descended a wide set of switchback stairs that led out of the palace, my fingertips grazing the coarse sandy walls as I went. He led me under an arbor with deep green clusters of ivy vines weaving through its openings and glinting like emeralds. Their existence in an underwater world remained a mystery to me. As I pulled my gaze from the arbor, my steps faltered—my mouth hanging open. It was an honest-to-goodness underwater garden with plump, deep red roses, floribunda with its rich yellows colliding with the hottest pink, and bourbon roses with a pale yellow that still managed to stand out. "How?"

He smiled knowingly. "Impressive, isn't it?"

My gaze fell upon a pond that sparkled with a variety of colorful fish. Among them, some were plump and adorned with crimson red dapples on a white backdrop; some sported spots of candy apple red on coal black, and others displayed a vibrant orange shade akin to a beautiful sunset, with flecks of white mimicking clouds on their tiny scaled skin. The pond kissed the grass neighboring the pathway—its mouth narrowing into a river that carried on in the distance. "Impressive is an understatement."

"The river carries outside the dome, so the fish who occupy its waters have the liberty of coming and going as they please." He breathed deeply. "The Elemental who tends to this garden is one of the best in all the queendoms."

"There's an Elemental for gardening?"

"There's an Elemental calling for just about everything. Dome lighters, healers, artists, architects, water purifiers, cleaners and organizers, strategists, ambassadors." He held up his wrist, the tattooed side facing me. "And, of course, protectors. Dax and I share the same, along with the other Guardians of Atlantis."

The intimidating image of Draevyn flashed through my mind. My strides quickened to hide my blush. "Myles told me about Mom's mark."

"Ah. Myles. Good male. Always teaching." A solemn smile lifted his lips. "Your mother had the same symbol you'll likely have when it is revealed during your Elemental Ceremony. It stands as the most esteemed Elemental marking, a sacred indication of royalty. Every female descendant in your mother's lineage has proudly borne this mark. Once revealed, it'll be hard for anyone to contest the goddesses' chosen queen, regardless of the Melysah's scheming." I brought my nose to an iceberg rose, inhaling its luscious, sweet scent, the deep yellow tendrils tickling my nose. "Our Elemental gardener has won tons of awards for her work," he continued as he smelled an iceberg in a different cluster, "although I doubt there will be any friendly competitions with the other queendoms...after what happened."

We continued strolling down the garden path with casual steps, the thick aromas snaring my senses as I absorbed every detail. "Everyone keeps mentioning the other queendoms."

"Yes. There are four in total, including Atlantis. The Water Fae rules our queendom. Then, we have the Queendom of Corenathia, the ones we believe responsible for sending the Fire Fae after us. The Air Fae rule over the Queendom of Airelandia and the Queendom of Earthos is comprised of the Earth Fae. Each Queendom is ruled by a female leader with the same Elemental marking you'll likely have. They're the reason for my recent absence. We demanded an emergency meeting with the other realms." He sighed heavily. "I'm definitely not your mother when it comes to communicating with the queendoms. I have no idea how she did it. Most of the time, I feel like strangling the other queens," he confessed, tilting his head. "Not the Airelandians, of course. They're our closest allies. The Queen from Earthos remains a mystery, though. She's kept me thoroughly entertained just by existing with that stone-cold, unreadable face of hers. When we're in the Council of Queendoms, I simply stare at her, trying to figure out whether the Earth Fae are friend or foe."

"Queendom," I said, mulling over the word. "It's difficult to say after hearing Kingdoms my whole life."

Dad let out an amused chuckle. "Yes, after being raised in the Above World, I can understand why you would find the word unusual. Soon enough, it will roll off your tongue without a second thought."

"And where do the Akani come from?"

I could have sworn I heard a low growl. "They're the rebels who seek to destroy everything your mother has worked so hard for. They don't want any more humans in the realms, and despite having a few humans in their ranks, the Fae among them would rather not have humans here at all."

The corners of my mouth dipped in a frown. "That's terrible."

"Hhmph. You don't even know the half of it."

We made our way down the winding flagstone pathway in companionable silence until the light pounding of hurried footsteps came from behind us. I twisted around, and the mesmerizing green eyes of my rescuer met mine. His long brown hair flowed behind him, and his intimidating form caused my breath to hitch. Every movement of his body held such lethal grace. Draevyn bowed at the waist; his eyes still locked on mine. "Your Highnesses." His deep baritone voice sliced deep—I the butter, he the knife. I fidgeted from foot to foot as I pulled the hem of my tank. Not the most regal attire for such a title. Aurelio's earlier advice about dressing to impress had me regretting I didn't listen.

"Commander Eliron, I believe you have yet to meet my daughter, Asherah."

"It's a pleasure to meet you, Princess."

I couldn't breathe. His eyes remained locked on me, a risky move considering my father—his King—was standing right beside me.

"Commander Eliron, what news?" he queried with one brow rising.

Draevyn tore his gaze away from me, addressing him, "I've requested a switch in post. I would like to guard the Princess from now on."

I felt the ground fall away beneath me. He was requesting to guard…me?

Dad's brow furrowed. "What about the training of the rural posts?"

Draevyn's gaze shifted to me again and left just as quickly. "I'll still train with them and have Mayana fill in for me in my absence."

"Mayana is doing a fine job guarding the Princess. I'd just been complimenting her today when I relieved her."

"Of course. She's one of my best guards. I would trust no one else with the job, but I'd feel better if I were the one to guard the Princess."

Dad regarded him skeptically. "And Dax knows about this switch?"

"No, Your Highness," he advised, his gaze ticking over to me again. "Not yet."

"Commander Eliron, you're one of the best, most

skilled Guardians we've ever had. Your talents are unparalleled. I admire you for wanting to protect Asherah. She is most precious to me, as you know. But you're sure you want to do this? It's well below your station."

Draevyn swallowed, his Adam's apple bobbing—the first sign of unease I'd ever seen from him. "Yes, I'm sure. I've already volunteered to train her in defense arts. It'll help with that cause."

Dad shook his head. "Draevyn, you know you have my unending support on this, but you'll have to clear it with Dax. He is the General, after all."

"That I am," a deep male voice called at his back. Dax meandered his way to us, sizing up Draevyn with those cobalt-blue eyes—his long pale hair tied with a leather strap at the base of his neck, some strands visibly shorter than others from the attack. His wide, muscular arms crossed. "I think I already told you I'd prefer for your assignment to stay in the rural posts with Mayana guarding the Princess."

"You did," Draevyn admitted, straightening his spine.

"Then, why, pray tell, are you going against my orders?"

Draevyn's nostrils flared on an inhale. "It has to be me."

"No. It does not."

Draevyn's fists clenched at his sides. "It. Has. To. Be. Me."

Dax dropped his own white-knuckled fists at his sides and closed the distance between them, the scales at their muscular chests nearly brushing. He was now only inches away from Draevyn's face, glaring at him with the heat of a hot branding iron. "Commander Eliron, I've known you since you were in cloth diapers sucking on your mother's tit, and that was nearly one thousand years ago." My eyes widened with that revelation. "You've never given a rat's ass about guarding the royal family. When you were old enough to swing a sword, you insisted on sparing with me because you wanted to train with the best. You've broken ribs and bones throughout your body hundreds of times to achieve your rank. What. Gives?"

Again, Draevyn's eyes slid to me and back to Dax. The gesture didn't escape Dad's notice as he pinched his chin between his thumb and forefinger, observing Draevyn with a perplexed expression.

"I'm the best person to protect Princess Asherah. She's our future Queen."

In an awkward yet intense moment that seemed to stretch on forever, Dax and Draevyn maintained their standoff. Dad and I shared a look, his shoulders lifting in a shrug. It was only when Dax let out a deep sigh that I knew Draevyn had won. "Fine," Dax conceded, dragging a hand down his face. "I approve of Commander Eliron's appointment as Asherah's guard," he said in a relenting tone. "But you must be present for training in the rural posts. They'll need your expertise now more than ever."

Draevyn nodded. "I'll see to it that arrangements are made." He pivoted, bowing to us. "Your Highnesses, forgive me for taking up your time." He wheeled around and strode out of the garden, leaving a sense of confusion in his wake.

"Do you think he's acting strangely?" Dad inquired.

Dax shook his head. "Understatement of the millennia. But he's not wrong. With the Akani becoming stronger by the day, I feel much better having his presence in the palace. Much as I hate to admit it."

Nothing more was said on the matter. Draevyn Eliron was to be my guard, and nothing could calm the eruption of butterflies in my stomach.

# CHAPTER 9

MY HANDS BRUSHED DOWN THE FEATHER-light fabric of my traditional Atlantian garment. The pant legs kept loose to my legs—the stunning lavender shimmering with my strides. It tightened at the waist, and the top of the jumper-like garment looped around my neck. While the outfit was lovely, I was beginning to pick up the vibes of the Atlantians I'd encountered and read the room perfectly.

I'm to be their Queen, and I wear the fashion of a human.

Never in a million years would I have thought I'd feel so exposed by the display of my skin. A swimsuit had been my work attire, for crying out loud. The looks and whispers stayed with me everywhere I went. Just yesterday, I'd tried to venture around the palace in search of the dining hall at Mayana's encouragement, but the constant ogling of the palace staff halted my attempts, and I returned to the safe space of my quarters. Being the center of constant attention in Atlantis had me on edge. I longed for the days when I could grab my board and disappear upon the waves for hours on end. How different my life had become.

When I returned, I'd received a letter from Myles requesting that I meet him at the university the next day. A sense of excitement sparked at the prospect of exploring a new place. Plus, my studies were one way I could honor Mom and the throne she had occupied.

Per Myles's letter that had been enclosed in a beautiful leather tote, the royal Elemental commuter would meet me outside the palace gates early that morning. I shifted from one foot to the other before the thick wooden drawbridge—a charming moat peacefully drifting many stories below. The stiff strap of the tote dug into my shoulder, but I adored the gift Myles left for me. It had been filled with a smooth, light brown suede journal, a decorative black marble pen I was scared to use, and a strange tablet made of a gray stone with nothing upon it. I'd twisted the tablet in my hand earlier that morning, trying to figure out what it was. I'd have to remember to ask Myles about it. Mayana stood silent but observant at my back underneath the stone barbican as we waited. I'd wondered just when Commander Eliron was scheduled to change his post.

"Ah, there he is," Mayana informed. I glanced at her over my shoulder—a warm smile cresting across her face. "This is where I leave you, Princess."

"Thanks, Mayana."

She bowed before her long strides carried into the palace.

The sound of waves lapping against a boat drew my attention to the moat below, and my eyes widened. Draevyn appeared with a short, curvy female in a boat-like structure that ascended out of the moat and up a long ramp that led to the entryway. A narrow cabin sat at the back of the tiny boat—the deep dark wood gleamed beyond polished perfection. As it approached, intricate carvings that detailed every panel came into view, a crest I could only assume was my family's carved into its side. I gasped as I noticed the wheels at the bottom of the boat moved of their own accord. No engine sound had reached my ears, and no animal had pulled it. The female with short dark hair faded on the side, and a little length at the top chuckled as it stopped in front of me—her brown eyes beaming from within a smooth, round face. "It has been a long time since I've seen someone in shock like that. I've missed that reaction." She rose from her seat at the tiny helm and curtsied. "My name is Braeliah Morvyn, Your Highness. I'm your Elemental commuter." She cut a thick, scaled arm in the air with a dramatic flare. "And this is your canoa, otherwise known as a boat with wheels where you're from."

Draevyn jumped out of the canoa without missing a beat, placing a set of moveable wooden steps before me. I had yet to pick my mouth up from the floor. Forgetting myself, I shook my head. "Pleased to meet you, Braeliah. I'm Asherah."

"Oh. I know. And I'm super pleased to make your acquaintance, Your Highness. Your presence has caused quite a buzz."

I felt the corner of my lips tilt up in a solemn smile. "I'm sure it has."

A rough, rugged hand dropped into my line of sight. My gaze shifted to Commander Eliron, and I forgot how to breathe as I placed my hand in his. His face remained impassive as he helped me into the canoa. Draevyn motioned toward the back. "You are welcome to sit in the cabin if you'll be more comfortable."

"And miss the entire ride?" I quipped, sitting on the bench before me and plopping my tote on the floor. "I wouldn't dream of it."

"Right. Of course," he murmured so low I thought I hadn't heard it.

Moments later, he sat on the opposite side of the bench as Braeliah slid into her seat before us. With a flick of her wrist, the canoa rolled into motion. "I understand you haven't had much time outside of the palace, Your Highness," Braeliah called over her shoulder. "We'll catch the Shingu River on the other side of town so you can take in the sights and sounds of Borike'n. Then, it's straight down the river to the University." I couldn't contain the giddy grin; my eagerness to observe the town filled me with glee.

A tingling sensation prickled my neck and swelled in my chest. I glanced over and found Draevyn's eyes intently appraising me. He quickly snapped his head forward, but not before I caught the slight twitch of his sensual mouth.

My brow immediately dipped of its own accord. Draevyn Eliron was a puzzle I was desperate to figure out. A part of me wanted to thank him profusely for saving my life. Another part of me wanted to ask...

"Have I done something to offend you?" The words tumbled out in a voice only he could hear.

Draevyn's widened eyes whirled in my direction. "No, Your Highness."

"Ash. You can call me Ash."

"Ash," he said as if mulling the words carefully on his

lips—deeply hypnotic cupid-bow lips made for so much more than talking, lips that suddenly grinned. My eyes drifted to meet his, and I felt the heat of a blush on my cheeks.

*Way to gawk, Ash!*

I cleared my throat, twisting to hide my embarrassment. My gaze held on the cobblestone roads lined with cozy sandstone facade buildings that glimmered as we rolled past. Fae and humans of every different color—some scaled, some brown, some pale as moonlight—milled about. I was instantly fascinated by how normal it all was—butcher shops, bookstores, coffee houses, and wine bars. The sound of children's laughter peeled through the air as we passed by a playground between two sandstone buildings. There was no commodity here that one couldn't find in the Above World. It was an honest-to-goodness underwater world. "You're positive you're not upset with having to guard me yourself?" The question slipped out of my mouth unbidden before I could help it.

My attention went to the male beside me again, his spine perfectly straight as he scanned the area around us and said, "No, I'd prefer it be me."

"It just seems that your skillsets might be needed elsewhere in Atlantis."

He shifted his gaze to me once more, softening. "This is a very important post, Asherah."

Damn, those butterflies that fluttered in my stomach. "Just Ash is fine."

"If you wouldn't mind, I'd like to call you by your full name." The deep tone of his voice did delicious things. My name fell from his lips like a prayer. "Asherah." A deep tug in my gut left me unable to move as a wicked heat spread deep in my core. "You are very important. It is my honor to guard you."

I felt like I'd just witnessed a crack in his carefully laid facade. "You are very hard to read, Draevyn Eliron."

Draevyn's gaze traveled over my face. "I'm…bothered by you."

I cringed. "Bothered by me?"

He shook his head. "That didn't come out right. I meant no offense."

"Then, what exactly did you mean?"

"Hold on tight!" Braeliah called from the helm as the road ended, and the canoa descended a ramp into the Shingu River with a mighty splash. I held my focus on the surroundings before us, feeling vastly confused by his comment. Sandstone buildings bracketed the river on either side. Dozens of villagers hustled in and out of their homes, starting their day—some in Atlantian garments while the Water Fae donned their scales. Little cafes peppered the riverfront, their patios packed with people sipping on their morning coffee and freshly baked pastries, the mouth-watering smells drifting across the river. Bright-colored flowers hung from the perfectly lined balconies above each store—drapes floating on the wind from open doors to welcome the day. In the distance, a large structure sitting atop a stone mountain came into view, taking my breath away. The spire at the top of the structure reached toward the top of the dome. "The university's official name is Cibao Univeristy," Braeliah informed with a hint of pride in her tone. "It means stone mountain in the native Atlantian language. It's the finest in all the Queendoms. You'll find many Fae from the other realms flocking here for their studies."

"It is why it is so heavily guarded," Draevyn added. "It is why I must be with you at all times. With the recent attack, we don't know who to trust, and this would be the easiest place for them to enter."

I nodded in understanding, grateful for the turn in conversation. "Are they permitted to enter the town?"

"Only with an escort. The students here have been heavily vetted, but we can never be too careful."

A sudden sense of dread built. "Am I taking classes with the other Fae?"

"No, no. You'll be studying with Myles separately. Unfortunately, there's a plethora of ancient texts and other resources we cannot extract from the university. Otherwise, we would have done your sessions at the palace." Draevyn frowned. "You don't need to worry, Asherah. I'll be right beside you the entire time. You have my word."

My vision narrowed. "How difficult it will be for you, with you being so *bothered* by me and all."

He rubbed a hand down his face with a sigh. "I deserve that. I do." The silence grew between us, but his following words sent my mind reeling, "It's not that I am bothered. It's more like I am…enchanted." My breath hitched. That voice. It did wicked, wicked things.

"We've arrived at the gate, Draevyn!" Braeliah called. He rose on swift feet, striding to the side of the canoa. I looked upon him in open fascination as he gracefully leaped off the side and into the water, his webbed feet disappearing below the surface. Before I knew it, I was leaning over the side and watched his form swim toward another form in the water. I squinted. "Is that another Water Fae? Underwater?"

"That sure is. That's Rally. He's the university gate guard. He ensures all the students and faculty coming in and out of the gate have proper identification."

"But underwater?"

Brealiah laughed heartily. "Of course, Your Highness. That is the normal way. The canoa is just a luxury for the Fae."

The normal way. Another reminder that I wasn't normal. Wasn't one of them.

"Soon enough, you'll be swimming the waters yourself to gain entrance, leaving me to my lonesome," she supplied with a confidence I didn't feel.

I winced, glancing over my shoulder at her. "I highly doubt I'll be ready to swim the waters in my Fae form any time soon." I'd never attempted it. Didn't even know how. I hadn't even been in the water since I'd arrived.

She flitted a hand. "Probably for the best, Your Highness. We can never be too careful with all the drama unfolding. But if you were to swim these waters, Draevyn would accompany you."

Water splashed onto the deck, causing my whole body to jolt backward as a pair of webbed hands firmly gripped the side of the boat. Draevyn pulled his bare torso out of the water—his glorious bicep, chest, and shoulder muscles on full display. I couldn't help myself, not when the lines of his incredibly well-defined lower abdomen pointed toward the very visible bulge just beneath his scales. At least I had the presence of mind to snap my mouth shut before he swung his muscular legs over the side wall. But my eyes hadn't gotten the message. They tracked every movement as he rose to full height as if pulled by a magnet. Water droplets dripped from the dark tips of his long, brown hair. By some unseen magic, the water that covered his body drifted off the contours of his chiseled body and dropped into the Shingu River with a faint splash. Draevyn shook out his now dry hair, and a smirk that spoke a thousand words emerged. I was caught gawking again. Mortified, I wheeled around to Braeliah, who held tight to her own mischievous smirk.

"Not bad accompaniment if I may say so myself, Your Highness." She winked just as the black portcullis ascended—the gears grounding in a high pitch. I swiftly slid onto the bench without another word.

The canoa glided through the dark tunnel before us, the faelit torches flickering their orange light against moss-ridden walls. Draevyn positioned himself a little closer this time, I noticed—his body only a foot away from mine.

"How do you all do that?" I ventured.

"Do what?"

"The water came off of you."

"Ah. That." He held out his palm, and a small sphere of water from the Shingu collected above it. In the blink of an eye, it took the shape of a rose and froze into solid ice before he guided it to my lap.

I traced a fingertip over the biting cold stem. "That's amazing."

Draevyn laughed. "Soon enough, you'll master water play."

My brows knitted together. "Water play?"

Draevyn flicked his hand. The ice rose flew from my lap and twirled in the air. "Yes, water play is not just some cheap parlor trick. As a Water Fae, we can manipulate water, freeze it, collect it. There are different levels of power each Fae possesses." The rose melted back into water and took the shape of an arrow. It shot across the canoa and into the water with a plop, my wide eyes fixed on the spot where it disappeared. "It can also be used to defend yourself," he warned.

Another set of torches drifted by. "That might come in handy."

"Indeed. Let us hope you learn fast. The thought of you defenseless is an obstacle I'm not too pleased with."

My gaze returned to my lap as I swallowed past the lump in my throat. "Right. Because I'm so human." I'd never felt so insecure; it was a new feeling to me, I realized.

"Look at me," he demanded. I pulled my head up and regarded Draevyn's mouth in a tight line, his sea-green eyes fierce. "You are Water Fae. The fact that you were raised in the Above World doesn't change that. You may need to work harder to learn everything you missed, but that doesn't make you any less Fae. The sooner you accept that, the more powerful you'll become. Never let your obstacles dim your light."

A newfound respect for him grew and went beyond this natural, strange attraction I felt for him. I gave him a slight smile. "Thank you."

My attention was drawn to the light filtering in from a vast cavern ahead of us, its jagged teeth swallowing the canoa as we sailed into it. A set of rough stone steps met a sandy, shallow shore—a ramp arching on either side of the grand staircase. Various canoas, with mostly humans and other Fae onboard, ascended the ramp or drifted slowly back into the water, gravity be damned. I beamed as several Water Fae emerged from the water. Droplets floated from their being and returned to the water as they strode forward. Something lit within me—a fierce desire to be like the other Water Fae, something potent awakening in my soul. I wanted to feel the webbing between my toes and fingers.

The attention of the other students and faculty clustered in the arrival area shifted when they realized the approaching canoa bore a royal crest. Some of them outright snickered, and their whispers echoed off the cavern walls. *Right. I'm not normal anymore.* My smile dropped, and I let loose a sigh.

"What's that frown about?" Draevyn asked.

"I'm not used to all the…" I began, motioning to the endless stares in our direction.

Draevyn's eyes narrowed at the onlookers. He rose from his seat and approached the side of the canoa, his big imposing frame blocking me from their view. They began scurrying away like frightened mice in the midst of a predator.

"Effective."

Draevyn glanced over his shoulder, smirking. "They'll not make you feel uncomfortable on my watch."

I gave him a genuine smile, my heart emitting a subtle swell. I gasped at the slight tug at my chest, and his smile vanished as he broke eye contact. I didn't know what to make of it; the overwhelming feeling.

But something told me he did.

And I didn't care for the mood swings either.

The canoa gave a sudden jolt at the top of the ramp. "That'll be Myles there in the entryway, Your Highness," Braeliah called.

Myles stood before a large stone archway with a brown leather messenger bag resting on his shoulder and gave a short wave. Dozens of Fae and humans crowded the vast hall behind him. I was grateful for our arrival; the interactions with Draevyn were becoming too much— too everything. I needed to get out. My hand snapped out, grabbing the strap of my tote. I leapt from the bench, trying to make my escape, but the steps to exit the canoa had disappeared from where they lay moments before.

I scanned the deck, but paused when Draevyn cleared his throat behind me. I swiveled around as he held them up with his eyebrow quirked. "Looking for this?"

My lips pressed together in a firm line. "Yes, actually I am." I snatched the steps from him, placing them outside the canoa. My silk-shoed feet thudded against the wood as I descended.

"You know, I could have helped you."

I turned and closed the distance between us. "I think you'll come to find…Commander…that I'm perfectly capable of doing some things on my own." I pivoted to Braeliah, who was biting her lips to keep from laughing. "Thank you for bringing us here."

Her eyes were alight with knowing. "It is my pleasure, Your Highness."

I strolled toward a very puzzled Myles, hoping to the goddess Draevyn wouldn't follow, but his steps sounded behind us as we strode into the hall. It seemed there was little I could do to escape Draevyn Eliron.

Deep down, I knew I didn't want to.

If I hadn't known Cibao University was hundreds of miles under the sea, I would've thought it resembled any other age-old university in the Above World—with a few exceptions, of course. Most of the students and faculty we brushed past were Fae, with their pointed ears proudly on display. Others were clearly human, gathering with the Fae in small groups as if they weren't immortal creatures. The cool tips of my fingertips rose to my own pointed ear, softly massaging its tip—the shape a frequent reminder that I was one of the Fae despite my still feeling human.

"Cibao University has been here for almost as long as the dome has. Naturally, we couldn't build any structures underwater without our blessed dome elemental. The very first dome elemental created the dome for the protection of humans. It's a scared elemental calling held by only one family in Atlantis," Myles informed me as we slid between another group of students in the grand hall, its arching windows casting light across the vast space. I fell into step beside him as curious stares swiveled our way, some of the Fae outwardly scowling at my Atlantian clothing. I could have sworn I'd heard Draevyn's low, rumbling growl behind me. "At Ciboa, we are proud to house faculty from every realm and believe in a well-rounded education," Myles continued as we approached the end of the hall. "It is for this reason that Cibao is so renowned. Unfortunately, the other queendoms do not embrace this practice, preferring to only employ their own."

"Why?" I asked. We ascended an imposing stone stairwell, my silk-clad feet tapping on each step. I refused to look behind me when a few light curses by several students were murmured in my wake. I assumed Draevyn's massive form was parting the crowd at the foot of the stairs.

"You'll find that the other queendoms are less liberal than Atlantis. Airelandia is the closest ally to us. They, too, believe in educating their citizens with faculty from other realms. Corenathia, not so much. Earthos—the Earth Fae—tend to keep to themselves. There's no telling what they do or do not do—let alone teach—in their realm. Some of their people attend Cibao, but the students and faculty are bound to secrecy. The curriculum the former learns and the latter teaches must be approved. It is something they take very seriously. If they reveal any unapproved information regarding their realm, they are spelled to forfeit their life on the spot." Myles angled off to the right at the top of the stairs, and we dodged a few more students heading in the opposite direction as he led us down a narrower hallway lined with thick oak doors.

My brows knitted together. "That sounds terrifying." A few more gasps and curses sounded from behind. I dared not look.

"Yes, it is. It is why asking an Earthonian about Earthos' customs and culture is considered offensive and rude. I strongly advise you never to risk it. Best to stick to friendly conversation."

"But why would they do that to their people?"

"Because when the ancient Earthonians witnessed the realms destroying each other during the last ice age, they decided to write solitude into law. Their ruler at the time cut off all connection to the other queendoms. The approved curriculum the Earthonian faculty teaches is very specific. They must only educate the students of Cibao about the history from *before* Earthos closed its realm. Even then, the information the students are taught is incredibly limited." Myles entered an empty classroom on the right-hand side of the hall, and a sense of nostalgia consumed me: the countless hours dedicated to my education, the times I'd missed a party here and there to study, much to Chrissy's disappointment. Those days seem so far away now that I found myself deep in the depths of the ocean in an empty classroom, with rows of weathered wooden chairs and blacktop tables, so much like my alma mater in the Above World. A pang of longing to study amongst the other students went straight to my heart. While I understood the reasoning, it would've been nice to get to know some of the others.

I quickly shook it off and stepped further into the classroom. There was no sense in dwelling on the what-ifs of life.

Myles set his bag on top of the desk at the head of the classroom. I slowly twirled and scanned the room.

Perfect rows of wooden tables spread to the back of a high-ceiling room. Dark, navy-blue shelves lined the back wall and reached the ceiling, housing hundreds of books. I squinted at the highest shelf to see if I could read the books there, but no luck.

"This will be our classroom for the foreseeable future. We'll attempt to cover all things, but we'll start with the most important: your safety." I turned to him then, his expression heavy with grave warning. "The other heirs also attend university. Remember, we don't know who is a friend and who is a foe now. The Akani may walk these halls alongside you, and we may not even know it. You'll need to be on your guard," Myles's gaze drifted to the hallway, the silence deepening as sessions began and the multiple doors on either side echoed shut. "And speaking of guards, you must get used to Commander Eliron following you around. He must be with you at all times. It's for your safety."

I peered out the open door, the now empty hallway silent. I couldn't see Draevyn, but I knew he was there, the odd feeling blooming within. The whole damn thing was puzzling. Frustrating.

Utterly confusing.

My jaw tightened as I nodded at Myles. He raised a knowing brow, but I cleared my throat and placed my bag on the table before his desk, ready to begin my studies and forget the looming presence in the hallway.

# Draevyn

# Chapter 10



*Get it the fuck together, Draevyn!*

That blasted phrase ran on repeat as I monitored the hallway, stewing over my idiocy. The Princess and the Secretary were just inside the classroom, and I was glad of it. I hadn't been affected by any- one like this since I was a Faeling, and even then, nothing compares to…her.

And I'd likely jumped straight out of her favor on the ride over.

This territory was foreign to me. All of my life, I'd had one goal in mind; to be the best Guard- ian the regimen had ever seen. It was a lofty goal. Many a warrior had accomplished this, but I want- ed to be the best. So, when my Elemental Mark confirmed what I'd already known in my soul, I began my pursuit. There were endless decades of studying techniques and researching the greats. I can still recall Dax's beet-red face when he'd finally relented and agreed to train me. I'd been outside of his quarters in Calichi, our esteemed Guardian outpost, pestering the enormous Viking who stood inches taller than me until he snapped and threw my head against a wall multiple times. With his fingers digging into my throat and blood trickling down my neck, I cited my intentions. I could still hear his rumbling tone telling me, "You'd better be sure this is what you want because to be the best, you'll have to make certain sacrifices the rest of your fellow Guardians aren't prepared to make." I understood exactly what he'd meant. My fellow Guardians wanted their leisure time to be with their mates, or go home and visit their families. My family wasn't the least bit happy about my being a Guardian, and I didn't have a mate. Problem solved.

I trained. I ate. I slept.

And yes, on occasion, I fucked.

But matters of the heart were a whole other thing entirely. I'd never had the time for it, never cared to.

Until now.

So, as I fidgeted like a young sapling yards away from the source of my reaction, I thought of ways to gain her favor.

Perhaps a better canoa ride on the way back. Maybe in the cabin where it's quieter. I could teach her about our ways.

But that was what Myles was doing right now. That was pointless.

Perhaps a walk in the gardens.

But that might be too intimate. Too forward.

I needed to start small; help her in some way. Perhaps I'd suggest that we practice morphing. That seemed to be a point of frustration for her. I couldn't stand to see her face fall every time she witnessed a Water Fae looking at her with anything other than respect. It would serve her purposes well and keep me from wanting to pound the face of every single one of those who looked upon her with even an inkling of disapproval.

Plus, I desperately wanted her to cover that island-kissed skin of hers with scales. The constant semi beneath mine was beginning to chafe.

A telltale rustling sounded from within the room, indicating they were wrapping up their session. I afforded myself a moment to take a deep breath into my lungs.

It was time to step out of my comfort zone.

# CHAPTER 11

MYLES HAD ALREADY DEPARTED BY THE time I'd packed the texts he'd instructed me to read for my next lesson. I hurried from the room, knowing *he'd* trail me the second I passed through the doorway. Sure enough, I could feel his presence looming at my back.

"How was your lesson?" he asked, increasing his pace with those long muscular legs to come up beside me—his scales shining against the light pouring in from the window of the stairwell landing. One small advantage to his presence was the sea of people parting for us as we approached. Silver lining and all that.

"It was good," I told him honestly as we began our descent down the wide stone staircase. "He didn't go into much. Just the basics. The other realms, which Fae rule them, which ones aren't our friends and which are our enemies and all that."

A Fae male rammed into my shoulder as we reached the foot of the stairs, pushing me into Draevyn's side and sending my tote flying against my back. The growl that ripped from Draevyn's throat gave pause to everyone in the room, including the Fae male who hadn't been looking where he was going and likely regretted it at that moment. He held his hands up and stared at Draevyn with wide eyes. "Sorry, man."

The heat gathering at my hip made me infinitely aware of his hand that had steadied my fall. I turned, my eyes trailing from the prominent chest blanketed in tunic-like scales to his chiseled jaw clenched tight. You could cook an egg with the heat rolling off of Draevyn's face as he shot the Fae male a venomous look. I carefully reached for his bare elbow, my fingertips brushing there. It seemed to be the distraction the Fae male needed to get away and for Draevyn to look down at me with those intense green eyes that resembled the clearest tropical waters. After a long, heavy moment, Draevyn reached out and lifted the tote from my shoulder, placing it on his. Apparently, chivalry wasn't dead. "Thank you."

"You okay?"

All I could do was nod.

His warm hand came to the small of my back, guiding me forward—the crowd giving us a clear path to where the canoas waited in the dark, musty cavern at the other end of the hall. "Tell me more about your lesson."

Right. My lesson.

"I mostly wanted to know how the tablet worked. I've never seen something that's been spelled like that. Pretty neat," I remarked as I gave him a brief sidelong glance.

The corner of his mouth twitched before he said,

"Yes, I guess that would be pretty neat. It's much different from the technology in the Above World. It's a shame it took them centuries to match what we can do with our magic."

I tilted my head as we exited the hall and paused in the waiting area for Braeliah. "I didn't think of it like that, but I suppose the Fae have had faelights and tablets for a while then, huh?"

"Yes, for as long back as I can remember."

I shook my head in wonder. "That's wild."

"Very wild."

We both chuckled as we shared a look, and I realized it was the first time we'd laughed together. And I liked it.

Draevyn looked toward the ground and cleared his throat. "I was wondering, Princess, if you wanted to perhaps practice morphing into your scales? No need to panic. Just the basics." He smiled warmly at my wide eyes. "Basics are the theme for the day, yes?"

I returned his smile. "Yes, it is."

His head dipped in a nod. "Perfect. Then, that's what we'll do."

We stood before the Shingu River, a slight tremble traveling down my spine. I expelled the breath I'd been holding and glanced sidelong at Draevyn, who waited with his arms crossed. "There's nothing to it, Princess. You need to get in the water first."

My brow quirked. "Easier said than done, don't you think?"

A shrug.

We'd been standing before the river at the edge of

the palace gardens for, give or take, five minutes while I worked up the nerve to step into the water. I gestured to my clothing. "I…uh…what about my clothing."

The devilish smile that emerged on his face could melt iron. "Well, you are welcome to unclothe yourself if you'd like, but you'd be gloriously nude going in."

I was sure I would die of mortification. "I just meant—"

"You're stalling, Asherah."

I blew a raspberry. "Yes, yes. I know."

He strode into the shallow water of the river with a splash, his webbed feet leaving footprints on the muddy bank. When he was hip deep, he turned to me and beckoned. "Come."

I put one foot in front of the other, the cool water rising to my knees and then my thighs as I gingerly stepped toward him. I placed my hand in his awaiting one, and the tingling sensation in my chest gave a little tickle. I brought my steady gaze to his eyes. "Okay. I'm here."

"That's half the battle," he teased. "We'll start with your lower body and work your way up. Your feet have webbing that protects your soles from puncture wounds or anything of the sort. It's why we don't wear shoes. There's no need."

My brow furrowed as I stared down at my feet in the clear water. "So, how do I…you know. Morph?"

"To be a Water Fae is in your very blood. You need to will it. I'm guessing that you feel a slight itch all over your lower body."

I hadn't realized it, but my wet skin was pricking slightly. "I do feel that, yes."

"Most faelings begin feeling that itch a few years after birth. You wouldn't have felt it being spellbound as you were. But now that you're unbound, as soon as you come into contact with water those scales will be begging for you to let them loose. Close your eyes, Asherah." My eyes closed as the soothing tone of his voice washed over me. "Imagine the thin layer of webbing between your toes, the iridescent skin draping all over your feet and rising to meet your beautiful blueish-green scales at the base of your ankles." With each word from his lips, the vision began to take hold in my mind as if I were glancing down into the water and seeing my feet and ankles in my Water Fae form. "Those scales travel all the way to cover the sunkissed skin of those beautifully shaped legs."

His words had me short of breath, but the itching sensation began to subside as I saw my legs blanketed with scales in my mind.

"They rise to the breathtaking curves of your hips and over the flat planes of your abdomen rising still to cover your..."

The flowing river of the Shingu was the only sound for a few heavy seconds. I didn't dare open my eyes when I quirked a brow. "Yes?"

He cleared his throat. "To cover your chest."

"Suddenly, out of adjectives?"

The deep rumble of his chuckle was such a beautiful sound I longed to hear more of. Without warning, I felt the warm breath from his mouth at my tipped ear. "Open your eyes," he whispered.

When I did, the wall of muscle at his now bare chest greeted me before he backed away. "Look at yourself, Asherah."

The light reflecting off the surface of the river briefly assaulted my eyes before I beheld what I saw below. A thin layer of skin stretched between my toes, and blueish-green scales rose underneath the sheer layer of my Altantian jumper. My mouth dropped open as my gaze roamed over my legs and torso, observing the scales fanning and rising to the top of my breasts and spreading outward to the center of my upper arm—the cool air kissing my bare shoulders in contrast to the comfortable warmth my scales emitted on my skin. My breath hitched as I took in the exquisite pattern that carried all the way to my wrists. As I held my arms out, the light glimmered across them. "This is amazing."

"So beautiful," he whispered. That had my head snapping to him, a pure look of wonder on his face. We were lost for a moment, just he and I in the shallow part of the river, drinking in every detail of each other like a spell had been cast that neither of us wanted to break. I could get very, very lost in him without any intention of being found. Draevyn was the first to shatter the spell as he cleared his throat and briefly looked away. "Very nice job. The shape suits you well."

The tips of my fingers brushed over the fanning in an A-line off-the-shoulder style. "I don't know how I did this."

He ran a hand through his long, dark brown locks. "Soon enough, you'll be able to manipulate the scales into any design you wish. It takes some practice, but many Atlantians fashion their scales into dresses, tunics—"

"Tails?"

His mouth quirked. "Like a mermaid, you mean?" He continued when I gave him an apprehensive nod, "Yes, there is some truth to the whole mermaid mythology. We can fashion our scales into a tail. It's rather useful for traveling at great speed with the other predators of the deep. Or we can swim just as fast with our scaled legs and webbed feet." His shoulder lifted in a shrug. "The scales are meant to give your body warmth, to protect it from puncture."

The question was out of my mouth before I could stop it, "Then why couldn't the scales save my mother?"

There was a darkness that spread across his features. "We can't figure out what happened on the yacht after you all escaped that evening. Normally, our scales can protect us from puncture and fire to a certain degree. My theory? Something kept them from donning their scales. It's possible she and Dax were injected with something. I…" he shook his head. "I wish I could give you a better answer, one that you deserve, but there was very little we could tell from the yacht since it had been so badly burned. And Dax's memories of the day…well…he hasn't been able to speak of it. It's as if he's blocked it all out. Like the details are too painful to recall. I don't fault him for it."

Truth be told, I didn't blame Dax either. If I'd been on that yacht and watched someone I revered and swore to protect die before my eyes, I wouldn't want to remember it either.

He let out a loud exhale and waded a little deeper, the deep 'v' of his abdomen dipping below the water's surface. "At any rate, the scales are meant to protect you from all types of predators, even the ones within the queendom. There are many a human female who wishes they had scales to protect them from pathetic, weak men who take things without consent."

I tucked a stray hair behind my tipped ear. "Oh. I hadn't thought of that."

"Yes, not having scales presents a certain level of vulnerability," he cautioned, his palm coasting over the water's surface absentmindedly. "It's why I wanted to help you." He held that strong, rough hand out to me.

"Come. Let's practice breathing the water."

Breathing the water.

Totally normal.

The slick pebbles and rocks pushed against the soles of my feet as I carefully stepped forward, placing my smaller hand in his. Draevyn leaned back into the water and kept his eyes on me—pulling me to the center of the Shingu. When he let go of my hand, I swam in open fascination as my webbed feet flicked just enough to keep my head above water.

There was one question I was dying to ask but didn't. My cheeks heated a bit at the thought of it.

"What—pray tell—is causing the blush across your face?" he asked with the most amused smile.

Well, now I'd done it. "H-how does…how do…"

"My, this must be a good question for you to be this flustered."

I dashed the back of my hand across the water, splashing him in the face. His broad laugh reached his sparkling eyes.

"How does the Water Fae relieve themselves…or have sex while in their scales?"

His laughter stopped abruptly. I nearly melted into the Shingu when the commander of Atlantis bit his lip before providing his answer. "Well, Asherah. The answer to the first is the same for the second. If we are in the company of another and want to be discreet, we part our scales to relieve ourselves." His glimmering green eyes glazed with naked hunger. "The area of my body used to bring females to pleasure is called a cock pocket, and when I use it, Princess, I part the scales there too, just as you can if you were to fuck a male."

My cheeks heated with an immense flush. His carefully crafted words sounded like a sinful promise.

"Any other lingering questions in that wonderful mind of yours?" he asked, his murmur echoing off the surface of the water.

I could do nothing but shake my head. My voice seemed to have momentarily disappeared.

"Perfect. Then, let's practice."

My mouth fell open. "What?"

His brow lifted to his hairline. "Breathing the water, not parting the scales."

I looked away. "Right."

"Dip underwater."

Wanting nothing more but to end the awkward tension, I took a deep breath into my lungs and dipped below the water's surface—my arms cutting through the weight of the water. What waited for me below caused my eyes to widen. Every spec, every piece of debris, every jagged rock edge and smooth surface could be seen with perfect clarity. I reached out and plucked a sodden leaf from the current, marveling at the shades of dulling brown and deep hunter-green.

*"Can you hear me, Asherah?"*

I jerked back, my gaze immediately seeking out Draevyn, who looked upon me with careful patience. *"It's okay. We can mind-to-mind talk underwater in our Fae form."*

*"Can you hear me?"*

*"Yes. Clear as a bell."* His grip came around my hand as he pulled me closer to him. *"The water serves as a source of oxygen. You'll need to let go of your breath first."*

A deep panic engulfed me. My head shook vigorously back and forth.

*"It's okay, Asherah. You'll not drown. Breathe the water in."*

My scales began retreating, and my tanned skin took

over as he held firm to my hand.

*"It's okay."*

*"Stop saying it's okay, and let go of my hand!"* I shot back, spearing him with a glare.

The second he released me, I swam for the water's surface, inhaling deeply as I breached. My breaths came in quick succession, and my heart pounded in my chest—a deep sense of failure immediately taking hold.

Draevyn rose a moment later, and his dark and stormy gaze landed on me. "What happened?"

I shook my head. "I just…couldn't wrap my mind around it."

He nodded resolutely. "Perhaps it was too much, too soon."

"I'm sorry," I breathed.

"No need to be sorry," he consoled. His muscular arms cut through the water as he began swimming for the riverbank. "Come, let's get back to the palace."

I left a part of my heart on the Shingu River that day. I couldn't help but feel I had failed my first test as a Water Fae and let Draevyn down.

# Chapter 12

"Y**OU LOOK LIKE AN ABSOLUTE DREAM,** Your Highness," Reneah, my chambermaid, said as she beamed at me from around my shoulder, gazing at my reflection in the mirror. Her very human features gave me a sense of calm—a sense of normalcy in the world of the Fae. Reneah had been a constant companion in the weeks since my arrival in Atlantis. During those first few weeks, she'd silently enter my quarters and exit on tiny stealth feet. I'd heard her, but didn't have the energy to see who'd entered the room. With Mayana standing guard in the hallway just outside my quarters, I felt reassured, allowing myself to remain secluded within the confines of my room.

One day, I'd been tucked into the comfy velvet armchair in the living room—a generously spacious area that sat in front of a granite-surfaced sandstone kitchen with all the amenities that I needed—when in came this young human woman who looked to be a little older and a foot shorter than me. She'd worn the traditional chambermaid uniform—a light blue tunic and tapered black pants—that I'd seen the rest of the palace staff in. It was her big brown eyes that went wide at what I held in my hand that caused her wide lips to break out in a smile. "You're reading Tales of a Shattered Kingdom. I love that book."

Right then, I knew she and I would be instant friends.

And these past few weeks, whenever I was in a funk I couldn't seem to lift myself out of, Reneah was there to ensure I was fed, bathed, or give an uplifting smile when it seemed my grief would never ease. Perhaps it never would, but with Reneah's help, I could go about my day more easily.

Reneah's angular face, with its fair skin, deep brown eyes, and thick dirty blond hair tied tight at the base of her neck, was likened to a fairy godmother about to send her fairy goddaughter off to the ball as she gave me a final head-to-toe assessment. Admittedly, that's what I felt like. I brushed my slender hands over the smooth silk fabric of my teal dress. It looked even better with all the alterations and adjustments Aurelio made—something both Aurelio and Reneah spoke of for nearly an hour when he'd dropped off the dress earlier that week, the two of them thick as thieves.

I glanced at the clock on the shiny mahogany nightstand, noting only an hour left. It sent my emotions into a cascading waterfall, landing in the pit of my stomach. The dread of being in front of so many people was a steady hum that grew in intensity as day turned into night. Mom's warm smile flitted about in my mind. I'd do it for her. It's what she would've wanted. I inhaled deeply.

"That's it," Reneah encouraged. "Deep breaths. Remember, you were born for this. And you're going to rock the ballroom." Her wide lips lifted in a mischievous quirk. "You hold that chin high and look that wicked witch, Melysah, right in the face with nothing less than condescension."

I burst into a chuckle, wheeling around to her. "Wow. Reneah has a mean girl side."

Reneah placed a hand on her hip. "I've been known a time or two to let the lioness spring forth," she said with a wink. "And my feelings are warranted. When your mother wasn't around to stop Melysah, she'd take full advantage of the royal staff. Melysah was tough on the humans, giving us all sorts of random projects. But she left the Water Fae to tend to their regular palace duties. She could be quite awful, that one. Despite having her own home in town, she'd take up residence in one of the spare rooms of the palace. And that's when the demands would start. Personal trips to the stores, waiting on her and her merry band of lovers long into the evening, fetching them all sorts of different things the palace staff still gossips about. It left me praying every night before bed for Neleah's return to Atlantis. She was a buffer for us, and even though we'd never utter a complaint to Neleah because of the pressure she was under, she could sense the ease of her staff when she returned. She may have even caught Melysah ordering a few human chambermaids a time or two and shooed her off. So, this evening? You'd best believe I'll be your biggest cheerleader from the sidelines."

My head tilted. "From the sidelines? You're not going to the ball?"

Her smile fell. "I'm afraid not. It wouldn't be my place."

I wrinkled my nose. "And why not?"

"Well, the Elemental Ball is for the Water Fae, Guardians, Council Members, and their invited guests, Your Highness."

"Quit calling me 'Your Highness.' Just call me Ash. Do they not let humans into the ball?"

"Oh! No, no. It's nothing like that. On the contrary, Atlantis is very kind to the humans. Or at least…"

My brow furrowed. "At least what, Reneah?" I asked when she fell silent.

Reneah wrung her petite hands at her middle. "Well, ever since the coming of the new ice age, tensions with the humans are getting a little sticky. We've never felt unwelcome in Atlantis. It's just…some of the Fae are boldly expressing frustrations at the prospect of welcoming more human refugees. And the next second, they're looking at us like they'd rather not have Atlantian-born humans here either. For many of us, Atlantis is the only home we know."

I cocked an eyebrow in surprise. "You've never been to the Above World?"

Reneah jerked back slightly, a stray strand of her golden hair coming loose from behind her rounded ear. "Goddess, no. We're not permitted. Our people took an oath to protect Atlantis. Part of that protection means that our people are to remain here. We take that very seriously. Even suggesting that the Atlantian humans visit the Above World is considered sacrilegious—and no offense, but I don't know if I'd want to. Yes, I hear it's amazing up there—the hills, mountains, waterfalls, and crystal blue skies. Aurelio and Myles show us pictures of all their travels, and they're breathtaking. But the near-constant wars and killing are terrifying. It never stops, and it seems to be designed that way." Reneah sighed. "Granted, it looks like we're gearing up for a war of our own. My only hope is that the Atlantians rally behind the humans who will likely need a place to call home, just like our ancestors."

My lips pulled back in a grimace. "Well, you shouldn't feel like this isn't your home. That's not right. Atlantis is more your home than it is mine."

Reneah smiled timidly. "It makes me happy you think so. Your kindness toward me, as a human, tells me everything I need to know about you. Would you mind if I confessed something?"

I fluttered a hand. "Not at all."

Reneah's head dipped in a nod. "Your mother and father are catching a lot of flack for raising you in the Above World; however, I think it's wonderful. And I'm not alone in my thinking. Many Atlantian humans were deeply moved by their actions. It was as if they could foresee that we'd need an advocate."

Something clicked in my mind. All the sacrifices my parents made, and the tension Dad was now dealing with seemed all the more significant. It meant something to their people—our people—who were born human in Atlantis. And it gave me an advantage no other royal had had until me—empathy.

"Anyway, I'm sure you'll see a few humans milling about, but they must be invited." She glanced at the ceiling thoughtfully. "It's kind of like the Oscars in your Above World. All the glitz and glamor with all the fans waiting outside."

I felt a pang of sympathy for Reneah. I hadn't realized the Elemental Ball was exclusive. "Couldn't I just invite you? As my guest?"

Reneah's eyes went wide. "Holy shit. Shoot. Crap." Her hand flew to her mouth. "Pardon my language. Oh, my word. But I couldn't. What in the world would I wear?"

I laughed and motioned around the room. "We live in an underwater palace. There has to be something we can find for you."

Reneah let out a girly squeal and jumped up and down. "Aurelio is going to freak out when I show up. Can I hug you? Is that even appropriate?"

I couldn't suppress the laugh that tumbled out of me as she gripped me in a tight hug. "Of course, you can. We're friends."

Reneah pulled back. "Friends?"

I nodded. "If that's okay with you."

Reneah smiled radiantly. "Friends it is, Your...Ash."

I gave her shoulders a squeeze. "Now, let's find you something to wear. I'm sure there is something in my mother's closet, yes?"

I almost laughed again at the shock written on Reneah's face. "You want me to wear something from the Queen's closet? That's just mad."

"Why?"

Reneah pressed a hand to her throat. "She was...the Queen. I couldn't do that."

I placed a hand on my hip. "Sure you can. She would've been honored to have you wear one of her dresses."

Reneah blew out a breath. "Okay, fine. But nothing too elaborate. As it is, Neleah was much taller than I am."

"Heels?"

"Definitely." Reneah locked her arm in mine. "Let's go to her quarters and see if we can find anything suitable."

My curiosity spiked. I'd never seen the inside of my

parents' quarters in Atlantis. Why hadn't I thought to see it sooner?

We emerged from my quarters and found Mayana standing guard—her back ramrod straight and her trident proudly at her side.

"Mayana. I wasn't expecting to see you."

Mayana bowed at the waist—her midnight black braid falling over her shoulder. "Your Highness, Commander Eliron is preparing for this evening's ceremony and ball. I'll be on guard till he relieves me."

I don't know why I felt disappointed.

A lie. That was a lie.

I could still see the tick in his jaw from our last meeting in my head. He hadn't spoken to me about my failed lesson, and I hadn't worked up the courage to open the front door of my quarters and speak with him about it either.

Reneah squeezed my arm, pulling me from my thoughts. "Come. We need to hurry."

I gave Mayana a slight smile as we proceeded down the hallway—her near-silent steps sounding behind us. We descended the staircase at the end of the hallway, our quick strides carrying us to a floor that mimicked mine. As we entered the luxurious room, Reneah explained, "These are your parents' quarters. Well, technically, they're your quarters, or it will be once you are crowned. Your father isn't here yet but should be at any minute. I'll hurry and see what I can find." She disappeared into a set of double doors just inside the darkened bedroom where I could just make out the large four-poster bed.

With Reneah leaving me to my observations, I padded across a living room three times the size of mine. A stone fireplace reaching to the ceiling loomed over a small table nestled between two sitting chairs before it.

A few metal photo frames sat on a long sea glass table against the window at the back of the room. I stopped before it, taking in the photos within the frames. A smile spread on my face when my own image stared back at me. I remembered the day as if it were yesterday. We visited Yosemite for the first time, and the image captured my cheeks burning bright red with the effort of completing a hike to Bridal Falls.

Another frame sitting just behind the others caught my eye. I placed the Yosemite picture on the table, and the cool metal of the other frame bit into my skin as I picked it up. My parents sat on a vast, sandy beach in the Above World, their pointed ears on full display, indicating the beach's exclusivity. Their laughter could be heard through the weathered black-and-white photo. My heart squeezed to see them so happy.

I squinted as something caught my eye on my father's chest. It resembled the very same tattoo-like Elemental markings I'd seen on the wrists of so many of the Fae, and they both shared the same style on the left side of their chests. I traced the cool glass of the frame with a fingertip, my brow furrowing as I tried to remember ever seeing a mark like that on them. But I was certain this was my first time seeing them.

Someone walked through the open door behind me, breaking me from my musings. I glanced over my shoulder and found Dad searching the room in confusion until his gaze fell on me. "Ah. Found our quarters, have you?"

I smiled. "Reneah is raiding Mom's closet for a dress. I've invited her as my guest to the ball. I figured she could find something to wear. I don't think Mom would have minded, but if you think it's a bad idea—"

He dashed a hand in the air. "Of course not. I'm sure your mother would have loved for Reneah to wear one of her dresses to the ball, just as I'm certain it would mean the world to Reneah. She misses Neleah just as much as us," Dad assured me. His gaze shifted to the frame in my hand as he pointed to it. "What is that you have there?"

I held it up, giving it a gentle shake. "It's a picture of you and Mom on the beach." My gaze drifted back to the photo. "When was this taken?"

He plodded toward me, a small smile on his lips as he came to stand at my side. "That was back in nineteen fifty-three. A few of us traveled to a secluded beach in the Above World; hence the Fae features." He huffed a laugh, shaking his head. "Don't ask what we were laughing at. It was probably insignificant, but I'm glad Myles caught the picture anyway. It's a good one of us." His Adam's apple bobbed on a swallow. "A good one of her."

"And the markings on your chests? I don't remember ever seeing those. What are they?"

A pause. "Those are our bondmate marks, and you wouldn't have seen them since we'd always had our glamour around you."

I twisted to him. "Bondmate marks?"

He nodded, his gaze fixed on the photo. "They're a representation to the world as bondmates."

I returned the frame to the table, the metal briefing clinking against the glass. "Oh. I didn't know you all were into tattoos."

He laughed. "They're not tattoos, Sher. They're marks much like the Elemental mark you'll receive today. They are goddess-blessed, a sign that one is your fated mate. Your bondmate."

My brows dipped as my arms slid into a cross. "Myles and Aurelio mentioned they were bondmates, and that it's a pretty permanent thing."

"It is. It's not like the Above World and marriages on

paper filed at a courthouse. They're your mate for as long as you live, and for the Fae, that's a pretty long time."

My eyes shifted back to the image of my mother, the way her mouth parted in a carefree laugh. "And what happens if your bondmate dies?" When he didn't answer, I glanced back at him. I couldn't help but notice the slight glistening in his eyes.

"Besides feeling like something tethered was cut directly from your soul? Your bond mark changes, as I've come to find out." He let his scales drop on the upper left area of his chest to reveal a now very different mark than the one in the photograph. It appeared the same with one major difference—its curving lines that swirled at the ends were now just an outline of the marking itself. The inside turned back to the color of his flesh. He traced it with his finger. "You see, the goddess believes in love, yes? So, the mark is meant to be filled again if one finds love after their bondmate passes." He sighed heavily. "Although I can't even imagine someone replacing your mother. The thought sickens me."

I didn't know how to feel about that either, but I squeezed his upper arm in comfort. "If it helps, I can't imagine you with anyone else but Mom. But it seems this goddess is a pretty smart lady."

He chuckled, bringing the back of his hand to wipe a tear that escaped. "Yes, that she is. That goddess. Always up to something."

"I think I got it!" Reneah called from the closet. Just a few moments later, she dashed into the room in a ruby-red dress that hugged every curve of her body, her hands traveling over the fabric to straighten the creases. When she looked up, she froze at the sight of Dad. "Oh, my goddess!" She curtsied low. "I am so sorry, Your Highness."

"Don't be," he assured her, his voice going soft. "You look beautiful, Reneah. Neleah would have loved to see you in her dress. *And* going to an Elemental Ball. She would've been pleased. Thank you for accompanying my daughter. You can steer her clear of all the busybodies and the troublemakers."

Reneah nodded vigorously. "Absolutely, Your Highness. I've got her."

I let loose a sigh. "Ugh. Now I'm even more nervous. Can't we just do the Elemental Ceremony?"

"And miss all the fashion?" Reneah exclaimed, bringing her palm to her throat. "Blasphemous!"

Within a few minutes, Reneah changed back into her clothes with my mother's ruby-red dress in tow, leaving Dad to prepare for the ball and me to further deliberate over bondmates—those questions rattling around in my head long after I departed his quarters.

A sense of dèjá vu traveled down my spine as I strode up the stone pathway to the Temple of Atabey—the scene eerily reminiscent of my mother's Wylemei. The memories of Atlantians with tears streaming down their faces as Mother's body passed them by—some human, some Fae—rattled through my mind. And yet, a part of her presence strolled along with me, an essence of her so palpable it felt like a warm blanket had been thrown over my shoulders. It had the ticking of nerves dialing down to a steady hum. The reverent energy emanating from the crowd rolled off them in waves—bowing as I passed them.

I silently recited Myles' instructions—where to stand

and who would be there with me—as my steps carried me to the base of the temple steps. So, it was no surprise to find Dad waiting with Dax at his side, standing tall and proud in their scales. Reneah informed me that everyone else dresses in ball attire after ceremonies. But I refused for my ceremonial experience to be lessened by my choice to wear my ball gown. I may not be able to don my scales at will yet, but at least the dress was extraordinary.

The other Guardians stood directly behind Dad and Dax in a near-perfect line—their glowing gold tridents on full display. As I came to stand before them, my eyes narrowed on a dangling piece of jewelry in the palm of my father's hand—the light of the fading day catching on it. He opened his palm, and a beautiful shimmering chain of little intertwined leaves fastened to a dangling teardrop diamond hung from his fingers. "This was your mother's," he told me. "It's a headdress. She wore it during her elemental ceremony. I know she'd want you to wear it, so a part of her is with you."

My vision blurred. I blinked away the moisture from my eyes as he placed the circular headdress on my head— the dangling diamond tickling my forehead. There was no avoiding the tightening in my throat when I witnessed the flash of pride and pain on my father's face.

"Thank you," I croaked.

He pulled me into a gentle hug before fussing with the headdress and positioning the large flowing curls of my long brown hair that Reneah styled to perfection behind my back. "You look amazing, Sher Bear."

"Thanks, Dad."

He cleared his throat. "Okay. Go ahead, honey. The Bohiti is waiting for you. I'll be right here."

My head dipped in a nod before I began my ascent up

the giant stone temple steps. My heart was a hammer in my chest, but a sense of calm so at odds with my current state caressed my building anxiety.

It tugged.

I halted, my gaze instinctively shifting over my shoulder and fixing on Draevyn positioned at the foot of the stairs. His handsome face brightened, and a slight smile lifted the corner of his lips. Despite the awkwardness at the end of our last lesson, I couldn't help but return it and felt instant relief when I witnessed the subtle dip of his head.

I let loose a breath I hadn't known I was holding and proceeded to the top of the steps, where a tiny female with glossy black hair that reached her lower back waited. The might of the Bohiti stood before me; a female filled to the brim with magical capabilities who led the high priestesses comprised of Fae from all realms. They existed as spiritual leaders for neither water nor fire, nor air or earth, but for all. I now understood what Myles meant about the fearsome high priestess. She was pure power, like stepping into an aura that could be felt but not seen.

The emerald diamond of her similarly fashioned headdress dangled off the bronzed skin of her forehead as she bowed before me. The smile upon her lips as she rose reached her glowing almond-shaped obsidian eyes. "Welcome, Princess Asherah. I am the Bohiti Loma. It's a true honor to reveal your elemental mark today." She gestured behind her with an elegant hand. "If you'll follow me this way."

The Bohiti led me to a dais just beyond the temple opening, her long white robes whispering across the marble floors. On top of the dais, a small bowl made of the deepest black lava rock was nestled between two glass pitchers and perched on top of a hip-high black marble pillar with clusters of rich gold veins snaking across it. I froze when my gaze caught on what lay at the back of the temple like an ominous shadow bearing witness—the pyre where Mom's body had turned to ash. Echoes from the beast of grief within my soul reared its ugly head, beckoning me to succumb to the dark depths of depression that awaited me, had engulfed me.

I immediately shook it off. I wouldn't go down that lonely road again. It did no one any favors, not with the weight of the realm on my shoulders.

Mom wouldn't want it.

And the beast of grief found sleep once again.

Two High Priestesses stepped out of the shadows and into the hue of the warm blue faelights that dimly lit the temple, their white robes flowing behind them on an errant wind. Unlike the Bohiti with her beautiful razor-straight hair, theirs had been parted down the middle and tied in a bun at the nape of their neck.

The Bohiti took my hand in her delicate one, turning my wrist over the bowl. One priestess reached for the glass pitcher filled with thick, golden oil while the other cradled a small rust-colored clay mortar in her palms. A fraction of the oil glowed like a beam of sunlight as it flowed into the awaiting mortar below. The Bohiti procured a small burlap packet from the inner pocket of her robes. The mesmerizing whispers of her incantation began flowing from lips, intertwining and weaving in a practiced dance of words. My mouth fell open of its own accord, complete and utter awe washing over me.

Whispers became murmurs when the two priestesses joined with the Bohiti in her incantation, and goosebumps spread down the arm hanging over the lava rock bowl. The contents of the small burlap packet were emptied into the clay mortar dutifully held within the priestess's hands without a flinch. The other handed the Bohiti a matching pestle that had laid in the shadow of the lava rock bowl. She began crushing the oils and the contents; the intoxicating earthy aromas of cedarwood, sandalwood, cloves, and deep red roses reached my nose as she crushed them beneath her pestle. The Bohiti gathered a bit of the substance on her delicate pointer and gingerly spread it over the sunkissed skin on the inside of my wrist. She then gently rubbed a thumb against my skin in a circular motion—their chanting growing louder and more frantic with each passing second.

A wild burning sensation spread just below the Bohiti's thumb, and my eyes widened as I beheld the black mark with ink of the darkest night sky beginning to manifest—an elemental mark different from any of the others I'd observed. Its swirling lines gracefully curved up and down, and a small black dot affixed itself at the base of the mark. A clear stream of water poured from the spout of the other glass pitcher, washing away the contents that covered my mark into the awaiting bowl below. It was stark black now, the lines definite and imposing.

The Bohiti leaned forward, a crease forming between her brows before she lifted her head and smiled. "You have the royal mark just as we expected, Princess Asherah. May the goddess bless your reign." All three priestesses bowed, their bright white robes kissing the floor before the Bohiti rose to guide me toward the temple entrance.

As my three-inch diamond-flecked teal heels clicked against the marble floors, I just kept staring at the mark— my mark—with a smile that made my cheeks hurt. All I could think, all I could feel, was that I'd hoped I'd made Mom proud.

"Princess Asherah, would you mind if I saw your elemental mark one last time?" the Bohiti asked as we passed underneath the massive metal bowl that hung on thick brass chains over the temple entrance.

I nodded, holding out my wrist for her inspection.

The crease between her brows appeared again, her fingers tracing over the small dot at the base of the mark.

The feeling of elation I'd felt a moment before began to dissipate. I tilted my head, ready to inquire about what had visibly perplexed her, but my attention was abruptly seized by the pounding footfalls on the entrance steps. I swiveled around, and my breath left me. My father's face was full of pride and joy. It was the first time he'd shown any sign of pure, unfiltered happiness in a while, and it instantly warmed my heart. He glanced down at my wrist. "The royal mark. I knew it would come through," he beamed. He wrapped me in his arms and lifted me in a twirl—my feet and dress whirling behind me. I instantly feared knocking into the Bohiti, but when he set me down, she had already retreated. My eyes fixed on her disappearing form, swallowed by the shadows of the temple. The faelights winked out in her wake.

# Chapter 13

The high domed ceiling outside the massive wooden doors that led to the ballroom within the palace loomed above me. Thousands of tiny crystals glimmered in beautiful hues of purple and blue from where they hung on the chandelier above the vestibule—hundreds of faelights amplifying their shine. I'd never been to this side of the palace, and my mouth hung open in awe as I took it all in. It was simply stunning, with its large sandstone pillars, archways, and imposing windows visible through the open doorway, along with the hundreds of people inside the ballroom I chose to ignore. "Amazing," I murmured.

"Yes, it is wonderful, isn't it?" Reneah mused. The bottom of her ruby-red dress hissed against the sandstone as she slowly circled me for the tenth time. She bent to tug on the teal fabric at the bottom of my mermaid-fit dress, ensuring all the creases were smoothed out. Having found satisfaction with her fiddling, she stepped back with a wide smile. "You look absolutely perfect."

The corners of my lips quirked into a light smile. "Thank you."

"Okay, I'll be waiting for you in the corner of the room," she declared, resting a hand on her hip. "You and your father will have the first dance. And don't make that face. You'll be just fine. Myles will introduce you to the crowd. The dance will be over before you know it, and then we can find some fabulous faerie wine, dissect people's fashion sense, and stare at all the handsome centuries-old Fae males from the corner of the room all night long."

I breathed in deeply. "Okay. I can do this."

Reneah's gaze slid over my shoulder. "Speaking of handsome males, here comes your father."

I twisted at the waist just in time to see him enter the vestibule. It was a shock to see him in human-style clothing. I realized I'd become accustomed to seeing him in his scales, a sobering thought. He straightened the black satin lapels of his tuxedo jacket—the matching vest peeking from beneath the opulent fabric. The crisp white dress shirt, stark black bowtie, and smooth pant legs lent to his regal look. Flustered but regal. I never had to wonder where my wallflower trait came from. That much was clear.

He looked up from the cufflink he was fussing with and finally noticed me before him. He raised his arms wide. "There's my girl." He wrapped me in a careful fatherly hug, his gaze sweeping over my dress as he pulled back. "I didn't have time to tell you before the ceremony, but you look wonderful, Sher. So much like your mother," he said with a bittersweet smile. He glanced over my shoulder to where Reneah quietly stood. "You did a fantastic job."

A scarlet flush crept across Reneah's fair complexion. "Thank you, Your Highness." She briefly peered into the ballroom. "Looks like Myles is ready for you all. I'd better get inside." Her hand reached out, gripping mine with a reassuring squeeze. "Remember to breathe, Ash. Keep your back straight and shoulders back. Posture is everything." With a final curtsy and a flick of those brown eyes to Dad, Reneah disappeared into the awaiting crowd beyond the open doors of the ballroom.

I blew out a breath and lengthened my spine as I snaked an arm through my father's awaiting elbow. Myles' voice carried over the hum of the crowd. "It is my honor to present his royal highness, King Regent Cathan Rosahan Delmar and Princess Asherah Delmar Rosahan."

The applause of the crowd echoed in the vast space of the ballroom as Dad pulled me forward on unsteady feet. Somehow, through the goddess's great mercy, I didn't trip—the sea of people parting before an empty area in the center of the room designated for dancing. A long, dark sliver of wood amongst the lighter floorboards became my sole focus to calm my erratic nerves.

"You're doing fine, Sher Bear," Dad whispered between polite nods and waves.

Desperate for any sort of distraction, I asked, "Why did they announce you as Cathan Rosahan Delmar?"

The sea of people continued to murmur their greetings when, at last, they began to dissipate as we reached the open space. "Because in Atlantis, we take the female's surname, as is tradition." As we reached the center of the room, he twirled me toward him—his arm coming to the center of my back. "Just place your right hand in mine, and we'll be done soon enough."

My nose wrinkled. "I don't know this dance."

An amused expression quirked on the side of his mouth as the music from the quartet in the corner of the ballroom began playing a tune I vaguely recognized. "Actually, you do." I listened intently as he guided us across the dance floor, my steps subconsciously following his lead. "Remember when you were a little girl? We spent the long family days together, just the three of us until the sun dipped below the horizon. You'd be swimming in the pool while I grilled fresh fillets or fat juicy burgers; your mother busy inside making whatever dish she could conjure?"

My brow rose. "Burnt mac & cheese?"

He let out a laugh that traveled through the ballroom despite the music. "Yes, your mother and her cooking. She was so great even the fire alarm cheered her on."

"Or so the sign in the kitchen told us," I quipped with a solemn smile. "Goddess, how I miss her."

"Me too," he murmured. He continued after collecting himself, "Anyway, I used to dance with you on the pool deck, remember?" He swirled us around again, my legs surprisingly matching every step my father made. My brow furrowed as he continued, "The steps I taught you when you were a faeling are from the traditional Atlantian dance. So, you do know it," he said, pride radiating in his eyes. The music moved to a crescendo, and he turned me—the flare of my dress fanning out and sparkling against the faelights. He gracefully pulled me into his hold and continued around the room.

The steps came back to me slowly, more confidently. I danced effortlessly past the crowd of onlookers in their beautiful finery of vibrant colors, noting a few surprised faces. I took comfort in the familiarity of something I had no idea meant something to the people I was expected to lead.

*A dance doesn't mean you can lead a queendom, Ash.*

My excitement dimmed at the thought.

Within a few more turns, the quartet finished the last strums of the song. I mirrored my father's movements, bowing to the crowd with shaky legs.

As soon as Dad strolled to the side of the room to greet one of the council members waiting for him on the edge of the dance floor, I escaped through the sea of whispers and luxurious fabrics, floral perfumes, and pointed stares. I let out a sigh of relief when I finally reached Reneah, who awaited me next to a buffet table filled with an assortment of delicious finger foods to nibble on: chunks of cheese in various yellow shades, small slices of white cheese with deep blue veins, rice crackers peppered with sesame seeds, bright green grapes, and savory empanadas. She handed me a plate with a little bit of everything. "You danced beautifully."

"Thanks," I replied while an empanada's rich, meaty flavors assaulted my tongue. I stifled a moan and pointed its tip toward the dance floor. "You're not going to dance?"

Reneah lifted a petite shoulder. "Maybe. I'd much prefer to analyze dresses from afar, though. I can never get enough of the fashion. We never see enough of it on the Fae."

I quirked my head. "You truly love the fashion world, huh?"

Her face brightened. "Oh, without a doubt. And what's not to love? Being able to make people feel beautiful through something that I created? That's power. Of course, I'm nowhere near Aurelio's level, but I enjoy make-up and design like him."

"Does he know this?"

"Of course. He's the ultimate fashion buddy."

I popped a luscious green grape in my mouth—its sugary juices flowing down my throat. "You've never thought of learning from him? Perhaps doing more of the design work?"

She held up her wrist for my inspection. "I have no mark. No calling. Humans in Atlantis generally follow the lineage of employment their families have been given. Although it's not frowned upon to seek a different line of work than my ancestors, I've always known my place is to serve you and your family. There's honor in that as well."

The thought of someone, especially Reneah, who'd been nothing but kind since my arrival in Atlantis, unable to pursue a career that matched her passion, didn't sit well with me. "As honored as I am for your help, you should ask him. See if he can teach you a few things," I pushed, placing my now empty appetizer plate on the neighboring table.

Reneah's brows furrowed. "Ask who? Aurelio?"

"Ask me what?" Aurelio questioned as he approached arm and arm with Myles—a curious gleam sparkling in his kohl-lined amber eyes. Gone were the bangles he'd adorned on his wrists, replaced with long dark sleeves that held tight to his slender arms. A perfectly tailored single-breasted indigo vest sat on a midnight black flare collar dress shirt. His black slim-legged pants lay in a cocoon of a train that flowed from the vest that he donned in one perfect piece of unstitched fabric. The indigo and diamonds of his stiletto heels were a work of art in itself.

"Yes, Princess. I will take all the gawking this evening," Aurelio teased with a sashay.

"I can't help it. You look fucking hot."

He dipped into a bow with a flourish of the hand

without a single strand of his perfectly combed dark hair moving out of place.

"He looks absolutely radiant," Myles said, the pride in his tone matching the gleam in his eyes. It made anyone desperate for an admirer to look at them the way he looked at Aurelio.

"If you keep talking like that, my love, I'll show you just how radiant I can be." Aurelio leaned in and placed a slow, chaste kiss on Myles' lips.

Color bloomed from his neck to his face as he straightened his matching indigo vest and tie with his free hand. There wasn't a single angle of his jet-black suit that was out of place.

"You both look marvelous," Reneah complimented.

"Thank you, love," Aurelio said to her. "Now, are you going to tell me what you were going to ask me? Or do I need to dump the faerie wine down your throat until you divulge?"

I grinned mischievously. "She was going to ask if she can be your design protege."

Aurelio gasped. "My protege?"

Reneah waved her hand. "No, no. I couldn't."

"But you can. I insist," Aurelio retorted.

"There's no reason you couldn't do both, Reneah," Myles assured her. "I believe it's important to stay current on the latest fashions, especially with the influx of humans entering the queendom soon. Aurelio will need all the help he can get. And I'm sure the Princess wouldn't mind."

"Not at all," I confirmed.

With the bittersweet defeat written on Reneah's face, I knew we'd won. She gave a solemn nod. "Very well. I'd be honored to be your protege, Aurelio." A smirk lifted on her ruby-red lips, and her face brightened. "I can't wait to work with all the fabrics and colors, and—oh!" She glanced just past Aurelio with a crease forming between her brows. "What in the world is she wearing?"

Aurelio's eyes drifted toward the entrance where Reneah was gaping—his face morphing into a scowl. "Oh my. She didn't."

"She did," Reneah breathed in mortification.

Aurelio's elegant masculine hand came to his throat. "But someone should have told her that color is drab on her. Who let her out in that?"

"Her complexion is far too fair for that color."

"Is she blind?"

"Blind or delusional," she said, peering up at Aurelio. The both of them burst into laughter. With them both blocking our view, Myles and I shared a look with a shrug, having no idea who they were speaking about.

"Well, now that I have a protege, I'm stealing you away." He grabbed Reneah's hand. "Let's go take a closer inspection." He peered back at Myles. "You don't mind, my love, do you?"

Myles smiled warmly. "Not at all, my dear. Go on. We'll be here." Within a heartbeat, Aurelio and Reneah disappeared into the crowd. "And you? How are you doing this evening, Asherah?" Myles asked me.

I tilted my head from side to side. "I'm as good as can be. Grateful I didn't trip over my own feet. That's a win, right?"

"You did more than just avoid tripping over your feet. You danced wonderfully." A server clad in a bright white dress shirt, black cummerbund, and pants offered us cups of faerie wine from where he expertly balanced them on his tray. Myles grabbed two, handing one to me. "A toast. To your future, Asherah Delmar. May we take down all of your haters, as the kids say these days," he said with a wink.

I clinked my glass against his. "To taking down the haters." I sipped from my glass, the full-bodied wine's rich, oaky, plum and blackberry tones slipping down my throat, my shoulders dropping a fraction.

We observed the crowd in companionable silence. The couples twirled with such grace across the dance floor, absorbing each beat with every step, moving with practiced fluidity. I couldn't help but sway to the music, longing to be one of them. Always the educator, Myles pointed out all of the important Atlantians to know, the dances, and what realm they came from. He never wasted any time teaching me, and I felt grateful for his dedication. Appreciated it.

After what must've been our second or third cup of faerie wine, Reneah and Aurelio returned to our corner of the room, still analyzing and critiquing. It wasn't until Dad approached and asked Reneah for a dance that the two stopped fashion-chatting. I bit my lips to hide my laughter at the expression of shock across her face and pushed her forward by the small of the back with my free hand. She seemed to catch herself and took hold of my father's awaiting hand.

As I watched the two swing around the dance floor, a tingling sensation began in the center of my chest. I could feel him before he broke through the crowd.

And I momentarily lost my breath.

Draevyn was otherworldly, coming to stand before me in all of his beauty. His twilight blue floral fabric suit danced with every crevasse of his massive chest, the gold-rimmed buttons pulling the jacket snug against his tight abdomen, the pants matching. His attire was flawless.

Draevyn looked upon me with those mesmerizing Caribbean green eyes flaring. Hungry. Short, loose tendrils from the half-tied dark brown hair at the back of his head hugged the panes of his face as he scanned me from the tips of my teal-painted toes to the emerald of my headdress. Someone cleared their throat, but our eyes remained locked on each other.

"My love, I think that's our cue," Aurelio told Myles from beside us.

"Cue for what?"

"To dance."

In my periphery, I saw them join the other couples on the dance floor. We continued in our battle of stares until he broke the silence. "Asherah. You rob me of breath," he said in his rich baritone voice.

My cheeks burned flaming hot. "Well, please breathe. I don't want to be responsible for you collapsing on the floor." Draevyn laughed through a smile that had likely brought countless women to their knees, his dimples deepening and causing me to squirm. "So, you've come over to protect me during the ball? I'll have to warn you. I'm a bit of a bore during these things."

Draevyn moved beside me, his hands casually dipping into his pockets. "I'm off duty this evening. I'm here of my own accord. I wanted to celebrate my Queen receiving her elemental mark." My heart danced at the words *my Queen* falling from his lips. Draevyn held out his hand. "So, let's see it then."

I blindly stared at the pure ruggedness of his hand for a few seconds before placing my wrist in his warm, awaiting palm. He began tracing the mark with a gentle touch, so at odds with the size of his hand, the size of him. His face held the utmost awe, and my breath hitched. "How remarkable. I don't think I've seen one up close before." His finger glided around the small circle at the base, causing the hairs on my arm to rise. His hooded gaze drifted to mine. "Are you cold, Asherah?"

"No," I whispered. My heart palpitated in my chest—the glass of wine nearly dropped from my other hand.

"You're shivering."

"M-maybe just a little then."

"Hhmmm." The tip of his finger began making a pathway beyond my mark and up my arm. "We should dance then. Perhaps that would warm you up."

All I could do was nod. Draevyn took the nearly empty glass from my other hand, placed it on the neighboring table, and laced his fingers through mine. He pulled me through the crowd of people—his bulging back muscles visible through his suit jacket before me. A few already in position for the next dance did a double take as we joined them.

Let them.

Our eyes remained held on each other as his arm came around my lower back and pulled me into his tall, muscular form, just enough that our bodies lightly grazed. I didn't know how it was possible for my face to flush any further, but it did. Draevyn's intoxicating, woodsy, earthy scent invaded my senses.

"So, how are your studies, my Queen?" he asked, the small quartet playing a slow-tempo waltz.

My eyes fluttered. "My studies?"

There was that dimple again. "Yes, your studies. With Myles."

I shook my head. "Right. My studies. Uh. They're doing good. Well, as good as expected, considering I know next to nothing about the people I'm supposed to rule or whatever."

Draevyn moved us skillfully out of the way of an on-coming couple, my dress fanning out around us. "Do I detect someone feeling sorry for themselves?"

I reared back. "Sorry for myself?"

Draevyn pulled me closer. "Yes, sorry for yourself. Everything here is new to you, Asherah. Cut yourself a little slack."

We whirled again, weaving around the ballroom, the onlookers following us with interest.

"It's not so much slack I seek. It's more the idea of being years behind everyone. I…I just don't want to fail."

"Well, from what I understand, you are anything but a failure. You excelled in your studies in marine biology. You're an amateur surfer and have won a few competitions. Doesn't sound like someone who is a failure."

I quirked a brow. "Been checking up on me?"

A shrug. "Maybe a little." He twirled us deeper into the crowd of dancing couples. "My point is you have the drive and determination to succeed already within you. This is just another thing for you to conquer." He stopped abruptly in the corner of the dance floor, carefully positioning us out of the way of the other dancers. I paused at the intensity of his demeanor. "You will do this, Asherah. You are meant to be our Queen."

"I don't even know how to stay in my Water Fae form. You were there when I spectacularly failed. When I failed you. And I'm so sorry to have upset you." I shook my head, my gaze dropping to the wooden floor. "I'm so behind."

The tips of his fingers came under my chin, pulling my head up. "You did not fail me. Did you think I've been upset with you all this time?"

"Yes," I admitted.

Draevyn's palms brushed over my bare shoulders, my skin pebbling beneath his touch. "I'm not upset with you, Asherah. I'm…not used to training a princess." He smiled sheepishly. "Most of my trainees are brutes who beg for pain, but I must learn to communicate differently with you." I opened my mouth to protest that he didn't need to make exceptions for me, but he placed a finger on my lips. "I know you can handle it." He let his finger slowly retreat to my shoulder. "But this is a lesson for me to learn. So, you're actually teaching me."

My brow quirked. "I am?"

"Yes. You are. And you're not alone, Asherah. We're in this together, you and I. The rest of us by your side," he said sincerely.

I swallowed. "Thank you. I appreciate that."

The song had long ended. People brushed by us as they moved off the dance floor, but we remained where we stood, immovable—observing each other like a newly discovered phenomenon.

"Well, doesn't this look intimate?"

Our gazes shifted to Melysah, who walked up to us—the pretentious smirk on her face revealing the evil lurking beneath. Her pearl-polished fingertips dug into the palms of her tightly clenched fists. The pale peach gown she wore probably would've looked stunning in any other color—a slit rising to the hip of her left leg. I had to wonder if this was who Reneah and Aurelio were speaking of earlier in the night, the contrast so at odds with her pale skin.

Draevyn's hand drifted down to my palm, his fingers threading through mine. Melysah's eyes tracked every bit of that movement.

"Councilor Velafyn," he said, bowing. When my legs began dipping in a curtsy, Draevyn held me firmly up, keeping me in place. His fiery glare locked on Melysah as he rose—the anger imminent with some message I was missing. It was only when Melysah's lips were pursed and a short curtsy followed that I understood his message loud and clear. I was not to bow to this female. Melysah was to bow to *me*.

"Your Highness," she said, managing to sound condescending. "Commander Eliron. It looks like you have become…closely acquainted with your assignment. You're taking your role as her Guardian *very* seriously."

"If by very seriously, you mean that I aim to protect Princess Asherah—the future Queen of Atlantis—at all costs from forces both inside and outside the queendom, then yes, Melysah. I do take this very seriously."

"I can see that."

"Was there something you needed, Councilor?" I interjected. "It seems other couples would like to dance, and we're in the way."

"No, Princess," she said, that evil smirk returning to her wicked face. "There's nothing in particular. Just wanted to say hello."

My head dipped in a curt nod. "And now you've done that. Drae, I'm thirsty. Want to get something to drink?"

"Absolutely," he said, sliding my hand through the crease in his elbow and giving Melysah his back.

"Oh. And *Drae*?" she called from behind us. "I'll address your proximity issues with General Lumeya tomorrow. We wouldn't want you falling prey to pretty distractions and causing harm to our queendom."

I turned back, my lips thinning. "The hell you will. You are not to do anything at all. Am I clear, *Councilor*?"

Melysah's smirk dropped, and her jaw clenched when more than a few of the people around her began whispering.

"Am. I. Clear?"

"Crystal," Melysah bit out, her cheeks flushing.

"Excellent. Let's go, Drae."

Something like surprise flickered across Draevyn's face as I slid my arm on his. We didn't wait for her reaction. We pivoted and strolled toward Reneah and Aurelio, who waited for us a few feet away, their eyes wide.

"What the hell was that all about?" Reneah asked.

"Melysah being Melysah," Draevyn said, seething.

"About what?" Aurelio asked with a scowl.

"Draevyn's apparent proximity issues to me. And she can go fuck off. I can be friends with whoever I damn well please."

A smirk emerged on Draevyn's face. "We're friends now, are we?"

"Only if you behave," I teased, giving his arm a comforting squeeze.

"Well, *friends*," Aurelio said, his eyes traveling between us. "How about we take this party elsewhere? It's becoming too stuffy in here. Myles is held up with Cathan chatting with an elder Fae, and Reneah and I have dissected every possible outfit in the ballroom."

"I'll grab the faerie wine," Reneah said.

"Sounds perfect," I said.

As we followed Aurelio and Reneah out of the ornate ballroom doors, Draevyn's breath hit the tip of my ear. "You are deliciously fierce, my Queen."

And a blush heated my cheeks anew.

"Her dress was peach! Pale peach!" Aurelio wailed in a fit of laughter.

My eyes welled with tears—my abs and cheeks sore from smiling so hard. The faerie wine crept through my veins, making me feel more relaxed than ever since arriving at Atlantis.

"It completely drowned her out. She was the absolute worst," Reneah chimed in.

"Just like her wretched soul. And I mean that sincerely. I offered to help her once, and she told me my style choices were dreadful, and the goddess must have made a mistake the day she gave me my mark."

"She didn't," I said aghast.

"That witch," Reneah seethed. She reached out and squeezed his knee from where she sat at his side on the couch across from us. "You don't listen to her."

Aurelio patted her hand. "Oh, I know, sweetie. She doesn't bother me."

Draevyn's arm brushed the back of my neck from where it lay across the back of the plush leather couch—the twin to the one Reneah and Aurelio occupied on the other side of the leather ottoman. The warmth of his body close to mine gave me comfort. I could still feel his hand against the small of my back as we walked the short distance to Aurelio and Myles's quarters in the palace, his eyes tracking every movement around us. When Draevyn left to use the bathroom, I couldn't fight the burning in my cheeks when Reneah and Aurelio wagged their eyebrows at me. I quickly shot them a look before he returned.

"You've come a long way from your assignment as Melysah's guard, huh, Draevyn?" Aurelio asked.

This was news to me. "You were her guard?"

"Hhmph. Yes. She was my assignment for a time when I was a private. Apparently, she thought I was at her disposal for everything."

"What do you mean by everything?" Reneah inquired.

He let loose a sigh as he drank a sip of his faerie wine. "At first, she wanted me to fetch her things. Her purse. Her notebook. I'd run all over the place. I'm almost certain that was her intention. But then the requests took a strange turn. She'd ask me to stand in a certain spot, which for me wasn't a challenge. Standing versus wielding a trident wasn't a challenge. What set me on edge was the way she periodically looked at me, the casual glances. Finally, a few weeks into the assignment, it all peaked when she asked me to kneel on a pillow beside her desk. It clicked, then. And I outright refused. She was treating me like I was her—"

"Submissive," Aurelio finished, eyes wide. "Oh, my goddess, Draevyn. It's almost as if she were grooming you into it."

"Grooming?" I asked curiously. Draevyn fidgeted slightly. "You mean so that she's your dominant? A sexual kind of submissive?"

Draevyn shook his head. "It doesn't matter what she thought she would do with me. And to be clear," his eyes flashed as they bore into mine, "I have no problem with anyone's sexual kinks. That's their prerogative. And I certainly have mine." Goddess help me. How I wished the couch would swallow me up.

"I immediately told Dax the next day," he continued. "When one of the other privates, Kane Ruema, caught wind of what happened, he volunteered to be her Guardian. There's no telling what goes on between the two of them now. Word is he's happy to be her lap dog, and I'm happy to be—"

"Ash's?" Reneah cut in.

I clicked my tongue. "Oh, stop! He is not!"

Draevyn bellowed with laughter, making me smile.

"Well, it is undoubtedly an upgrade anyway. Am I

right, Draevyn?" Aurelio asked.

My heart skipped when his arm pulled me closer to his side. "Of course it is. I'm highly entertained when this one gets feisty and puts Melysah in her place. Plus, the view is far better."

I playfully swatted his thigh, my hand stinging with the impact against solid muscle. "You flirt."

We were interrupted when the front door opened. Myles lumbered into the room, the exhaustion heavy on his face. "Well, this is where you all skipped off to."

"You look terrible, my love." Aurelio placed his glass on a wooden tray that rested on top of the ottoman and rushed to Myles, helping him to remove his jacket. "Do you want a nightcap?"

Myles rolled his shoulders. "No, my dear. I'm afraid I've had quite enough, and I'm ready for bed."

"That's our queue," Reneah said, getting up and gathering the cups, bottles, and plates around the room.

"Leave it, Reneah. I'll get it in the morning," Aurelio said.

"No worries," she said with a smile. "You were hospitable enough to host us tonight. I've got this."

Draevyn stood from the couch, holding his hand out to me. "I'll escort you to your quarters."

I felt light as a feather as he pulled me up with ease, my face coming inches from his chest. "You don't have to do that."

"Actually, he does," Myles said, his eyes traveling between us with scrutiny. "He's your guard, after all."

I gave him an apprehensive nod. "Okay, then."

We said our goodbyes, Myles's gaze following us until we closed their front door. Silence enveloped us as we stood in the empty hallway alone. I wrapped my arms around my middle and began walking.

"Cold again?" he asked.

"Oh, no. I'm fine."

We didn't utter a word to each other as he led me to my quarters, the dome's moonlight filtering through the windows that lined the hallway.

"Do you think Melysah is going to say something to Dax?" I asked, finally breaking the silence.

A smirk lifted his lips. "That would be disobeying a direct order from her Queen. And what could she possibly say anyway?"

I shrugged. "That you and I were…you know…"

"Dancing?" We ascended the stairs that led to my floor, the warmth of his hand on the small of my back causing my breath to hitch. "I can't get in trouble for dancing with you."

We reached the corridor just outside my quarters, where Mayana stood guard and nodded in greeting. My heart kicked up a beat as I turned and faced Draevyn. "I guess it's stupid to get worked up about a dance, huh?"

Draevyn playfully pinched the point of my chin. "Let her think it was more than a dance. Truth be told, I don't care what she or anyone else in the queendom have to say." The moonlight cast shadows across his face, but it did nothing to hide the heat in his gaze. "You are my greatest assignment, Asherah. There's nothing anyone can do, save Dax, to reassign me. I refuse to leave your side."

My stomach dropped. "Right. An assignment."

He rubbed the back of his neck. "And my friend."

Feeling incredibly stupid for thinking this was something more, I glanced at Mayana, who now stood on the stairwell landing, observing us quietly. "If Mayana's here, I'm guessing your shift is during the day?"

"It is." Draevyn leaned in, his lips grazing my ear and

causing my thighs to clench. "But I'd be happy to protect my…*friend* throughout the evening if she ever needed it," he whispered. The stubble of his chin grazed my cheek as he pulled back, that ridiculous smirk causing his dimples to appear. He sauntered backward down the corridor with his eyes never leaving mine. "See you tomorrow, my Queen." He wheeled around and descended the stairs, leaving me in a puddled mess of confusion.

# Chapter 14

"Corenathia sits at the center of the Earth's core. Humans widely speculate that the Earth's core burns about four thousand to seven thousand kelvins. That would be about seven thousand to twelve thousand degrees Fahrenheit. The Fire Fae's skin has been goddess-blessed to withstand this heat and weaponize it. To yield it."

The muscles in my hand cramped with the effort to keep up with Myles' instruction, the pain traveling throughout my palm and down my wrist—my hand flying across the magicked tablet. Myles had promised at the beginning of today's lesson that soon he would start on simple spells that dictate notes versus having to write them out. As I shook my hand out, I sort of wished he'd begun with those lessons first.

Myles slowly paced before his desk. "As you

very well know, the Fire Fae rule this realm quite differently from all other realms. They see humans as collateral. While strict protocols are in place today, the Fire Fae took full advantage of the last ice age, enslaving every human who took refuge in their lands. They remain enslaved till this day."

I looked up from my notebook, appalled. "Even today?"

He winced. "Yes," he confirmed, the sorrow evident as his shoulders slumped slightly—so at odds with how he usually carried himself.

"But...but how is this still going on today?"

Myles inhaled deeply. "The Fae realms are far more complicated than the Above World, Asherah. Diplomacy is a delicate balance, and the power of the Fire Fae is very great. Challenging them could cause an all-out war that none of the other realms are motivated to pursue. Each queendom loves its people too much, with the exception of Corenathia. Their Queen does not value her people as much as the other Queens value theirs. She'll use them to whatever ends she needs to overcome any obstacle before her. She'll threaten whole families to serve her and torture them until they comply, and many do so in an effort to protect their families regardless of whether they support the mission of their Queen. And unfortunately, not every realm is willing to stand up to them. While each queendom has its own elemental abilities, it is very tough to combat the Queendom of Corenathia."

I blinked. "But can't someone just take them down?"

Myles chuckled sadly, shaking his head. "It's not that easy. I truly wish it were. The scrolls of the High Priestesses prophesize a Fae powerful enough to rule over all the queendoms, but that is all we have. A mystical foretelling that is less than dependable. Until then, we must use whatever tools are in our arsenal to get them to yield. Sometimes, it's the most frustrating dance imaginable. And it will test you, Asherah. Of this, I have no doubt. There will be days when you'll look a Corenathian in the face and attempt diplomacy when all you really want to do is drown their lungs with water."

A knock sounded at the door, and our gazes landed upon Draevyn—his jaw set. "Kane is outside. We're being summoned to the council room. Something urgent he refuses to disclose." His gaze slid to me momentarily, and my cheeks instantly heated. "Says he'll stay here and stand guard while we're gone. Shouldn't take too long."

Myles sighed. "Very well." He made rapid strides to the back wall, fingers grazing over the spines of books till he plucked one out and fanned through the pages. He hurried back and placed the book on the table before me. "This section is about the last ice age and Corenathia. Read it while I see what is so urgent that it can't wait. We'll go over it once I return."

With that, he and Draevyn strolled from the room, leaving me to read over what I could only assume would be some dark and disturbing shit. In the silence of the classroom, with only the ticking of the clock on the wall for company, I read page after page of the cruelty and vileness of Corenathia. The idea that humans were no more than slaves in their realm boiled the blood in my veins. This was proving to be the hardest lesson yet when the next words leapt off the page:

*When Corenathia agreed to the accord, splitting the humans evenly between the realms, they failed to disclose their ill intentions. It came to the attention of the Queendoms Council nearly a century later when a spy, at a significant personal risk, procured the inner workings of Corenathia. Since the realm is protected by a fire dome only the Fire Fae can control, there was little the other queendoms could do to infiltrate Corenathia and save the humans.*

"Fucking assholes."

"You must be learning of Corenathia," a cool voice called from the doorway.

My head snapped up. A man who visually appeared to be in his mid-twenties leaned against the door jamb, his medium build taking up half the doorway. His bright orange hair loosened a little from behind his tipped ears as he tilted his head, observing me with his deep brown eyes—an amused smirk lifting his lips. A feeling of unease emerged.

"And you are?"

He casually stepped into the classroom with his hands in the pockets of his loose leathers, his gaze never leaving me. "So, it's true then. The heir of Atlantis exists. I wouldn't have believed it if I hadn't seen it with my own eyes. You look so much like your former Queen." He gestured over me. "With the exception of the human attire, of course."

"Yes, I exist. *And you are?*"

His smile grew as he leaned against the desk at the front of the room, crossing his arms over his dark green tunic. "Lux."

"Lux. Okay. Well, hi, Lux. Is there something I can help you with?"

His shoulder lifted in a shrug. "Nothing in particular. I just wanted to meet you."

"Well, you've met me." My eyebrow rose. "And now, I have to get back to my reading."

"Of Corenathia?" he asked curiously.

I paused, not knowing how much I should or wanted to share with Lux, but decided there was no harm in telling a nosey student what I was studying. That's what we were here for, anyway. "Yes, of Corenathia."

"Interesting." He pushed off the desk and strolled around to me. "And what do the Atlantian texts say of us? Is it everything as evil as they say we are?"

My heart plummeted, and my eyes widened. My inability to defend myself against any other Fae became strikingly apparent as a sense of helplessness spread throughout me.

I shot up from my chair, walking backward to the next row of desks, my feet tripping over the legs of the table at my back. "We?"

Lux held his palms up. "Relax. I'm not going to hurt you."

"You'd be the first Fire Fae not to do so."

There were now several rows of tables separating us, but I could have sworn I saw sadness fall over his gaze before his carefree composure returned. "That was warranted. I understand why you're cautious."

I was saved from retorting when angry male voices sounded down the hall. Lux's eyes held mine, almost pleading. Truth be told, I didn't know what to make of that look. "Remember that not everything is as it seems, Asherah. And if you ever want to know the truth, find me."

I could feel my nostrils flare. "I think I can decipher the truth for myself, thank you very much."

Lux sighed, his hands falling to his side in what looked like defeat.

"You were supposed to guard her, not seek fresh air outside these walls!" That voice was distinctively Draevyn, and my shoulders eased as he entered the classroom. Myles and an unfamiliar guard followed behind him and stopped short within the doorway, their lips parting and their eyes bugging out of their sockets as their gazes fell on Lux. Draevyn's trident materialized out of thin air, the glow causing his scales to glimmer.

"Prince Lux. What exactly are you doing here?" Myles demanded.

Lux placed his hands in his pockets. "I just wanted to introduce myself."

"There's a time and a place for such diplomatic introductions. I think it best if you return to the class that you are presumably missing. We wouldn't want you to fall behind in your studies."

"No, we wouldn't want that." Lux turned back to me. "It was a pleasure meeting you, Your Highness. Until we meet again." Decerning that his time was up, Lux rushed out of the room.

Draevyn's trident disappeared as he approached me. His face, full of concern, did nothing to calm my nerves. "Are you alright?"

"Yeah. He just wanted to introduce himself. No harm done."

Myles came up to my side. "Did he say anything to you?"

I shook my head. "Nothing bad or threatening."

Draevyn wheeled around and glared at the other guard. "You can return to Melysah now, Kane. I think you've caused enough trouble for one day."

A malicious smile broke on Kane's face. "By trouble, you mean reporting what *must* be reported as required by my superior? I hardly think it's trouble. It's called accountability, Draevyn. You should try it sometime."

"How *dare* you?" Draevyn charged toward Kane, but Myles's arm caught him in the chest, holding him back.

"That's quite enough, Kane. All is done. Please go

back to your assignment."

I watched as Kane stepped backward through the doorway with a vile grin, disappearing a moment later. I made my way to my desk and pulled my chair upright. As I slid into my seat, I had a sinking feeling this was about Melysah, figuring she made good on her threat. I pinched the bridge of my nose on a slow exhale. "Do I want to know what that was about?"

Draevyn's face was pinched as he leaned against the table across from mine. "Melysah figured that if she couldn't follow through on a threat because of your order to stay silent, she'd have her lapdog do it."

Myles folded his arms. "Dax will be visiting you soon to discuss your relationship with Draevyn," he said in an almost fatherly tone.

I threw my hands in the air. "Am I not allowed to have a friend?"

"Calm down. Calm down. You're allowed to have friends." His gaze traveled between the two of us. "You're also allowed to have more than that if that's what you want." I could feel my cheeks heat. Myles fluttered a hand in the air as he continued, "But there are protocols for this sort of thing."

"What Asherah and I have is not a *thing*." I could feel my heart swell at his declaration. This indescribable pull that made zero sense kept a hold on me and my heart.

But we were just *friends*, right?

Right?

Myles slid his hands in his pockets, regarding Draevyn. "I really don't care what you call it. Quite frankly, it's none of my business. That's between the two of you and the goddess." His attention shifted to me. "Dax just wants to speak with you. Just chat with him. There's no harm done. This is just Melysah trying to stir the pot."

Draevyn huffed his displeasure. "She's doing more than just stirring the pot when the Prince of Corenathia is strolling into the room with our one and only heir."

"Indeed, but remember. If the rumors are to be believed, Lux is every bit his mother's victim. I don't think he meant any harm. And with regard to Melysah, we cannot sink to her level. We must keep the line, especially with her. She's the most knowledgeable council member ever to hold a seat. She knows more about the council rules and politics than Roarvyn, a fact that crawls under his skin. If you two were smart, you'd try to hide whatever it is you feel for each other for as long as you can. Her obsession with you is well known. She'll not take kindly to being upstaged." He reached forward, sliding the book I'd been reading across the desk. "Now, let's get back to your lesson."

But I could hardly focus on anything else that afternoon, nor did I want to.

The Prince's words kept rolling through my mind.

*Remember that not everything is as it seems, Asherah.*

Even though I'd expected the knock at the door the following morning, it still set my nerves on edge when I heard it. Reneah peeked her head into my bedroom and gave a slight wince. "He's waiting in the sitting room."

I nodded and placed my latest textbook, *Medieval Diplomacy: Airelandia and Atlantis*, on the side table. My shaky steps carried me into the living room where General Lumeya waited. Gone were the days when I could take an interest in someone, or they take an interest in me, and we could decide what we were to each other without interference.

Friends?

But even as I thought it, it didn't seem right.

He'd mentioned that we were more than a "thing." I couldn't disagree if I wanted to. It's hard to call someone a friend when my body reacts the way it does to Draevyn Eliron. Regardless, one thing was for sure. I didn't want to have this conversation.

I really, really didn't want to have this conversation.

Dax's note came early in the morning as I devoured a breakfast of fluffy eggs with bell peppers, onions, and bella mushrooms. The savory flavors from the homefries accompanying them still lingered on my tongue. After those first few days of holing myself up in my room, I can still recall the first time my breakfast magically appeared across the kitchen island. Reneah, having sensed my confusion, had explained that there are elemental fae responsible for cooking. Being catered to like this wasn't something I was used to, and I made it my mission to find out where they cooked such delicious food so I could thank them profusely.

As I entered the sitting room, I found Dax sitting on a reading chair in the corner—mindlessly chewing on his thumbnail and staring out the window with a contemplative look. I cleared my throat, and he snapped to attention—his massive form rising abruptly to bow.

"Good morning, Your Highness," he said, his warm smile spreading across his masculine face. "It's good to see you."

I smiled in return. "Good to see you as well, Dax. I hope you've been feeling better."

His head dipped in a nod, strands from his bright blond hair falling forward. "The goddess has given me the strength to go on. Well, as best as she can possibly provide. I'm great in physical health. But I still have quite a bit of work to do with my mental health, if that makes sense."

My heart squeezed for Dax. What he must have seen then, and what he must have felt now. I didn't want to imagine. "Yes. It makes perfect sense."

Dax motioned with a meaty hand to the sitting chairs by the window. "Shall we?"

I moved across the ornate Persian rug to perch on the edge of the chair—my hands folded neatly in my lap.

Dax plopped down and rubbed the back of his neck. "Well, there's no easy way to go about this, so I'll not sugarcoat it for you. I believe you know why I'm here?"

Thoughts of the Elemental Ball flashed through my mind. The way Draevyn had laced his fingers through mine as if it were the most natural thing in the world, the way he held me as we danced, the way I lost myself in those stunning green eyes like it had been my own personal, tropical oasis, the confidence in his words and the way he treated me. *Friends*, he had said, but more than a thing. "I do," I answered Dax because regardless of what we were to each other, we weren't just Guardian and Princess.

He let loose a breath. "I'm reassigning Draevyn to the—"

"No."

His brow rose. "No?"

"Please. Do not do that."

He raked his fingers through his hair. "Why him, Ash?"

I swallowed past the lump in my throat. "I don't know." *Please don't blush. Dear goddess, please don't blush.*

"That's not a good enough reason. Any one of my

Guardians would do the job well."

"I know, but…please. Just leave him assigned to me."

The glare of his cobalt-blue eyes was heavy with concern. "You realize you'll be pissing off one of the most strategic council members with," he flourished his large hand, "whatever is going on between the two of you?"

"We're just friends." When he gave me a look that said he didn't believe a word out of my mouth, I straightened my spine. "Besides, I will not be bullied."

Dax quirked a thick, blond brow. "You're sure you want to go there with Melysah?"

"Yup. Pretty sure."

"Be that as it may, Draevyn may be in violation of some code of conduct. I'll need to report this."

"You will not. I mean." I glanced down at my hands. "Please don't. That won't be necessary. He hasn't done anything wrong."

Dax gave me a knowing smile. "Maybe not wrong according to you, but in the eyes of the Guardians and the Council, he may have stepped out of line."

I grimaced. "Please leave him assigned as he is, and please don't report him. Commander Eliron has been incredibly helpful to me. This realm…it's all new to me. I feel safer with him at my side. This is nothing more than Melysah attempting to create drama."

Dax gripped his chin in his hand. After a long pause, he said, "I wouldn't be doing you any favors if I didn't tell you this. I've known Draevyn since he was a faeling. I've watched him work hard to achieve his status. There were times I'd catch him in the training center long after everyone had departed for the day, going over and over his movement to perfect it. He has poured many hours, weeks, and years into his craft. I've never seen anyone like him. As his mentor, watching him grow into the male he is today has been a point of pride for me. I could depend on him like none other in my guard.

"His elemental calling has always been his sole focus, which is why his recent behavior—particularly with you—has me both perplexed and worried." I felt a phantom vice grip around my lungs, robbing me of air as I awaited his answer. "Yet, oddly, it also has me confident that there is no one else I'd rather have looking over you. I'll keep him assigned to you so long as whatever is brewing between the two of you—and don't deny it—doesn't distract him from his duties."

My shoulders sagged. "Well, thank you. Draevyn's been…great." There was no hiding the heat on my cheeks because Draevyn Eliron was not only great but also mysterious.

And charming.

And alluring.

And intoxicating.

I voiced none of those things.

"I'm glad to hear it, but be mindful. Melysah will have her eye on you now, on the both of you. She's a pain in the ass, one I'll gladly handle for Draevyn and for you, but it won't be easy."

I gave him a solemn nod. "Thank you. It means a lot to me."

Dax rose from his chair. "And now, I shall return to your grumpy father in the Above World."

"Grumpy?"

Dax's shoulders bounced with a chuckle. "Yes. This isn't his calling at all. He longs for your coronation day so that he doesn't have to deal with Fae politics anymore. It's not his thing."

I nodded, the weight of my responsibilities settling hard and heavy in my gut. "Well, I'll let you get to it. Tell my Dad I love him."

Dax's face brightened. "Of course, Your Highness. But you can tell him yourself. He returns this evening to prepare for the upcoming meeting with the queendoms." I twitched a bit, and Dax's keen eye noticed. I wasn't looking forward to meeting the other queens. I didn't feel ready for it, but Dad insisted I be there as a sign of our strength. "Try not to worry yourself too much. It's your first queendoms meeting, but you'll get the hang of it."

I gave him a solemn smile. "Thanks, Dax."

He dipped in a brief bow and lumbered out of my quarters, leaving my nerves unsettled save for one tiny victory.

I would still have my guard.

# Chapter 15

"Take off your clothes, Asherah."

I stood on shaky legs before the dome wall just beyond the palace gardens. Aside from the gates to Atlantis, it was the closest entrance into the ocean depths and was only accessible to very few, according to Draevyn. "Friends don't tell each other to take off their clothes." I couldn't have felt more mortified if I tried.

"It will be a better incentive for you to keep your scales," he commented from behind me.

I slowly twisted around and gave him my best eye roll before returning my attention to the dome wall. His low chuckle reached my ears, but I couldn't share in his humor. My anxiety was busy holding my body hostage.

With the upcoming meeting with the queens, both Draevyn and Dad felt it was best if I practiced holding my scales. Nothing would be more insulting than if I were to show up in human clothes, apparently. "You just want to see me naked," I said, trying to match his humor.

His feet crunched across the sand that led to the dome wall entrance until the heat from his body crested across my back, and my breath hitched. "You're a stunning female, my Queen. I'll not deny your beauty. Ooof!"

I elbowed him in his well-defined abs, earning myself more hurt than him. "Shameless flirt," I scolded, rubbing at my elbow.

"Only with you."

Anyone would be a fool not to smile at a comment like that. So, I did as I dropped my hands to my sides and inhaled deeply, my eyes held tight to the darkness beyond the wall. "I'd feel better if I went with my clothing on."

"How about a compromise?" he asked as he approached my side. "Why don't you remove your clothes before entering the water?" He held his palms up. "I promise I won't look," he said, but his devilish smirk expressed something else entirely.

My brow rose to my hairline. "Why don't I believe you?"

The smirk dropped, and the heat in his eyes could be felt all the way to the Atlantian outposts. "You should. Because if you ever honor me with the sight of your exquisite body, it will be because you choose to."

Was it possible to melt into the sand?

I broke his gaze as I glanced at the ground, my curtain of dark hair hiding my blush before I cleared my throat. "Compromise it is, then." I motioned toward the wall. "Go ahead."

He stepped forward and pushed his tall, muscular body through the wall of water, swiveling back toward me when he was halfway submerged. "I must warn you. It is quite cold without your scales." His tropical green eyes dropped to the stiff peaks visible through my sheer, lavender Atlantian jumper before he disappeared beyond the wall. I could've sworn I'd heard him huff a laugh.

I blew a raspberry. "Nothing to it but to do it," I murmured to no one in particular. With one final scan of my surroundings, noting nothing for company but bright, plump rose bushes and bright green-leafed trees that whispered against a phantom wind, I dragged the straps of my jumper down my arms until it dropped to the ground at my feet, my undergarments following a moment later. Goosebumps grew across my tan skin as I slipped off my matching silk shoes. I was naked as the day I was born, standing before the massive, dark-as-night wall of water. On an exhale, I closed my eyes and envisioned my webbed foot as I pressed it through the barrier. The biting cold water assaulted my toes, causing me to wince before the webbing formed to protect them.

Suddenly—or perhaps for a much-needed distraction—I remembered the times when winter bled into spring in the Above World, just brisk enough to be uncomfortable, but warming slightly that the pool water was beginning to increase in degrees. John and I would challenge ourselves by jumping in and seeing which one of us could last the longest without hauling ourselves out of the pool and launching ourselves in the hot tub. Being the competitive beast I'd always been, I'd stuck it out the longest. It's why, with my foot and part of my ankle already through the barrier, I decided the best strategy was to simply jump in.

Without breaking my concentration, I hurtled forward.

"*Shit!*"

This was so not the pool. Thousands of tiny pins pricked across my skin, paralyzing my entire body. It was too much. It was way too much.

In an instant, Draevyn's form emerged from the depths with lightning speed as his hands came to gently grip my face. "*Morph, Asherah. Your body cannot sustain this temperature. Morph!*" he demanded, his deep voice sounding in my mind.

I didn't even care about my sheer nakedness in front of him as I nodded my head vigorously and concentrated on the one area of my body that felt warm, my toes wiggling with heated relief. I imagined that warmth spreading up my legs, desperate for it. My body began to shake as that warmth finally hit my abdomen and spread across my breasts. And as my arms became blanketed by my blue-green scales that shimmered against the light emanating from within the dome, another problem emerged.

Eventually, I would need to breathe.

As if sensing my rising panic, Draevyn encouraged, "*You're doing beautifully. Just one last step, Princess. You can do this. You are so strong. Breathe for me.*" He held so much confidence in me that it was impossible not to try and honor him—this Commander of Atlantis who had patiently stood by my side, teaching me everything I needed to know without condescension me or causing me to feel anything less than what I'd been called by the goddess to do.

So, I breathed.

The brine of the saltwater speared my throat as I drank it down. I gulped until my need for breath overwhelmed me, my eyes going wide as they held on Draevyn's face.

"*Almost there,*" he said, his thumbs brushing across my cheekbones. "*Through the nose.*"

When you surf as much as I did in the Above World,

you always think about drowning and what that sensation may feel like—not being able to take a breath and dying a slow, agonizing death. But when the water entered my nostrils on an inhale, my beating heart did not give out. My body didn't go into shock. I simply…breathed.

My gaze traveled over Draevyn's face, noticing the light bluish-green sheen on his olive skin as my lungs began to pump—the strands of his long brown hair drifting around him like tiny serpents. Water flowed in and out of my mouth and nose as easily as air, and the drumming beat of my heart slowed to a steady rhythm.

A smile lifted his sensual lips. *"There you are."*

*"Your skin is iridescent."* I raised my hand and brushed my fingertips across his prominent cheekbones. A swoosh of water sounded on an intake as he gasped. *"Almost blue, yet green."*

*"Yes, that's the layer of protection that spreads across our unscaled skin for protection,"* he advised as a lavender blush began to spread across his skin. He reached for a strand of my hair, twisting it around his thick finger. *"You'll notice your hair and scalp will also have the same sheen."* He set it aside reverently, regarding me again. *"How are you doing?"*

*"I'm…okay. It's weird. The breathing."*

*"The water provides the oxygen that your Fae body requires."* His hands slid down my arms, but I felt nothing save a slight pressure. He twined his fingers through mine. *"Let's swim out a bit. It'll give you a chance to practice using your webbing."* A faelight formed in the center of his palm, and he cast it ahead of us—the light's blue glow breaking through the darkness ahead, illuminating thousands of tiny particles floating around us. *"We'll practice summoning faelight as well. It's important for you to know how to do so when swimming in the open water. This way."*

Draevyn pulled me alongside him as my feet fluttered behind me, cutting through the water. After a few kicks to adjust to my webbed feet, an overwhelming feeling of fluidity took over—some natural part of my being awakening. I pulled slightly ahead of Draevyn, and a smirk emerged on his face. "*Challenge accepted, Princess.*"

My webbed feet fluttered behind me, my muscles beginning to cramp with the effort to outswim my mentor, my…friend. The corners of my lips lifted as I kept pace with him, but he expertly swam ahead, the scales at his feet forming into one large tail. My eyes widened as I took in all the beautiful ridges and creases. It was the stuff of fairytales and legends. He twisted around while still managing to swim ahead of me. "*You'll need to do better than that.*"

"*You have nearly a thousand years on me!*"

His face lit up, the faelight's warm blue glow causing a mesmerizing shimmer across his tail. "*Then we'll spend the next thousand years trying to outswim each other. Won't we?*" He winked as he swiveled back, winning him a broad grin he couldn't see. "*Don't worry. I can still feel that smile of yours.*"

I gave him a one-finger salute and kicked my feet to fasten my pace, gaining on him. I could swear I heard him laugh. His iridescent tail flapped in front of my face, and I dared myself to reach out and touch it, but he turned abruptly, and I propelled right into his chest. "*Ow,*" I said as I cradled my nose. I ashamedly buried my face in his chest to hide my embarrassment, brushing my fingers over my nose. "*I don't think anything's broken.*" Except for my pride, but I didn't voice that.

"*Let me take a look.*"

"*I'd rather you not.*"

"*Oh, come on. Let me see.*" His fingers came underneath my chin, lifting my face, still held in a wince. His gaze roamed, and his finger gently prodded at my nose. *"Not broken, thank the goddess. It might be a little sore."* His gaze locked on mine, and something lit within my chest. *"Still breathtaking, my Queen."*

Irrational emotions weren't something I'd indulged in during my time in the Above World. I'd never had the impulse to leap and kiss a guy or a male like the one in front of me. I'd taken lovers to my bed, but none that had piqued my interest for more than a short time. The initial attraction eventually fizzled out, and we'd become nothing more than a mutual itch to scratch on occasion. I was Asherah, the wallflower. I made methodical, rational decisions. But in this moment, with the heat of a thousand suns in Draevyn's gaze like an alluring invitation, I wanted to consume him.

Ravish him.

With unmistakable reverence, he cradled my upturned palm in his. *"You'll need to practice summoning faelights,"* he said, his telepathic tone soft. *"The ability to cast a faelight comes from a very ancient magic, a gift from the goddess."* He summoned his faelight to hover over our joint palms. *"The same will used to summon our scales is the same will used to summon our faelight. Make this faelight grow, Asherah. Will it."*

I focused on the sphere of blue light, the little mass swirling with an ebb and flow of tiny bright waves within. I imagined that sphere growing, and my mouth parted slightly when it grew large enough to the circumference of our hands.

Draevyn slowly dropped his hands from mine. *"That's it. You're doing great. Now, keep your focus and cast it a few feet away."*

A smile formed on my lips as I flicked the light into

the shadows with ease, but what my light illuminated caused my smile to flatten. Every muscle in my body went rigid. A group of Water Fae hovered beyond the faelight, not even ten feet away. My heart sank into my stomach when I beheld the scowls and various states of righteous anger across their iridescent faces.

The leader of their little pack ventured forward, and a darkness came across his face. "*Commander Eliron. You're a little ways away from the safety of the palace gardens.*" He dared to glance at me, an uneasy feeling skittering down my spine. "*Seems you've taken your pet Princess for a stroll in the deep.*" He shifted his attention back to Draevyn, who glared at him with equal malice. "*Unwise, given the state of things in Atlantis.*"

"*How dare you disrespect our future Queen,*" Draevyn seethed. "*Do not look at her. Don't even think about speaking to her again.*" Draevyn summoned his trident, the golden glow bathing the area around us. I surveyed the group, counting five in total—five against one because I didn't know how to defend myself.

"*Stay behind me,*" Draevyn ordered. He casually twirled his trident, golden streaks of light trailing behind the tips of the mighty weapon. When their leader summoned his own weapon—a long, golden blade that glowed so similarly to Draevyn's trident—he paused his advance. "*So, it would seem the Akani have recruited a blacksmith elemental,*" he remarked as he positioned himself to strike. "*Good to know.*"

And what happened next…

I wouldn't have believed it if I hadn't seen it with my own eyes.

Draevyn struck first, the male's sword ascending to block his trident. Draevyn seized the opportunity, his hand snapping forward to grab the male's wrist in a vice grip. The male's muffled scream could still be heard despite the ocean depths. So could the crunch of his wrist as he released his blade. Draevyn scooped it up in his free hand and swiftly struck across the male's throat. The male's eyes went blank as he drifted away on an errant current. I hadn't even noticed Draevyn disappearing in the darkness, like a shadow in midnight water, leaving me with only my tiny faelight for company.

But I could imagine the dance with the small glimpses I witnessed in the shadows.

His trident would appear in an explosion of golden light, strike, and disappear. Another male dead. A similar explosion. A female dead. His fierce, muscular body cut around the group, eliminating them with a speed barely visible to the eye, fae eyesight or not. Golden blades emerged and disappeared like strikes of golden lightning. The tiny flashes bathed Draevyn's face in a brief light, revealing the look of a furious warrior—one who was prepared and determined to protect. That same light showcased the fear of the Akani who dared to kill him.

Dared to kill *me*.

Draevyn's trident appeared yet again and struck true in the torso of the fourth, the male's body jerking as Draevyn dislodged his trident. He scanned the area, summoning faelight to shed light on the damage before us, blood drifting into the water like thin red drapes on a rogue wind.

My brow furrowed. *"There were five."*

A bright light grew at my back, and Draevyn's face slackened. My heart kicked in my chest as I wheeled around just in time to see the bright golden blade of the last Akani aim for my chest. But before it could strike true, a beast emerged out of the darkness—its large jaws and gleaming white teeth snapping on the male and separating him in two in an instant. Water flowed in and out of my lungs as I tried to settle my erratic heart, but I couldn't.

Because as Draevyn swam up beside me and his hand wrapped around my waist pulling me into him, our gazes were held firmly on the massive form of the great white shark before us.

The great white shark flung the body of the male he'd held between his enormous jaws in the direction of a shiver of sharks who were already consuming the bodies of the other deceased Akani. It swiveled its mammoth head back to us, Draevyn's arm tightening around my waist. I felt his body stiffen when the shark lowered in a similar fashion to a bow.

*"Greetings, Princess Asherah."*

I jerked back into Draevyn's chest. *"You can talk."*

*"The goddess blesses us with the ability to speak to the one with the mark,"* the shark replied.

*"Is it speaking to you?"* Draevyn inquired.

I glanced back at him. *"You can't hear him?"*

*"Only the one with the mark can hear us. Speak to us,"* the shark provided. My gaze shifted back to the shark. *"My name is Tiburon, but you may call me Tibu. I am the King of the water world,"* he said, bowing again slightly.

*"He says only the one with the mark can hear them,"* I informed Draevyn.

I caught the dark creases shadowed across his brow in my peripheral, his wide eyes observing Tibu. *"Extraordinary. I've never heard of anything like it."*

*"Tibu. Thank you,"* I ventured, *"for saving my life. It*

*would seem I'm in your debt."*

Tibu swam at a leisurely pace back and forth in front of us as he said, *"There is no debt, princess. It is our duty. We've been guarding you these past twenty-three years—with much difficulty, might I add. You've given us quite a fright with you riding the waves as you do."*

It was as if a puzzle piece had slipped into the place. All of the encounters with sea life, the strange behavior, the inexplicable way sharks seemed to stay far away when I was in the ocean. *"It all makes sense now,"* I said mostly to myself.

*"What makes sense?"* Draevyn asked, his eyes never leaving Tibu and his arm not moving a single inch from around my waist.

*"Sea creatures, especially sharks, have acted so strangely with me in the Above World. I never knew why."*

*"Tell your Guardian that he must be vigilant in these waters,"* Tibu warned, his tone grave. *"While your kind may not be able to hear us, we hear every message they relay to each other in these waters. Your kind seeks to disrupt the goddess's will, which has become a grave concern to us. We've been observing from afar, but the activity has increased."*

I relayed Tibu's message to Draevyn, whose face paled slightly in the faelight. *"Thank you, Tibu. For your vigilance."*

Tibu bowed his head once more. *"And we thank you… for dinner. I must leave you now before the rest of these heathens eat all the good meat."* My grip tightened on Draevyn's arm, some inner part of me still aware of the nature of the beast that swam before us. *"Be careful, Princess Asherah. May the goddess protect you and your Guardian."* Draevyn and I watched as Tibu swam into the darkness.

*"Let's get out of here."* Draevyn slid his fingers through mine, and we swam with speed for the palace gardens.

# Chapter 16

A SOFT KNOCK CAME FROM THE BEDROOM door.

"Come in," I called as I adjusted the sleeves of my mint-colored Atlantian-style jumper.

Queens be damned, I planned to stroll into the Queens' Council Chamber with my human clothes. My mind drifted to Draevyn, to Dad, and what they might have to say about it. An over-whelming feeling of guilt tried to push itself to the forefront. I'd been attempting to block it out all day but failed to.

Earlier that morning, I'd soaked in the luxuri-ous black stone in-ground tub in my bathroom and rested my head on the lip—wondering if I was be-ing stubborn about summoning my scales or if this was just me standing up for the humans. As the intoxicating aromas of eucalyptus and chamomile rose on tendrils of steam and permeated the air, I'd tried to convince myself that my actions were noble, that this was about the humans. But as my scales shimmered through the breaks in the bubbles that blanketed the tub, I knew I wasn't being honest with myself.

Walking into this meeting with the queens in my scales was a declaration of sorts, one I didn't know I was truly worthy of. It meant that I had accepted my place, my mark. It meant that I had fully embraced being a Water Fae. Gone were the days of slipping into my favorite pair of jeans, my beloved tanks, and their witty sayings I loved so much. My clothes were my skin in many ways. They represented who I was. Accepting my Water Fae form meant I was a part of this realm.

And I didn't fully feel that I was. Especially not after my last encounter with the Akani. These thoughts repeated until the water grew cold, forcing me to end my bath and face the day that lay ahead.

The bedroom door slammed against the wall with a bang, causing me to startle. Reneah entered with her arms filled with a heavy-looking white coat and my brows furrowed. "What in the world do I need that for?"

She laid the coat across the bed. "This would be for your Quarterly Queendoms meeting."

"Goddess. Where in the world are we meeting? Antarctica?"

Reneah's deep brown eyes blinked a few times. "Um. Yes, actually."

I couldn't move. I absolutely detested the cold. Snow was meant to be admired, not experienced. I was Floridian, after all. "Uh, I was joking."

"I'm not," Reneah said, smoothing out the long, wool-like coat. "Hence why I'm here with your coat."

I gaped at her for a long moment. "You mean to tell me that the Quarterly Queendoms meeting is in Antarctica? For real, for real?"

She spun and placed her hands on her hips. "Yes, for real, for real. There's no better place for the meeting. The soil is frozen, so the Earth Fae can't use it against anyone. The water is frozen, so you can't use it against them. I suppose if the Fire Fae really tried, they could conjure a flame, but then they'd melt the ice and give you an advantage. And the Air Fae could use the air against all of you, but then you'd all freeze to death. It's not completely foolproof, and I'm told that the Queendoms council chamber is magicked by the goddess to keep the peace. So, it's an advantage for everyone."

"An advantage for everyone except for my limbs, which will be frozen to death." I shivered as a phantom chill spread through my body.

"Well, that's why I brought you your coat, silly. Besides, when you enter the portal, it'll take you directly to the chamber. So you won't be in the cold for long." Reneah paused, assessing my clothing while biting her lip. "You're sure you want to do this? I don't mean it disrespectfully, but it's a risk. The other queens will see it as a weakness, not a declaration."

I blew out a breath. "Yeah…yes. I'm sure."

Reneah's head dipped in a nod as she pulled the coat off the bed, holding it out to me. "You need to get going. Your father is waiting at the temple."

I took the coat from her, my eyes planted on the ground. "Right. The temple. The portal." They'd explained the portal to the Queendoms Council chamber. The idea of going through some magical void set me on edge.

Reneah dipped her head in my line of sight. "Chin up, Ash. Your father will be there with you, and Draevyn is going as well. You're not alone."

I flashed a warm smile. "Thank you."

I hastened for the front door, finding Draevyn in the hallway when I emerged from my quarters. He turned toward me as it opened. "Hello, Prin—" Whatever smile he'd had quickly fell, his lips forming into a thin line as he appraised my clothing.

The heat that crept up my neck couldn't be helped. I straightened to full height and I cleared my throat. "Hello, Draevyn."

He plucked the coat from my hand. "Come. Your canoa is waiting below. We don't want to be late," he said, a twinge of anger lacing his voice. The walk from my quarters to the front of the palace where Braeliah waited in her canoa was a blur of intensity, my heart thumping rapidly the entire time. I breathed in deeply as I slid onto the bench and kept my gaze on the floor before me despite feeling his furious gaze on me as we rolled toward the Shingu River.

When the canoa descended into the river with a mighty splash, I made the mistake of glancing his way. Draevyn skewered me with unflinching fury. "Why?"

I swallowed past the lump in my throat. "Why what?"

"You know what."

I straightened my spine. "I don't believe I do."

"Bullshit."

I gripped the ledge of my seat and looked away before whispering, "I have no right to be there."

The tension in our little canoa thickened. "Stop the canoa, Braeliah!" Draevyn bellowed.

"Yes, sir!"

The canoa gave a sudden jerk. Draevyn rose from his side of the bench to stand directly before me. I shrieked when his arms went underneath my legs and behind my back, lifting me to his chest. "What are you doing?" I cried out.

"Teaching."

"What do you mean *teaching*?"

Draevyn's swift motion caught me off guard; I hadn't expected his next move until he was leaping over the side of the canoa, holding me tightly in his arms. I couldn't even draw in a breath before the water engulfed us. Draevyn held me firmly to him as I squirmed in his grip, desperate to make it to the surface for air.

"*Morph*." Frustration and disdain were wrapped up in the tone of his demand. "*You know how to do this, Ash-erah*. Morph."

I paused my thrashing and gave him a pleading glare, but Draevyn was unflinching. I knew I was running away from a part of myself. He knew it, too. And when I beheld what lay beneath all the frustration, disdain, and anger laced in his penetrating gaze, I finally broke. It was the confidence, the determination, and the trust that had me call my scales to the surface, the edges whispering against my garments as they spread across my body. Draevyn dropped his arm from underneath my legs and palmed the side of my neck, my heart thumping as my air supply depleted.

"*You. Are. Water. Fae. Breathe the water in. Do it.*"

Despite being surrounded by water, I could feel the tears well in my eyes until finally, I submitted. My hands came up to grip his forearms as I opened my mouth, taking in the Shingu—breathing it in.

"*That's it. Breathe.*"

My toes became scrunched in my silk slippers as the webbing emerged. His coarse thumb traced back and forth across my jawline in a soothing motion as a small smile finally emerged on his breathtaking face. "*There you are.*"

I breathed a few more pulls of water, our gazes fixed

on each other, the shock of what he'd done dissipating. The world outside the river waited for us, but I couldn't bring myself to care.

"*I want you to listen to me carefully,*" Draevyn began. "*You do have a right to be there.*" He grabbed my wrist, turning it over. "*Do not forget that the goddess herself gave you this mark.*" He traced the protective layer on my fingers with a gentle touch. "*Do not forget that regardless of where you were raised, this beautiful coat lies beneath the surface of your skin, along with those beautiful toes that are surely packed in those slippers.*" He caught my chin between a thumb and forefinger. "*There is not an inch of your being that is not Water Fae. Every part of your body is rightfully yours. No one can take that away from you, Asherah. You are meant to be here among us. You are one of us.*"

A long pause stretched before I dipped my head in a subtle nod. "*Yes, Draevyn. I'm Water Fae.*"

My heart positively swelled when his lips kicked up in a satisfied grin. "*I'm glad to hear it.*" His arms came under my legs once more, his other held firmly across my back. "*Now, let's go above water and get you dry.*"

His long, muscular legs cut through the water, propelling us through the surface. Draevyn summoned a wave of water at his feet, guiding us inside the canoa, where he gently set me on the deck. "We're ready, Braeliah."

"Yes, sir!" The canoa kicked into motion a second later.

I stomped my way into the cabin, leaving various puddles of water that formed on the deck from my soaking wet garments—Draevyn nipping at my heels.

"Let me help you get dry." He lifted his palm and pulled the water drop after drop from my body, sending it back through the cabin door and into the river. Within seconds, my hair was dry and cascading down my back, my clothes were impeccably dry, and when I looked into the mirror hanging against the wall of the small cabin, I had only to wipe away the small smudge of eyeliner to erase the last remnants of Draevyn's *lesson*.

I turned to him fully, unsure whether to be outraged or thankful.

His hands flexed at his sides. "I know you're mad."

"You think?"

He gave me a sheepish smirk that had me fighting a smile. "But maybe just a little happy?"

I sighed and wrapped my arms around my middle. "Maybe. You could have picked a better time for your *lesson*."

"It was as good a time as any. And you needed this." He stepped closer to me, his body heat radiating from him—his gaze softening as he regarded me. "Take them off, Asherah."

I didn't dare to look away from him. I didn't dare look too closely at the significance behind his demand and this moment. I had donned my scales and intended to keep them. There was just one final act to make.

It was time.

A smirk emerged on my face as I held his gaze. "Why are you always trying to get me to take off my clothes?"

He said nothing as I pulled down the sleeves, my hands shaking. His stare became something else entirely as I revealed every scale on my body to him, what lay hidden under the garments that now rested at my feet. There was something almost predatory, instinctively primal, about the way he gaped at me. My scales displayed in the same style as they were the first day they had emerged. He crouched before me, never moving his eyes from mine as he removed my silk slippers. When he rose, he kept his body within an inch of mine, and I forgot how to breathe. Draevyn Eliron was mesmerizing. I couldn't look away. But he slowly stepped back and placed the garments and slippers on the bureau before the mirror, and I instantly missed his body so close to mine. "You are ready," he said, bringing us back to the moment.

My hands fidgeted before my waist. "I don't feel ready."

He encompassed my hands with his. "I will not lie to you and say that the other queens will welcome you with open arms. The Queen of Earthos will likely be a silent participant. Airelandia is your closest ally who typically keeps the peace, which will be needed because the Queen of Corenathia is a viper. I want you to listen to me carefully. You do not show her weakness. Do not give her the opportunity. She'll take it and attempt to provoke you at every turn. You rise above it. You hear me?"

Draevyn's intensity cut right through my self-doubt. I willed another deep breath. "I understand."

"Good." He broke out in a radiant smile. "You look stunning in your scales, Asherah Delmar."

I tsked. "You shameless flirt."

"Only with you," he said with a wink.

I couldn't help but laugh. He joined in, and our laughter filled the small canoa cabin, cutting through the intensity. Draevyn's methods might have been slightly extreme, but I felt better about facing the other queens. "Thank you."

"Anytime, my Queen. Anytime."

We climbed the steps to the Temple of Atabey, where Dad stood, chatting with the Bohiti Loma—a long wool coat similar to mine draped over his arm. When we caught his attention in his periphery, he excused himself to greet us.

"Hey, Sher Bear. How are you feeling?" he asked, pulling me into one of my favorite hugs.

"About as you would expect."

He drew back. "So, nervous as hell then?"

"Yup."

His head dipped in a nod, his dark hair lightly brushing the olive skin of his forehead. "Sounds about right. But at least you've mastered your scales. That makes me a proud father."

I swallowed past the lump that instantly formed in my throat. "Thanks, Dad."

His dark brown eyes traveled over my shoulder. "Draevyn. Good to see you." I couldn't help but notice the clipped tone.

"You as well, Your Highness."

I cleared my throat and raised a brow at Dad, to which he cocked his head in question—a smirk pulling at his lips. He held his elbow out to me. "Shall we?"

"Like I have an option," I muttered, lacing my arm through his.

Our brisk steps carried us to the back of the temple just past the pyre. I didn't give it much attention, and the way Dad blocked it from my view told me he understood my unease. A tall archway with its tip pointing to the top of the temple occupied the furthest wall. Oddly enough, there was no entryway, just a solid wall of sandstone blocks within it. My brow furrowed when our steps could go no further. Draevyn stopped silent as a predator in the night just a few feet behind us. "Um.

How are we—"

"Coming! Coming!" the Bohiti called from behind us, launching across the vast open space of the temple with a comforting smile. She skillfully crushed ingredients in her fire-red clay mortar and with a matching pestle. "For as often as I've done this, you would think I'd be prepared. And yet, I always seem to run on HPST."

"HPST?" I asked.

"High Priestess Standard Time," she informed with a wink of her obsidian eye. Draevyn's amused chuckle reached my ears. She deftly gathered the substance in the bowl on the tips of her delicate fingers. "No matter what we do, time seems to slip away." Her long, silky black hair shifted as she wheeled around to the archway, smearing the substance on the stone before her. The Bohiti lathered every crevasse of a symbol etched in the stone that I hadn't initially noticed. My eyes narrowed on the symbol that matched the one on my wrist, save for the dot. When thoroughly satisfied with her work, she set her bowl on the ground and began her incantation, the spell rolling off her tongue with practiced ease. While her words were unfamiliar, my scales began to prickle with awareness. I gasped as the symbol before us expanded into a large black mass as dark as a midnight sky—a twinkle or two winking in the expanse.

Dad stepped forward, and my breath quickened. When I didn't move—couldn't move—he glanced my way. "It's okay, Sher. I've done this a million times. I promise you'll be fine."

Panic swelled up inside me, threatening to consume me whole, but when Draevyn's hand brushed the small of my back, the panic began to ease. "You can do this, Ash," his soothing, baritone voice encouraged.

I blew out a breath and reached back, threading my

fingers through his. "Okay. Let's do this."

The gesture didn't escape my father's notice as that knowing smirk returned to his face. He squeezed my arm tight to his side as we stepped beyond the archway with Draevyn in tow. Pure, black darkness enveloping us, snuffing out the light of Atlantis.

The immediate euphoria that followed was entirely unexpected. In college, I rarely had time to partake in parties or any of the extracurricular activities students were into. Chrissy often recanted her escapades—both of a sexual nature and of the substances she experimented with. Those stories are the only knowledge I had to describe what it felt like to indulge in the million types of substances that run rampant on college campuses. But as I fell through this vast expanse with only a few specks blinking in a brief wink, I'd have to imagine those simple human pleasures were nothing in comparison. The portal was ten times any feeling of pleasure I'd ever had. And I didn't know if I had the willpower to break from it.

When small, bright particles of light began gathering before us—the different colors shifting into bright greens, deep golds, and cerulean blue—my teeth clenched. The picturesque landscape, with its rolling hills of the whitest snow and the bluest of skies, was not enough to deter my longing to stay in the void.

To stay indefinitely.

"No," I murmured. "No, no, no."

The void was safe and warm. It invited me like a cozy fire on a cold winter day.

'*But even fire can burn, Asherah.*' A familiar feminine voice penetrated my void lust. '*Step into the light.*'

My breathing accelerated as I tried to reason with myself, some small part of me fighting like hell to remember who I was.

Asherah.

Heir.

Save the humans.

I breathed in deeply, focusing on the picturesque landscape before me. The familiar voice—one I began to recognize as my mother's—encouraged again. '*Step into the light.*'

And when the arch before me solidified with a sea of blinding white snow beyond, I stepped into the light.

I'd have to remember to express my unending gratitude to Reneah when I returned to Atlantis for the heavy coat she'd made sure I'd left with. The frigid wind cut into my bones as I clung to my father's arm. A stark white sea of snow reached as far as the Fae eye could see, meeting the crystal blue horizon before us. There was no telling which direction we were headed. There wasn't a single structure or any other living being in sight. I found out just how much cold my protective layering of skin could withstand as the biting wind assaulted my face. My teeth began to chatter, and tiny frosted drops gathered on my lashes. Dad pulled me forward as Draevyn placed a hand on the small of my back, pushing me against the wind. I glanced at Dad in confusion, hoping my facial features conveyed my question since I found myself incapable of forming words with my tongue frozen to the roof of my mouth.

"Just a few more yards," he called over the roaring wind.

Draevyn moved in closer to shield me from the on-slaught when I began to shiver violently—his thick, brown wool coat flapping in the wind behind him. My webbed toes stiffened with every step, the cold becoming increasingly unbearable. Dad stopped abruptly and knelt in the snow, tugging me down to join him. My mouth would have fallen open had it not been frozen shut. A puddle of water sat untouched and unmoved, like a tiny, hand-sized lake surrounded by miniature blinding white mountains covered in snow. How any unfrozen water existed in the frigid temperature remained a mystery, but I knew better than to question the magic of the Fae. I was beginning to learn that anything was possible.

Dad led my hand to the puddle of water, and upon touching the surface, the landscape before us rippled. An array of colors emerged like a mirage in a snowy desert landscape. A pathway made of tiny stones of blue and gray led to a charcoal-colored stone building with tall Roman columns supporting a dark metal dome roof. They lifted me from the ground, rushing forward.

The moment our feet hit the pathway, the air around us warmed considerably—my fingers and toes welcoming the heat with profound relief. My teeth chattering began to subside, and I breathed a few lungfuls of cool air.

"I'll never get used to that," Dad complained, shaking out his coat.

Draevyn blew into his palms and rubbed his hands together. "It makes me desperate for the warmer Atlantian waters. Goddess, it's cold."

As the warm air defrosted my limbs, I removed my heavy coat and surveyed the area before the chamber, noticing all the intricate details. Lush green moss bracketed the pathway, a small stream trickling alongside. My brows furrowed. "I thought we weren't allowed water here?"

Dad tilted his head. "We're not allowed a massive amount of water, but the stream is more symbolic than it is useful to us. I imagine the other queens' entrances are also decorated with their elements. But, unfortunately, it's inside the chamber where your powers will be rendered useless."

I breathed out a sigh. "My powers *are* useless."

Draevyn cut me a scolding look. "None of that, Asherah. Your powers are not useless. You need to go in there confidently."

"He's right," Dad agreed, placing his cool palm on my shoulder. "If you show even an ounce of self-doubt, the queens will eat you alive. Remember, you are meant to be here."

I nodded, not feeling even the slightest bit ready for the inevitable meeting. "So, what happens now?"

Draevyn took the coat from my hand. "You and your father will enter the chamber. I'll stand guard outside."

"When we enter the chamber, there'll be a large round table with four chairs. Yours will be directly in front of you," Dad advised as we strode down the pathway, the stones crunching beneath our feet. "Only the queens are permitted to sit in those chairs. You'll take your place, and I'll stand behind you as your regent. There'll be lots of talking. Plenty of arguing, I'm sure. Try not to intervene this time and simply observe. They'll no doubt try to needle you."

I blew out a harsh breath as we reached the chamber door. The tall, imposing frame with its dark metal handles and fastenings loomed over us. I gripped the handle and pushed it open—the ancient wooden door squeaking on weathered hinges—entering with all the confidence I could muster. I risked one last glance at Draevyn, soaking in all the encouragement in his Caribbean-green gaze—his dark hair framing his gorgeous face. I let loose a breath as Dad closed the door behind me and hung his coat on a steel hook on the wall behind the door.

A round oak table sat perfectly positioned in the center of the round room—a few weathered books and light leather journals scattered on its surface. A pair of females sat in two of the four opulent upholstered chairs surrounding it. Tiny dust motes floated in the air, the near-blinding sunlight casting its rays through a tall rectangular window on the opposite side of the chamber. I took in the multiple ancient tomes and aging scrolls lining the walls that seemed to reach the darkest corners of the circular, dark metal roof. As my steps carried me to the table, their heads snapped in my direction—my father's clipped steps sounding behind me. The females stood, staring at me with two very different types of expressions; one with a warm smile, the other with a look of trepidation, both just as intense as the other.

"Hello, Princess Asherah," the female said with a warm smile—her dark brown eyes observing me with interest. Wings with feathers of the brightest white unfurled behind her, complementing her beautiful, dark chocolate complexion. Her long black hair hung in perfect curls down to her waist. She was, in short, a marvel—the stuff tales of angels were written about. "I am Queen Laenah Karaya of Airelandia. And this is Queen Ayi Jiba of Earthos," she said, motioning to the female beside her. Queen Ayi's forest green eyes scanned me with neither contempt nor approval, long locks of her fire engine flowy red hair shifting as she nodded in greeting.

"You must call me Laenah, of course," she beamed, her hands folded primly over her white satin trumpet-style dress. Why I was expected to don my scales while the queens so clearly could do otherwise would be one of the first questions I'd ask as soon as we breached the realm of Atlantis.

"It's a pleasure to meet you. And please, call me Ash," I replied. I gave Queen Ayi a passing glance and found her intense glare still upon me—no first name given. Fair enough.

"Regent, good to see you again," Laenah addressed Dad. "It's always nice to have a male presence in the Queendoms chamber."

"Says you," Queen Ayi murmured.

He bowed slightly. "It is nice to see you both as well."

The chamber door flung open with a violent thud against the wall, startling us all. I thought it might've been a gust of wind, but it turned out I wasn't so lucky. A fierce female with facial features set into a severe expression strode powerfully into the room. Her bright blond hair was pulled tightly at the back of her head, causing her prominent cheekbones to stand out. The deep red fabric of her floor-length gown floated behind her in a gust of wind. She neither greeted nor acknowledged anyone in the room; she strolled to the chair neighboring mine and slid into her seat—slamming the weathered journal she'd been carrying upon the table.

"I don't think I need to remind you, Regent, that your attendance here is a privilege," she seethed, thumbing through the pages of the journal to a fresh blank page.

I quirked an eyebrow at him. He cleared his throat. "Yes, Queen Sessi. I understand. I'm here as Regent and to support my daughter."

Queen Sessi's steely gray eyes lifted, landing on me. They traveled from the tallest standing strand of my dark hair to the tips of my webbed toes and back. "Yes, yes. Support your daughter. It's a wonder how she'll manage when she is crowned Queen. Whatever will she do without her Daddy?"

"Enough of the dramatics, Sessi. We have important matters to discuss," Queen Ayi admonished. She folded the skirt of her rich emerald green dress beneath her as she sat on my other side, and my head did a double take. It was no dress Queen Ayi wore but hundreds of palm-sized leaves skillfully drawn together to form her gown. I couldn't help but admire the intricacy.

"Indeed. And better to discuss these things diplomatically," Laenah added, sitting with a plop in her chair—her bright wings vanishing as she shuffled it forward with a loud scrape against the stone floor.

Sessi pulled a black marble pen from its home on the side of her journal with a huff. "Polite diplomacy is more your thing than mine, Queen Laenah. I prefer a more blunt approach."

"No shit," I heard Dad murmur under his breath.

Sessi scowled in his direction. "I hope you understand that you do not get a chair at this table, *male*," she said contemptuously.

"Yes, Queen Sessi. I understand," he replied in a borderline tone of boredom. "I stand by my daughter. Nothing more."

I perched delicately on the black velvet of my chair, feeling impossibly small around the three queens. *Imposter. You're an imposter.*

*No, you are not. You are meant to be in that chamber.*

Draevyn's voice bellowed in my head. Whether it was real or my subconscious, I couldn't tell.

I breathed carefully, shifting my gaze to the right to find Sessi's eyes boring into my skull. "I understand condolences are in order," she said dryly.

I could hear the blood rushing to my head. "You

dare to offer condolences when one of your own took her life?"

The other queens stiffened in their chairs, their eyes pinging between us. Sessi's perfectly pink lips pursed in a thin line, and her head tilted with predatorial precision. "I said they were in order. I never said I would provide them."

Laenah clapped her hands together. "Of course, yes. Our sincerest condolences for the loss of your mother. Neleah was a lovely female and Queen."

"My condolences as well," Queen Ayi provided as she gave a terse nod.

They glared at Sessi expectantly, but she only scowled back at them before waving her hand in the air with a sigh. "Yes, yes. What they said. Now, can we please get back to the meeting?"

I wanted to rip her throat out and scream how she'd been responsible for ordering Mom's murder, but I remembered the words Dad gave me a few days ago in a warning. *There is no proof of her involvement yet, and we mustn't accuse the Queen during the meeting.* But goddess, how I wanted to.

Laenah cleared her throat. "Right, the first item on our agenda—"

"An item needs to be added to today's agenda," Sessi rudely interrupted. She sat back in her chair, twining her burgundy polished fingers in her lap. "Please add the topic of Princess Asherah's existence. Perhaps now that she's present, the Regent can answer the question we've been asking of him these past few months. We need to know how she existed without our knowledge." She glared over my shoulder where Dad stood.

Laenah scribbled down on the parchment before her. "Right. Item has been added. Moving on. The first topic to discuss is the plan for the upcoming ice age."

Sessi scoffed. "I do not see why we need a plan. We already know what must be done."

"Which does not align with what the goddess calls us to do," Queen Ayi voiced in a tone that left no room for argument. "Going against the goddess's wishes will call her fury upon us. The Queendom of Earthos will have no part in it."

"She is right, Sessi," Laenah agreed with a grimace when Sessi turned her steely gaze in her direction. "We cannot go against the goddess's wishes. This is Atabey's will."

Sessi huffed and leaned forward, placing her clasped hands on the tabletop. "May I remind you that the scholars in Corenathia have interpreted the texts differently. We will have our humans. They are a gift to the Fae from the goddess."

"The hell they are." I couldn't hold my tongue with that decree.

Sessi shifted her attention to me, an evil smirk pulling at her lips. "Ah, of course. The little human want-to-be *would* have a problem with us fulfilling our roles as the masters of the human race. No matter where she was raised, they've instilled those human-empathizing Atlantian values. Always trying to save the poor, innocent humans."

I tilted my head. "You say that like it's a bad thing."

"You act like humans have any other purpose than to serve us. We are the superior species. That's what the goddess wants, and for a millennium, your queendoms have treated them like they are called for something more." She turned her attention to the queens. "Look at what's happening in the Above World. They've become too brazen, too comfortable. They look at their short lives and figure that if they're only on earth for a little while, who cares if they destroy the world? It doesn't affect them. They won't be here anyway, but their children will. And they don't even care about their children's future."

Queen Ayi let out a soft chuckle. "That is rich. You speak of caring for children like you actually care about your own."

"Queen Ayi," Laenah hissed. "Please try to be civil."

"Furthermore," Sessi continued without a denial, "they are destroying each other."

"And we're what? Not destroying each other?" Queen Ayi remarked, her red brow lifting.

Sessi lifted a shoulder. "Our conflicts are completely avoidable if you all would just conform."

"The Queendom of Earthos doesn't answer to you. We answer to the goddess and no other. Please remember that the next time you decide to spew your extremism." Queen Ayi paused, turning her attention to Laenah and myself—her rich green eyes in stark contrast to her cream-colored skin. "At the request of Queen Sessi Nacan of Corenathia, our scholars have reviewed the texts and concluded that the humans' true nature is not to serve the Fae but to live in unison with us. Therefore, the Queendom of Earthos will be happy to take in our share of the humans before the ice age commences. We will sign the proclamation."

"Wonderful," Laenah beamed, her bright white teeth peeking through her dark, full-lipped smile. "As stated in the previous queendoms meeting, the Queendom of Airelandia will also sign the proclamation. With Queen Neleah's initial creation of the proclamation, that makes three queendoms—"

"Does it, though?" Sessi interjected. "As far as I understand, Atlantis doesn't have a Queen."

"No thanks to you." The words escaped my lips before I could think better of them. The room fell eerily silent. I caught Dad's curse under his breath behind me.

Sessi's face turned beet red. "What exactly are you accusing me of, Princess?" She spat the question through gritted teeth. Frustration and disdain were laced with every word.

"You know exactly what I'm accusing you of."

"Where's your proof?"

"The proof is in how the Fire Fae attacked me both in the Above World and Atlantis. The proof is in the way I sit in this chair, and my mother doesn't."

"Princess Asherah," Laenah said with kind eyes, "unfortunately, those are very tall accusations to make against a queen with no evidence. I feel for you and your father. I feel for the whole queendom of Atlantis, but we cannot accuse Queen Sessi of such a thing. Those were a few rogue Fire Fae."

I heard what she didn't say: those were a few rogue Fire Fae until we could prove otherwise. I shifted my attention to Sessi. "The Queendom of Atlantis will have their Queen."

Sessi smiled knowingly. "That's not what I hear. I hear that your little council is quite set on booting you out. How very diplomatic of them. How very against the calling of the goddess, with that mark upon your skin. It seems the Atlantians only want to follow the goddess's rules when it serves their purpose, does it not?" Sessi leaned back in her chair. "With that said, the proclamation is void until the Queendom of Atlantis has a Queen."

"They will have their Queen," Dad answered.

"No one invited you to speak, Regent," Sessi hissed.

"But now that your mouth is moving, perhaps you could explain why you never informed us of your Heir."

"That is mine and Neleah's business. Not yours. We don't go around telling you what to do with your children. Otherwise, we might encourage you not to squirrel them away for their entire existence."

"How dare—"

"It would be nice to know why you did it, Regent," Laenah interrupted. "It was a bit of a shock to find out you had a faeling and didn't tell us." I could have sworn there was hurt in her brown eyes.

His hands landed softly on my shoulders. "Neleah and I did what we thought the goddess would want for our daughter: for her to understand the humans and their nature and for Asherah to develop compassion for them before the coming ice age. No heir has been raised amongst the Above World humans. Given that Asherah has grown into a wonderful female with a heart that encompasses the whole world, I'm confident we did the right thing, and I know Neleah would say the same.

"Our desire to keep her existence from the rest of the realms was simple; we wanted to protect her. And seeing how the moment others discovered her existence, her life was perilous, it appears we did the right thing."

"How touching," Sessi said, sarcasm dripping from her tone. "Anyway, we'll wait to see what the Queendom of Atlantis does with their Heir. Since the rest of the items on the agenda deal with the upcoming ice age and we are clearly at an impasse, this meeting is officially over." She stood precipitously, her chair screeching against the stone. "This has been so enjoyable, as always." She gathered her journal and strode for the chamber entrance. "Until next time."

My gaze followed her until the chamber door clicked

shut. A renewed energy filled my soul, my calling more evident than ever before. I wouldn't let that spawn of hatred take one single human into Corenathia, and I'd fight till my last breath.

# Chapter 17

"Well, you can't expect her to attend the Queendom's council in her Fae form. She'd burn through her clothes!" Dad had said to me of Queen Sessi when we'd returned to Atlantis that day. Being held to a different standard than the other queens was a hill I aimed to die on, but I let the issue rest for now.

There were more important things at hand.

I strode behind Draevyn, the strong muscles of his bare back flexing with every step of his long, muscular, scaled legs as we approached the guard house of the Fotuto outpost. He was every bit the formidable warrior everyone treated him like. Every Guardian we'd passed on the walk from the Shingu saluted the Commander with an arm reverently crossed over their chest. And when their gazes carried to where I walked behind him, their eyes went wide before they bowed.

Draevyn had requested I travel with him for the day to Fotuto, one of three outposts in Atlantis. Fotuto was founded on the southern border, Calichi to the north, and Jimagua—a twin to the Calichi outpost—to the west. "It'll be good for you to meet your guard," he'd suggested when we returned from the Queendoms Council. "They need to see you."

And so, stepping well out of my comfort zone, I'd agree to go with him in two days' time when he left to visit his regiment. Unlike Calichi and Jimagua, Fotuto was an underwater outpost located outside the dome at a higher elevation than the rest of the Atlantis—the natural light from the Above World visible above. At least, that's what Draevyn informed me as we swam through the Shingu that morning. My heart raced with excitement to see it.

A grey stone arch protruded from the dome wall at the end of the matching stone walkway—the dome wall rippling within as Guardians entered and exited the outpost. A Guardian stepped out of the guard house, greeting Draevyn with a hand across his chest and a smile. "Commander Eliron. Welcome back."

"Officer Celiryn. Good to see you again." Draevyn motioned to me with his trident. "Princess Asherah is accompanying me today."

Officer Celiryn's gaze flicked my way, and his eyes widened. "Princess Asherah." He bowed at the waist. "It's an honor."

My cheeks flamed. I'd never get used to the formality. "It's a pleasure to meet you as well."

Officer Celiryn returned his attention to Draevyn. "The Guardians are at the training ground with Major Yaralyn."

"Ah, that's perfect. We'll head there first, then."

Draevyn's trident disappeared in a flash as he placed his hand on the small of my back, sending a flourish of butterflies in my stomach. Based on the smirk he gave me, it was clear he noticed. "This way, Princess."

When we stepped through the wall of water, I had a brief moment of panic, as I always had, but I pushed beyond my fear.

But I wasn't prepared for what lay beyond the wall. I gasped on an intake of water. It looked like something straight out of a fairytale.

Brightly colored yellow and blue fish formed schools, gracefully swimming through the large arched openings of the circular underwater structure. Deep green algae blanketed the faded grey stone, extending nearly four stories above us. Bunches of mustard brown kelps decorated each level of the outpost, columns with ancient etchings lay in perfect rows with red sea whips dotting the multiple levels high and low. Hundreds of Water Fae swam through the various openings passing through the atrium, all throwing curious glances our way. Light from the Above World filtered in from its center, casting its watery rays on a spire that pieced the ocean above it, a large shell affixed at the very top. Draevyn pointed to it. *"That there is called the Fotuto, after which the fort is named. If we're ever invaded, that shell is magicked to send a signal throughout Atlantis. Many historians argue that this very well may be the founding site of Atlantis, something the scholars at Cibao passionately debate. But no one truly knows."*

I took in the light that filtered in through the top. *"We're so close to the Above World. How have the humans not discovered this?"*

Draevyn smiled like an excited child with a secret to tell. *"Lots and lots of deterrent spells cast by the most gifted priestesses in Atlantis.*" He laced his fingers through mine, an act that was becoming so natural, yet it still sent heat to my core. "*Let's go see Mayana in action. She's on faeling duty today.*"

"*Faeling duty?*"

"*You'll see.*"

Draevyn pulled me through an archway to the left of the outpost, a low hum of voices filtering through my mind as we approached a clearing surrounded by brightly colored coral, forming a large arena—giant stone steps hugging the entire area. Dozens of young Fae males and females—no more than thirteen years old by the looks of them—faced Mayana in a perfect row at its center. We slowly swam outside the arena, careful not to disturb them.

"*Again,*" Mayana instructed.

In unison, their tridents suddenly materialized in their hands, and they pitched it forward in the sand before them, tiny grains bursting up from the sea floor from the disturbance.

Mayana swam above the wall of sand, her face beaming. "*Nice work! Let's try a few more times. Focus on distance this time.*" Her attention flicked our way, and the corners of her mouth curled upwards into a wide grin. "*Princess Asherah. Commander Draevyn.*"

The group of faelings turned toward us, some swimming in front of others to get a view of us, some in webbed feet, others in full, long, scaled tails. I flicked my webbed feet a little closer to Draevyn as he said, "*Don't mind us, Major. I'm showing Princess Asherah around the outpost today. We don't want to disturb.*"

Mayana gave us a flourish of the hand. "*It's no worry at all, is it, cadets?*"

The resounding no from the group filtering through

in teenage voices brought a smile to my face. They were so young, which prompted a million and one more questions I had for Draevyn.

*"Okay, cadets. Let's go again."*

The group reluctantly swam in formation—some of them casting final glances over their shoulder, not at me, I realized, but at Draevyn—before readying themselves for another throw. Draevyn and I watched in silence for the better part of an hour as I absorbed the scene before me. So young, and so many. And already showing such skill. I admired how they effortlessly cast their tridents with a form I was envious of. I studied one male faeling in particular and the way his face contorted in outrage as he impaled his trident in the sand like he was envisioning something. Or someone. I searched the hundreds of them, all called to serve our realm. At their age, I was in the Above World, trying to figure out how to stand on my surfboard. Yet, these faelings were training to be warriors. Why?

*"What questions do you have in that pretty little mind of yours?"*

I raised an eyebrow. *"How could you tell I had questions?"*

The corner of his sensuous lips lifted in a smirk. *"I'd be surprised if you didn't."*

*"Well, since you asked,"* I began, as I motioned to the faelings, *"there must be hundreds of them. Are there normally so many?"*

I watched through the dark strands of hair drifting around his face as his smile slowly dropped. *"No, Princess. This amount of faelings training for the Guard is very unusual. It's…"*

Something tugged at my heart. I didn't like the way he'd gone silent. I reached for his hand, giving it an encouraging squeeze. *"It's what?"*

Draevyn shook his head. "*It's just that there are so many. When I received my mark, there were maybe ten of us that year. All these faelings you see here? They've just received their marks. It's very troubling.*"

I shifted my attention to the group, scanning over all the young Fae called for the Guard. "*And what do you make of it?*"

"*I don't know,*" he said softly in my mind. "*It's as if the goddess is preparing for something. Something big. And it sends a sense of dread into my gut if I'm being entirely honest.*" Bubbles flew from his mouth on a sigh as he flicked his head toward the outpost. "*Come. There's lots more to see.*"

I followed behind him as we swam to the second floor, where we entered a hallway—blue faelights flaring to life as we passed. Draevyn ushered me into a room with a large window cut out, providing just enough light to make the area visible. There wasn't much in the room. In fact, there wasn't a single piece of furniture in sight.

Draevyn faced me as he reached the far side of the room. "*You'll find no books or scrolls in this outpost for obvious reasons. This is solely for training and guarding the realm's southern end. This room is our only meeting room.*"

My brow furrowed. "*Is there nowhere dry in this outpost?*"

"*No, Princess. This outpost is to train our baser water element. The cadets are each assigned a room in the outpost. Save for a solid few hours of sleep, they train, and they feed.*"

"*And…how do they sleep?*"

Draevyn smiled. "*They float.*"

"*Float?*"

"*Yes, in the water. In their rooms, of course.*"

"*And what do they eat if there are no kitchens to prepare food or a place to have a dry meal?*"

Draevyn bit his lips to suppress a laugh. "*They feed.*

*On fish."*

*"It's so…"*

*"Strange?"*

*"Really strange, but amazing as well."*

Bubbles flew from his mouth as he let loose a laugh. He paused briefly as we hovered in the water before each other in the empty room. When his eyes scanned over me slowly, warmth spread across my chest.

And lower.

Draevyn seemed to catch himself and motioned behind him. *"This is our main meeting room. It's not much to look at, but it serves as the only meeting room."*

It was my turn to hold a laugh. *"You said that already."*

*"Did I?"*

*"You did."*

*"Oh."*

I bit my lip, an action that didn't go unnoticed. Draevyn shook his head before he continued, *"In Fotuto, they learn how to fashion their scales for war, where they learn the art of the trident, where they learn what it means to be a true Guardian of Atlantis. It separates the weak from the strong and lets us know who to keep an eye on for higher rankings."* He raked his fingers through his hair. *"Maybe we can… practice with your scales. Perhaps try fashioning them in a tail. If you'd like."*

My head dipped in a nod. *"I'd like that very much."*

Draevyn slid his hand in mine but paused before me for a minute, his tropical green eyes causing my heart to thump frantically in my chest. *"I love the way you look at Atlantis."*

*"And how is that?"*

*"Like someone who's discovered a hidden treasure. It's entirely refreshing."*

I squeezed his hand. *"Well, I'm glad to entertain you."*

*"Oh, you provide endless entertainment, my Queen. In so many ways."* He swam toward the door with my hand in his. *"This way."*

And we left the outpost behind.

Three football fields remained between where we swam and the outpost, well into the open water—a few fish brushing against our scales in greeting as we hovered before each other. Draevyn's tail glistened in shades of blue and green with deeper shades of purple on the feather-light tips. My gaze roamed over every scale, committing it to memory.

*"Just as you've fashioned your scales to rise to your collarbone or prefer to expose your arms on other days, you'll fashion your tail in whatever shape you desire."* He flipped his tail forward in the space between us. *"I prefer adding as many scales as possible to the fin so that I may cut through the water with ease."* With a flick of his tail, he began circling me, a giddy grin spreading across my face. It was a dream come true.

Instant mermaid, just add water, indeed.

Once he swam in a full circle, he motioned to me with a smile. *"Go on. Give it a try."*

I gave him a determined nod as I glanced down at my webbed feet and then to my scales just above my ankles—the bluish-green tint winking at me in return. Narrowing my gaze, the scales drifted over my ankles and under my heel, spreading over my toes. I thought about Draevyn's tail, the very shape of it—the power of it. I watched in open fascination as the ends of my tail spread nearly four feet wide.

The pure joy of Draevyn's smile reached deep into

my soul. *"Well done, Asherah."*

A pod of dolphins emerged from the deep blue shadows, their tiny clicks reaching my ears and their long tails flicking powerfully in their wake. They circled us, and I couldn't help but gape at them. We spun around, my body brushing up against Draevyn's. He glanced at me with a smirk. *"Friends of yours?"*

One of the dolphins paused a foot away. *"Care for a swim, Your Highness?"*

The dolphin was talking.

To me.

*"Let me guess. It's talking to you,"* Draevyn said dryly.

I nodded at him vigorously. *"They want to go for a swim."*

Draevyn tried to play it off with a carefree shrug, but his twitching smile betrayed his excitement. *"Then, let's."*

I shifted my attention to my new dolphin friend. *"Um…sure."*

And the pod took off.

Embarrassment coursed through me as I tried to flick my tail to keep up. My abdomen screamed with each effort. My brow dipped in concentration, my lower back muscles protesting as Draevyn and the pod swam nearly fifty yards away. I remained determined to figure it out. I observed his movements, the way his tail gracefully rose and fell, how his large fin gracefully flipped with perfect precision.

And I mirrored it.

My speed picked up until only a yard remained between us—Draevyn's long, flowy hair drifting behind him like long tendrils caressing the sea. With all my might, I pushed harder until I finally reached his side.

Draevyn gave me a wink. *"I knew you'd figure it out."*

Nearly two dozen dolphins easily cut through the water—some playfully swirling around each other. We followed in their wake, and pure elation cut through me. This brought new meaning to swimming with the dolphins—the movement of my tail becoming second nature as we traveled further into deep ocean blue waters, their light clicks sounding all around us.

I'd never felt so at home in my life. The scales felt more like a part of me, more like something I'd been missing my entire life in the Above World; like every time I'd entered the ocean, they wanted to spring forth and welcome me home.

I am a Water Fae, and the sea is my tribe.

And so, we swam with the dolphins, playing like children, our faces full of glee at simply being part of their little pod.

Draevyn slowed, and I came to a pause. *"There's something I want to show you."*

I gave him a nod as I wheeled around to my dolphin friend, who swam a few feet away. *"This is where we leave you. Thank you for the swim."*

*"It was a delight, my Queen."*

With a few playful twirls, they disappeared into the ocean depths.

In Draevyn's wake, I trailed behind as a towering ridge emerged—a colossal, jagged rock slicing through the ocean like a knife. Passing through a lofty, narrow opening, Draevyn conjured a faelight, its glow swallowed by the surrounding darkness. The light danced against the water's surface as we ascended to meet it. When my head slowly breached the water, I cast a faelight into the darkness and smiled in bewilderment. "Commander Eliron, do you have your own personal hideaway?"

Draevyn climbed the rocky shore with ease and a complete sense of familiarity. He glanced over his shoulder, a mischievous smile spreading on his face. "I have lots of personal hideaways, my Queen. But not everyone gets to see them." He reached his hand out to me.

My scales separated into legs as I placed my hand in his. "Well, I'm honored you've deemed me worthy of your hidden…is this a cavern?" I asked, my gaze roaming over the hundreds of stalactites dropping from the ceiling like midnight black monsters baring their sharp teeth.

"That it is," he confirmed, resting his hands on his hips. Draevyn's gaze swept around the room as if checking to make sure everything was where he had left it.

My feet gained purchase on the rocky ground that bit into my soles. The shore was nothing more than a fifteen by fifteen-foot space in front of a large pool of water. A tiny wooden crate sat in a corner with a stack of books on top. A few bottles of wine occupied the space within. Neatly folded woolen blankets and a rather beatdown pillow lay against its side. Draevyn motioned to it. "Would you like a drink?"

My lips lifted in a smirk. "Sure."

As he reached for a bottle to uncork it, my gaze traveled around the charming little cavern. "So, what is this place?"

"This is where I come when I need to escape the outpost," he informed me as the sound of the wine pouring from the bottle reached my ears.

"Ah, so you snuck away when you were a cadet?"

"Never as a cadet. But as a Commander? With that

many faelings and Guardians running around? Certainly." He placed two cups on the ground and grabbed the blanket. "I've already paid my dues. I deserve some quiet time."

I busied myself perusing the titles of his books, scanning the first one. "The Count of Monte Cristo," I murmured as I flipped to the first page. My eyes widened, and my mouth dropped open. "Um…Draevyn. I'm pretty sure the Monroe County Library wants its book back since it's been checked out for over a century." I provided him with my best scolding glare over my shoulder. "And you should always return your library books."

He spread the navy-blue woolen blanket across the floor and sat upon it—the groves of his muscles tightening as he leaned back on his arms. He patted the space next to him. "It must have slipped my mind."

"Frequented Key West in the past?"

A shrug.

I tucked that tidbit away for later. I dropped beside him with the book, carefully thumbing through the weathered pages. "This is amazing."

"Well, then, I'm glad I forgot to return it. It's yours if you want it."

I lifted an eyebrow. "If I can figure out how to get it out of your hideaway without ruining it."

"Exactly."

I shook my head. "Just how did you get it here anyway?"

Draevyn brushed my hair over my shoulder, eliciting a tingling sensation that shot down my spine. A gasp stuck in my throat as his eyes roamed over my bare shoulders and back and even lower to my bare hips. I may or may not have intentionally donned my scales on my breasts, stomach, and legs only.

I'll never tell.

"That is your next lesson. Shielding."

"And how do we do that?"

He pointed at the book.

I threw him an incredulous look. "You can't be serious."

"I am."

"Do you know how much this is worth? It's a first edition. I may ruin it."

He lifted a shoulder in a lazy shrug. "Well then, you better shield it properly."

I blew out a breath. "Okay, how do I do that?"

Draevyn held out a hand for the book, and I reluctantly gave it to him. He rose from the floor to crouch in front of the pool of water before us. "When you shield, you're essentially pushing the water away from the object you desire to protect. Think of it as your own personal dome magic." I gasped as he dipped the book into the water and then pulled it out. My gaze roamed over the aging pages. Not a single inch of it got wet. He flicked his head toward the pool. "Now, you try it."

I glanced around the room, trying to find anything else that might not be so valuable, but came up empty. Draevyn gave me a look that bordered on an eye roll. "It will give you incentive. Come on." I bit my lip and joined him in a crouch beside the water.

"First, you'll want to practice with your hand. Dip it in the water," he instructed. The cool water enveloped my hand as I pushed it below its surface. "Now, you'll want to connect with your water magic. Let it call to you and will the water away."

"You make it sound so easy."

"There's nothing to it. I have complete faith in you."

I honestly wished I had that same faith in myself all

the time. I would need it now. My gaze narrowed on my hand just beneath the water's surface. I felt the water, connected with it, and I could have sworn it brushed up against me like it was greeting me beneath my fingertips. My lips lifted in an excited smile as I answered its call and pushed it away. A thick layer of air materialized between the water and my skin.

"Nicely done, Asherah."

I pulled my hand back, examining it. Not a single drop trickled from my skin. It remained completely dry.

He handed the book over. "Before you push the book beneath the surface, connect with your water magic again. Then, dip it in."

I gave him a determined nod and shifted my attention to the pool before me. I called to my water magic, willing it to do my bidding. I swore I heard it whisper in return. On a deep inhale, I began lowering the book into the water. I watched in wonder as it pushed back on a tiny wave before enveloping it with a pocket of air. I couldn't hold back the laugh that escaped me if I tried.

Before I could lose my concentration, I pulled the book above the surface and beamed at Draevyn. His face was alight with something akin to pride. "You're a natural, my Queen."

My cheeks burned under his gaze. I cleared my throat, handing the book back to him. "Thanks."

He patted the area beside him. "Sit. Let me read to you for a bit before we head back."

For some reason, the idea of the Commander reading to me in his deep, baritone voice was both thrilling... and arousing. I dropped on the blanket beside him, my extended leg brushing against his as he began to read, "On the twenty-fourth of February eighteen fifteen, the lookout at Notre-Dame de la Garder signaled the arrival of the three-master Pharaon coming from Smyrna, Trieste, and Naples."

Draevyn's deep voice echoed across the walls, amplifying the tale. When he was deep into chapter two, a flicker of faelight illuminated the other side of the cavern. Draevyn paused his reading, likely to see what had captured my attention. "Ah…you've discovered the goddess."

"Is that who that is?" I asked as I cast a few more faelights to get a better look at the etchings on the wall. Long, flowing lines of hair were carved down the back of a female, a flower resting behind her tipped ear. Her lower half donned the very scales that blanketed the Water Fae. The mighty trident gripped in her hand almost shimmered in the faelight. With a shell held to her mouth, she blew a wind cyclone, a feather floating on the top. A snake rested at the base of her tail, and I had to suppress a laugh. It almost looked like a pet lovingly sleeping at her side. "It's stunning."

Draevyn smiled at the ancient carving like seeing an old friend. "Yes, that she is. The goddess is a great companion to have in my little hideaway. These kinds of carvings are not unusual. You'll find them throughout various caverns surrounding Atlantis. Whoever put them there, however, remains a mystery."

"Fascinating."

Draevyn hummed in agreement.

As the day slowly drifted by, Draevyn continued reading from his favorite book with only the goddess on the wall and the faint resounding drip from the stalactites looming over our quiet sanctuary to keep us company. It was the perfect end to my Drae day. As his soothing voice echoed across the cavern's walls, I dared to let my feelings for him venture beyond the friendship I felt.

And something within me flared a little brighter to life.

# Chapter 18

I GREW TIRED OF FEELING DEFENSELESS IN A world where everyone around me had extraordinary power at their fingertips. If Queen Sessi wanted to take humans into Corenathia to enslave them, she'd have to do so over my dead body. I vowed to make her mission as difficult as possible, but in my current state, I couldn't even fight off a minnow if I desired to.

Which is why, with each step I took, my excitement grew. I followed Dax as he entered the training facility where the Guardians trained—his long, pale hair brushing across his massive back with each step. The facility stood across the south side of the palace. It was nothing more than a sandstone building that resembled a warehouse, with its backdoors opening into a large, sandy training arena. Warm sunlight filtered across the grounds and poured through the windows of the facility. As I strode through the double doors behind Dax's towering form, I couldn't help but notice all the various tools designed to inflict pain: long, shiny swords encased in a glass cabinet, tall wooden staffs tucked into the corner, several nunchucks hanging from metal hooks in neat rows, bows and arrows resting just beneath them on a wooden crate.

But that wasn't what drew my sole attention. A wall of cascading water fell into a large, natural pool at its base, where several half-naked, incredibly gorgeous Guardians milled about—every inch of their ripped warrior's bodies on full display. Some appeared to be cooling themselves, their deep breaths indicating they'd just completed their training. Others manipulated the water into all kinds of shapes and sizes. Spheres. Discs. Arrows.

Jagged rocks of the deepest charcoal color framed each side of the descending waterfall and what appeared to be a cave peeked from just beyond the veil of water. I stood gaping.

"Impressive, isn't it?"

"Just a little."

Dax smiled in amusement. "This is where we start our training." He shifted his attention to the Guardians in the water. "Okay, everyone! Times up! We need to train our little Princess!"

I scoffed. "Little Princess?"

Dax tied his hair with a leather tie at the nape of his neck. "You'll want your scales covering as much of your body as possible. Wouldn't want you to get nicked. I've spent more time in the infirmary than I care to." I had no desire to visit the infirmary either. I summoned my scales to my collarbone and down to my wrists, leaving only my face, feet, and hands exposed.

A murmur of laughter echoed off the walls as the Guardians exited the pool. They each bowed—one of them openly scanning me from head to toe with a lift of his lips and causing my cheeks to heat—as Dax led me into the water until the water rose to my waist. It lapped against my scales, calm and inviting.

"Alright," he began, motioning over me. "It's clear you've already mastered morphing. Any questions on summoning your scales or morphing shapes?"

I lifted my hand, watching my protective skin shimmer against the light as I wiggled my fingers. "None so far."

Dax nodded, placing his rugged hands on his chiseled hips. "Very well. So, for your first lesson, we'll go over manipulating water, but most importantly, how to use it in self-defense. Soon enough, it'll become second nature, much like morphing." He held his palm in the air, and several tiny streams of water fell into it. "Water can be both a weapon and protection." The water thinned and moved up his bare arms, blanketing them with a thin layer of water, like a caterpillar crawling across his fair skin. "The water, while not impenetrable, can lessen the effects of some elements, can block out most of them. For example, if a Fire Fae were to catch us unaware and we cannot summon water quick enough, we may get burned." The layer traveled up his defined torso, thick neck, and bulging biceps until his entire body was covered in a glimmering shield of water. "But if we can summon our water shield, we can protect ourselves." Dax held his arms out, wiggling his fingers. Droplets of water floated before him, transforming into thousands of long, sharp-looking needles. He shot them into the waterfall with a flick of his wrist, and my mouth fell open. "We can also take down our enemies," he said with a sly smile. The water shield dropped unceremoniously back into the pool with a splash. "It'll take some time to train you to that level. So, we'll start with some basics."

Dax carefully grabbed my hand, laying it flat on the pool's surface, the water dancing over my fingertips. "Begin by mastering the art of communication with the water, attuning yourself to its essence, and absorbing the energy generously bestowed by the goddess. She is in all things. Close your eyes and call to Atabey."

My brow lifted. "Call to Atabey?"

His face turned gravely serious. "I know in the Above World, such things as calling to spirit or a god may seem…silly, like calling out to some phantom un-reachable being whose existence is debatable. But I hope you've seen enough proof with your own two eyes to know that nothing is debatable about Atabey. The god-dess hears you, listens to you. You have only to call her, and she will answer," he pointed at the swirls and curves inked on my wrist, "especially with that mark."

His words rang true. I'd felt it in the cavern that day with Draevyn, and my tiny experience was enough to know Atabey existed. I let loose a breath, closing my eyes and letting my other senses take over. I heard the crashing sound of the waterfall meeting the pool below and felt the push of the ripples under my hand. My sur-roundings came to life behind my eyelids. Just beneath the surface of the water, a blue string of light brightened, playful in its energy, as it snapped to and fro on an errant current, edging closer to my palm. It gave a few light taps, causing me to flinch.

"Don't be afraid of it. Embrace it," Dax encouraged.

I inhaled deeply, the blue string caressing my palm. Suddenly, it latched onto my hand and began creeping up my arm. My breathing accelerated, but I remained determined to be still. My eyelids squeezed, my natural instincts imploring me to open them, but as the energy reached my upper arm and spread to my collarbone and down my torso, a sudden calm came over me.

"Good. That's good, Ash. Now, give your palm a flex or two."

As my fingers expanded, I felt the flow of the water move at my command. My cheeks lifted into a grin I couldn't contain. The water called to me from some natural, deep-seated place within.

"Excellent. Now, turn your palm up and imagine a ball of water," Dax directed. "Not too big. Just a small sphere."

Turning my palm face up, I imagined a ball of water the size of a softball, the small streams of water tickling the lines of my palm as I imagined a perfect sphere.

"Open your eyes."

My lids slowly opened to reveal the exact shape I saw in my mind, the light catching on the different angles of water within as it rotated in my palm. My gaze snapped up to Dax, whose proud smile expanded on his face. "Water Fae."

Looking back down at my creation, I couldn't help but agree. "Water Fae."

A surge of energy rose from the water, and the sphere suddenly tripled in size.

"Whoa," he said, jerking back.

"What's happening?"

Dax's brow furrowed. "Not entirely sure, but I'd say the goddess is pleased." As if in confirmation, the energy beneath the surface intensified. He scanned the waters as if a living, breathing thing were about to emerge. The waterfall slowed until it came to a complete stop—a glowing blue tint similar to the one I'd envisioned reflecting off the water. Dax's cobalt-blue eyes went wide.

I shuffled in place. "Uh, has this happened before in

your training?"

"Not with a single pupil," he murmured. "Not even your mother when she was learning to connect with the goddess as a faeling." He shook his head, glancing back at the waterfall. "I've never seen the water react like this. The goddess gives us the power to move the water, to create shapes—even weapons. But never to pause its movement. And it's certainly never glowed like that. This is unheard of."

A ripple of worry traveled down my spine. I shook out my hand, and the sphere dropped back into the water, the waterfall resuming its journey to the pool below.

Dax's stare remained fixed, his arms crossing over his chest. "Hhmph."

I cleared my throat. "Great. Well. I love adding to my unusualness. Nothing like having a human-like Fae queen with never heard of powers to rule the queendom."

His gaze slid to me, his eyes so severe that I stilled. "You must not speak of this to anyone." He scanned the room, sighing in relief. "Thank the goddess that there was no one here to witness that," he murmured. "We need to keep this between you and me until I can determine exactly what just happened. Such occurrences aren't normal. Humans and Fae alike tend to fear the unknown. Promise me you'll say nothing."

"Not even my father?"

"I will tell your father. I keep nothing from him, but no one else must know. Promise me."

Despite my mind momentarily drifting to Draevyn at the thought of keeping something like this from my… friend, my head dipped in a nod. "Of course. I promise."

Seeming satisfied, he reached for my hand, turning my palm up once more. "Let's try this again. I want you to get comfortable with your gift."

I attempted to summon a few spheres throughout the remainder of my lesson with Dax, but comfort eluded me as I thought about the significance of my newly discovered talent. It was another anomaly to add to the growing list of oddities in this new world I found myself in. Asherah the wallflower. Asherah, the shark whisperer. And now, Asherah with the gift to stop water in its tracks. No, I wouldn't dare tell anyone about this.

# Chapter 19

I WIGGLED MY TOES AGAINST THE BANK before the Shingu River, my hands flexing at my side and sweat beading on my brow. I stared into the depths, observing the other Water Fae swimming toward the university—a few of them glancing up as they noticed us on the shore.

"The water isn't going to bite you," Draevyn teased beside me.

I provided him with my best scowl. "I'm aware. Thank you for that insight." I shook my head. Before I could talk myself out of it, I dove in, the water rising to greet me. My vision sharpened on the various mounds of brightly colored coral in beautiful shades of red, purple, and blue that decorated the perimeter of the river, with schools of brightly colored fish swimming in and out. Dozens of Water Fae swam by with a speed that made me desperate to match. However, there was one notable difference between my scales and theirs.

I'd been warned about the Water Fae opting to display their skin and minimize their scales to the bare minimum. It wasn't unusual for most males to display their chests proudly or for females to don their scales on their breasts and legs only, exposing their stomachs, shoulders, and arms. "It's not appropriate," Reneah had told me when I'd asked if my scales looked okay that morning. In the Above World, wearing my swimsuit was an everyday occurrence. In Atlantis, royalty had to be covered and never exposed. I'd swiftly donned my scales without a further comment.

Draevyn, on the other hand, had no problem whatsoever with exposing his mouthwatering olive skin to the world. His broad chest came into view as he reached for the bag floating on my back, checking on the thin layer of protection he magicked to stay dry. It was entirely distracting and nearly impossible not to gape at his body. I couldn't help the heat creeping up my cheeks when he caught me ogling.

He gave me a sly grin. *"Enjoying the view?"*

I reached out to pinch the olive skin of his chest, but he caught my hand and threaded his fingers through mine. Draevyn had held my hand before, but the way he looked at me now had me clenching my thighs and lit something in me. As Draevyn and I continued this delicate dance in the gray area between friends and something more, I was afraid I wouldn't be able to snuff out my feelings if they were unrequited.

Hello, friend zone. Ash again.

"Ready, my Queen?" he asked, drawing me from those particular thoughts.

*"As I'll ever be."*

He winked as he pulled us into the current—my Fae instincts taking over as my feet moved of their own volition. Wanting to test how far I'd come, I kicked harder—the movement propelling me ahead of Draevyn. He smiled and matched my speed. Bubbles floated from my mouth with a giggle. Being with him was as easy as breathing—like he was an extension of myself. The thought both thrilled me and scared me, especially because I didn't know if he felt the same way. After everything that happened with John and Chrissy, I felt more cautious with my heart than I'd ever been before. My grin dipped into a frown as I tried to hide my face from Draevyn.

Tried and failed.

"*What's the matter?*" he asked, swimming up beside me.

I plastered on my best impression of a smile. "*Nothing.*"

His lifted brow told me he thought otherwise, but he thankfully left it alone.

The swim to Cibao was over in a blink as the gate loomed before us. With a quick check-in with the guard, it wasn't long before we were climbing the stone steps and striding down the brightly lit hallway to the classroom where Myles awaited. As usual, Draevyn remained just outside the door to stand guard.

"Morning, Myles."

"Good morning, Asherah," he said with a kind smile, gesturing to the desk before his. "Take a seat. I see you've survived the wrath of the queens."

"Barely," I quipped.

Myles' shoulders shook with laughter. "Yes, well. Cathan tells me you did quite well in your first queendoms meeting. And because this was a hot topic of discussion between the four of you, we'll review the last ice age today."

I pursed my lips in mock thought. "Um, yes. Especially the part about humans being our rightful slaves."

Myles sighed. "Yes. That. Queen Sessi loves to throw her theories around. It's complete rubbish, of course."

"She's hell-bent on trying to convince the other queens just how right she is, though."

"Yes, she'll do that. And you must be prepared with the truth."

I extracted my journal and pen from my bag. "One thing has been bugging me, though. The Fae put so much dedication and devotion into the goddess. Why would Queen Sessi risk challenging the goddess' will to push her agenda to enslave the humans? Does she not fear the goddess?"

Myles crossed his arms and leaned against the desk.

"She believes the goddess wants the humans enslaved."

"That's stupid."

He lifted his shoulder. "That's Sessi. It always has been, and I suppose it always will be. And that's what you'll be fighting against. That's what makes us Atlantians. We see things the way the goddess intended. Not some distorted version of the truth."

It made my blood boil in my veins. Sure. Humans were imperfect beings, but given everything I'd seen of the Fae, so were they. Myles circled his desk, grabbed the chalk they lay on the lip of the board, and began writing across it.

My eyes narrowed. "Chalk?"

Myles looked over his shoulder, wiggling it in the air. "Magic chalk. It never breaks and never leaves residue on your fingers. Very different from the Above World." He turned and resumed his scribbling. When he stepped back from the board, it read:

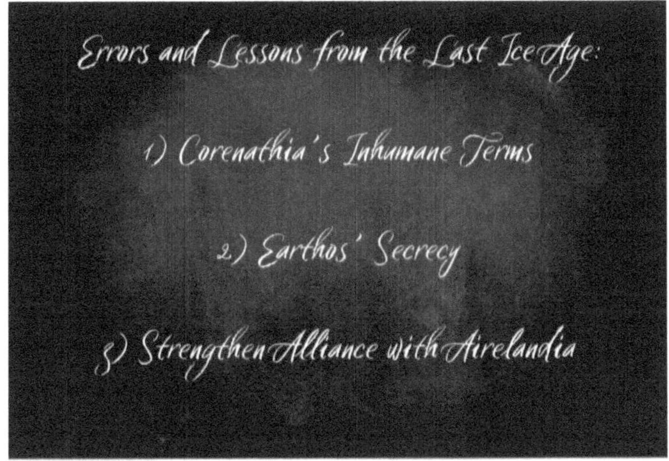


"During the accord of the last Ice Age, which took place roughly twenty thousand years ago, many errors occurred that could've been prevented, but the gravest was not standing as one against Corenathia's terms, the very same ones that left them to operate independently with no checks and balances of any kind. We were met with great resistance when any inquiries regarding their land provisions and the care provided to the humans were made. Our ancestors wrote multiple scrolls and tomes expressing their deep regret that they never demanded a better treaty between the queendoms and Corenathia to ensure the humans were treated with dignity." Myles reached for a hunter-green book on the corner of his desk and thumbed through it with his brow furrowed. When he reached his intended page, he placed the book before me. "If you will read the first paragraph in this passage, please."

I glanced down at the passage—the page browned with age and weathered at the edges. "Lessons for the New Ice Age" was written in a deep, bold black at the top of the page. I read, "It was imperative that every human be documented and recorded in the High Priestess archives, no matter which realm they were assigned to. While it was initially difficult to secure such a proclamation from Earthos, Airelandia and Atlantis immediately began recording their human populace's lineage to better understand and support them as they established themselves in the realms. Earthos—while reluctant to divulge any information at first—eventually committed to the practice. Corenathia refused to commit to a proclamation based on claims from their scholarly research. They believed the goddess intended for the humans to serve the Fae. Such mistakes cannot be repeated. Any future accord must have Corenathia's cooperation." I glanced up at Myles. "No pressure then, huh?"

He smiled ruefully. "I'm afraid the task lies squarely on your shoulders to negotiate these terms."

The only experience I had negotiating anything at all was with Professor Larson when I pleaded my case for an extra day on my mid-term paper. I'd won my case, but I was on penguin-feeding duty for an entire week during his vacation to Tahiti. It took weeks to get rid of the fish smell on my hands. Now, I was expected to convince a nasty queen to reveal the inner workings of her realm. A sense of deep unease crept up my spine. "And she never mentioned what happened to the humans in her realm during the last ice age?"

"From what we understand, there are barely any humans left in her realm. But it's hard to tell exactly. Our informants are reluctant to reveal too much for fear of prosecution."

"That's terrible. I don't understand how her scholars determined that humans are supposed to serve the Fae. What does she even mean by that?"

"That dates back to the original goddess' text.

The wording states that 'all humans shall be set free by the Fae.' That part about 'set free?' That's what the Corenathians hang on to. They believe the Fae are responsible for granting the humans their freedom…or denying it; therefore, they are meant to serve them. Serve us. We believe 'set free' is related to the word before it. Shall, not maybe. Not someday. Shall be set free. But the Corenathians have distorted their scrolls for their own grotesque purposes, changing the wording to match their own beliefs."

My brow dipped. "How can they change the goddess' own words?"

"The same way all ancient texts, both Fae and human, have been altered since the beginning of time. They do it in plain sight and then gaslight their people into believing it was necessary; however, the true core of the texts rarely changes if you look closely enough. And that message—that prophecy—has never been altered to our knowledge."

"Prophecy?"

His head dipped in a nod. "Yes. The scrolls point to a prophecy interpreted before the last ice age. They speak of a Fae who is the key to peace, one who will possess a sacred set of abilities."

I tilted my head, a few rogue strands of hair tickling my shoulder. "What abilities?"

"Abilities of extraordinary power, all four elements. No Fae in history has ever possessed all four elements. It's unheard of. When one Fae mates with a Fae with an opposing element—let's say water and air—only one element carries to their offspring. Never more than one." Myles gazed absentmindedly at the floor. "We keep hoping the chosen will present themselves before the next Ice Age, as the text suggests."

I fidgeted in my chair. "Do we know when the next Ice Age starts? Do the texts mention anything about that?" They'd spoken over and over about the approaching Ice Age. I'd assumed—given how long the Fae live—that it was thousands of years away. I internally dreaded the answer.

Myles rubbed the back of his neck. "I'm afraid it's already begun. The weather patterns have been incredibly unpredictable, as prophesied in the Scrolls of Atabey. There's a powerful hurricane in the Above World even as we speak."

My stomach dropped. Hurricanes weren't uncommon where we'd lived. I'd been through several in my lifetime. They'd only recently become more catastrophic. More destructive. Lethal. "Where?"

Myles winced. "I'm afraid the eye of the storm is over The Keys at this very moment."

I leapt from my chair, the back slamming against the desk behind me. "We have to go."

Myles gave me an incredulous look. "To the Above World?"

I threw my tablet and books in my bag. "Yes. They'll need our help. The storms are getting worse every year."

Myles held up his hands. "Wait, wait, wait. You don't have to set off in a panic. We have Guardians already assisting. Our magic protects them as much as possible."

I hefted my bag over my shoulder, the leather strap biting into my bare skin as I glared at him with determination. "I still want to be there."

"Given what happened, it's much too dangerous for our future Queen to visit the Above World. We can't lose you, too. It's much too risky."

I glared at him dead in the eye. "If I don't take any risks for the humans, for my friends, then what kind of

Queen will I be?"

He stood motionless before his shoulders dropped, a sigh leaving him. "You mustn't go alone."

I glanced toward the door. "I won't be."

Myles followed my gaze and placed his hand on his hip. "Very well. But when you return, we will thoroughly review Earthos' secrecy and our alliance with Airelandia. Understood, Princess?"

My hand cut into the air with a salute. "Understood, boss." I rushed out of the room, Draevyn's light smile disappearing when he saw my face. "What's happened?"

"There's a hurricane in the Above World right over The Keys. I'm going to help."

Draevyn's lips thinned as he nodded. "I'll go with you."

I released a breath I hadn't realized I'd been holding. "Thank you." We were going to the Above World, and I didn't know what we'd find there. The dread seeped into my veins as we hurried down the hall. What would John and Chrissy say? How exactly would I explain my absence? I'd left the Above World as a graduate, ready to start my career as a marine biologist. As far as they knew, I was living out my dream in California. That version of myself seemed so far away. Now, I'd have to pretend I was still that girl and not the woman I'd become. John's handsome face, growing beet red the way it always had when he'd caught me doing something I wasn't supposed to, flashed in my mind. Not a phone call, text, or smoke signal. That's precisely what he was going to say. In an oddly masochistic sort of way, I was looking forward to it.

# Chapter 20

Being a Princess of a realm whose primary cause is to protect humans worked in my favor. With Myles' assistance, we coordinated the transfer of supplies from the mainland to the areas that were hit hardest by the storm. Hundreds of pallets were moved with extreme proficiency by the guards: cases of water, diapers, formula, canned goods, blankets, clothing. Everything moved underwater at lightning speed with not a drop of water touching it. Thank the goddess for water magic. All I could do was watch in awe. When the supplies reached dry land, we began coordinating the deliveries to the people in shelters who needed it most.

Once everything had been delivered and the Guardians and volunteers had returned to Atlantis, I gave my aching body a moment to settle. Only then did I let the devastation sink in and finally headed home to see what was left of it.

Weathered fragments of wood dusted every inch of land. Kelly green palm fronds lay clamped between debris, and smoky-colored gravel had been pulled from the neat confines of their pathways. Shattered glass littered the ground under hunks of metal that used to be cars. That's what greeted us as we reached the neighborhood I once called home.

I moved cautiously down the road, the pieces of debris crunching underneath my sandals with a cracking sound that carried across the silence surrounding us. The mellow, humid wind steadily pushed bits of salmon pink insulation in tiny circular vortexes across our path.

Mostly decimated.

Some houses had survived, but the strength of the hurricane-force winds was evident in the damage to the paneling on those that remained. Chipped paint in bright colors of lime green, tangerine orange, yellow as bright as a fresh banana peeled back from the homes they'd accented. Cars tossed from the storm surge rested in various positions blocks from their owner's house. The people of the town-proclaimed Conch Republic understood the risk of living on these tiny islands entirely surrounded by water. They took that risk for the freedom of living in a beautiful, peaceful paradise. To fish endlessly, to surf, to relax, to watch the stars blink in the middle of a pitch-black night. The Keys were a way of life unlike any other. Perhaps it was wild to live so exposed to the elements. It was their choice to do so, but as I surveyed the damage before me, I wondered how many would return to risk it again. At what point did it become too much?

I paused in front of my home, and my mouth dropped open. Dad's beloved electric Mini Cooper sat in the driveway with not a single scratch on the shiny black paint. The debris that surely traveled a great distance landed a foot away from hitting any part of it. As my gaze scanned the area around my home, I realized there was a foot of distance between any piece of debris and the entire house. A boat from the channel behind the home sat a foot away; the metal bent as if it slammed against the side of the house but couldn't reach it. There wasn't a single dent in the bright metal roof.

Draevyn came up behind me as I gaped. "It's warded for protection."

I glanced back at him, his dark brown hair flowing behind him on a gentle breeze. His faded, heather gray Hurley t-shirt stretched deliciously over his chest, reaching to the washed-out jeans that hung low on his hips. When I asked him where he got the clothes, he simply stated that a commander is always prepared. He'd even brought his own footwear. There shouldn't be something so captivating about his feet in sandals, but here I was, admiring them. "Don't you think the neighbors will get a little suspicious?"

A shrug. "Haven't you noticed that your house has never been damaged during hurricane season?"

I stared off in the distance as I tried to recall my parents ever calling an insurance company to file a claim. Weird.

I blew out a breath and gestured around the front lawn. "Well, welcome to my home. I guess."

Draevyn's lips lifted in a smirk. "Oh, I've seen your home before."

My brow rose. "You have?"

"Of course. We've all helped protect you and your family in one form or another. We've just never stayed above water for long periods of time." Draevyn tilted his head in thought. "Well, I have. For other reasons."

I slid my hands into the pockets of my white-washed

denim jean shorts. "And what reasons are those?"

Another shrug. "Curiosity, I suppose." He gave me one of those radiant smiles I'd never tire of seeing.

I cleared my throat and scanned the empty street behind me. There wasn't another human in sight, just debris for miles in either direction. A couple of houses down, the second story of Mr. Parker's home lay on the ground in front of his garage, and my heart squeezed. He'd just lost his wife a few years ago. How was he supposed to come back from this? My vision distorted when unshed tears welled in my eyes, a few escaping down my cheeks with a blink.

Draevyn's essence wrapped around me before his strong arms came around my middle, his warmth seeping in against my back as he pulled me into his chest. He rested his chin on my head, and the protection of his embrace was a welcomed distraction from my chaotic emotions.

"It's okay," he whispered against the shell of my ear. "I've got you."

I wrapped my arms over his and squeezed. "These were my neighbors for so long. It'll be so hard to come back from this. If they can come back at all."

Draevyn turned me in his arms and cupped my face—his thumb brushing away a stray tear. "They'll need your strength, Asherah. Remember what's about to happen in the Above World. These homes shouldn't be rebuilt. The ice age is fast approaching. Your friends? Neighbors? All these families. They'll have new homes in Atlantis, where they'll be safe."

Reality sunk its claws into my mind. My friends and neighbors wouldn't only join me in Atlantis; I'd rule over them. Possibly. Sessi may very well be their ruler, and that thought sent a shiver down my spine.

Draevyn ducked down in my line of vision. "Hey. Where did you go?"

I shook my head. "It's just…the thought of them joining us in Atlantis. The thought of them believing any of it is real. The possibility that my friends and my neighbors may be assigned to Corenathia. To Sessi."

"That won't happen."

"How do you know, though?"

"Because you can request that they stay with you. In Atlantis."

"But that just means some other poor souls will be stuck in Corenathia. It's a death sentence. Why even go at all?"

His rough hands brushed up and down my arms, the contact of our bare skin eliciting a different kind of feeling that was entirely inappropriate for the moment. "This is why checks and balances must be made. I have faith you and the other queens will come to a compromise. But let's try and not worry about it now." He gazed behind me. "I don't suppose you know where everyone is taking shelter?"

I sighed. "I think I do."

He took my hand, and I gazed down at where his hand encompassed mine. I didn't know where the lines were with us anymore. When I was with him, it felt natural—like surfing a wave meant just for me, my board perfectly in sync with the surface of his curl. That feeling in my chest expanded the more time I spent with him.

"Lead the way," he said, his baritone voice a seductive calling my heart could only hear.

I cleared my throat, briefly looking down at my feet. "Right. Um. This way."

We left the ruins of my neighborhood and carefully meandered through the debris to where my friends would surely be—the friends who were likely going to rip me a new asshole for leaving without a word. I welcomed the balmy air into my lungs as we headed toward The Blue Fin.

Just as I'd predicted, most of the neighborhood was at The Blue Fin, which was likely the only place with electricity and backup generators for miles. Bobby had the wisdom to install solar panels four seasons ago. The regulars laughed at him for succumbing to "new energy hype," but now, those same haters sat inside, eating hot, savory bar bites and welcoming the cool air the A/C provided them. A couple dozen people milled about—the upbeat music blaring from the jukebox clashed starkly with the somber mood of the patrons inhabiting the space. There wasn't a face in the place that wasn't as solemn as the next.

Plywood covered every window and one-half of the double doors we'd entered—the entire dive dark save for the overhead can lights bathing every person, table, and chair in a warm glow. It warmed my heart to find the place completely intact. "There appears to be a ward on this place as well," Draevyn had told me before we'd entered the dive. I couldn't help but feel touched by the gesture. My parents knew what this place meant to me and the town.

"Ash?" a voice called from the bar. Bobby grew ashen like he'd seen a ghost but quickly replaced his shock with a dashing smile. He dropped his rag on the bar top and rushed toward me. "What the hell are you doing here?" His big arms wrapped around me, squeezing to the point of suffocation.

"Hey, Bobby," I greeted as I broke out in laughter.

He pulled back. "They said you ran off to Cali and forgot all about us."

I gave a quick flick of the wrist. "Psst. How can I forget about you all?"

He folded his arms across his chest, his bright yellow *Resting Beach Face* tank bunching slightly. "Well, you never came to say goodbye."

I winced. "Ugh. I know. I know. I'm sorry about that. They needed me to start as soon as possible. I couldn't help it," I said, the lie falling too easily off my tongue.

Bobby's eyes drifted behind me, and a smirk crept up. "And who is this?"

I cleared my throat. "Bobby, I'd like you to meet Draevyn. My…um…man friend."

*Man friend?*

An amused expression bloomed on Draevyn's face before he shook Bobby's offered hand. "It's a pleasure to meet you."

"The pleasure's all mine." He gestured to the bar. "Sit. I'll get you your favorite bacon tater tots you like and an IPA. Thankfully, the storm didn't wash that away. What can I get you, man?"

"IPA is good."

"Perfect."

We slid into the final two weathered stools on the corner of the bar while Bobby fetched us our crisp, cold beers. The euphoria of coming back to a familiar place wrapped around my soul. Some places lived rent-free in your brain: a family home, a favorite surf spot, or perhaps a middle school hallway where you had your first kiss. For me, The Blue Fin would forever be my place. Everyone who walked through the door was like family.

Even now, they greeted me like a long-lost family member finally coming home. As Draevyn and I snacked on our bacon tater tots—the rich, savory flavors eliciting my taste buds—I took my time with introductions. While some greeted Draevyn with interest, others remained wary of the newcomer at the bar. But soon enough, Draevyn fell into an easy conversation with them. The patrons told stories of escape and near misses from the storm and plans to clean up the town. We mentally noted every plan so we could help.

"I've enlisted some friends to come by and help tomorrow," Draevyn told them between sips from his pint.

"Excellent! We can always use more help," said Paulie, a local fishing junky who preferred fish to people, which is why, most days, he came to The Blue Fin only for an hour or so to grab dinner and scurry home.

"And if they're as big as you, that's even better," Magda—the owner of the *Live and Let Dye* hair salon—called from down the bar, her thin lips smirking and auburn brows wagging on her weathered face.

"Well, you're in luck because they're bigger than me," Draevyn replied with a wink.

Magda began fanning herself with a cardboard coaster. "Oh, my lady loins. I can't wait for tomorrow, then."

The whole bar erupted in laughter.

Draevyn casually slung his arm over the back of my stool, his thumb brushing back and forth over my shoulder, causing my skin to pebble. I sagged as I leaned into him a bit. The tunes from the jukebox filled my soul like a potent energy. I hadn't felt this carefree in so long.

Here, I was just Ash—a local Keys girl. I wasn't an heir or a Queen.

In here, I could just be.

"Ash?" a voice called incredulously from behind. I

swiveled on my stool, meeting John's wide grey eyes as they bounced between me and Draevyn. "What are you doing here?"

I hopped off my stool, my hands flexing at my sides. "Hey, John."

Behind him, Chrissy gracefully strode through the door, fiddling with her keys as she jammed them in her shorts pocket. She stopped in her tracks when she caught sight of me—a smile emerging so bright that one might need sunglasses to block out the shine. "Ash!" She ran at full speed and pummeled me in a hug, squeezing my ribs to the point of breaking. When she finally granted me mercy, she pulled back, her smile dropping into a flat line. "Where have you been? Why haven't you called? Is everything okay?" Her gaze shifted behind me, and her mouth slowly dropped open. "Please tell me you're climbing that."

Heat immediately crept up my cheeks.

John cleared his throat, his dark brow lifting at Chrissy before awkwardly moving in for a hug of his own. As much as I dreaded the twenty million questions about to be flung my way, I missed them immensely. As I stepped out of his embrace, I felt Draevyn's tall form looming behind me, his hand protectively landing on my hip.

"Um. John, Chrissy, I'd like you to meet Draevyn. Draevyn, this is Chrissy and John. My friends."

John held out his hand. "Nice to meet you, man."

Draevyn, ever the gentlemen, shook his hand with a nod. "Pleasure."

"Hi, I'm Chrissy," she beamed, reaching forward and shaking his hand enthusiastically. "But she just said that, so you know that."

Draevyn's lips lifted in an amused grin. "Yes, she mentioned that. Nice to meet you."

"I'm Ash's best friend."

"Yes, she mentioned that, too."

"The name's Chrissy. With a 'y'. Not an 'i-e.'"

"Pleasure to meet you, Chrissy, with a 'y.'"

"Ash?" John interrupted. "Can I speak to you for a moment?" He gestured to the far corner with a stern look on his face.

I gave Draevyn a questioning look, which he returned with a nod before I followed John with my heart kicking in my chest. An irrational feeling of being caught filled me despite the absurdity of it. I'd done nothing wrong. When we reached the dark corner, John twisted around and placed his hands on his hips, causing me to feel like I had.

"Where. Have. You. Been," he asked in a tone that held all the authority of the Captain I knew. The one that had left butterflies in my stomach but now didn't. Not even a flutter.

"I had to go."

"Uh–huh. I get that. But Chrissy and I have been calling you non-stop. And every time I see your Dad, he tells me the same thing."

"And that is?"

"That you're doing great but you're super busy."

Weird. Dad never mentioned seeing John or Chrissy. "Well, he wasn't wrong. I was…am…busy." How I wished I could tell him the truth. Before I grew to have any feelings for John, he'd always been my friend, the boy who met me at the head of the street to walk me to the bus stop, the one who met me after every class that wasn't across the campus in both middle school and high school. The boy who grew into the man before me. I had to crane my neck to look up at him—a fact he used to rub in my face during our senior year of high school.

But there was hurt in his gaze now, and it wrestled with my heart.

"You could have called."

I avoided his gaze, glancing down at the floorboards. "I'm so sorry."

"Is it Chrissy?"

My head snapped up. "No. Not at all."

His steel gray eyes drifted over my shoulder. I followed his line of sight. Chrissy's hands gestured in the air around her—her face lit animatedly. Draevyn appeared at ease with the conversation, chuckling at whatever story she recanted. "Yeah, I guess you wouldn't be bothered with our relationship, with meaty long locks over there."

That got my attention, my brow furrowing as I looked back at him. "Meaty long locks?"

John shrugged. "I mean, if you're into that sort of thing."

"Jonathan Tyler Adams, do I detect a hint of jealousy?"

"Psft. No. Don't look at me like that. I'm serious. It's cool if that's what you're into." He let loose a sigh. "I just wish you would have called."

I reached up and squeezed his broad shoulder. "I know. I'm sorry. Where I live…eh…doesn't have the best reception." I fluttered my hand in the air. "Marine life and all. You know."

John snorted. "Okay, big shot. I forgive you. But make an effort next time. And I'm not the only one who missed you, you know. Chrissy's been feeling awful. Thinks you couldn't handle…you know…"

I pinched the bridge of my nose. "You all really have nothing to worry about. Don't worry. I'll talk to her. And I *am* truly happy for you both. It makes me happy knowing you have each other and looking after one another. It's one less thing I have to worry about."

He tilted his head, his dark brown hair shifting. "Worry about? What's there to worry about?"

I gestured around me. "You, Chrissy, Bobby, the whole town."

"Yeah. Yeah," John said, waving it off. "It's The Keys. This shit happens all the time."

"It's getting worse."

He blew out a breath. "I know. It is. That I can't deny."

I desperately wanted to tell him everything right there and then. But I couldn't. I flicked my head toward the bar. "Let's get you a beer and catch up. It'll give you a chance to get to know meaty long locks over there."

John chuckled, slinging an arm over my shoulder as we lumbered back to the bar. "Good to have you back, Ash."

"Same, John. Same."

With the more challenging conversation of the two complete, I returned to the ease I'd felt before John and Chrissy arrived, my mood sinking into pure happiness when Draevyn pulled my stool closer to him and eased into conversation with my friends. And knowing what lay ahead, I soaked in the moment like the warm rays of the sun after an afternoon rain.

"Last call?" I asked Draevyn as I pulled the stainless-steel refrigerator door open. He slowly drifted around the living room, taking in each photo that hung on matching frames on the cream-colored walls.

"Sure."

I grabbed two Fizzy Finny IPAs—The Blue Fins award-winning brew—from the fridge and shuffled to the gray sectional that took up most of the room. The darkness beyond the patio slider was an ominous reminder of the devastation around us. I sighed as I cracked open my beer and plopped down on the soft cushions.

"Where was this one taken?"

My gaze narrowed on the eight-by-ten photo, recognizing it immediately. "Surf competition in Newport Beach. I was in high school. It's one of the only competitions Mom attended. I begged her to frame it. She thought that I liked the photo. She doesn't…didn't know that I wanted it framed because I wanted to remember a time when I came before her work." The guilt gripped my heart. "Work. More like taking care of an entire queendom. All while I was a little brat wanting her to be at my surf competition."

He twisted around with a sympathetic gaze. "You couldn't have known, Asherah. It's not your fault."

"I know. And yet, I still feel guilty anyway."

Draevyn picked up his beer from the coffee table, opening it as he sat beside me. "You're holding yourself accountable for something you couldn't control. Queen Neleah wanted you to have a full life in the Above World— a good life. And based on the pictures that decorate the walls of your home, I'd say she accomplished that goal."

He wasn't wrong. The moments I'd had with Mom were some of the best. "It wasn't that I didn't feel loved or anything. I just wish I had more time with her. More memories."

Draevyn placed his arm over the back of the couch, the hairs on the back of my neck brushing his arm and sending shivers throughout my body. "I hate to break it to you, but had you been raised in Atlantis, you likely would've seen her even less than you did in the Above World. Every minute of her day was always scheduled. Just look at your father. How many times have you seen him since arriving in Atlantis?"

Again, he wasn't wrong. I nodded as I smeared a bead of condensation across my beer can—the cold aluminum biting into the tip of my finger. "And soon, that will be me."

"And soon, it will be you," he gently smiled. "However, you'll be Queen, and you can set your boundaries. I think it's important that you set those soon so they know not to cross those lines."

"Boundaries for what?"

Locks of his brown hair fell forward as he tilted his head. "Well, there'll be things you'll want in your life—a mate, faelings of your own. One day." My cheeks heated, and his eyes roamed over my face, his dimple revealing his pleasure. "You do want those things, yes?"

I cleared my throat. "Um…yeah—yes." My eyes narrowed. "How does the whole bondmates thing work anyway?"

His brow arched. "Has no one ever told you?"

I huffed. "Barely. Well, Myles and Aurelio have, and Dad gave me some info. But not much."

Draevyn's thumb caressed my shoulder, slowly moving back and forth, causing my breath to hitch. "Every bonded pair I've spoken to states that it starts as an itch just over the left side of the chest," his gaze dropped over me, "or breast in the case of the female." I remained stock still, my pulse picking up speed. "Then, there's an undeniable pull, a tethering that makes you want to be around the person, that makes you constantly aware of them."

I swallowed. "Really?"

"Really."

"How interesting."

"Very."

I'd felt that pull in my chest from the moment I'd set eyes on this beautiful male; I could swear I felt it tug a little harder as he looked at me with lust in his eyes. "What else?"

He placed his beer on the coffee table and turned to me fully, his thick, muscular thigh settling slightly over mine. "Well, when the couple begins feeling the bonding signs, they attend the bonding ceremony together and present their union before the Bohiti for the goddess's blessing."

"Bonding ceremony?"

"Yes, it happens every Ostara, what you call spring in the Above World. We pay homage to the goddess's blessing of fertility." Draevyn moved my hair over my shoulder and I stifled back a gasp. "It's one of our most sacred rituals." There was no denying the heat in his gaze as he continued, "It's a very sensual time of the year and can get a little…erotic; the bonded pair taking their pleasure, going mad with lust until the morning hours as the bond solidifies through their union." He leaned forward, his face a mere breath away from mine. I gasped as the tip of his finger traced tiny swirls above my left breast. "Once the couple has presented themselves to the Bohiti for the blessing, a bond mark appears," he swirled dangerously close to my nipple, dipping beneath the top of my tank, "right here."

"Oh," I breathed. His tropical green eyes hypnotized me, relaying exactly how he felt without uttering a single word.

Draevyn leaned in further, and I closed my eyes…

…just as the front door slammed open.

Draevyn leapt from the couch, placing himself in front of me as footsteps sounded down the entryway. Dad entered the living room with Dax a second behind him, their eyes traveling between the two of us. My father's face was set in a questioning look, while Dax's was lit with amusement. My cheeks were absolutely burning.

"Well, doesn't this look fun," Dax teased.

Draevyn bowed to my father. "Regent."

"Draevyn. How nice to see you here. Alone. With my daughter."

"Dad," I hissed. I pinched the bridge of my nose.

He fluttered a hand. "I get it, Sher. You're a grown woman. Etcetera, etcetera." He shifted his attention back to Draevyn. "I'm not about to tell you how to do your job, or that she's still in a shitload of peril."

"I understand, Your Highness."

"Good. The other Guardians are on their way."

My head jumped up. "Like, right now?"

Dad jerked back. "You didn't think we'd have our future Queen up here with just one Guardian, did you?" he asked, quirking his brow.

"The Blue Fin is an amazing establishment," Dax called from the kitchen with his head half in the refrigerator. "Fine food. Fantastic music coming out of those speakie thingies. Ah." He pulled a Fizzy Finny from the top shelf and cracked it open, taking a long gulp. "And *delightful* refreshments." He turned to Dad, looking affronted. "How come you never brought us any of these? They're fantastic."

"Because a beer run for the Guardians wasn't exactly a top priority."

I sighed. "I'd better get to bed," I announced as I rose from the couch. "I'm going surfing in the morning."

"Then, I best be off to bed as well," Draevyn said.

Awkwardness and tension filled the spacious living room. I had to wonder which bed Draevyn would have ended up in if Dad and Dax hadn't shown up. "I'll show you to the guest room."

"Or the man cave with the other Guardians," Dad quipped.

My brow lowered. "That's downstairs."

"Yup. And Dax is sleeping on the couch, so you'll be well protected."

"No. Draevyn stays near me." I looked to Dax. "Not that I don't trust you or anything. No offense."

Dax raised his beer. "None taken."

"I feel more comfortable with Draevyn," I pleaded. "It's not like he's sleeping in my room. He'll be in the room next door."

Dad let loose a sigh. "Fine. Okay." He glanced over his shoulder at Dax. "You still good on the couch?"

"Of course," he replied with a Cheshire cat smile.

I guess we'd have a babysitter then. "Good night, Dad. Dax." I gestured for Draevyn to follow down the hallway that led to the bedrooms—Dax and Dad flicking on the big screen TV as the sounds of football filtered down the way. I entered the guest room, flicked on the light, and wheeled around to Draevyn. "Sorry about that," I whispered.

My breath hitched as he stepped into me; his hands reached up to cup my face. "Nothing to be sorry about." I couldn't help but lean into the warmth of his palm as his next words took my breath away. "Would you honor me with a kiss from those beautiful lips before I go to bed, my Queen?"

The entire world faded. "Yes," I whispered.

The left side of my chest tingled, and I didn't move

as Draevyn leaned in, his full lips capturing mine in the most electrifying kiss. His soft tongue pushed past the seam of my lips and slowly danced with mine to a rhythm only our hearts could hear. His strong arms wrapped around my lower back, clasping me to him as my fingers threaded through the thick strands of his hair. Draevyn Eliron's kiss set my soul on fire. It captured every beat of my heart, and I knew right then that I was incapable of letting him go.

He slowly pulled back, his hooded eyes caressing me. My heart nearly melted when he began to smile. "Thank you for honoring me. I shall never forget that kiss."

A familiar scarlet heat warmed my cheeks. "I don't think I'll forget either."

He huffed a small laugh. "You'd better get to bed if we're getting up early."

I drew out of his embrace and let out a reluctant breath. "Okay." I slowly moved toward the door, my hands lingering on his arms a moment longer.

Just before I shut his door, I couldn't help but notice how he rubbed over the left side of his chest.

My soul filled to the brim as my aching muscles worked to keep myself on my surfboard. It had been far too long since I'd felt the beautiful pain, and I relished it. I breathed in the warm, humid air as I bobbed on my board, watching Draevyn as he skillfully rode a wave to shore. His form was perfection, and from the way he cut and commanded each wave, it was clear he had some experience. My smile held the entire time I watched him.

When Draevyn joined me far out in the water, the

tingling sensation grew anew like a frenzied nest of bees stuck in my chest. I bit my lip as my gaze roamed over every chiseled ridge of his torso on display. The water dripped from his long, dark hair, and his aqua-marine eyes held mine, full of an easy joyfulness that was very unlike the demeanor of the Commander I knew. I'd never seen him so relaxed before. It was nice to see him enjoying himself.

"I'm impressed."

His gaze swept over me as he rose to sit on his longboard. And for good reason. I'd worn my favorite pink hibiscus bikini that left let little to the imagination. His bright blue swim trunks bunched on his muscular thighs as his long legs straddled his longboard—his biceps bulging as he leaned forward on his arms to steady himself. I'd never wanted to be a surfboard as much in my life as I did at that moment. His shoulders reached for his ears. "I might have had some practice over the years."

"Yes, I suspect having decades to practice has helped."

He winked. "It does."

My lips tightened, and my eyes playfully narrowed on him. "Just how often have you come to Above World to surf?"

"A few times," he said with a mischievous smile.

I folded my arms over my middle, my abs tightening with the effort to steady myself. "Why do I get the feeling you're keeping something from me, Draevyn Eliron?"

His laugh was infectious. "I'm not keeping any secrets from you, my Queen."

"Uh-huh. Right."

His laughter died, the smile dropping from his face. "In seriousness, though, I think it would be best if we didn't keep secrets from each other."

The thought of my last training with Dax zoomed

into my mind, and I bit the inside of my cheek. I'd promised Dax I wouldn't tell anyone, but Draevyn had become something…more. And it didn't feel right not telling him something important like that, especially something that was still puzzling me. I pinched a clump of wax from my board between my pointer finger and thumb as I confessed, "There's something I have to tell you then."

His head gave a slight tilt. "You can tell me any-thing."

"But you can't tell anyone."

He rowed a bit closer, bringing his board parallel to mine. "You have to know, anything you say stays between us. Always. And I hope you'd do the same for me."

My brow furrowed. "Of course."

"Then, tell me."

I pressed the clump of wax on the board as the sun's blistering rays heated my skin. "The other day, during my training with Dax, I…I stopped the flow of water."

The water lapping against our boards was the only sound for a long moment as I beheld the shocked expression on his face. "You stopped the flow?"

"Yes. The waterfall just seemed to…pause." I provided every detail: how the current beneath the water also seemed to stop, the bright blue light that flared from the water, how Dax said not to tell anyone except Dad. I left nothing out, desperate for any advice or similar stories he may know of.

Draevyn ran his fingers through his now damp hair. "I've never heard of such a thing happening."

My shoulders sagged. "Great. Guess I'm back to weird things happening with zero explanation then."

He reached out, taking my hand in his. "Asherah, this is extraordinary. *You* are extraordinary. Don't look at a gift like that as something to be upset about. Every magic, every ability, is a gift from the goddess. Do not dishonor her gift by clouding it with frustration. Whatever it is, we'll figure it out together."

Right then, I knew with certainty that I was right to tell him about what happened that day in the training facility. My instincts implored me, and even though he couldn't explain what could've happened, my entire body and soul felt lighter with my confession. My lips lifted in a solemn grin. "Thank you. For listening."

"You do not have to thank me. I hope to share a million secrets with you throughout our very long lifetimes."

I tilted my head. "Oh yeah? Will you tell me one of your secrets then?"

Draevyn glanced down at his board, chasing a rouge water droplet with the fingertip of his free hand. "Every time I'm around you, I have this strange sensation in my chest," he confessed. I gasped, and his gaze drifted up to mine. "I know you've felt it, too," he said, as he carefully placed his hand between my breasts, "right here, right where the call of a bondmate should be. It scares me to no end because I've only heard of the power between mates. And now that you're here, ever since you entered the gates of Atlantis, I've known you are infinitely special, like a remarkable tether to my soul that left me desperate to get to know you. I've watched you see your new world with a fascination that is entirely refreshing. I love seeing Atlantis through your eyes." He shook his head. "You are a beloved gift I feel so unworthy of. But somehow…somehow, the goddess has found me worthy. And I hope you will, too. I'll do anything in my power to build the foundation of a long and happy life with you. This is how I wish to honor the one whom the goddess has blessed me with; the one who has captivated me with her beautiful mind, an incredible heart, and…" he paused, his eyes roaming every inch of my exposed skin, my legs straddling my board baring nearly everything to him, "a body that has left me intoxicated with an all-consuming lust I'm no longer capable of containing." My heart picked up speed, his words eliciting a slow ache that spread to my core.

I moved as if by some magnetism, pulling myself on his board and straddling it before him—his hooded gaze following my every movement. Draevyn flicked his hand, calling on his water magic to steady his board. When the air around us rippled, I quirked a brow at him.

"Glamour," his white teeth peeking as he grinned.

I inched forward on my arms until my legs draped over his thick thighs—my surfboard bumping into his board as the leash tied at my ankle pulled it with me. Draevyn licked his lips as his eyes roamed my inner thighs, spread wide before him, and slowly carried up my body like a gentle caress. My head felt light, but the exhilaration of being this close to him gave me the courage to ask, "Do you think I'm the one whom the goddess has blessed you with?"

His breath coasted across my lips as he replied in a seductive tone that had my toes curling, "Has the energy between us not been evidence enough? I do not think, Asherah. I know." He claimed my mouth, and I lost myself in the way his lips melded perfectly against mine. The feel of him was overwhelming.

Consuming.

Draevyn's fingers dug into my thighs as he pulled me onto his lap, his rock-hard length growing harder by the second against my slit. His strong hands trailed over the back of my neck as our tongues tangled in a seductive dance. This energy between us was so right. I had to have more.

I *needed* more.

My hips rocked frantically against his straining cock, the fabric of my bathing suit rubbing against my clit and fueling my desire. Draevyn made a low noise in his throat, which only added to the liquid heat between my thighs. The fabric of my bikini top created a delicious friction against his bare chest. He sucked my lower lip between his teeth, and a moan escaped me. My low ache continued to build until it became nearly unbearable. His warm lips trailed down my neck, nibbling and sucking, causing my breathing to accelerate. I leaned my neck to the side, giving more of myself to him.

"You are a dream I never want to wake up from," he whispered against my skin. He slid his arms around my waist, pressing me firmly against him. "And as much as I never want to wake up from it, we have to stop." I couldn't hold back the whimper that escaped me, which he deftly captured with his mouth. "The things I plan to do to you, the way I plan to take you, require more than the surface of a surfboard. Although the sounds you make, the little moans, have me desperate to sink my cock into your silken heat. I want to bottle it for my own personal pleasure forever." I breathed out a moan as his words went directly to my core. "When I take you for the first time, I want to worship every incredible inch of your body, like taking you on my own personal alter upon which you lay everything bare to me." He brushed his lips gently against mine. Slowly. Sensually. "But I'd never withhold my female's pleasure if that is what you need." His fingertips traveled over my bikini top, teasing the tight bud of my nipple between his fingers before venturing lower to trace the fabric of my bikini bottoms, my center aching for his touch. The desire in his gaze was a palpable thing as he asked, "What do you want, my Queen? Do you want me to give you relief?"

My hands gripped his neck as I moved against him. "Yes. Please. Yes."

The words were barely out of my mouth before he pulled the fabric of my bottoms aside and dipped his fingers through my slick folds. I sucked in a breath as they slowly ran from my entrance to my sensitive bud, coating them with my arousal. "Fuck, Asherah. You're so wet for me," he breathed against my ear as he nibbled the lobe in his warm mouth. I felt as if he were everywhere, yet still, it was not enough. When Draevyn skillfully circled his fingers in slow, painful circles over my throbbing clit, each mind-blowing flick caused my hips to buck. I cried out as his finger entered my heat, his thumb rubbing rapidly against the swollen nub. My thoughts were a cloud of desire, making it nearly impossible to breathe. Despite his glamour, the rest of the world didn't exist. I was his captive, and I never wanted him to let me go.

When his second finger joined the first, I arced into him—his tongue drawing a line from my neck to my collarbone. "Such a perfect Princess," he murmured against my hot skin, "ride my hand like you'll ride my cock. Show me how you like it, Asherah." His words undid me. My hips rocked harder and faster against him as I shamelessly rode his hand—the sensation was so overwhelming that I thought I might faint from the feel of him.

"Come for me," Draevyn commanded.

And I refused to deny the commander his due.

Wave after wave of pleasure tore through my body, and my hands dug into his hair, gripping tightly. He continued his quest to expel every bit of desire until my body was utterly spent, and when he deemed me worthy, he slowly removed his fingers from my heat.

As I came down from the high that was Draevyn Eliron, I lay my head upon his shoulder—his arms coming around me and holding me tightly to him. We bobbed in the water, holding each other for what felt like an eternity before he pulled back, bringing his forehead to mine—an expression of pure bliss as if he'd won a divine lottery flashing across his features. "It's an honor to begin this adventure with you, Asherah Delmar."

But I couldn't help but feel that the honor was all mine.

# Chapter 21

The afternoon we'd arrived back in Atlantis, our webbed toes had barely dug into the sand at the front gates when Draevyn was called to train in Calichi, the northern Atlantian outpost. "That's the life of a commander," he'd told me in between chaste goodbye kisses. He'd left me weak in the knees in the hallway before my quarters with a promise that Mayana would be there shortly to guard me. Unfortunately, Mayana couldn't take care of my...baser needs.

It had already been a week since the remarkable, incredible, toe-curling memory that played in my mind and dreams on repeat. Upon waking from the tantalizing dreams he'd frequented, I had to take care of the ache between my legs a time or two. It was a dream—I vowed—that was worth repeating in real life. Until then, I was stuck waiting for Draevyn to return.

Thank the goddess for the distraction of my

training.

I stood in front of the waterfall in the Guardian training center, my webbed feet in the shallow end of the pool. The training center had been cleared out per Dax's request. The drapes over the windows had been drawn to deter anyone from witnessing our training. There had been several since the time we'd discovered my ability. It was why I stood in the pool playing with the flow of the waterfall, just because I could.

Pause.

Flow.

Pause.

Flow.

The sound of the door swinging open captured my attention. I swiveled to the entrance just as a broad smile emerged on Dax's face. His large, muscular legs carried him to stand before me with two tridents in his hands. My brow furrowed while my lips lifted. "Two tridents?"

Dax wagged his bushy blond eyebrows. "It's time you learned the art of the trident."

My heart skipped in elation as I stepped out of the pool to meet him. "And I suppose that's my trident?"

One of his tridents vanished into thin air while he rested the other across his hands, presenting it to me. "Actually, this is your mother's trident."

I swallowed past the lump that had suddenly formed in my throat. I brought my finger to the long part of the golden trident. My eyes went wide when it grew brighter at my touch.

"That's called the stem," Dax informed me. He turned the trident upright, placing a finger on the tallest pointed end. "This is the tip." He pointed to the bottom. "That is the base." Dax held my mother's trident out, encouraging me to take it. I did, carefully—the golden glow flaring to life. "Your trident is yours alone, Asherah. It will call to you and help you wield its power. Others can use it, surely, but it will not sing the same way for everyone." He stood back a few paces, his face alight with something akin to pride and perhaps joy. "Go ahead. Give it a little twirl."

I stared at the trident in my palm. When I was little, probably around nine or ten, Mom bought me the longest twirling baton with a bright white rubber tip on one end and a neon pink ball on the other. For an entire summer, we hung out on the pool deck, my mother relaxing on her favorite lounge chaise with a bright smile as she regarded me. "You're doing amazing, Sher," she told me. "Keep practicing." I must have practiced for hours on end, just twirling and twirling until blisters eventually formed and calluses replaced them months later. It was my favorite thing in the world to do to pass the time, besides hanging out with John, of course.

So, when Dax instructed me to twirl, it was like riding a bike for the first time in a very long time. My fingers slowly danced with the stem as it began swirling in a perfect circle. The progression was a little wobbly, but as my muscle memory roared back, I twirled my mother's trident faster—bright trails of gold chasing the tips and stem like a sparkler on the fourth of July. I couldn't help the pure laughter that escaped my lips.

"That's marvelous, Ash. You're a natural," Dax beamed.

I paused my twirling regarding him. "My mother. She…" I swallowed past the rising emotion and continued, "She gave me a baton once. She'd always encouraged me to practice."

Dax's face softened, the grief lightly flickering in his cobalt-blue eyes. "Neleah was always the smart one of us. Leave it to her to figure out how to train you without officially training you." He blew out a long breath, gathering himself. "Now, your trident is an extraordinary weapon. Only the Guardians and those belonging to the Queen's bloodline may acquire them." He pointed to the tip. "That sharp point can break through just about anything. And I mean anything. Scales. Bone. It's strong enough to break through stone. So, it's vital to handle it delicately." His cupid-bow lips lifted in a smirk. "Unless, of course, we're training. In which case, I want you to be very indelicate."

I returned his smirk. "I wouldn't want to hurt your pretty little face."

"Hah, you can try, Princess," he challenged. Dax called his trident, the stem appearing in his hand in the blink of an eye. "That is how you summon your trident." It vanished yet again. "And that is how you dispel it."

My brow furrowed as I concentrated on the stem I held in my hand. "Well, how do I do that?"

"The trident is a part of you now, Asherah. Once your mother passed—may Atabey rest her soul—its power transferred to you. Think of your trident as a sentient being. Command it to dispel."

My gaze locked on the golden trident. With everything I had, I shot the command down my arm. My hand became weightless as it suddenly vanished.

Dax's broad laugh reached his eyes. "Excellent, Ash. Now, same thing. I want you to summon your trident. Will it into the palm of your hand."

I gave him a firm nod, my gaze fixed on my palm once again. I envisioned the bright, golden stem and felt the weight of it in my hand before it appeared in a blink. Dax broke out in applause, and I twirled it once with a bow. "Well done, Princess. Well done."

I placed the base of the trident on the floor beside me. "What's next, my valiant mentor?"

Dax motioned to the pool. "Follow me."

The cool water rose on my scaled legs as we entered the pool until we were waist-deep. "For this next lesson," Dax began, as we faced each other, "we'll focus on summoning a wave beneath your feet. This particular trick can be very useful in everyday life, whether you want to lift yourself out of the Shingu or to a higher ground. The more powerful the Water Fae, the higher the wave."

I lifted a cool eyebrow. "And how tall can you make your wave?"

With a challenging look, he began to rise out of the water, the long locks of his blond hair flowing around him as a wave lifted him nearly three stories in the air, the water churning beneath his feet. Only a foot remained between his head and the ceiling. Dax lifted his shoulder in a half-shrug. "I could go higher."

I breathed off an impressed laugh. "Well, then. I'm glad you're on my side."

He wagged his brows as he summoned his trident, lowering his wave to about six feet above my head. "Our ability to wave carry gives us the perfect advantage against our enemies. It guarantees you'll always have the high ground." He dropped into a fighting stance; his trident held back for the strike as the gentle roar of his wave echoed above the splash of the waterfall. "It can also give you a full view of any battlefield." He flicked his head to the water before me. "Try it."

My gaze held on my webbed feet below the water's surface, but I shot Dax a questioning look. "What am I supposed to do?"

He huffed a laugh. "Same as you did with the trident, Princess. Remember, the water is sentient. Will it to do your bidding. Go on. Try it."

I dropped my gaze to my feet again, focusing on the water surrounding them. A tiny current began drifting between my toes and pushed beneath my feet. I lifted only slightly, and my mouth dropped. "I think something's happening."

"Well, make it happen more," Dax called above me.

"Smart ass," I murmured, and I thought I heard his faint chuckle. I couldn't tell for sure, though, because my gaze remained on my feet as I rose another foot in the air. I held my arms out to steady my weight, the water now pushing against me. Only my calves remained below water.

"You've got this, Ash. Just a little higher."

I poured all of my focus on the current beneath my feet until a wave pushed me entirely out of the water. I glanced up at Dax, who was only a few feet above my head now, absolute joy pulling at my lips. "I did it!"

Apparently, my excitement broke my concentration because the wave below my feet suddenly dropped in a flash. I crashed into the water below, the water's surface smacking into my back as I plunged into the pool. When I resurfaced, I couldn't help but feel mortified.

I wiped my eyes as Dax's knowing smile met my gaze. He gracefully lowered himself into the water before me. "It will take time. I can tell by the look on your face that you're being hard on yourself."

Yes, I was. Would I admit it, though?

Likely not.

"Give yourself some credit, Ash. You did well for your first time. And summoning and dispelling your trident like that? It takes Guardians several days to achieve that task. That was very well done." He patted my shoulder. "You should be proud."

I let loose a breath. "Thanks, Dax."

"I don't give compliments lightly. It's well deserved." He glanced at the time on the wall. "I need to be going."

"I think I'll stay here for a bit, if that's okay?"

"Of course. Practice makes perfect, as they say," he said with a wink.

For the rest of the afternoon, I practiced everything I'd learned. And with my mother's trident swinging through the air, I could've sworn I felt her with me.

# Chapter 22

THREE WEEKS.

It had been three entirely long weeks since I'd seen Draevyn. The distance was clawing at me. He'd be gone for long periods of time. I understood this, but I found myself moping more than coping.

Communication was limited during his training. Whether he thought of me as much as I thought of him had been a mystery. Until one day, Mayana delivered a long, rectangular package to my quarters. "For you," she'd said, her dark lips lifting in a knowing smirk. I immediately ripped it open when I saw Draevyn's perfectly crafted writing on the brown parchment wrapped around it. It said, 'To my surf mate' and instantly brought a smile to my face.

When I opened the box, a single white marble pen lay surrounded by navy velvet padding. The note inside read:

*Dear Asherah,*

*The days are long without you. I long to hear your voice. Actually, I long for many things, but I won't put the descriptive details in this note in case it is intercepted.*

*Use this tablet pen to write to me from your stone tablet. It is magicked to send messages to mine. I may not be able to respond right away, but I promise to return your message when I can.*

*Always Thinking of You,*

*Draevyn*

That first evening, with my new tablet pen in hand, I was like a schoolgirl with the worst kind of crush. I devised a million different messages to send him before I finally settled on, '*Thank you for the pen. -A.*' I cursed and threw the pen across my fluffy duvet while silently chastising myself for not writing something more heartfelt. I'd decided to step away from the tablet and set it on my nightstand while I buried my face in my hands, not wanting to see his response.

The tablet echoed my words for an entire day until, on the following evening, while sitting in bed with a puffy pillow supporting my back, I noticed that the writing had shifted from white to a vibrant green. My brow dipped as I lifted the tablet from the stand and read the note, '*You're welcome. In truth, the pleasure is all mine. I patiently await to see how you've been…beyond the gratitude for the pen. -D.*'

I had to admire his subtle way of calling me out for my lack of communication after the beautiful note he'd sent. So, I attempted something more. '*Everything here is boring without you. The company isn't as great.*' I thought long and hard before I wrote the next sentence. '*I can't stop thinking about our last surf session together.*'

There. I'd done it. I'd actually written something more like…well…I don't know what it was, but it was definitely beyond the perimeters of my comfort zone.

Given how long it took him to respond the first time, I was pleasantly surprised minutes later when the writing on the tablet was replaced by his message in green. '*I think of it often. I'm thinking about it now. I must confess, it's increasingly hard to write and stroke at the same time.*'

The vision of him bare-skinned and stroking his considerable length sent an instant heat to my core. I'd only felt it against me that day, which prompted my reply. '*I plan to be the one doing that for you when you return to me.*'

It took nearly a full half an hour before his response appeared. '*I definitely wasn't able to write after that response. The vision of you touching my cock needed my complete attention. I plan to hold you to that promise. Dream of me. -D.*'

And dream of him I did.

The days rolled by with us exchanging messages. Some were far simpler. He'd told me his favorite color is green. He'd promised to send a tablet pen in my favorite color—coral. His mother's family is Air Fae. His cousin, Jamevyn—also Air Fae—is a Guardian for Airelandia, and they often spar for sport. Other messages were far more flirtatious and had me begging the goddess for his training to finish so he could return to Atlantis.

I attempted to bury myself in my studies—the trade history between the queendoms paled in comparison to the romance books I thoroughly enjoyed. As I sat on a high back chair at the kitchen island, I let loose a heavy sigh and turned the page of the heavy tome. This was my third activity of the day.

My second activity had been forming water spheres and throwing them against the wall. I even practiced forming a wall of water as I lounged in my comfy reading chair. I tried to grow it as tall as the ceiling before it came down, crashing on me. It was why I remained grateful that I'd mastered creating a protective layer over the old tomes that littered my coffee table as my *first* activity of the day. I feared Myles's wrath if even a single drop of water managed to land on the ancient texts. I shuddered at the thought.

My studies were becoming easier as time progressed. Dax had begun training me in basic martial arts. Without the excursion of surfing every day, I welcomed it. I wasn't a ninja by any means, but I did enjoy the art of the fight. Dax was a fantastic instructor.

"Keep this up, and I may steal you for my guard," he'd teased one day.

I'd tried to steady my breathing. "And do this all day, every day? You've lost your mind."

He shrugged. "Perhaps. But I've never been one for politics. At any rate, I'm jesting. There's no way I'd want anyone else ruling Atlantis."

Ruling Atlantis. Me. It still caused my nerves to jump. I'd also heard what he didn't say that day; he'd rather have me than Melysah and the council ruling over Atlantis. I couldn't disagree with him. Melysah had her lap dog, Kane, following me everywhere. Granted, he wasn't assigned to me, so that was a plus. But the look the male gave me every time we crossed paths made me desperate to get away from him. I didn't like Kane Ruema. Not one bit. I could still feel his creepy gaze in my mind, the storm-gray eyes that tracked me everywhere, and I couldn't suppress the shiver.

A knock sounded at the door.

*Probably Mayana again.*

That was the other…thing…that was different. Mayana—goddess love her—was very diligent at her job. She was my shadow everywhere I went. While I appreciated her dedication to keeping me safe, there was only one Guardian I wanted at my side.

The door flung open. "Just leave me alone, please." The door slammed shut a second later, my entire body jolting.

I immediately hopped off my seat at the sound of Reneah's voice and beheld the anger that lit her features. "What's going on?"

Reneah blew out a breath. "You've been assigned a new guard."

Panic swelled inside me, and my nails dug into my palms. "Please tell me it isn't Kane."

"I'd be lying to you if I did."

"But where is Mayana?"

Reneah winced. "She's in heat, I'm afraid."

I went rigidly still. "What do you mean by 'in heat?'"

Her brow furrowed. "Has no one explained female Fae menstrual cycles to you?"

"Um. No. Do they need to be explained?" I asked, crossing my arms over my middle.

"Well, yes," her lips lifted in a smirk, "especially if you plan to take a certain hunky commander to your bed."

I pinched the bridge of my nose. "Does everyone know my business?"

"No, but I'm your chambermaid and friend, so I do notice everything. Not to worry. I only divulged that tidbit to Aurelio, who also knows, by the way. Your secret is safe with us," she assured, her dirty blonde brow wagging.

I waved a hand in the air. "You were saying something about menstrual cycles?"

"Oh. Right. So, females only menstruate every ten years. When they do, they let out certain…eh… pheromones that drive the males wild. If a female is unmated, it can get a little intense, especially if the attention is unwanted. So, some females—like Mayana—choose to reside in the solitary colony until it passes. Some females decide to give in to the baser primal instincts and take a male or a few to their bed since the fertility rates are so low amongst the Fae."

That was news to me. I rested my chin on my hand as I tried to recall my first menstrual cycle and…

"Holy shit."

Reneah's brown eyes went wide. "What happened?"

"Nothing. I just remembered my first cycle." I shook my head. "It was nearly nine years ago. It was one of those rare times when Mom was home and not on a work trip. I remember running into her room at the first sight of blood, and she immediately sent my father away."

"Presumably to reassign the other Guardians in the area, if I had to guess. Your parents would be immune to the heat, thank the goddess," Reneah provided.

I gripped the back of my neck. "But what about the pills?"

Reneah tilted her head, tiny dirty blonde strands falling forward and framing her angular face. "What pills?"

I immediately raced for my bedroom, sifting through the drawer of my nightstand until I retrieved the case containing my birth control. Mom had provided them just after my first menstrual cycle, claiming they stopped the bleeding altogether and kept me safe from getting pregnant. I told Reneah as much when I handed them to her, where she stood in the middle of the brightly lit living room. She gave me a withering smile and handed them back to me. "I'm afraid these are just sugar pills."

I stared at the metal container, the circular pills almost smiling up at me and laughing for believing a ruse. "But why would she do that?"

"Because in order for you to believe you were human, you'd have to have a regular period like the human women in the Above World do." She reached out and gave my upper arm a gentle squeeze. "I wouldn't hold it against your mother. She was just trying to do what was best."

My head dipped in a nod, but it still hurt to know she'd lied to me. "So, I can't get pregnant?"

"Yes, you can." Reneah took my hand and guided me to the chairs by the window. I slid into the seat, thankful to be off my shaky legs. "It's just not as easy as it is with humans. You'll get your cycle every ten years. And when you go into heat—like Mayana has—you and your bondmate will seclude yourselves for days on end, making love until the frenzy passes. And hopefully, create a little faeling. But I wouldn't get too discouraged if it doesn't happen the first time. It may take a few tries. You and your mate will have a long life of trying, long after I'm gone from this world. But hopefully, the goddess will give you a little faeling for me to spoil before I'm gone."

My gaze drifted between her eyes, and I caught the slight pain there. "I don't want to think of you as gone from this world."

She reached across the way and patted my hand. "Then let's not think of it." Reneah glanced behind, a mischievous smile emerging on her face.

"Uh-oh. What is that smile about?"

She rose from her chair. "I've thought of a plan. I'll be back in a few." She whirled toward the door, and it was nearly half an hour before she returned, her short legs making rapid strides across the living room as the sparkling purple sequence of her spaghetti strap dress rode up her thighs. "You better get your ass off that chair if you want to escape that asshole Guardian and have a little fun tonight."

I leapt from my chair and dropped my text on the side table. "Um, you look hot. And where are we going?"

"That is privileged information," she said with a wicked grin. "Come. And hurry."

"Do I need anything?"

She grabbed my hand, her brown eyes positively gleaming with impish delight. "Nope. Just yourself. Hurry. My accomplice is waiting."

Reneah dragged me out of my quarters and into the hallway, checking both ways before dashing down the stairs. I was surprised when our hurried steps carried us to Myles and Aurelio's floor. Reneah gave a soft knock on the door. It swung open to a grinning Aurelio. "I see you have the goods."

"I do, Master Accomplice."

Aurelio shut the door behind us. "Perfect!"

"Just what are you two up to?" I asked, unable to hold the chuckle that bubbled up inside me.

"We're tired of you moping," Reneah said. "And studying. And then moping some more."

"And then studying some more," Aurelio remarked with a dramatic roll of his amber eyes.

"And more moping. It hasn't failed our notice that

this all came about when a certain commander was assigned to the outposts for training."

"If I didn't know any better," Aurelio cut in, "I'd say this happened for one of two reasons." He held up his perfectly manicured pointer finger. "Either one, you are sad because your commander is not guarding you or," he added his middle finger, "you prefer your commander to any Guardian assigned to you."

"Or both," Reneah remarked.

I felt my cheeks flame. "Um…isn't that same thing?"

Aurelio's eyes went wide. "Oooooh. She's got it bad."

"Real bad," Reneah agreed.

"Say no more, our dear future Queen. We have exactly the type of distraction you need after weeks and weeks—"

"And weeks of moping and studying and moping." Reneah grabbed my upper arms. "We're sneaking out and going out on the town."

"But won't Kane come looking for me?"

Reneah and Aurelio shared a look before Aurelio spoke, "I'm sure he'll be fine for a while."

My brow rose to my hairline. "What did you all do to him?"

"Nothing," they said simultaneously.

Aurelio clapped his hands together, his signature gold bangles clanking together. "Now, if anyone asks, we can tell them I was teaching you an essential skill this evening." Reneah rushed into the bedroom.

I shifted on my feet. "And…that is?"

"I'm teaching you to glamour properly." He waved a hand over me. "We'll need to change your hair color for sure. How does going blonde sound?"

Reneah bounded into the room with a deep, red

dress and a smile a mile wide. The dress didn't reach any-where past mid-thigh.

"What is *that*?"

"*That* is the dress you'll be wearing tonight."

I chuckled and tilted my head, eyeing the spaghetti straps and tight-fitting material. It wasn't the worst dress in the world. "Where in the world are we going?"

Aurelio's brows wagged. "We're going to your first Atlantian night club."

Reneah practically jumped up and down. "We're going dancing!"

"And not just any dancing at any club. We're going to your first foam party at Muse!"

I reared back. "Foam party?"

"That's correct," Reneah confirmed. "Now, let's get you in this dress and get out of here before someone suspects you've been smuggled out of the palace."

With that, Aurelio and Reneah did what they do best: pamper and preen. Within no time, the three of us stood in front of a floor-length mirror doing final checks on our outfits. Aurelio whirled around, checking out his ass in his skinny black jeans—his hot pink tank top clung to him like a second skin revealing an impressive set of washboard abs. "Oh, yes. I'm ready for all the foam."

Reneah's dirty blonde curls that reached her shoulders bobbed as she adjusted her dress. "Let's hope this thing doesn't ride up too much throughout the night."

"And if it does, perhaps someone can remove the cobwebs that have been collecting there," Aurelio teased.

Reneah swatted his upper arm. "Oh, stop. Not all of us can have a hot male at our beck and call."

"Well, you could," Aurelio replied with a smirk.

Reneah gave him a pointed look and resumed her final check.

I appeared relatively the same, but it was my hair that stood out in stark contrast. It was pale blonde. "Well, how did I do?" I questioned. I didn't know how I managed to learn so fast, but my glamour seemed to have held after a few attempts. I only hoped it would hold throughout the night.

"You look marvelous, darling," he complimented from behind me, beaming with pride. "I'm impressed you managed to learn so quickly. They'll never be able to tell it's you." Aurelio checked his watch. "Time to move. Our chariot awaits."

We exited the door and moved silently down the halls, pausing every now and then so Aurelio could check the corridors. Within minutes, we were at a palace side door I'd never been through before. When the door swung open, Braeliah perched on top of her canoa in the canal that sat parallel to the outer wall.

We all hopped onto the canoa with Reneah faux whispering to Braeliah, "Greetings, getaway accomplice."

Braeliah glanced at us over her shoulder. "I have no idea what you're talking about. I'm simply transporting you and your…blondie friend out for a night on the town," she said with a wink. With a flick of her wrist, we were off.

I'd like to tell you that Muse was just like any other club in the Above World. But what I witnessed made my cheeks burn aflame as I squeezed through the crowd sandwiched between Reneah and Aurelio. Sure, there was foam. Seafoam.

And lots and lots of nakedness.

Several dark alcoves ran along the perimeter, with Fae forms barely hidden and moving on plush red-colored bedding behind sheer curtains. On the dance floor, multiple hands, arms, and legs wrapped around various wet, bare-skinned bodies as they moved to the rhythm, the foam barely concealing anything at all.

Aurelio cut through the crowd—the foam gathering on his shoulders as he strode for the roped-off dais as dark as any of the alcoves. He addressed a very tall, broad male who resembled a bouncer with scales in lieu of a black suit standing at the base of the stairs. As he let us through, I didn't miss the curious once-over he gave me as I passed him.

Reneah pulled me onto the bench seats that lined the cornered-off lounge. At least, the exclusivity of our V.I.P. area would pass Draevyn's approval…if he could look past the fact that we did, in fact, sneak out of the palace to come to Muse. My gaze traveled across the room, every detail leaving me in awe. Water sculptures moved fluidly in different shapes—one shaped like a Water Fae dancing to the music in the air above the crowd appeared vividly real. Another water sculpture traveled around the room as it morphed into different sea animal shapes.

"It's incredible, isn't it?" Reneah said in a raised voice that carried over the pounding of the music.

I didn't need a mirror to know my mouth was hanging open as I said, "I've never seen anything like it."

A Fae female approached our table carrying a serving tray with practiced ease—her black hair cut in a pixie style that complimented her severe cheekbones. She cast a bright smile at Aurelio "Aury!"

"Nina!" He leaned in, placing a gentle kiss on both of her cheeks in greeting. "It's been so long."

"Too long. I hear you've been rather busy with the new arrival. How is the new Queen? Is she less on her high horse than the last one?"

Well, that was an interesting tidbit. I'd never once considered that Mom might be viewed in a negative light. Up until this moment, I'd only heard high praises for Queen Neleah.

He flitted a hand in the air. "Oh, our future Queen is extraordinary, to be sure. And a vast improvement in the fun arena." He glanced over his shoulder and gave me a wink. I couldn't stop my grin.

"Well, I'm glad to hear it," the server replied. She glanced around at the rest of us with a welcoming smile. "So, what will it be for you all?"

Reneah clapped her hands together. "How about we start the table with three Dirty Water Faetinis?"

My forehead scrunched. "Dirty Water Faetinis? What in the world is that?"

"That is the house specialty," Aurelio beamed.

"And they're fantastic," Nina endorsed enthusiastically. "Three of those coming right up."

I narrowed my eyes at both of them as she strolled away. "I don't know if I like the sound of this."

Reneah playfully slapped my knee. "Oh, come on. Live a little. You're in the best company, and no one even knows who you are. You look smoking hot, and you haven't had a single moment in Atlantis to be anything other than the future Queen. Enjoy this!"

"She's right, Ash," Aurelio remarked as he plopped down on Reneah's other side. "Be unapologetically you tonight. There are no Fire Fae here to harm you, no royal duties to tend to. No one even knows that you're you. So, let's dance and have fun. Ah! There's Nina with our drinks."

Nina gracefully strode before us and placed the drinks on the low table before issuing a wink and proceeding to the next table. Aurelio held his faetini up. "To the future Queen, may everyone see her as brilliantly as Reneah and I do."

"Absolutely," Reneah agreed.

Our glasses clanked together as I smiled, taking a sip. I moaned as the most magnificent martini—or faetini—ever to touch my lips traveled down my throat. The light hints of strawberry and cucumber graced my taste buds and went down like water. I pondered whether it was wise to drink too many of these, but quickly dashed that thought away when the liquid began coursing through my veins. A sense of warmth spread throughout my chest, and my limbs dropped in relaxation. "You all are truly the best. And I wouldn't make it without the both of you."

"Well, you would, but it would be dreadfully boring," he said as he took another sip.

As the night progressed, the faetinis kept coming—each of us drinking our fair share—until Reneah and Aurelio finally dragged me out on the dance floor. I'd never heard club music like the kind that pumped through the room. It was almost as if a spell had been cast and possessed my body until I could do nothing but move. There wasn't an inch between me and the next person. Everyone danced and swayed as if under the same spell. It was joyous. Freeing. And touch? Touch felt incredible. Hands moved over arms and skin, without being violating in any way—almost as if each touch and caress were a way to honor the other person's body.

When Reneah dragged me back to our table for a quick break, I reveled in the throb of my red-heeled feet. "Ugh, I haven't danced like that in so long."

Reneah's eyes suddenly went wide as they scanned my face. She leaned into my ear. "Your glamour is slipping a bit."

That sent a jolt of shock to my stomach. If anyone recognized me, the night would be over sooner than I wanted it to. Worse, someone from the Akani could recognize me, which put my friends at risk. And I wouldn't have that.

Aurelio stood a foot away chatting with a group of Fae when Reneah grabbed the back of his shirt and pulled. When he wheeled around, she pointed at me, and his amber eyes widened. He came to stand in front of me, blocking me from view as he bent down. "I believe someone has had a few too many faetinis to hold their glamour. Can you remember what I taught you?"

My head was a little fuzzy, but I remembered. "Imagine the change. Will it to happen."

He nodded. "That's right. Do that again. Come on now."

I blew out a breath, imagining the pale hair and slightly paler skin, and felt the glamour pull taut over my head. "Is that better?"

Aurelio straightened with a smile. "Much."

I breathed a sigh of relief, reaching for my glass to take a cooling sip. Crisis averted. I swayed to the beat in my seat, and Reneah grabbed my hand once again. "Let's go back out there."

We squeezed through the crowd, venturing back onto the dance floor. The euphoria grew with each beat, causing my hips to sway and my neck to loll. The sea foam fell from above, cascading down my bare skin and sinfully red dress, and I tipped my head back, letting it soak my too-blonde hair. I danced without a care in the realm. I was amongst my people for the first time, soaking up their energy and being one with the Fae. All the various states of undress bothered me less and less as I danced the night away.

It wasn't until a pair of very strong arms snaked their way around my waist that I gave pause. I knew those arms. I dreamed of them often. His muscular chest pressed into my back as he swayed with me. I tipped my head back on his shoulder, my eyes finally meeting his green ones after weeks of separation. "How?" I asked in his ear.

Draevyn nudged his nose against my face, bringing his lips to my ear, "Your glamour slipped." His teeth gently nipped my lobe. "But there is nowhere I won't find you, no matter what glamour you use. You can change your hair any color, but nothing can glamour the curve of an ass I've shamelessly studied and memorized." His tongue darted out and sinfully licked along my neck, causing my breath to hitch. "You've been naughty, Princess."

I turned in his arms and found his aquamarine eyes swirling with lust. "And what are you going to do about it?" I challenged.

Draevyn's rough hands skated over my hips, suds of seafoam gathering on his arms. He brought his soft lips close to mine. "Come with me."

He intertwined our hands and pulled me through the crowd. I cast a glance behind me, and Reneah and Aurelio were nowhere to be found. They likely saw him coming a mile away. *Traitors.* But I couldn't bring myself to care. The energy rolling off of Draevyn felt like desire, passion, and outright knee-dropping lust combined. My feet fluttered in my stilettos in an effort to keep up with him as I followed him out onto the street before Muse.

He dragged me into an alleyway, and I felt the glamour he cast over us a second before his mouth was on mine. Warm. Demanding. Seeking. He pushed me against the wall, his fingers threading through my barely blonde hair. I could scarcely breathe as I drank him in—all the tension from the long weeks without him snapping something inside me. I clawed at his back as he let loose a delicious masculine groan against my mouth. I couldn't get enough of him.

Draevyn pulled back. "Remove that glamour off your hair," he demanded. "I need to see you."

I quickly dropped my glamour. He leaned in and nuzzled my damp, dark strands, inhaling deeply. "Yes. I've missed that smell. I've missed you." His hands gripped my ass and pulled me against him. His hard, thick length dug into my stomach, and a moan escaped my lips.

"And I missed you," I breathed.

A serious expression crested his features. "But you have been very, very naughty."

I bit my lip. "You mentioned that."

His fingers threaded through my hair at the nape of my neck. He tugged just enough to bring my gaze up to him. "The entire guard is out looking for you. And your accomplices."

A playful smirk lifted my lips. "Who says there were accomplices?"

"Don't be cute. You know there are dangers out here. Genuine ones."

I lifted my shoulder. "Again, what are you going to do about it?"

He groaned in a way that had me clenching my thighs together, adding to the ache that had been building since his arms snaked around me on the dance floor. "I will punish you. Thoroughly."

"Somehow, that doesn't sound like a punishment at all," I whispered.

Draevyn's tongue darted out and traced the seam of my lips before my mouth parted for him, his kiss hungry. Demanding. His rough hand brushed up my thigh and underneath my dress to exactly where I wanted him. He pulled the thin fabric of my red lace thong to the side and slipped his fingers between my slick folds, wet and drenched with my desire. "Already wet for your punishment, I see." My head tipped back against the wall, and my mouth fell open when he swirled his skillful fingers against my swollen clit—my hips jerking against him in response.

But I wouldn't be the only one receiving pleasure.

Not tonight.

I swung him with all my might against the wall, his eyes widening in amusement. "Let me show how I like to be punished." I dropped to my knees before him, the coarse ground biting into my knees. He leaned his bare back against the wall, his hooded gaze watching me trace a finger over the seam of his cock pocket, my eyes begging for permission. When the seam parted, he bit his lip as his glorious cock sprung free in front of me. His manhood was glorious, all length and girth. My tongue darted out, licking around his hot, smooth crown.

"Ash," he hissed through his teeth.

"I'm ready for my punishment, Commander," I hummed against his skin. His eyes never left mine as I took him into my mouth, the tip reaching for the back of my throat as I began moving him in and out in a steady rhythm. His hands splayed against the wall behind him as he breathed in deep, quick breaths. His hips reluctantly pitched forward at first, but as I pulled back and swirled my tongue along the entire length, his restrain snapped.

There was something erotic about watching this man lose control. He was like a newly discovered addiction.

And I was the addict.

Draevyn grabbed the back of my head and pumped

frantically in and out, my mouth straining to take in the depth of him. My need to please him had me gagging around his enormous cock, but I was determined to bring him to pleasure.

"I want you to feel yourself, Asherah," he gritted between clenched teeth. "I want you to come and moan around my cock as I come."

I wasted no time with his command. I gripped the base of his thick erection firmly with one hand as my other hand reached between my thighs, landing on my throbbing core—my fingers moving frantically over my sensitive nub, issuing the release I knew was on the brink. Within seconds I was moaning around his cock, the vibrations tickling my lips and my eyes watering as he pounded with abandon into my mouth.

Draevyn grunted his release, the sound echoing off the alley walls and causing another wave of pleasure to crest through me. I swallowed every last bit of his release as the warm cum shot down my throat. When his hips slowly rolled to a stop, I gave him one last lick around his swollen head. He lifted me under my arms, his mouth crashing into me, licking, tasting each salty remnant of himself on my lips. He slowly leaned against the wall and gently wiped the wetness around my mouth with his thick thumb. "You are exquisite, my Queen."

I rose on my toes and kissed his lips softly. "The feeling is mutual."

The warm skin of his chest pressed against my cheek as he held me against him. We said nothing for a few minutes as we came down from the energy born from our reunion. His hand drifted lazily up and down my back in a soothing motion. "Remind me to thank Aurelio for this dress."

"Who said Aurelio was involved?"

"Pfft. Oh, please."

"I won't snitch."

"Hmph."

"Well, isn't this the most intimate scene?" a voice called beside us. I lifted my head, and my heart kicked up. Kane Ruema stood at the head of the alleyway appraising us—his deep brown eyes roaming over our intimate embrace. Draevyn pushed us off the wall, placing himself in front of me. I realized, then, that our glamour must have slipped.

"Kane," Draevyn replied in a cold tone.

Kane prowled forward with an evil smirk on his face. "Well, knowing our future Queen is safe puts me at ease." He glared directly at Draevyn. "Not as much at ease as you both seem to be." His nostrils flared as he inhaled deeply. "Smells like a lot of ease."

Draevyn lurched forward, but I held him back. "As you can see, I am alive and well."

Kane's brows rose. "Very well, from the blush on your face," his gaze dropped to my legs, "and the red skin of your knees."

"That's enough, Ruema."

Kane held his hands in the air, laughing. "Hey man, I'm not judging." His eyes shifted back to me, roaming over my body in a way that made me cringe. "If I had the chance with the Queen, I'd take it. She's damn fine."

I couldn't stop Draevyn's forward momentum as his fist met Kane's face. I pulled him back with all my might. "Stop it."

Kane shook his head and straightened, wiping a thumb across his lip where Draevyn made contact and glancing down at the blood that decorated his skin. "I'm sure Dax would love to hear about this. I know for certain Mely would." He stepped backward, holding his gaze on Draevyn and then flicking it to me. "You two enjoy your night. I'll let the guards know you're safe." He twirled around and casually strode down the street.

Draevyn shook out his hand. "Fucking asshole."

I sighed. "Yes, well, that asshole is going straight to Melysah."

"It doesn't matter. He was planning on doing that anyway, whether I hit him or not." He cupped my face with his good hand. "Hey, don't let him ruin an excellent evening."

The corner of my mouth twitched upward. "I thought I was in trouble."

"Oh. You still are. But I can tell by how happy you looked in the club that this was a good night. And whether I agree or disagree with jeopardizing your life, I can't fault you for wanting to have a good time, even though I would have preferred that you take a guard."

"Mayana is in the solitary colony."

Draevyn's lips rounded in an 'o'.

I breathed out a sigh. "You're not in any trouble… about us?"

Oh, the smile that came across his face could melt icebergs. "No. I'm not. I anticipated others finding out about us at one point or another. Better sooner so everyone can get used to it. The only thing that might change is my assignment as your guard."

I reared back. "I don't want that to change."

"Neither do I, but I don't know if Dax can stop the reassignment if Melysah keeps insisting. I plan to do everything in my power to stop it." He claimed my hand in his. "But let's not worry about that now. We need to get back to the palace."

As Draevyn and I strolled down the streets of Borike'n toward the Shingu, a distinct feeling of unease crept into my mind. Kane's assignment during Draevyn's absence had to be strategic, and Melysah may very well be ahead of a game I wasn't aware we were playing.

# Chapter 23

It turns out Draevyn and I had a true ally in Dax. Melysah had brought the incident in the alleyway to his doorstep. He'd heard her every word and had given her all the attention she desperately sought. Then—in so many words—he advised that he'd never presume to tell her how to run the council and asked Melysah to stop trying to tell him how to run the Guardians.

At least, this was the story relayed to Draevyn. He'd told me as much as we ascended the steps for my lesson with Myles—the light filtering in from the tall arch windows catching on the lighter brown strands of his hair. "I don't think you'll have anything to worry about," he assured me with his hand on the small of my back.

We sifted through the crowd of students in the hallway. "What is with her? And why do I get the feeling that there's more to the story than I'm aware of?" I inquired with an arch of my brow.

Draevyn let loose a long sigh. "A long story for another time."

"Hmph," I replied. I left him in his usual spot beyond the classroom door, throwing him an expression that promised retribution if he didn't give me the details later.

When I stepped into the room, I paused. "Roarvyn?"

His crossed legs rested on top of the desk, and his chair was tilted back as he casually thumbed through a book. He glanced my way with one of his charming smiles rumored to bring the females in Atlantis to their knees. Quite literally, from what I hear. "Welcome, Your Highness."

I cautiously stepped forward. "What are you doing here?"

Roarvyn's chair came to rest on the ground as he rose and bowed with a flourish—strands of his long, brown hair falling forward. "I am here for your lesson, of course."

"Huh." I strode to my usual table just before his desk. "And Myles is?"

"Occupied in the Above World, I'm afraid," he informed, crossing his arms over his scaled chest.

"I see." I slid into my seat and extracted my journal, giving him a small smile. "And what are we learning today? How to disarm women and make their panties melt with a look?"

His face brightened, his gleaming teeth peeking. "Why? Is it working? Because if so, I believe my work here is done."

I snorted. "Yeah, okay."

Roarvyn bellowed with laughter. "Regardless of all my experience with the…how do you call it in the

Above World? The birds and the bees?"

"I know plenty about the birds and bees—"

"I'm here to teach you how to survive the council and when needed, manipulate them."

I jerked back. "Manipulate them?"

He tilted his head with a mocking grin. "Oh, you sweet little thing. You don't believe Melysah *isn't* studying every tome in Atlantis to see how she can get her way? Aw," he cooed, shaking his head. "I didn't take you for a simpleton."

My blood boiled. "I'm not a *simpleton*. I've been thrown into a world I'm still learning about, fuck you very much." The words were out of my mouth before I could think better of them.

Roarvyn reared back, his hand coming to his collarbone. "Oh, she bites. Good. You're gonna want to hold on to that fight, Princess."

He sauntered to the bookshelves at the back of the room, his fingers trailing over spine after spine until he plucked a crimson-clothed book from a shelf within reach. He deftly thumbed through it and placed it on the desk before me. "If you would read amendment eighty-eight of the Queen & Council Accord, Asherah."

My eyes briefly scanned the page, and I began reading, "With changing times comes necessary amendments to the accord between the Queen of Atlantis and her council. While ultimate say rests with the Queen on many issues, let it be stated that should the heir apparent contain or possess any qualities beneath the status of the ruler of Atlantis, the council may take a vote to allow a different bloodline to fulfill the role of Queen. Council members are encouraged to review the Scrolls of Atlantian Royal Families, which can be found in the High Priestess archives." I tapped the edge of the book, glancing up. "So, there's an actual road map for replacing me. Has it ever been done before?"

He rubbed the light stubble on his chin. "No. This is an amendment presented not that long ago. So, you'll need to consider who stands to benefit. Read the author marking at the bottom of the page, if you would, Asherah."

My gaze trailed to the bottom of the page till I found the name written there. I flinched. "The year of our goddess one-thousand sixty-eight. Proposed and codified by Melysah Velafyn."

Roarvyn came to my side, peering down at the text with an expression of disapproval. "Our dear Melysah is in this for the long game."

I shook my head. "Were you there when this was written?"

"No, no. I hadn't graced this earth with my presence till the twelve-hundreds, but I did ask my father about it in detail. He was on the council with Melysah. Never trusted her. Always thought she'd had ulterior motives. When he dug deeper, he found something that confirmed his suspicions twice over." He grabbed one of two aged, weathered scrolls that decorated his desk. "These are the Scrolls of Atlantian Families on loan from the High Priestess archives. The Bohiti made me promise to return them within the hour, or else she'll issue my punishment. I might return it a minute or two late to see what that punishment entails," he declared with a wink. He carefully spread the scroll out on top of my desk and tapped his finger on the name listed at the top. "As you can see, Neleah wasn't the Queen's only daughter. Queen Asu had seven total, meaning her legacy would live on. It was more than secure with that many faelings in line for the throne.

"But not every daughter was pleased that Neleah had a direct line to the crown." His finger traced one of the branches. "One of the seven daughters was Behuko Delmar. Now, Behuko wasn't a fan of Neleah's. To say the least. Being the second eldest, she was pretty nasty and defiant, always trying to upstage your mother at every turn.

"One day, things took a nasty turn, and she and her merry band of devotees captured Neleah and beat her within an inch of her life. She survived. Barely. Her attackers were sentenced to death, but not before they sang like a canary about who was responsible for organizing the attack. When they learned of Behuko's involvement, she outright denied it and, in a heated moment, decided she would defect to Corenathia."

I could feel my face pinch in disgust. "Corenathia? How is that even possible? I thought they didn't like the Water Fae."

"Oh, but they do love the drama. They welcomed the Atlantian Princess with open arms, especially one that had taken a liking to one of the princes of the realm. And most definitely a Princess who hated the Queen of Atlantis as much as Corenathia did. Behuko wed the Fire Fae Prince, Fynlor, but not only did she wed him. In defiance of her mother—our beloved Queen—she took his last name, unheard of in any of the realms.

"Fast forward a couple hundred years, and their daughter, Yari, is born in Corenathia. Imagine their horror when Yari turns out to be a Water Fae. Blasphemous! But her father doted on her nonetheless. The little family lived in service to the Queen of Corenathia. They were staunch supporters of all the cruelty and beliefs about the humans that the Corenathians still believe to this day. Those ideologies were passed on to little Yari. Yet despite Yari's belief in those ideologies, she never fit in with the Fire Fae. She and Behuko would always be outsiders to the Corenathians because of their water affinities.

"It wasn't until Yari was eleven that one of the Corenathians decided he'd had enough of a Water Fae in the high court. They snuck into Prince Fynlor's home to kill little Yari; however, the Prince was a very gifted Fire Fae. He arose from his sleep when he sensed the intruder's energy in his home. When he opened his daughter's bedroom door, he was shocked to discover one of their trusted friends in Yari's room, and he was momentarily stunned. That moment cost him his life. If Behuko wasn't directly behind Fynlor as he turned to ash, I suspect Yari would've been the next to die. But Behuko took him out. She and Yari returned to Atlantis after Fynlor's death, but Behuko died of a broken heart, leaving Yari to a queendom she grew up resenting.

"She lived the rest of her days in Atlantis, spewing her hatred of humans. She was the first of our kind to begin a rebel movement. Like Behuko, Yari had her loyal little band of supporters. She married a Water Fae, and when her daughter was born, she taught her to believe in those same hateful Corenathian ideologies. Please read the final name on Behuko's branch for me if you would."

My gaze dropped to the final few names on Behuko's branch—Prince Fynlor Velafyn, Behuko Delmar (surname renounced) Velafyn, Melysah Delmar (surname renounced) Velafyn—and everything clicked together.

My head snapped up. "Melysah's next in line for the crown."

Roarvyn smiled slowly. "Well, well. She does catch on. Yes, Your Highness. She is next in line—after you, of course—for the crown. She takes your ability to rule away? It goes directly to her. This plan of hers goes back centuries. Melysah has had plenty of time and preparation to devise her strategy."

I huffed, rubbing a hand down my face. "And I'm an interloper who just got here."

"Stop." Roarvyn's face had gone serious. "You will stop. I'll not have that kind of attitude from you. Not now and not ever. You may have just gotten here, but I've spent a lifetime observing the game unraveling before me—staying devoted to what Neleah intended for her queendom. I'll not fail her, and I certainly will not fail you. I am your ally. And you have many who are willing to help you. We'll see this through, but you must overcome this ridiculous idea that you don't belong here—quite the contrary. Of all the Fae and humans in Atlantis, you are the best suited for this role. You understand the humans, and you have something Melysah doesn't."

I swallowed past the lump that had formed in my throat. "And what's that?"

"Empathy." He spread his hands on the desk, leaning toward me. "I have your back, Ash. I have your back in that council room when you feel the weight of it all. We all do."

My heart was warmed by his support. There was a game I honestly felt unprepared for occurring within the council chamber. I'd take every ally I could find, and the look in his eyes told me Roarvyn was one of them. I gave him a solemn nod. "Thank you."

He tapped his knuckles against the top of the desk. "Good. Now, prepare yourself for a full afternoon of the council ins and outs, my future Queen. By the time you leave this room, you'll be an expert on all the council politics."

I meandered out of the classroom in a total daze, my mind foggy from information overload. Roarvyn didn't hold back a single council detail, and as I dodged a few students giggling and chatting on their way to their lessons, a faint buzz expanded in my ear. I hadn't even noticed when Draevyn lifted the bag from my shoulder, his lips tilting up in a smile. "Rough day?"

I sighed. "Just a lot of information. Like…a lot."

He placed himself before me as we cut through the crowded hall, the skin of my hand tingling when he threaded his hand through mine. As we reached the dark cavern that led to the Shingu, I glanced up in time to catch his lips lifting slightly. "Do you want to go with me to the gardens for a bit? Get away from everything?"

"You think that's a good idea?"

A shrug. "It seems to me that you need it." We shuffled across the sandy shore, the water lapping at our webbed toes. "Come. The Shingu leads to one of my favorite places in the palace gardens. No one will bother us there."

As we entered the river, I shamelessly let him pull me through the water, my emotions drowning me inside. So many revelations regarding the Atlantian council came to light, and the prospect of dealing with it all weighed heavily on my soul. Who was an ally? Who would seek to undermine me by using archaic rules in a book with binding so sensitive it could break upon opening it? Give me all the marine life in the world, all the different species, and their qualities any day.

Underwater politics?

Not so much.

It wasn't long before we were breaking through the surface of the Shingu. My breath caught as I took in the scene beyond the shoreline. A small clearing was covered in a carpet of lush green grass, and towering rose bushes painted in hues of red, orange, and yellow adorned the surroundings. Arches lined the walkways, leading to the other side of the gardens. The palace loomed in the distance, its faelights glowing against the setting sun, casting a soothing calm over the land. At the heart of the clearing, a stark white gazebo stood, bathed in the warm glow of copper Moroccan lanterns. Vermilion orange-colored cushions and pillows lined the floor, creating an inviting and serene atmosphere. Draevyn's enthusiasm could be felt a mile away. "Amazing, isn't it?

"It's so beautiful."

His strong arm snaked around my waist as he guided me up the steps. "I used to come here to unwind when training became too much, which was nearly every other day."

I leaned into his warmth. "Dax was that hard on you, huh?"

He huffed a laugh. "Some days, I could barely walk, and then it wouldn't matter how much rest we would get overnight. We'd be up training hard again the next day. There were some days I swore my arms would fall off. I'm pretty sure that's what Dax intended anyway." He dropped my bag in one of the gazebo's octagon corners and threw himself amongst the sea of pillows in such a childlike fashion that it warmed my heart to witness his elation. He patted the cushion beside him for me to follow suit.

I tucked myself snugly into his side, extending my legs before me—my scales shimmering against the warm glow of the lanterns—and rested my head on his muscular shoulder. I let loose a sigh with all my worries and fears about the dreaded council carrying into the wind and let my body go limp. The Shingu moved lazily along its path, the dome wall sitting just beyond dark, but providing a window into the ocean floor that encompassed Atlantis. Every now and then, some large gray sea animal moved back and forth in curiosity. "This is just what I needed." The lantern light glinted in his eyes as I brought my lips an inch away from his. "Thank you."

Draevyn pressed his soft lips to mine in a chaste kiss, igniting my core. "You're welcome, *nanichi*."

My brow furrowed. "What does *nanichi* mean?"

His thumb moved in lazy circles over the scales at my hip. "It's a term of endearment reserved for those who mean something. Something more. Like, let's say, a bondmate."

Butterflies took flight in my stomach. I couldn't help the smile that emerged on my face. My lips were pulled to his once more, the essence of him driving deeper into my heart.

As he ever so slowly broke our kiss, he placed his head upon mine, his thumb now tracing a pathway on my bare arm.

"Tell me more about you," I pleaded.

"What did you want to know?"

"Well, everything."

His chest vibrated with a chuckle. "Everything is a lot."

"Where are you from? I mean. I know you're from Atlantis, but what part?"

"I grew up in the outskirts, right along the southern border of Atlantis. It's called Sabana. It's a farming town where most gardening and farming elementals live.

They're responsible for feeding the whole of Atlantis and trading produce and wine amongst the other queendoms."

"So, your parents are farmers, then?"

He brought a leg to cross over the other. "Yes, and they're really good at it too. Vegetables, meat, poultry. They also produce some of the best wine in the farming country."

"They must have been shocked when you were called to join the Guard."

"Understatement of a lifetime. They were furious."

My fingertips crested the ridges of his abdomen as I lazily traced over his scales there with a deep furrow on my brow. "But they have to be proud of you now, yes?"

My head bobbed upward as his shoulder lifted in a shrug. "I suppose they are now. It took them a while to come around. They weren't keen on having their only son become a Guardian when they'd planned for me to enter the family business. It also didn't help that they'd waited an eternity for the goddess to bless them with a faeling."

"Because the Fae have trouble conceiving?"

His body stiffened. "Because the Fae have trouble conceiving."

I rose to lean against my arm to take in the expression of solemn concern that graced his features. "Why do you think that is?"

He twisted a strand of my dark brown hair within his fingers as he said, "Because we are blessed with a longer life span, but faelings? Not so much. Faelings are such a blessing among us. It is why some Fae choose to take humans as their partners. Their conception rate is much higher. Of course, the human life span is so short. The choice is not an easy one. The way I look at it, it's a guaranteed heartbreak. I couldn't bear it—falling in love with someone only to lose them a few decades later. And then watching your children die a few more decades after that."

"Sounds tragic," I murmured.

"Yes. Quite." He gazed off into the distance, his green eyes holding untold grief. It had me wondering whether a human woman had captured his heart in the past.

"Have you ever been in love?"

"Hmph. When I was coming into my manhood, I used to think I loved Melysah." I felt my heart constrict and desperately tried to control my breathing. "I wasn't aware she of the evil manipulator she is today. I was very taken by her beauty at first. I courted her for a while until I realized that her beauty was a mask for something much darker. I slowly began to withdraw from her. But one day, she showed up at my quarters in the Guardian wing of the palace. She requested I accompany her to Guake'te—the bonding ceremony—to see if we were goddess-blessed as bondmates. I refused to present her."

I picked at a wayward thread in the seam of a neighboring pillow. "The rejection must have been heartbreaking for her."

"It was. Still is, apparently. I regret ever courting her. What I felt for her was lust. Nothing more. I had no idea what love was back then."

My breath hitched. I didn't dare look at him as I asked, "And you know what love is now?"

His fingers came under my chin, lifting my gaze to his. "And now, I know without a shadow of a doubt that I had no idea what love was. I had no idea what it meant to find your perfect bonded mate. Not even close." His breath crested across my lips as his deep baritone voice murmured, "Now…I'm so dangerously close to losing myself in someone who deserves it."

His hand slid into my hair at the back of my neck—pulling me to meet the warmth of his lips. I lost myself in his kiss, in the sensation of his tongue. He devoured me, pulling me down to the cushions till I lay over him. Panting. Breathing. Taking. Needing. I wanted to experience it all with this marvelous male.

Draevyn tipped me on my back, the length of him pressing into my thigh. His mouth traveled down my neck, his tongue moving in delicious swirls, causing my toes to curl. When his lips met the scales at my collarbone, he glanced at me with a heated question in his eyes.

And I answered.

I willed the scales over my breast and abdomen away, the cool late afternoon air pebbling my skin as I bared myself to him. He paused, his gaze roaming over me with such reverence, such adoration, that my core instantly melted with every careful caress upon my breast. "So beautiful," he whispered against my skin as he captured my taut nipple in his warm mouth. My back arced into him, gripping the thick strands of his silky dark hair as he teased the tip of my other nipple between his skilled fingers. My core went molten as he sucked so hard that I felt it all the way down my body. I let loose a moan of complete desperation.

"I don't believe this is what they had in mind when they asked you to be her Guardian, Draevyn."

The cold voice had Draevyn jumping to his feet. My scales rose back up my body as I bolted upright. Melysah stood on the pathway just outside of the gazebo, seething. "You dare to fuck her in public?"

Draevyn balled his fists. "What are you doing out here?"

The nostrils of her defined nose flared. "I can go wherever I please."

"And you just so happen to be in the outer gardens?"

I wanted to smack the evil grin off her face. "Perhaps." Melysah turned, meeting my furious gaze. "I would watch yourself with him."

"What I do with him is none of your business," I bit out.

Her perfectly sculpted brow rose. "Want to bet?"

"That's enough, Melysah," he admonished.

She began walking backward. "For now. I'll see you all around, but hopefully not as much as I've seen today." She spun on her heels and disappeared beyond the garden.

Draevyn ran a hand through his hair. "I'm so sorry. I should have realized…"

I placed a hand on his calf. "Realized what?"

He landed on his knees before me. "Now that she knows about us, we'll be watched."

I reared back a little. "But why?"

"This is who she is. Her little games with me. They're what she lives for. If she can't have me, no one can."

"But I thought what happened between the both of you was history."

"It's history to me but not to her. She's never stopped pursuing me, no matter how often I've told her that I feel nothing for her." His eyes narrowed on the pathway. "There's only one sure way to get my feelings across."

My heart rate kicked when the words settled. "And what's that?"

Draevyn's face flashed with pure unguarded delight. "We present ourselves before the Bohiti at Guake'te."

# Chapter 24

Guake'te.

The bonding ceremony.

My thoughts were a mess of all things: excitement and fear and longing. I had to imagine that Guake'te was equivalent to a marriage ceremony in the Above World. And Draevyn mentioned it so casually, like he knew with his whole heart that I was his bondmate.

And I couldn't disagree with him.

I'd never felt for anyone else the way I felt for Draevyn Eliron. If falling in love with someone meant losing yourself in them so irrevocably, then I never wanted to be found.

My thoughts continued to distract me as Atlantians packed every inch of space, and the gentle buzz of their conversations permeated the room. Villagers from all over Atlantis checked in with a female named Iris just beyond the massive double doors. As they entered, the villagers clustered in groups, waiting their turn to speak with the King.

And the Heir.

I hadn't even known the throne room existed until Dad sent a letter requesting I meet him there for the town hall. I had to pick my mouth off the floor when my eyes landed on the very ornate, very elaborate wooden throne that sat on a dais at the head of the room—an intricate trident carved directly at its center. Dad had to ease me into the chair, some inner part of me protesting that I didn't belong in that seat. Roarvyn's voice growled in my mind, and my ass landed on the cushioned upholstery.

My spine remained taut and immobile beside Dad on the dais—my fingers drumming on the armrest of the wooden throne. I had no idea what to do or what to say. I remained a silent observer of all the Atlantians who came forward. Dad's hand came to rest on top of mine, settling my fidgeting without breaking his conversation with the man who'd come forward to complain about a sliver of land they felt was rightfully theirs.

"I'll have the appraiser sent immediately to assess the land divide."

"Please, Your Highness. It would be much appreciated. The only thing I want is to move on from this in peace. There's nothing as terrible as a feud with neighbors."

He smiled gently. "Understood. In the entryway, please find Iris. She'll be happy to schedule a time for you."

"Thank you, Your Highness," he said with a bow.

He'd heard every issue with a grace I knew I'd try to mimic for years to come without coming close: land disputes, trade negotiations, business agreements. We'd heard just about everything.

A human woman no older than thirty stepped forward with a scowl. Her eyes raked over me from head to toe before she bowed in greeting. When she rose, her eyes landed on Dad. "Your Highness, I've come to address the issue of the Atlantian humans and their permanent residence in the realm." The collective gasp in the room could be heard all the way in the outer gardens. I didn't think I could stiffen any further, but I did.

The smile faded from his face. "Why is there a question about the permanent residency of Atlantian humans?"

"Forgive me, Your Highness. There are rumors of a movement to get rid of us."

"Such rumors shouldn't be entertained," he said in a firm tone.

"And yet, they're entertained by many in the realm. Our families have been a part of Atlantis for centuries. This is our home." Her gaze shifted to me again. "While we are…honored that there is an Heir to the throne, many wonder if we'll be truly safe from the threats under the rule of the future Queen."

I'd never seen my father's face turn so red. "I will not hear of this."

The woman bowed again. "I mean no disrespect, Your Highness. I only meant to relay the rumors in the exact details. We worry about our future."

"You have nothing to worry about."

"Says you." The distinctly male voice carried from the back of the room. You could have heard a mouse fart for how silent the room went. The sea of people parted. A male Fae stepped forward, his steps sure, and his steely gaze held on Dad. "What she speaks is true. Every word." He glared at the human woman with such loathing that I pitied her. "We question whether we want the dilemma of the humans coming to Atlantis—whether we want any humans here at all. The Fae founded Atlantis. It should be for the Fae," he declared boldly.

Dad rose from his throne that resembled my own, yet smaller; his fists squeezed so tight his knuckles whitened. "I will not have anyone in this queendom question the will of the goddess."

The male's arms stretched wide. "What goddess, Your Highness? Where is Atabey? We only have our texts that mention her existence. She hasn't appeared in a millennia. At least I'm brave enough to say the quiet part out loud."

"I don't think that's bravery coming out of your mouth."

His meaty hand gestured over me where I perched on the throne. "And now we have this…Heir, raised among the humans. We deserve to know why. Because from where I'm standing, it sure looks like she's ill-qualified to lead a queendom of the Fae," he spat. My breathing accelerated—the male was the epitome of all the fears I'd held so deeply inside.

"Enough," Dad said, his hand slicing definitively through the air. "I will hear no more of this. Atlantis has been and will always be a safe haven for the humans."

The most sinister of smiles emerged on the male's face. "Yes, but if there's no Heir, then we have no more human coddlers on the throne."

Before I could register the threat, the male conjured metal through the open door of the throne room. I'd only heard of metal elementals briefly in my studies with Myles, but to witness it up close was another thing entirely. The metal came to him in the blink of an eye, forming into a small, thin arrow pointing straight at me. My eyes widened when he flicked his hand and sent the arrow through the air. Months and months of Dax's training thrummed through my body. I dodged to the right—the arrow knicking my upper arm. I instinctively conjured water from the fountains that ran the length of the room at a speed that equaled the male's. Frozen spikes formed before me in a blink, and I sent them careening toward the male exactly where Dax had taught me to kill a Water Fae. His eyes widened, and his mouth fell open when all three spikes lodged themselves through his head, mouth, and neck—the impact sending him to the ground. I hyperventilated as I watched the life slowly leave his body.

Silence.

Pure, motionless silence save for my rapid breaths filled the throne room.

A hand landed on my shoulder, Dad jostling me gently out of my stupor. "Sher, it's okay."

But it wasn't okay. I'd just killed a male. My body began to shake.

"Sher, listen to me. He would've killed you. You were simply defending yourself." I couldn't move my eyes from the male's body as it twitched with its last vestiges of life. In my periphery, I caught Dad gesturing to someone at my side. If I hadn't been in shock, I'd have known who it was by the tingling sensation in my chest. "Take her to her quarters."

Draevyn's arm came around my shoulders, gently guiding me down the steps of the dais on shaky legs and away from the male whose deep red blood seeped along the grout of the stone floor. The weight of stares bore down on me heavily as I left the room.

"Let that be a lesson to all who dare to doubt," I heard Dad say—his voice echoing off the walls of the throne room. "Asherah Delmar is the rightful Heir to the throne and is a Fae through and through. She'll be there for her people, both Fae and human. May her line forever reign over this realm."

DRAEVYN

# Chapter 25

The blood drained from Asherah's face as we climbed the steps to her quarters. Mayana's forehead creased with concern as we reached the landing, clearly not expecting us for another hour or so. Asherah's quick, uneven breaths and fidgeting hands were a clear indication that she wasn't dealing with this incident well. Her hands shook as she reached for the doorknob. I'd been tracking every step, every breath, every movement. To say the town hall hadn't gone the way we'd planned was an understatement.

Asherah entered her quarters in a daze, leaving the door open in her wake. As I passed, I leaned into Mayana's ear and murmured, "Do me a favor. No one comes through this door. Not the maids, not Atabey herself."

Mayana's charcoal-colored eyes widened. "And Cathan?"

I blew out a breath. "I doubt he'll come up here any time soon. But even him if you can."

Mayana's perfectly pleated braid swayed as she shook her head. "What happened?"

"Too long of a story to get into just now." My gaze drifted to the open door. "And she needs me. Just hold them off if you can."

"Yes, Commander."

I closed the door behind me with a deafening click, my steps carrying me to her bedroom, where I knew she would be. Sure enough, Asherah stood in the middle of her room, her slender arms folded and her stare fixed on the floor. My heart ached for her, knowing that she'd never taken someone's life, knowing that it was tearing her apart. The first kill was never the easiest. The motherfucker deserved to die for attempting to take her life. I didn't care if he was a fellow Atlantian. He threatened my future bonded. I should've been the one to take that asshole's life—to spare her the feelings that are likely gripping her soul at this very moment.

Oh, but how she had looked when she sent those spikes through the Fae's face. Confident. Measured. Lethal.

Beautiful.

My cock stiffened. What that said about me, I didn't know. I also didn't care. Asherah was magnificent. It took my Guardians years to develop the kind of fluidity I'd witnessed. She was—in short—extraordinary.

I carefully approached her, noticing the trembling in her shoulders. My arms slid around her, lending her the strength of my hold. It did very little to ease her shaking. "Take a deep breath, *nanichi*."

She blew out a measured breath. "I just killed a male," she croaked.

I rested my chin on her head, the strands of her brown hair tickling my skin. "It was self-defense. You did what you had to do."

"But did I?"

"Yes, Asherah. You had to. It was either you or him. Would you have preferred it to be you?"

"No," she whispered.

I turned her around, her eyes glistening with unshed tears. My thumb instinctively wiped one that had escaped down her cheek. "You have the heart of a warrior, one that has never been tested. You passed."

Her bottom lip began to wobble. "Then why do I feel like a failure?"

I stepped into her, cupping her face. "Because in that heart of a warrior is also the heart of someone with compassion and empathy. You are not only a Queen who's captured my heart but a Queen who will capture the hearts of her people when she stands and fights to protect them. Whether they see that now or later doesn't matter. I know it. Your father knows it. Dax and the entire damn guard know it."

Asherah closed her eyes, the tears streaming steadily down her face now. "Make me forget," she whispered.

Her request sent an instant jolt to my cock. My thumbs brushed against her damp cheekbones. "How should I make you forget, Asherah?"

Her mesmerizing eyes searched mine as she said, "Take me, Draevyn. Make me feel something else. Please."

I really should insist that the first time I bed her be something special, something romantic—with faelights flickering around the room and soft, soothing music, perhaps the scent of rose or jasmine permeating the air. But the way her hooded gaze held me captive let me know that what she needed from me right now was a distraction—a taking.

And I would deliver.

"Drop your scales, Asherah."

She took a step back, and I lost my damn breath when each scale slowly receded to reveal her exquisite body. Her emerald eyes glistened with the remnants of her tears, the lush sweetness of her lips parting as she revealed her slender shoulders and full breasts that fit perfectly in my able hands. The warm, sunkissed skin of her tight abdomen caused my length to push harder against my scales, begging for a hot, wet heat to plunge into. The light dusting of curls at the apex of her thighs was the perfect home it sought, with deliciously sculpted muscular thighs I needed wrapping around my head. My perfect, beautiful future bondmate. I couldn't wait to make her mine.

"Take me," she breathed.

That was all the invitation I needed. My scales dropped, and I relished in the way her gaze fixed on the evidence of how she aroused me. I waited no more.

I took her.

My lips reached hers, the salt of her tears spreading across my tongue as our kiss turned ravenous. The telltale pull in my solar plexus hummed to life, wanting me to take her and make her mine. Bonding ceremony be damned. If Asherah Delmar wanted me to make her forget, I would give her this.

We were a frenzy of touching, kissing, nibbling. Desperate kisses given and taken as we gripped for dear life onto one another. I gently pushed her to lay before me on the bed, her body completely bare for me as she crawled back. I could scarcely breathe seeing her on display like this for me—rose-colored nipples tightening and ready to be sucked and lashed and licked. The silken swell of her breasts heaved as she labored to steady her breath. I nearly lost control when Asherah's beautiful, heated gaze locked on mine just as she parted those lovely legs—her pussy already glistening and ready for me. A primal instinct took over my body. No one. No one would ever take her away. She was *mine*.

Kneeling at the altar of Asherah's parted legs, my tongue licked a line on the inside of her knee and ventured down her delicious thighs—the lines of muscle had my cock aching with need. I placed soft, chaste kisses along the way until I reached what I could no longer resist. I sought out those beautiful blue eyes that mesmerized me, pleading for permission.

"Please," she begged, biting her luscious bottom lip.

I threw her legs over my bare shoulders, licking the petal soft folds of her soaking slit. She tasted of sweetness. Perfection.

*Mine.*

I sucked her tight, swollen bud into my mouth, and my eyes nearly rolled back in my head when she jerked beneath me, moaning my name. My hand splayed against her stomach, holding her to the bed. I was desperate to hear that fucking moan again. My tongue swirled endlessly around her clit, and a deep sense of satisfaction arose when her fingers combed through my hair, gripping me to her sex. My control was completely decimated; my hips thrust into the soft bedding, the friction giving little relief for what my cock desperately wanted. I speared my tongue through her opening, my length aching to be inside her. Her little breaths came up short, and her legs began to tremble. Knowing I was so close to summoning her ultimate pleasure, I devoured her and placed my thumb on her swollen bud to bring her to release. Her hips bucked against my face as her climax tore through her body.

"Draevyn. Get inside me. Now," she breathed.

I could feel the smirk emerge on my face. "Is that a command, my Queen?"

Her answering tug underneath my arms, pulling me above her, was answer enough. I reached down and gave a few strokes on my aching length before I ran the throbbing head through her slit, coating myself with her desire. With my gaze held on hers, I pushed the head of my aching cock into her tight pussy. We gasped in unison as I thrust my hips forward and sank into her wet heat. Of all the times I envisioned this moment—all the times I'd finished myself at the mere thought of burying myself inside her—it didn't compare to the reality. The warm center of her welcomed me, and my body felt like it had finally come home.

To her.

To my Asherah.

Her delicate hands dug into the muscles of my ass, and she pushed me further into her. I could no longer hold back. I slammed into her, Asherah's body arcing into mine. My hands landed on the headboard above her, my hips snapping forward, thrusting harder, her tight walls clenching around my length. Her smooth legs wrapped around my hips—her pert breasts jumping in rhythm with my thrusts.

She was pure perfection.

"You take my cock so beautifully, my Queen." I couldn't hold back my groan when the muscles of her sheath fluttered around my cock. "Fuck. You're so close. Come with me, Asherah."

My arms slid behind her back, lifting her, her nipples like pebbles against my chest as I thrust into her over and over and over. Her hips met mine in a perfect rhythm of bliss. I steadied her with one hand and reached for her clit circling it.

"Draevyn," she cried as she bucked in my lap.

And that was my undoing.

Asherah sent me over the edge, and my release spilled inside her warm heat. I felt it then, that inexplicable, undeniable connection to her. And as the last drips of my cum shot into her core, my soul whispered, '*My mate. My mate. My mate.*'

*Mine.*

We panted into long, lazy kisses, my hips slowly rolling—riding the last crests of our waves of pleasure. With her arms held tightly around my neck, we both sank into the bed—limbs exhausted, minds muddled. We said nothing further. Didn't need to. We just held each other until the afternoon light dimmed and the stars breached the sky. Asherah's eyes finally drooped with the exhaustion of the day. And as she fell asleep in my arms, I took pleasure in her steady breaths and the knowledge that she would officially be my bondmate.

One day.

# Chapter 26

My eyelids slowly opened to a crackling fire in the fireplace just beyond the bed, where we lay under my white fluffy duvet. Draevyn's skin warmed mine as his heart beat against my ear. I gathered he must have gotten up at some point to light the fire, the warm air blanketing the room a welcome feel against my naked body. My fingers began tracing circles across the firm dips of muscle on his chest. I was content to lie there forever and never face the world beyond the bedroom door again—a world filled with what I'd done and what I must continue to do. A heavy sigh escaped my lips.

"What's wrong, *nanichi*?" he murmured, the vibrations of his deep voice tickling my ear.

I draped my leg across his hips, positioning myself on top of him, my chin coming to rest upon his firm chest. His hooded gaze did things.

Really delicious things.

"I don't want to leave the room," I confessed.

Draevyn chuckled as he tucked a wayward strand of hair behind my tipped ear. "I'm afraid we must leave the bedroom if you are to rule the queendom."

"I don't want to rule the queendom."

"I know you don't mean that."

I sighed. "I don't mean that."

"We're going to need to work on your mental toughness."

My brows dipped. "Are you saying I'm not mentally tough?"

"You were never taught to mentally prepare yourself to take a life in self-defense."

"No. They failed to teach that in marine biology."

"Yes, they wouldn't need to." Draevyn's hands went under my arms as he dragged me up his body—a chaste kiss rewarding my journey. "But I digress. There's an even more important reason to leave the room."

Another kiss. "Even more important than ruling the queendom?"

The tips of his rough fingers traced lazily up and down my spine, and my skin pebbled. "We need to present ourselves at Guake'te."

His aqua-green eyes sharpened on me. I'd had lovers in the past, none that were too memorable. They were simply there to scratch an itch. But Draevyn was something entirely different. There was no denying what I felt when we came together as one—the inexplicable pull I felt in my chest, almost like a tether that was barely there before, that had strengthened instantly. I didn't know how this male I'd only met a few months ago, who seemed so familiar to my soul in so many ways, managed to crawl into my heart. But he did.

"I felt it," I admitted in a whisper.

He rolled on top of me, his lips claiming mine as I

gripped the long strands of his hair. He pulled back a little, and his smile was so bright, it was blinding. "Thank Atabey. I dreaded it was just me." He bent down, pressing his soft lips between my breasts right where I could've sworn I felt the tether. "It's right here, isn't it?" he asked. I could only nod as he coasted his lips to capture my pebbled nipple in his warm mouth. His masterful tongue swirled around the tip, his lips wrapping around the stiff peak and sucking it vigorously, causing my core to tighten. A moan escaped my lips, and he hummed in delight against my breast. "I live for that sound you make," he said as he captured the other rosy bud, giving it the same mind-blowing treatment. I rocked my hips against him, desperate for the friction. His amused gaze lifted to me with a smirk. "Patience, my Queen."

Draevyn rose to kneel between my legs, his rough hands coming to my knees and pushing them apart—exposing me to him. I bit my lip at his appraisal—his eyes worshiping me, devouring me. "Your pussy is already wet for me, Asherah." He reached down, sliding a finger through my desire till he reached the top. His deliciously skilled thumb circled my sensitive bud and continued its assault as if possessed. Swirl after swirl caused my composure to slip. And I didn't care that I was wild with lust and need. I lost myself to him—his ministrations sending me into madness.

"Oh my God," I called as my legs began to twitch.

"Yes, Asherah. Today, I am your god. And I command you to come for me."

Draevyn's fingers thrust inside me, stretching me, as his thumb tortured me into ecstasy. My release came as he curled his finger on the most sensitive spot. No shame could keep me from grabbing his arm and grinding against him.

"More," I begged.

He removed his hand from my core, and I whimpered at the absence. But absence suddenly turned into anticipation.

Draevyn lifted my legs to rest on his shoulders and lined his straining erection up to my throbbing center—the thick tip pushing inside me. "Your wish is my command."

His hips pitched forward and he was deep inside me. I screamed in ecstasy at the intrusion. His considerable girth stretched me wide to the point of pain, but the pleasure that followed erased the sting. His hips pistoned into me as his tongue swirled on the inside of my ankle. My fingers dug into the soft cotton sheets to steady myself through the delectable pounding. His fingers pressed into my hips as he lifted them to hit the most delicious spot. "You are mine, Asherah," he growled. "My bonded. My mate. *Mine*. Say it."

"Yours. I'm yours," I cried.

He circled my clit again, and I shuddered around him. With two quick thrusts, he came with the most toe-curling groan. I'd never tire of watching him lose himself. It was my new addiction.

The tether to him pulled, and we gasped—his strong body collapsing beside me and his lips claiming mine most sensually. We lay there staring at one another with our heads digging into our cushy white pillows. I'd never tire of the adoration I saw there. I'd never thought anyone would look at me that way.

"I can't wait to start our forever," he whispered.

The smile that emerged on my face was so at odds with the internal conflict awaiting within. "Me too." But my gaze briefly shifted to the bedroom door, where the weight of the world hovered—waiting for us to emerge.

But not yet.
    Not yet.

# Chapter 27

Knock at the bedroom door pulled me
from my sleep, the grogginess encouraging me to
fall back asleep against the hard chest I slept upon.

"Um...Your Highness?" Reneah called in a
sing-song voice from the other side of the door.
"You'll be late for your lesson if you don't wake
up. And I have it on good authority that Myles gets
very moody if everything doesn't happen according to schedule."

I groaned and lifted my head to the amused face
of my Guardian, his sleepy eyes at half-mast. My
gaze traveled down his body, and I found his eyes
weren't the only thing at half-mast. "I'm up," I
called.

"So am I," Draevyn murmured. He pulled me
fully on top of him.

I groaned. "Not helping."

"I heard all of that!" Reneah called. "Ugh. I'll be in your father's quarters preparing for his arrival. Please don't be late!" A few moments later, we heard the front door close.

Draevyn brushed my hair back from my face with a smile that could melt metal. "Good morning."

It was truly unfair that he had that mouth-watering chiseled chin and long velvety hair and looked like a god. And was so incredibly naked underneath me. "Morning."

"I want to stay here all day," he confessed as he pushed his hardening length into my belly.

I bit my lower lip. "Me too."

He leaned up and kissed me ever so gently, his warm lips lightly pressing into mine. "Reneah's not wrong."

"About?" Another kiss stolen.

"Myles. He does get moody when people aren't on time."

I sighed against his lips. "Well, you're not giving his moodiness a reason to win here, are you?" I shifted my hips, pressing into him.

The most delicious moan sounded from the back of his throat as his hands came to still my hips. "I will take you in every way possible. But later. I promised Dax I wouldn't let our relationship interfere with your duties. Time to get up." He smacked me on the ass, causing me to yelp, and I reluctantly got into motion.

Within thirty minutes, I hurried down the hallway to my classroom, Draevyn scurrying behind me to keep up. My heart sank into my stomach when we reached the doorway. Kane Ruema—lap dog extraordinaire—stood sentry just outside my classroom.

"This can't be good," Draevyn murmured.

With each step, Kane's evil smile grew on his face.

"Ah. If it isn't the happy couple come to grace us with their presence."

"What's this about, Ruema?" Draevyn bit out.

He peeled his creepy gaze away from me. "I've come to relieve you. Dax has summoned you. Something urgent."

Draevyn's forehead creased. "What's it about?"

Kane lifted a shoulder in a lazy shrug. "How am I supposed to know? That's none of my business."

Draevyn sighed, turning to me. "I'll be back before you're done with your lesson." He squeezed my arm and strode down the hall. My eyes held to his retreating form, an uneasy feeling spreading throughout my body.

"Don't worry, Eliron," Kane called after him. "I'll take great care of her."

I wheeled around to face Kane. I could feel the heat rising off my head as that infuriating smirk returned. "I don't think I'll be needing your care."

"That's okay. I wasn't really going to protect you anyway. Those fancy words were just for show." I reared back as he leaned into my ear, his hot breath against the shell of my ear, causing me to cringe. "Have fun in your...lesson." Glaring at me indignantly, he pulled back and resumed his stance by the doorway.

I'd had about enough of this asshole. I pushed him in his chest, his back slamming into the wall. "Stay away from me."

His mocking laughter carried after me as I dashed into the classroom, but my stomach plummeted further.

"You're late," Melysah said from the desk at the head of the classroom, her arms folded against her scaled middle.

My fingernails bit into my palms as I clenched my fists. "What are you doing here?"

Melysah's pale blonde brow lifted. "Teaching, if one would get here on time. Sit."

I swiftly took my usual chair, glaring at her. "Where is Myles?"

"Obviously not here."

A sense of uneasiness cemented itself inside. "Seems a little coincidental; Draevyn and Myles, gone at exactly the same time?"

Without taking her gaze off me, Melysah lifted her delicate hand and flicked her wrist. The door slammed shut with a loud thud—the bookshelves behind me rattling from the impact. "You will learn to curve your temper and respect me."

"In my world, respect is earned."

"This isn't your world, Asherah."

"The fuck it's not."

"Language."

"Manners."

Melysah stood leaning on the desk, her frigid eyes boring into me. "You're an arrogant little thing, aren't you?"

"I don't know about arrogant, but I'm certainly not going to put up with your shit."

It was then that I saw it, the fire that brimmed in Melysah's irises. She held up her hand, and a deafening crack sounded from the classroom door. My eyes went wide as a solid wall of ice formed within the doorjamb. With every instinct screaming for me to run, I leapt from my chair, but was immediately thrown back when a thick chain of ice wrapped around my torso—the tail ends winding tightly around my wrists and binding me to the chair. "What do you think you're doing?" I bellowed, part in anger and part in genuine fear.

"What? Scared of a little ice, Princess? You're expected to rule this queendom, yet you have no idea how to melt it and save yourself? Do you think you're ready because you can form a few ice daggers and send them through a Fae male's face? You silly, little amateur." Melysah casually strolled in front of my desk. She leaned in and inhaled. "Silly little slut, too, from the smell of it. Draevyn's scent is all over you."

It was my turn to smirk. "Jealous?"

Melysah's face flushed. "We're going to play a little game, you and I."

"That's funny. I'm not in the mood for games right now."

I gasped when Melysah sprung forward, her fingers painfully digging into my cheeks. She procured a tiny bottle with a clear liquid I hadn't noticed was sitting in her hand. I struggled against her hold as she uncorked the little bottle with her thumb and poured it into my mouth—the liquid burning a path down my throat like the most potent whiskey and causing me to gasp for air. She placed the empty bottle on the desk and watched with sick satisfaction as my scales suddenly retreated from my body. The ice chains bit into my naked skin. Her severe gaze appraised me from the brown hair of my head to my bare toes. "I really don't get what he sees in you. Pathetic." My heart kicked in my chest. I was completely beholden to this mad woman, and I didn't know what she was capable of.

But I was about to find out.

Melysah breathed out an annoyed sigh. "I'm going to quiz you on your Atlantian knowledge," she continued, her lip curling in disgust as her gaze roamed over my naked form, "and you're going to tell me the answer." She came around my desk to stand at my side. "We're only covering Atlantis, the very queendom you're intended to rule over." She mockingly patted my cheek. "This should be easy for you…Your Highness." She twirled and strode toward the front of the room. "Question number one. Who was the first Queen of Atlantis?"

"Atabay."

Melysah's thin lips pulled up in a grin. "Wrong." She lifted her hand—a thin pin of ice forming—and shot the pin forward. The sharp tip pierced the top of my foot. Before the pain could register, Melysah sent water down my throat, stifling my screams; my Water Fae form immediately fought to be released, but it was useless against whatever potion she gave me. "The first Queen of Atlantis was Siseree the Chosen. Let's try again. Shall we?"

The water exited my throat, and I gulped a breath. "You are in so much trouble."

"Because I'm threatening their precious little Princess? What are you going to do, Asherah? Run and tell them? Can't handle this female-to-female, I suppose. Seems to be a family trait."

I saw red as I straightened my spine. "Next. Question."

Melysah tilted her head. "Huh. Well, perhaps I'm wrong. We'll find out, won't we?" She clasped her hands behind her back. "Who was the first Queen to negotiate a treaty with Airelandia?"

"Queen Huelema."

"Wrong." I cried out as Melysah sent the next pin into my other foot. "Queen Huelema negotiated the treaty with Earthos. Not Airelandia."

And so it continued for the better part of a half-hour—Melysah peppered me with her questions. With each one, I fought to answer, fought to remember everything I'd learned with Myles or Roarvyn. Even when I knew the answer, it was a struggle to get the answers past my lips—the pain becoming too much to bear. Rivers of sweat dripped profusely from my brow and down my neck despite the cold, biting freeze of my chains, and my head lolled. Nearly eleven pins stuck through various spots in my feet. The pain throbbed down to my bones.

"Final question." Melysah's pearl-polished fingertips dug into my cheeks as she squeezed tightly. She leaned in within an inch of my face—an evil glint shining in her pale blue eyes. "I'll remove every one of those pins in your pretty little feet if you can answer this one question. It will all be over."

I spit in her face. "Fuck off."

Melysah wiped the phlegm from her cheek and slapped me. Hard. That slap rang loudly in my ears—my cheek throbbing, the muscles in my neck pulling as my head whipped to the side. "You little wench."

I slowly pulled my head back…and smirked. "I'm ready for my question," I croaked.

Melysah's nostrils flared. "Whose line is the *rightful* line to the throne of Atlantis?"

Roarvyn's lesson came roaring back. I refused to utter the name Melysah wanted and opted for the truth. "Neleah Delmar." A pin shot through my calf. I stifled a cry in my throat despite my wince and breathed through the pain.

Melysah's glare was one of pure, unguarded evil. "I'll keep asking the question until you get it right. So, you'd better get it right. Whose line is the rightful line to the throne of Atlantis?"

"Neleah Delmar."

Another pin. The other calf. More pain.

Blinking stars blanketed my vision. I closed my eyes to ebb the tide. It wasn't until my hair was pulled and my scalp burned that my eyes flew open—Melysah's beet-red face inches from mine.

"Whose line is the rightful line to the throne of Atlantis?" Melysah seethed. "Say my line, Asherah. Say it!"

I didn't care anymore. Even though it felt like the gravest betrayal, I didn't care if I uttered Behuko's name. I wanted this to be over.

But something within me remained resilient. I lifted my chin, my mouth sneering. "Neleah Delmar," I whispered.

Melysah began to breathe heavily and screamed in my face—flecks of spit hitting my face as she bellowed, "It's Behuko Velafyn! Behuko Velafyn is the rightful line to the throne, you entitled little bitch. And I will have my crown!"

My head snapped forward as she released the grip on my hair and stomped toward the exit, shattering the wall of ice with a flick. The scattered pieces slid across the stone floor. Before Melysah opened the door, she turned and flicked her wrist. All the pins of ice shot out of my feet and calves at once, and I screamed in excruciating pain.

Melysah folded her hands primly in front of her waist. "You failed today, Asherah Delmar. I'll leave those ice chains around you until they melt or until you figure out how to melt them yourself. The potion will wear off within the hour. Nevertheless, it'll give your feet time to heal. Draevyn won't be back to find you. He's been mysteriously called home. And your father is in the Above World. Myles, along with him. You're all alone—your first true test. Let us see if you can keep this secret lesson between us. Let us see if you're female enough to keep this all in the family." A moment later, she threw open the door and slammed it behind her. And despite the pain, I treasured the silence.

# Chapter 28

Melysah had spoken true. It took nearly an hour for whatever potion she poured down my throat to wear off, and when my scales returned, I let out a sigh of warm relief as it protected me from my melting chains of ice. It turns out I was pretty good at turning ice into water, a lesson I learned fairly quickly as the chains fell to the floor in a melted slush. Draevyn had swum home immediately after receiving the urgent message. While his family had been happy to see him, they had informed him that they'd never summoned him. That's the message that appeared across my tablet that evening in his signature green ink, along with his decision to stay the extra day to spend time with his family. I'd shifted in my bed, my feet still slightly aching, as I read his promise to return tomorrow afternoon.

And with Mayana assigned to the outposts, that left none other than Kane Ruema guarding my quarters.

I wanted to scream.

I couldn't take the rising tension anymore. The deep-seated feeling of loneliness, the looming prospect of failure, the idea that I'd have to watch my back even more now that Melysah had gone full psycho, and her lapdog standing guard just outside my door. I refused to tell the others what happened. I refused to cower to that wench. I could handle her, female-to-female.

For the time being, though, all I wanted to do was fall into a familiar comfort, which is why I found myself standing in front of the Fae Flings Bookstore in Borike'n, with the villagers exchanging pleasantries as they purchased their produce from the corner store, the smell of freshly baked bread from the bakery drifting across the street to where I stood. With my heavy wool coat wrapped snuggly around me, I stepped into the store—a grin pulling at my lips as the tiny bell above my head gave a jingle. This wasn't just any bookstore. It was a fantastic concept, really. Sure, there were mysteries, fantasies—books that were all things paranormal. But if it didn't have romance, it wasn't welcome at Fae Flings. It made me want to run to the Above World and open a store just like it, but then I remembered that there wouldn't be a future for me in the Above World. There wouldn't be an Above World at all. Not until the ice age passed.

The smell of freshly roasted coffee and sugar-sweet pastries hung in the air as I perused the shelves lining the quaint bookshop. Reneah, like me, shared a love of all things romance books. She mistakenly let slip about her frequent visits to the establishment. Reneah offered to accompany me anytime I'd like, but with the sudden urge to escape the palace and Reneah nowhere to be found, I decided to go on a little solo adventure. It turns out that the unguarded door we'd snuck out of to attend the foam party comes in handy in a pinch, especially when you give an asshole guard the slip as he's got his back to the door he's supposed to be guarding.

I gripped the hood of my cloak tighter to my head, chancing a glance around the room. As I suspected, the place was empty at this time of day, with it being mid-week and the university classes in session. My refusal to go to another class while Myles was away had nothing to do with Melysah and everything to do with the fact that I was a grown-ass female and needed a mental health day. At least, that's what I'd told myself. After all, there's no better therapy than book therapy.

Impressed by the variety—the store featuring both Fae authors and human authors—I selected a shifter romance I had yet to read before my abrupt departure from The Keys and padded toward the checkout counter. I couldn't help but notice the various drinks available; their infamous Lick It Lattes and Spankuccinos—not to be confused with their Spunkuccinos—were just a few of the popular favorites I'd heard about. Their coffees ranged from Suck It Light Roast, Medium Build Roast, and my favorite, Dirty After Dark Roast. The small sample Reneah had kept in my quarters served as my only introduction to the stuff, and I'd developed a lowkey craving for it.

The middle-aged woman behind the counter greeted me with a soft smile—her light brown hair pulled in a tight ponytail at the back of her head. "Would you like a beverage with your book?"

"Dirty After Dark Roast, please."

"Perfect." She waved a hand in front of a glass sphere on the counter. It brightened to a light blue. "And which surname will this be charged to?"

Right. Money.

I'd forgotten how currency worked in Atlantis. The glass sphere magically cataloged each house's monetary holdings. No credit cards or cash were needed. The currency elementals handled the books of all Atlantians. Still, a surname was required to make a purchase, and the sphere would either burn bright with the correct surname or dim completely if the wrong one was provided. My cover was about to be blown. "Delmar," I whispered.

The woman leaned in. "I'm sorry. I didn't catch that. What name was it?"

I quickly twisted around to make sure I was the only one around and cleared my throat. "Delmar," I said a little higher this time.

The woman's back went ramrod straight, her eyes bulging. "You're not…are you?"

I pulled her cloak a little tighter with a wince. "I am. And if it's alright with you, I'd like to keep my presence here quiet so I can be in peace. Just for a bit."

The woman's face brightened. "No worries, Your Highness. Your secret is safe with me," she said with a wink. With a flick of her wrist, she murmured my surname under her breath, and the glass sphere burned bright blue.

I breathed out slowly, my shoulders sagging. "Thank you."

The woman pushed the crisp, new shifter book across the counter. "Of course. My name is Ezra. I'm the owner of this naughty establishment," she beamed. "I think you'll find the seating in the back room to be the most discreet. It's where we send our customers who don't want to be disturbed, so they can be comfortable during their visit. I'll get your coffee ready for you and bring it right over. Cream and sugar?"

"Please. And thank you." I picked up my new book and padded to the quiet back room, where the warmth from the fireplace enveloped me, and more bookshelves lined the walls. With the wainscoting wrapping around the room, it felt more like a home than a bookstore. Two sets of wingback chairs bracketed small tables in front of two arching windows, the bright light shining through and providing plenty of reading light.

As I pulled the chair back, my steps faltered, and my brows furrowed. An outstretched foot with a male-looking shoe rested on the floor before the other table. I found it curious that a male would seek refuge in a romance bookshop but to each their own. I admired any male who embraced the romance genre. While I wouldn't dare to blow my cover, I was fascinated to see who it was, but his cloak made it impossible to see his face. Apparently, I wasn't the only one who wished to remain unseen. I respected his right to privacy and took the seat facing away from him.

Minutes into the first chapter of my shifter romance, the sound of a rattling cup on a saucer captured my attention. Ezra placed my coffee on the shiny wooden table with a cheery smile. "Here you go, Your Highness," she whispered with a quick glance to the neighboring table. "That is a wonderful book. I just finished it last week."

"Seems really great so far," I agreed.

"I'm sure you'll love it. I'll leave you to it. Let me know if you need anything else." She turned on her heel out of the room.

I couldn't remember the last time I'd enjoyed a quiet afternoon just reading. The fire crackling in the fireplace seemed to be the only peaceful, soothing sound as I delved into chapter after chapter—the rest of the world fading away around me. It was why, when my eyes absorbed every word of chapter fifty-five and the heroine finally escaped the secret lair of werewolves, I failed to notice the male behind me rising from his seat. It would take several seconds longer before I noticed him standing beside my table. My eyes left my book and scanned the perfectly polished shoes, the perfectly pressed trousers, and the button-down shirt, all the way to the face that regarded me with curiosity: the one belonging to Lux Nacan, Prince of Corenathia.

My book dropped on the table with a thud. "What are you doing here?" I whispered hissed.

"I would ask you the same thing," Lux said with no lack of amusement. He reached for my book. "It appears I have my answer, though."

I snatched the book back, glaring at him. "I thought this would be a safe place to relax and get away."

"It is."

"Then why are you here?"

"Because it's a safe place to relax and get away."

We regarded each other like two opponents sizing one another before a match. A tinge of unease crawled up my spine as I glared up at him from where I sat, feeling like he had the high ground.

"Everything okay over here?" Ezra interrupted, her gaze bouncing between us.

Lux turned toward her, his expression softening. "Everything's fine, Ezra."

She placed a comforting hand on his arm, her brows knitting. "You're sure, Your Highness?"

My mouth parted.

"Of course. I was just about to keep the Princess company. Another Dirty After Dark Roast would be great." He twisted around to me. "If that's okay with you?"

I wanted to say *hell no*, but I realized there was a budding curiosity I couldn't deny. What was the Prince of Corenathia doing in a romance bookshop in Borike'n in the middle of the day?

He was likely asking the same question about me.

My gaze shifted to Ezra. "Make that two."

"On my tab, please," Lux insisted. "Thank you, Ezra."

She pulled a velvet curtain across the doorway I hadn't noticed upon entering as Lux slowly slid into the chair across from me, his cautious gaze never leaving mine. A book poked out of the inner pocket of his cloak. I flicked my head toward it. "I think it's only fair you show me what you're reading."

A subtle blush crept across his face before he reached into his pocket, retrieving the book. He slid it across the table, and my eyes went wide. "Midnight Dragons? But this is a why choose romance."

His face reddened further. "I'm aware."

"But you're…"

"A male. Last time I checked."

I scoffed. "I know you're a male."

"But you're welcome to confirm—"

"I will not."

A shrug. "Didn't think so, but it was worth a shot."

It was my turn to blush. I returned my attention to his book. "This is one of my favorites."

Lux perked up at that. "Is it now? What do you like about it?" he asked, his penetrating gaze making my stomach flip. I fell silent as Lux regarded me, his chin resting on his hand with an elbow upon the chair rest. "Oh, come on now. This is a safe space. Is it the idea of having multiple men at your mercy? Or is it the M-M-F-M-M that does it for you?"

I straightened my spine and lifted my chin. "Both."

The corners of his full lips lifted. "Interesting."

The tell-tale clattering of coffee cups alerted us to Ezra's approach. We remained staring at each other as she placed the cups before us and exited just as quickly.

Lux reached for his cup, taking a long sip. "So, what classes are you missing today, Princess?"

"None," I replied, picking at a thread on my cloak. "Myles is out of town. I decided I didn't want to have sessions with Melysah."

"Ah. Melysah."

My head snapped up. "Are the two of you acquainted?" I asked.

"Acquainted," he said, face unreadable. "I know more of Melysah than I care to know, from her head down to her perfectly polished toes."

I winced, taking a sip of my delicious coffee. "Maybe I don't need to know." I decided to change the subject. "What classes are you missing?"

He raked his fingers through his fire-red hair. "Intro to Corenathia."

"I would think you could teach the class yourself."

He let loose a charming chuckle. "That's exactly why I'm here. Professor Wyles and I have an understanding; he keeps me informed of the tests I need to take. Additionally, I must answer any questions about life in Corenathia. For some reason, the fool has an interest in my realm." I held back my surprise at the veiled negativity of that statement. "I come here to have a little free time of my own," he continued, "I try and blend in like a normal Fae, giving me just a little glimpse of what it's like to be unknown. It's a win–win for everyone."

I felt a pang of sympathy for him. It was the very reason I sought refuge in the back room of the bookshop; I just wanted a little slice of normal again. "I get it."

Lux tilted his head back and forth in introspection. "Yes, but at least you know what it's like to be normal. At least…your parents had the sense to send you to the Above World to grow up. That must have been freeing compared to the confines of Atlantis."

My lips pursed. "I never thought of it that way."

"They cared."

"And your mother doesn't?" The question slipped unbidden from my lips.

"No," he answered through a tightly clenched jaw.

"Hmm. Touchy subject?"

"You have no idea."

"Enlighten me."

Lux leaned forward, resting his arms on the table, his mouth tightening. "I meant what I said when we first met, Asherah. Things aren't always as they seem. Both of us were raised differently. There are rights I could never dream of having in Corenathia that I enjoy here in Atlantis. I very much value my freedoms here."

I couldn't help but to prod further. "Do you plan to stay here?"

His shoulders sagged. "I wish I could, but I can't." He seemed to check himself and gestured around the room. "So, I'll take my freedoms where I can."

"I'm sorry." I lowered my gaze to the table. "I'm sorry. I didn't…I just wanted to understand."

Lux's hand entered my line of vision, resting upon mine. "It's okay, Asherah. Really." I looked up and felt the warmth of his gaze. "It's nice to spend time with someone other than myself."

I gave him a genuine smile. "I suppose it is."

Lux's gaze held where his hand rested upon mine, his brow furrowing. He turned over my wrist and observed my elemental mark. With his other hand, he traced the tiny circle that had set my mark apart from my mother's. "That is so curious. It's different from Queen Sessi's."

My brows lifted. "Your mother has the same?"

"All the Queens do." His eyes narrowed as he gave the circle another rotation with this fingertip—his fingers much smoother than Draevyn's. "But yours has a dot. That's puzzling."

"You think it means something?"

"It must. Atabay's marks are very intentional."

I pulled my hand back to my lap, feeling suddenly uncomfortable. "And you'll tell your mother?"

Lux's jaw went tight. "No, Asherah. I will not."

"I'm sorry. It's just that…you're a Fire Fae."

"I know what I am, but I'm capable of keeping my own secrets. You don't have to worry. Not even my mother's spies know of my visits to Fae Flings. I've become somewhat of an expert at keeping my comings and goings from their traitorous lips." His fingers drummed on the table as he continued staring at the place where my hand had disappeared underneath the table. "Have you looked into it at all?"

I shook my head, my thumb rubbing at the mark. "I honestly haven't thought about it."

"You should. I'd be happy to help."

I debated whether I should agree to meet my enemy Prince again. It wasn't the best idea, but sitting in the bookstore sipping coffee in solitude did things to one's mental faculties. "Sure. That would be great."

Lux reared back. "For real?"

"For real. You'll have to let me know when. I won't always be free like this. Just reach out to Reneah, my chambermaid. My friend. She'll let me know."

His eyes lit up as he rose from his chair and placed his

book back in his pocket. "Sounds like a plan. I'll see you around, Ash."

"Same. Enjoy your book."

He winked. "I always do."

I managed to sneak back into the castle undetected—the sound of my silk-slippered feet ascending the stone steps that led to my quarters barely ricocheted off the palace walls. When I turned down the hallway, I almost breathed a sigh of relief, but I lost that breath as I stopped in my tracks.

"You fucking brat. Do you have any idea how much trouble I'm going to be in?" Kane seethed through his teeth, his face burning scarlet. "I was told to escort you to your lesson. Where the hell have you been?"

I crossed my arms, holding my book tightly to my chest. "I don't believe I owe you an explanation."

The veins in Kane's neck throbbed. "You don't believe you owe me an explanation?"

"No."

His gaze shifted to the book I held tightly to my chest. He stormed forward, snatched it out of my grasp, and began reading the back of the book.

"Follow Ella and her four dragon shifter men," he spat the words through gritted teeth, shoving the book back at me. "A smutty shifter book. This is what you ditched your lesson for, huh? Does the throne of Atlantis mean nothing to you? You'd rather ditch learning about your people to read book porn?"

Anger spiraled in the pit of my stomach. "How dare you!"

Before I could register his movement, Kane slammed me up against the wall. I winced from the impact as his fingers dug into my throat. Real genuine fear snaked down my spine. For some foolish reason, I'd never registered Kane as a threat, but as he glared at me with pure loathing, I knew I'd made a grave mistake.

"You little entitled bitch. You come to Atlantis all high and mighty like our people owe you something. Like we should bow down to you. Yet, you wear no crown. You have no power." He leaned in closer, his hot breath tickling against my ear, causing me to cringe. "You will never be Queen, and I'll enjoy every minute watching you try." He released my throat, and I slid down the wall, gasping for air. "You can guard your damn self," he bit out as he descended the stairs, leaving me on the floor.

I leaned my head back against the wall, my breaths steadying and his words wedging themselves in my mind. I didn't want anything he said to cement itself.

But it did.

When did all of the drama end? Melysah's outward hatred for my existence seemed to have no end—constantly looking over the shoulder to make sure she or her lapdog didn't accost me. It was exhausting.

In truth, I understood Kane's departure left me vulnerable, but I'd rather be vulnerable than at his mercy. I picked myself off the floor and entered my quarters, locking the door behind me.

The tears started to fall a second later.

The door to my quarters opened a few hours later. By then, my tears had stopped flowing, but the puffiness around my eyes couldn't be helped. Based on the way Draevyn's smile fell when he took in my appearance as I lay on the living room sofa with a throw covering me, I knew I wasn't fooling anybody today—least of all him.

I don't know why I started tearing up again at the sight of him standing in my doorway. Maybe it was the feeling of loneliness welling up inside me. Perhaps it was those damn feelings of not being good enough to lead this queendom despite the encouragement of those around me. The incident in the throne room. Melysah and her fucking lessons. Kane Asshat Ruema.

Take your pick.

But as the warmth of Draevyn's arms encompassed me, I just let them fall again. And I was grateful that he was there to catch them.

When I was finally able to catch my breath, I reached for a tissue on the coffee table and blew my nose in the most unattractive way. "I'm sorry. I didn't mean to break down like that," I breathed.

A slight grin pulled at his lips as he fetched the trashcan for my snotty tissue. Ever the knight in shining armor, this one. "Do you want to tell me why you're crying?" he finally asked.

And so I told him. Every last detail. Melysah's teaching methods, her remarks about Behuko, and her quest for the throne. Kane.

And I had the common sense to stop when I noticed his face growing red after informing him of the incident with Kane in the hallway. Gone was the Draevyn who'd dried my tears. He was the Commander now. "I'll kill them both with my bare fucking hands."

I shook my head. "You can't."

"I can."

"I mean, I know you can, but there's something bigger happening here. Can't you see? The Akani, Melysah's quest for the throne, Kane doing her bidding. We go after any of them, and we lose a chance to study the game."

His eyes searched mine as his mouth hung open slightly—my words settling in. "I'm getting some wine. Would you like some?"

Wine sounded great right about now. "Sure."

Draevyn rose from the couch, pouring the thick, burgundy liquid into two crystal glasses that sat on top of a charming bar cart against the wall of the darkened living room. His worried expression was unmoving as he handed me my glass. "They can't keep coming after you like this: game or no game. And you're right; there *is* something bigger going on, something I can't hide from Dax. Or your father. I need to summon them, Asherah. We'll need their help. We can't do it on our own."

I held his gaze for a long moment, his eyes imploring me before my head dipped in a nod. "I trust you."

He blew out a breath. "I'll ask them to come to your quarters."

With the message sent to meet us in my quarters, he seemed more relaxed, his thumb tracing the intricate patterns on his etched wine glass as we waited for them to arrive. "You know, you're allowed to take a break, Asherah."

A wince came across my face. "Am I, though?" Kane's words churned over in my head.

Draevyn turned fully toward me. His knee rested against my thigh as he said, "I'll not lie to you. Some may frown upon you taking a little time to yourself with the looming ice age and the prospect of more humans arriving in Atlantis. But they don't understand the pressures you're facing, not completely anyway. So, it doesn't matter what they think or if they understand. They don't know about Melysah's scheming or challenges in the council weighing down on your shoulders. So, you took a mental health day. That's okay. Your mind is a priority and is more important than their opinions. If your mind isn't just as strong as your body, not only are you at an extreme disadvantage, but you're setting yourself up for failure. It's important to take time for yourself, especially in moments of chaos. How can you survive if you don't take care of your health?"

I thanked all the brightest stars in the sky for Draevyn, his words meaning more to me than he knew. I squeezed his hand. "Thank you. For understanding. Even if others aren't going to."

The dimple on his cheek emerged. "You're welcome." His brows furrowed when he caught sight of the book lying on the coffee table. "Just what were you trying to read anyway?"

I huffed out a laugh. "Just a romance novel."

Understanding dawned on his face. "Ah. You went to Fae Flings. Good coffee," he said with a wink.

"Yes, the coffee was good." I debated whether to tell him the next bit but decided it was best not to keep it from him. "The company was interesting, too."

"Ezra? Yes, she's a bit eccentric, isn't she?"

"Yes, she is. But I wasn't talking about Ezra."

"Oh? And who kept you company? Did you make some new romance book buddies?" he asked, sipping his wine.

I tapped a nail against my glass. "Um…yes, actually. The Prince of Corenathia is my new book buddy."

Draevyn spit out his wine, the drops sprinkling across the table. "What the hell were you doing with the Prince of Corenathia in a romance bookstore?" He wiped his mouth on the back of his hand.

I grabbed my book and dried the droplets of wine with a clean tissue. "I know, right? Strange finding him there. Apparently, he's a frequent customer."

"At Fae Flings?"

"Yup. I was just as surprised as you are."

Draevyn's mouth fell open a bit. "Did he say anything to you?"

"Well, not at first. He kept to himself for a bit. We were the only ones in the shop at the time. Lux was reading his book, and I was reading mine. I think he may have heard Ezra whisper to me. I guess she wasn't discreet enough."

"Hmph. Not a bad place to pick up the ladies, I guess."

"Actually, I don't think he was there to pick up anyone. He was reading a really good book. I read it a few years back." I patted his leg. "You have to be in romance circles to know about those. So, he has to be a fan."

Draevyn knitted his eyebrows. "I'll be damned."

Now came the part I was afraid to tell him. Would he or wouldn't he accept our new ally? I cleared my throat. "He sat with me for a bit and had a coffee. He seemed to take an interest in my elemental mark."

His nostrils flared. "Why would he want to know about that?"

My shoulder lifted in a shrug. "I don't know. He noticed my mark was different from his mother's."

"All the Queens have the same mark."

"All but me." I flipped my wrist over. "There's a dot just below. His mother, the other Queens. They don't have a dot. But mine does." My gaze flicked up to his blank expression.

And then it dawned on me.

"You knew that already, didn't you? You noticed it at the Elemental Ball when I first received my mark."

Draevyn's eyes searched mine for a beat before he replied, "I did. I didn't think much of it, to be honest." He reached out, his thumb moving idly back and forth over the mark.

"He wants to help me research the mark, why it's different."

Draevyn froze. "And you trust him?"

"I know," I said, sighing. "He's a Fire Fae. And a Prince."

"It's risky."

"It is. But there's something about him."

"Something about him?" Draevyn quirked an eyebrow. "Should I be worried?"

I tsked. "No. Not like that. What I mean is that he doesn't seem evil. He seems…lost? Maybe that's not the right word. Despite my first impression of him, my gut tells me something's going on. Something maybe he can't—or won't—tell me." I stared off across the room. "Could his mother compel him to silence?"

"To be sure. She's a master compeller, probably one of the best in existence. You think she may have compelled him to secrecy?"

"Wouldn't you if you were sending your son to live amongst your enemy?"

Draevyn stroked the stubble along his jaw. "Yeah. I guess I would. What do you think he knows?"

"I think he knows about the mark. I think he knows what the dot means. Or he at least knows where to start looking. The only other person who'd had that reaction was the Bohiti Loma, but if she knew what it meant, she didn't say anything."

"She might not have known then, but she may now."

"We could ask." I glanced at him sideways. "That's if you want to go with me."

He gave me a most delicious grin. "Of course."

I nodded. "I'll wait for Lux to get in touch with Reneah. He wants to do some research in the library. I'll probably need some help meeting with him in secret."

Draevyn let loose a long sigh. "Why do I get the feeling I'm going to get in trouble for this?"

"What could you get in trouble for?"

"For helping you conspire with the Prince of Corenathia."

"We're not *conspiring*," I said, rolling my eyes.

"Then what shall we call it?"

"Studying."

Draevyn bit back a smile. "You take lessons alone, Asherah."

"Well, we'll have to be sneaky about our study sessions then. If they ask, he's my study partner. We'll call it Fae cooperation."

Draevyn tapped the tip of my nose. "You're adorable when you're conspiring."

I opened my mouth to retort, but a knock at the door interrupted us. The door opened, and Dad and Dax strode into the room.

"Got your note, Commander," Dad said.

"Goddess, I can't stand that woman," Dax exclaimed. "She's ridiculous."

"You're telling me," I murmured.

They came to stand before us, Dad resting his hands on his hips. "Tell us everything."

I let loose a sigh at the challenge of retelling all the details to them, but I painstakingly did—both of them falling in the chairs across from us as I unleashed everything. "Plan or no plan, Kane will be held accountable for his actions. What he did…it's unacceptable," Dax said in a guilt-ridden tone, his eyes filled with everything I didn't want him to feel.

"It's not your fault, Dax."

"But he is my guard. And he's my responsibility. For that, I'm sorry."

"We need to stop them," Dad declared, the bags under his eyes more prominent than the last time I'd seen him. His gaze rose from where it was absently held on the floor. "Are you okay, Sher? You know I want nothing more than to run out of here and formally reprimand her for what she's done. Games and politics aside. What she did was not okay. Not even a bit."

"I'm fine, Dad. Really. I just want to figure out what the plan is." I tucked a wayward strand of hair behind my ear. "Any ideas on what we should do?"

"Well, for starters, I'll have Myles advise the council not to send Melysah to teach your lessons anymore. She's become unhinged."

"That's an understatement," Draevyn agreed. "When it comes to Asherah, she can't seem to control herself." He rubbed his chin. "I do have an idea, though," he continued. "Dax has given some of us a couple of days rest after being a complete hard ass at training."

"That's entirely subjective," Dax said defensively, crossing his arms.

Draevyn cleared his throat. "I'd like to take Asherah to Sabana…to meet my parents."

Dax winced. "You think that'll be relaxing for her? You know how your father will feel about—"

"It's not intended to be relaxing," Draevyn interrupted, glaring at Dax. "I mean, I'm sure she'll find our home relaxing, but it's more for her protection."

"And to meet the parents," Dad said, his brow arching. I ducked my head as my face instantly heated.

"I don't think that's the flex you think it is, Cathan," Dax chided.

He squinted at Dax and Draevyn. "What are you two not saying?"

Draevyn rested his head on the back of the couch. "It's such a long story."

"In short, Draevyn's parents—well, more his father—wanted Draevyn to take over the family business," Dax supplied.

Dad tilted his head. "But your elemental mark is for Guardianship."

"Much to my father's disappointment," he replied in a flat tone.

I fidgeted in my seat. "I thought they were over it."

Draevyn twisted his head to look at me. "It's never over for a fourteenth-generation farmer."

My eyes went impossibly wide. "Fourteen generations?"

"Yup," Dax mused, "and there's no telling what he's going to say when he finds out about you." Dax wagged his bushy blond brows.

And, yup, my face just got hotter.

The room fell silent, with all types of things left unsaid. Dad was the one to break the silence. "Will she be safe with you and your family, Draevyn?"

He leaned forward, placing his elbows on his knees. "The safest, Your Highness. You have my word."

Dad nodded. "Very well. Are you okay with that, Sher?"

I had no idea what I was getting myself into, but the tension in the palace could be felt a mile away. The whole reason I went to the bookstore was to escape all the madness. "I think a trip to the farmlands is a good idea. I can get to meet the Atlantians out there."

With one final look at Draevyn, the little fleeting look of concern that crested his features stirred my worry anew.

Draevyn left with Dad and Dax to make arrangements for the trip to Sabana. With the events of the day pressing in on me, I decided a little self-care was in order to let my worries wash away. The steam rose from the water pouring into the massive black stone tub—large enough for a few adult Fae.

A jar of rose-scented bath salts rested on the side of the tub. When I tipped the glass jar, tiny salt crystals plunked into the water, the rich rose scent immediately permeating the air. The warmth of the water climbed up my body as I lowered myself. I let loose a sigh that was a borderline moan, resting my head on the edge of the tub, my eyes coming closed. It was only when I heard the sound of Draevyn returning that I opened an eye.

He padded into the bathroom without a word, his eyes immediately zeroing in on my naked body, just visible beneath the surface. His gaze was hungry. Thirsty. Longing. After the time apart, I had no doubt my gaze wasn't any less of those things.

Succumbing to the uncontrollable urge, I fixed my hooded gaze on him and moved my hands slowly up the contours of my ribcage. I took my nipples between my thumbs and forefingers, twisting them, biting my lip softly, enjoying the growing expression of hunger on his face.

Draevyn swallowed hard. "You mean to torture me,

Asherah?"

With a teasing smirk, I moved one of my hands across the panes of my tight stomach to its destination between my thighs, cupping my center and rubbing the sensitive nub I desperately wanted him to explore. "I mean to entice you," I told him in a seductive tone I hadn't recognized was my own.

"Consider me enticed."

My lips parted as my finger danced a rhythm on my swelling bud. "Then, what are you waiting for?"

Draevyn needed no more invitations. His eyes fixed on the hand that ramped up my desire as he dropped his scales, revealing every inch of chiseled body and glorious manhood—ready for taking. He was akin to a god, the faelights flickering and casting shadows across his beautiful body as he massaged his long, raging length. I could've come just by watching him, but luckily, I didn't have to.

With a grace only a Guardian possessed, he stepped into the steaming water and swam to me, floating over my body until his lips were mere inches from mine. "I'm going to devour you now," he whispered, his breath minty and warm as his tongue delved into my mouth. A soft moan of pleasure escaped my lips as his strong hands traveled down to my ass and gripped me tighter to him— pinning my hand between us. I instantly reached for his length, gently stroking—his skin so tight and full within my grasp. Draevyn let out a toe-curling groan, fueling my aching core. That sound would drive me to madness. His hand came to mine, stopping my movement. Draevyn sucked my pouting bottom lip in his mouth. "Not yet, *nanichi*. Let me take care of what you started."

With his eyes never leaving mine, Draevyn slowly dipped below the surface. I gasped when his lips grazed my inner thighs, nibbling a path until he finally reached where I desperately needed him. My entire body shivered as his skilled tongue licked through my folds, finding my swollen bud ready and waiting for him. And then he sucked.

Hard.

I bucked into his mouth and couldn't help but wrap the long strands of his hair around my fingers to steady myself. In my naivete, I wondered when he'd come up for air. But Draevyn didn't need air, of course. He planned to stay underwater until I found my release. The thought of my release becoming his oxygen was entirely arousing.

His delicious tongue circled my aching clit in torturous swirls, my thighs twitching at every rotation. His thick fingers found my entrance and pushed inside, thrusting with the movement of his tongue. I tilted my head back, bright stars appearing behind my eyelids.

"Draevyn…I'm going to—"

He gripped my pussy tighter to his mouth—devouring, licking, sucking.

Taking.

I rode the waves of pleasure that coursed throughout my body. But I needed more.

I wanted more.

Draevyn rose out of the water, smashing his mouth to mine, his tongue seeking with such need it made my legs weak. He broke away and twisted me around, guiding my hands to the edge of the tub. His hot breath crested across the shell of my tipped ear as he breathed, "Keep your hands there." His thick, muscular thigh nudged my legs apart. He moved my hair over my shoulder, placing soft kisses along my back while his large hands caressed the aching peaks of my breasts. His tongue traced a line between my shoulder blades, causing my skin to pebble in its wake. The warring sensations were entirely overwhelming. I ached for him to take me, my desire building yet again.

Draevyn's hands moved from my breasts and coasted over the curves of my hips until he reached my bottom. When his fingers dug into my ass, parting me for his viewing pleasure, I couldn't hold back my gasp. He groaned in delight. "Your pussy is simply divine," he said in a dark, masculine voice. I didn't know if my face was flaming red from the hot steam rising from the water or the vulnerability of being so exposed to him, but when he guided the tip of his engorged shaft to breach my entrance, I forgot to feel embarrassed. He slid his thickness into my wet heat. My moan echoed across the walls as he stretched me wide. "That's it, Asherah. Fuck. Look how well you take my cock." He reached into the water, pulling my knees apart and wrapping my legs back around his waist until my front floated on the surface. "Hold on tight."

And then he moved with abandon.

Draevyn's nails dug into my quad muscles as he pounded into me. These were not the actions of a man who wanted to make love. These were the actions of a male embracing something instinctual. Something primal. I was his to devour, and I gladly handed my body over to him for his pleasure.

I tightened my grip on the edge with each thrust of his powerful hips—the rough stone biting into my palms. The feel of him moving in and out of me, the water lapping against my torso with every slap of his body against mine ramped up a desire in me so potent I could scarcely breathe. Just when I thought I could take no more, Draevyn anchored me with one hand on my hip and reached for my throbbing clit with the other—driving me to madness with the precision of his fingers rubbing over and over and over. My body was his musical instrument. My sounding cry was his melody. I squeezed around him as my release tore through me. "Draevyn!"

"That's it, my Queen. Fuck. You feel so good coming around me." The most erotic masculine moan escaped his lips before the pace of his hips heightened, the water splashing where our bodies met. His hands came to press against mine on the ledge as he molded tightly to me. He grunted his release with one final thrust of his pulsing cock.

As we came down from the height of pleasure, he leaned up to massage my lower back, touching his way up to my shoulders. "I'll never get enough of you."

I let out a blissfully spent sigh. "Neither will I."

Draevyn guided my back to his chest, his satisfied length slowly pulling out of me as I rested my head upon his shoulder. We floated together until the water cooled—just the two of us in silence, the struggles of tomorrow waiting patiently beyond the palace doors. I would deal with it.

Tomorrow.

# Chapter 29

The Shingu River's various canals ran throughout the queendom, serving as a freeway to travel between towns. My exposure to Atlantis had been limited to the confines of the palace, Borike'n, and Cibao University. An anticipatory thrill ran through me at the chance to see more of Atlantis; more of my people.

The only underlying current that ultimately kept my elation at bay was the prospect of meeting Draevyn's parents. I'd heard enough to know that I may not be welcome. Even the idea that we'd become intimate might alone be problematic. With all the drama happening at the palace, it was the last thing I wanted. I'd always been respectful of my friends' parents. They generally tended to like me. But there was one loud and glaring reason Draevyn's parents wouldn't like me.

Because I was the future Queen.

Which would eventually make their son the

King.

I vowed to be the Queen of Atlantis no matter what obstacles stood in my way. Besides honoring Mother, I didn't go through the hours of training and the endless lessons just to give up now.

But there was one single, solitary thing that had grown on me: the idea of Draevyn Eliron being by my side. This fascinated me. He'd given my life something I didn't even know I was missing. I was unsure if I could let him go. I simply hoped he felt the same.

From what I'd learned of the Fae, I understood that bondmates were forever. If his parents weren't happy about it…well…forever is a long time to deal with their disappointment. I wouldn't choose that for Draevyn. I refused to be the cause of any more disappointment from his parents—a disappointment I felt was vastly unwarranted given the success he's had as a Guardian. I cared for him too deeply to cause him any more pain. There was no changing my destiny, but his destiny at my side was his choice. Aside from this all-consuming…passion that had grown between us, I wasn't sure he understood what it meant to be my bondmate. And that scared me.

"*We're almost there*," Draevyn informed from where he swam a few yards ahead with the other Guardians who traveled with us—a tentative smile on his face. He paused and reached back, taking my hand in his. In the distance, a set of stone steps leading out of the water came into view. Bright-colored coral and sea-green plant life bracketed the bottom step. My heart began to kick in my chest as I gazed at the bright daylight above. Draevyn gave my hand a gentle squeeze. "*It'll be okay*, nanichi."

Why did those words not bring me any comfort?

Our speed slowed at the foot of the stairs. We began ascending the slick steps, and when my head breached the surface, a gasp escaped my lips. Various warehouses lined the shoreline, the port teeming with Water Fae entering and exiting as they milled about their day. The savory scent of food carried from a corner cart with a line of people waiting to purchase their meal. The heavy scent of spices assaulted my nose, and I breathed in every delectable scent. Workers entered and exited large canoas in well-practiced formations, loading and unloading various crates with proficiency. Tons of canoas were tied to every available dock. This was a whole other part of Atlantis I had yet to explore, and the sight warmed my heart. They were so similar to the humans in the Above World. It gave me hope that they could be saved by seeking refuge in a small town like Sabana.

The sound of hushed whispers began reaching my ears. A few of the workers had stopped to stare at our entourage. One by one, they froze. Some dropped their crates to get a better look over their shoulder. The heat rose in my cheeks.

"Draevyn!"

A beautiful female with long jet-black hair called out to him—a male with equally dark hair at her side. It was only when they reached us that I realized who they were. Their youthfulness threw me off, but the resemblance to Draevyn was undeniable.

The woman threw her slender arms around Draevyn, squeezing him tightly. "My *guali*. It is so good to have you home."

"It hasn't been that long, *Bibi*," Draevyn said with a chuckle, returning her affection with a strong embrace of his own.

She leaned back, her olive-skinned face beaming. "You look so handsome. Have you grown?"

The male next to her scowled. "Oh, stop fussing

over him, *liani*. He's been a grown Fae male for centuries now. He doesn't need his mother fussing over him." He shook his dark-haired head and held his hand out to Draevyn. "Hello, *guali*. Nice of you to come home again so soon." I hadn't missed the subtle dig, which Draevyn gracefully ignored.

Once Draevyn grasped his hand, his father yanked him into a hug and patted him firmly on his back. His father's gaze widened when he realized Draevyn wasn't alone. His sea-green eyes—so much like Draevyn's—scanned the group behind him, myself included. "What's all this?"

Draevyn backed away, clearing his throat. "*Bibi, Baba*, I'd like to meet Asherah Delmar. Asherah, these are my parents, Samani and Zoriato Eliron."

Samani's mouth gaped open. Zoriato's lips tightened.

"Asherah," Samani finally managed to say. "As in, the Princess of Atlantis?" She swatted Draevyn on the arm, causing him to wince. "You brought the Princess of Atlantis here without warning me first?"

"I did warn you. I told you I was bringing—"

"A few Guardians and a female to visit—the first female you've ever brought home, mind you. You didn't mention she was *the* female the entire queendom has been talking about," she said, scoffing. "He brings royalty to my home like it's not the biggest deal in my lifetime. Typical male. There's no contesting whose son you are."

Both Draevyn and Zoriato managed to scoff in unison.

Samani strode forward, taking my hands. "It is such an honor to meet you, Your Highness."

"Please. Call me Asherah."

Samani's warm smile put me at ease. "Asherah, then. It's an honor to welcome you to Sabana and our home. I'm sure you've had quite a shock, yes?"

I looked down. "To say the least."

She squeezed my hand. "Well then, you'll be right at home while you're here. Zori and I want you to be comfortable."

Glancing up at Zoriato, I wasn't too sure about that. His expression was remarkably unreadable. I didn't know what to make of it. Shifting my attention back to Samani, I replied, "Thank you for welcoming me."

"Let's get a move on," Zoriato interrupted, taking note of all the Guardians. "I'm glad your mother always has the good sense to cook enough food to feed an entire outpost."

Draevyn squeezed his father's shoulder. "Don't worry yourself, *Baba*. They'll stay in the farming cottages, taking turns looking out."

Zoriato's forehead creased. "Look out for what?"

Draevyn sighed. "Long story."

Zoriato opened his mouth, but Samani beat him to it. "Let's all get home. We can discuss this over a nice meal and a few glasses of our signature wine." She motioned us toward the awaiting canoa. Samani had a natural motherly aura about her that instantly squeezed my heart. Given the way Zoriato had greeted me—the completely unphased, unreadable expression—I desperately hoped I'd at least find an ally in her.

Well, we were about to find out, weren't we?

The cool travertine tile met the warmth of my webbed

feet as I stood in the foyer. The beautiful Eliron home could've easily passed for one in the Above World—the ceilings were made of rich mahogany; the layout was open and homely. The inside of the home was just as impressive as the outside—the two-story perfectly nestled on the land surrounding it. There wasn't another home for miles on either side of the property. From what Samani had informed me as our canoa rolled through the charming streets of Sabana, the neighbors were kind and mostly kept to themselves. Where Borike'n was more events, celebrations, clubs, and chaos, Sabana was quiet, peaceful, and comforting.

Deep-brown plush leather couches sat in the center of the living room beyond the foyer, complimenting the cream-colored textured walls—the most beautiful paintings of farmland, countryside, and vineyards decorating them. Delicious, savory scents drifted throughout the room, and my stomach growled in anticipation.

Samani didn't miss the sound, her full lips spreading into a knowing smile. "You must be starving."

I grinned sheepishly. "Maybe just a little."

"Not to worry. We have plenty of bits and pieces to nibble on while we wait for Zori and Drae to return. Do you like faery wine?"

"I love faery wine."

"A woman after my own heart," Samani said with a wink of her brandy-colored eye. "Follow me. Or rather, follow the smell. It's the easiest way to find the kitchen in this house if you get lost."

Samani's long-black hair swayed across her back as I followed her through the home. We entered a kitchen that could only be described as a chef's dream. A large island sat at its center—the bright, white quartz countertops with bold gold veining flowing throughout provided plenty of space for a few people to sit and prep a meal. Matching countertops lined the back and sides of the sizeable kitchen, complimenting the smokey green-colored cabinets throughout. Samani stirred the contents inside a pot on top of a massive stove fixed in the back.

I slowly turned, taking in every detail—the long, beautiful wooden table with vibrant natural colors before a double set of French doors leading out onto a large patio with outdoor seating and a fireplace with a roaring fire. I'd never been in a home so inviting. "You have the most gorgeous home."

"Thank you," Samani said as she approached with two glasses of faery wine in her hand. "Although I suppose the palace is far more luxurious than this," she remarked.

I lifted a shoulder in a shrug as I gratefully took my glass. "Yes, the palace is. But that's not a home—at least not to me."

She gave a slight wince. "Yes, of course. Anyone would feel that way in such a big place." She gestured toward the patio. "Why don't you make yourself comfortable and warm by the fire? I'll get us something to nibble on."

"I can help," I volunteered.

She fluttered a hand. "No, no. It's no worry. Sit, relax," Samani said with a comforting smile before she drifted back into the kitchen. I proceeded through the French doors and placed my glass of wine on the low outdoor table. The comfy burnt orange cushions engulfed me as I plopped down on them—the heat from the fire in the weathered brick fireplace trailing over my scales. The crackling of the fire put me at ease as the distant sounds of Samani preparing a platter reached my ears. My shoulders sagged of their own volition.

Perfect rows of grapevines stretched for endless acres into the shadows of the dying day beyond the patio. Various questions rattled through my brain. What elementals were involved in the upkeep of the crops? What kinds of crops did they have? I noted all of them and would ask when Draevyn and Zoriato returned from getting the Guardians settled in and fed.

Samani strode outdoors on graceful steps. She flicked a delicate wrist, and a wooden cutting board appeared on the table with large red grapes, mustard yellow cheeses, and sesame seed-flecked crackers scattered upon it. I withheld my amazement at the sudden appearance of food on the table and would have to remember to ask Draevyn to teach me that one. Wasting no time indulging, I reached forward and grabbed a little bit of everything.

Samani slid into the seat directly across from me with a sigh. Her anticipatory gaze swept over me as she sipped on her wine. "So, tell me of your home in the Above World. I'm guessing it was much like this, yes?"

I nodded as I swallowed. "I miss it very much. It's the only home I've ever known. Not that I'm complaining about being in a palace. I hope that doesn't sound ungrateful. I just would've never imagined my life as it is right now. A Princess," I commented with a light huff. "All I wanted was to become a marine biologist."

Her silky hair shifted as she shook her head. "I can't imagine. What a shock it must have been to find out all the fairy tales in the Above World held some truth."

"To say the least."

Samani regarded me thoughtfully over the rim of her glass before asking, "You truly had no idea you were the Heir?"

I shook my head. "I wasn't even aware I was Fae.

Now that I've had time to process everything, I under-stand it was a difficult decision for my parents to make."

Samani stared off into the fire, the flames flickering in her gaze. "Yes, I must admit, when I first heard of your arrival to Atlantis, I could hardly believe it. I wondered what I would've done if I were in their scales. The Above World is a whole other world. Its rules, belief systems, and societal challenges differ slightly from the realms. I've rarely ventured up there. We have no reason to." She gave a shudder. "To have to wear clothes."

I chuckled. "I'm sure it would be a change. But, it's nice to express oneself through fashion."

Samani waved a hand. "Too much trouble, in my opinion. Scales are the way to go. Less hassle, and they're fashionable enough."

I'd never admit it to her, but every now and then, I'd slip on my favorite *All I Do is Beach and Wine* pajama t-shirt just for the comforting feel it brought me.

"You must really miss your mother," Samani said in an empathetic tone. "I'm very sorry she passed. We all are."

"Thank you. I miss her a lot." I tilted my head in thought. "Well, when she was alive, I also missed her a lot. Most of the time, it was just me and my dad. Mom was always away on business trips. Now I know those business trips were either trips to Atlantis or meetings with the human delegation in the Above World."

"That must have been very trying on you and your father," she mused.

"I won't lie. At times, it was frustrating. She missed a lot, but now that I understand why she was gone, I can't help but admire her. When she was home, she was a great mother. Sometimes, it would just be the two of us. We'd go to dinner or shop. Those are the times I miss the most. Not being able to hear her voice again. That does something to me." I shook my head. "What I wouldn't give to hear her, to ask her all the questions about how to be an Atlantian Queen and deal with all the politics." My eyes snapped up to Samani's gaze, full of a certain sadness. "I'm so sorry for rambling. It's not the happiest of topics."

"No need to apologize, Asherah. You're permitted to grieve and talk to someone about how you're feeling. Even if we don't know each other well, I'm always happy to be that person."

My chest tightened. "Thank you…so much. That means a lot."

The creaking sound of the front door opening on weathered hinges reached our ears; Zoriato and Draevyn appeared on the patio a moment later—a gleam of happiness on Draevyn's face as his gaze traveled between us.

"Looks like the Guardians are all settled," Zoriato remarked.

"They send their gratitude," Draevyn said to his mother. "The food was nearly gone by the time we left."

"Well, with the size of those males, that doesn't surprise me. It's a good thing we live on a farm." We all shared a laugh at that. Samani rose from her seat. "Okay, we've kept the Princess starving long enough. Why don't we migrate to the dining table and eat? Shall we?"

Draevyn snaked an arm around my waist as we made our way inside and leaned into my ear. "Everything okay?"

"Absolutely. Your family home is wonderful, Drae," I complimented as my hand instinctively wrapped around his back.

A look of pride crested across his features. "I'm glad you like it."

We paused in front of the doorway, holding each other's gaze a little too long to be appropriate between Commander and Princess. When I finally remembered where we were, I turned to find Zoriato's face with an expression that could only be described as mild shock. Samani and I hadn't spoken about my relationship with Draevyn. It was apparent that Draevyn hadn't breached that subject either based on his father's reaction. The heat instantly rose to my cheeks as I dropped my hand from Draevyn's back. I ducked my head and took a seat at the massive wooden dining table.

Zoriato kept his gaze on the both of us as he and Samani sat across the table—Draevyn sliding into his seat with an amused grin. With a flick of Samani's wrist, heaps of food appeared on the table: crisp romaine lettuce, crumbled chunks of feta, and shaved carrots in a large wooden salad bowl, accompanied by a mountain of lightly seared ahi tuna on a large porcelain plate. Steam rose from freshly sautéed peas and mushrooms, the hints of pepper drifting on a tendril. Samani dipped her head. "Our thanks to the goddess who blesses our meal this eve." The table was a mess of plates exchanging hands and glass filling to a brim. I speared a piece of tuna, taking my first bite, and had to stifle a moan, opting to close my eyes instead.

"It's good, right?" Draevyn beamed.

All I could do was nod and roll my eyes in ecstasy, which seemed to please his mother based on her satisfying smile. We ate peacefully in each other's company. They asked questions—mostly his mother—about Draevyn's training. Zoriato huffed around his food a few times, indicating that he may still have difficulty accepting Draevyn's elemental calling.

"Asherah was an excellent surfer in the Above

World," Draevyn said proudly.

"The sport with the board and the waves?" Samani inquired, her free hand mimicking a wave.

"Yes, that one. She's won a ton of competitions."

"That must have been very time-consuming," Zoriato remarked flatly.

"It was. I only stopped competing when I had to focus on my studies."

Zoriato's forehead wrinkled. "But isn't being a Water Fae an unfair advantage? Surely, you manipulated the water in your favor?"

I patted my mouth with a napkin. "Um. No, not exactly. My parents bound my powers, so they were of no use."

Zoriato's fork dropped on his plate with a clang. "I beg your pardon?"

I cleared my throat. "Well, they bound my powers and glamoured me. It was the only way they could raise me in the Above World in secret."

"That's blasphemous."

"*Baba*," Draevyn hissed.

Zoriato threw him an admonishing look. "I'll speak freely in my own house. That's just terrible not to grow up with one's powers. And without the protection of scales. It's completely reckless."

"Well," Samani calmly interjected, "there's little that can be done now. It is what it is. We're just happy she returned to her true home." She gathered a heap of vegetables on her fork. "So, Asherah, I'm sure you're happy to escape the drama at the capital, am I right?"

A huff of a laugh escaped my lips. "Yes, I've had quite a bit of drama, some I'd rather do without."

Draevyn casually touched my arm, drawing my attention. "And you've done remarkably well, *nanichi*."

Another fork dropped on a plate, startling me. "*Nanichi?!*" Samani exclaimed. Draevyn's parents went utterly still, Samani's mouth hanging open and Zoriato's mouth held in a thin line.

A scarlet blush spread across Draevyn's face. I would've laughed had the tone of the room not dropped into awkward territory. My nails lightly dug into his palm under the table as Draevyn cleared his throat. "Yes. *Nanichi.*"

Samani's mouth rounded in an 'o'.

Zoriato motioned between the two of us with his fork. "I take it, given how her scent is all over you, that this isn't some sort of diplomatic mission or assignment?"

"Asherah is still my assignment. She's still mine to look after." He glanced at me and smirked timidly. "During Asherah's training, she and I became close and," he paused, inhaling deeply before shifting his attention to his parents, "we plan to attend Guake'te."

"No," Zori said instantly.

Samani smacked him on the shoulder. "Zori, what's wrong with you? Your *guali*—"

Zoriato slammed his hands on the table, the plates and silverware clattering. "Yes, my *guali*! My only *guali*. It's bad enough that he isn't a farming elemental safely within the confines of Sabana, where he should be. Getting accustomed to having a Guardian elemental in the family was hard enough. Now, he plans to bond with the future Queen of Atlantis?" Zoriato rubbed his hands down his face, his reaction building the rage within me. "What an honorable future," Zoriato continued, "to sit at the Queen's side as a permanent fixture. A figurehead with nothing to do."

"My father sat at my mother's side," I interrupted, all the calm I possessed fused into my tone. "My father is not a figurehead. He is a great man who honored my mother with everything he had to the day she died."

Zoriato's fearsome gaze sliced into my soul. "Your father—while an honorable man he may be—has done nothing but your mother's bidding even after her death. Despite the Guardian elemental mark, he does not fight with the other Guardians. His mark means absolutely nothing."

"*Baba*, that's enough," Draevyn sneered. "I'll not have you speak ill of Cathan. Not in front of Asherah, and certainly not in front of me. We can debate the merits of being King consort. Those are welcome, but I'll not have you disrespecting Asherah or Cathan, a male I've always respected as my King and have grown even more to respect since my assignment. I can only hope to follow his example one day."

Zoriato scoffed. "You'd rather follow his example than your own father's, eh?" Zoriato threw his napkin down on the table and rose from his seat. "I need some air."

An uncomfortable silence followed his departure. I'd expected some resistance to our union but not hostility.

Draevyn's chair screeched across the tile as he stood, his face solemn. "I'll go speak with him."

I watched him as he disappeared beyond the patio through the rows of vines and into the darkness. Twisted back to the table, I kept my eyes on a stray pea in the middle of my plate, unable to look at Samani. A deep feeling of rejection settled in the pit of my stomach as I swallowed past the lump that had formed in my throat and murmured, "I'm so sorry."

Samani swiftly rose from her chair, saying, "No, no. Don't do that." She slid into Draevyn's vacant seat and took my hand in hers. "Do not apologize, Asherah. I want you to understand something. Zoriato is a complex male, burdened by generations of family farming weighing heavily on his shoulders. I'm not excusing his behavior. Quite the opposite, but Draevyn is his only *guali*, whom he loves immensely.

"We'd waited so long to have a faeling. There are no words to describe the joy we felt when we discovered I was with child. And when Draevyn received his elemental mark, Zori was beside himself with worry. Being a Guardian is such a dangerous elemental calling, even in the best of times. Now, with the state of things in the Above World and the Akani gaining traction within the realms…" she shook her head. "It's not just a small group of Fae and humans who support their cause now. The talk of joining the Akani has become normalized, especially in the outskirts of Atlantis."

A cold feeling of shock crept up my spine. "Are you…do you all…do you support their cause?"

Samani reared back. "No, no. That's not what I'm saying. Zoriato and I believe very much in Atabey's calling—may the goddess continue to bless us." Samani smiled brightly. "And she *has* blessed us. What an extraordinary gift. Zori can be upset all he wants. He can scream about it all he wants and take all the time he needs to let it sink in. Me, on the other hand? I'm absolutely elated!" She shook her head. "My *guali*. King consort. And—more importantly—happy," she beamed. "That's all a mother wants for her child, is to be happy."

My heart warmed as I beheld this female who was quickly growing on me, but the warmth was dampened by the conversation happening between Draevyn and his father. I couldn't stand for Draevyn to bear more of Zoriato's disappointment. I cared for him too much.

*More* than care.

In my heart, I knew exactly what that meant about how I felt for Draevyn Eliron.

# Draevyn

# Chapter 30

W ELL, THAT WENT WORSE THAN EXPECTED. Never in a millennia did I ever imagine my father's reaction when he learned of Asherah and me. Sure, I expected him to be worried. Disappointed, even. But furious? He wasn't even that furious when I received my mark.

Well...I mean...he was *somewhat* furious.

I can still remember his face when the elemental mark appeared across my wrist—the initial astonishment that flitted across, followed by the outright scowl of anger. I'd never intended to hurt him in any way, never thought I could until that day. My father was my hero. Still is in many ways.

The truth is it didn't matter what reaction *Baba* had to my elemental mark. Being a Guardian was all I've ever wanted since I was a tiny faeling. I'd begged my parents to venture to the capital for the Tournament of Champions—the once-in-a-decade competition between the Guardians of Atlantis. "No," *Baba* had told me, much in the tone he'd just had over dinner. "You need to pull your head from the dome clouds and stop dreaming of the Guardians. Now, go do your chores," he'd told me.

So, like any other young sprite challenging their limits, I snuck out and went to the tournament.

I'll never forget the pain in my arms from the amount of horse manure I had to shovel for my disobedience. But I smiled through the pain with each shovel full of horse shit. All I could think about was how I would win that tournament one day.

And I had.

Three times.

I was destined to be a Guardian. *Baba's* disappointment—while difficult at first—became second nature to me. I didn't need or want his approval. Atabey blessed me with my mark. I'll not shame the gift I received at her blessed hand.

But for *Baba* to show disappointment in who I'd hoped was my mate? For him to throw an adult tantrum about who I planned to present myself with at Guake'te in hopes of gaining our bondmarks?

That's a step too far across my boundaries.

Which is why I followed *Baba* into the fields that lined the property; the faery grapevines used to ferment the most delicious wine in all of the realms scraped across my scales as I shuffled further down the pathway. I watched—the corner of my lips twitching—as he vigorously plucked grapes from the vines, tossing them down in a large wooden bucket at his side. He continued his plucking and seething as I reached his side.

"I'll not be happy about it. You can forget that," he declared as he stomped down to the next set of grapes.

I casually crossed my arms. "I'm not asking you to

be happy about it, *Baba*. I'm asking you to show Asherah some respect. I'm asking you to show King Cathan and the late Queen Neleah some respect; Atabey rest her soul." I plucked a grape from a vine and popped it in my mouth, contemplating my following words with careful consideration. "She means something to me."

The vines shook with how hard he pulled his next few grapes. "Oh, I'll bet she means something to you. You're thinking with your cock pocket, boy."

"I most surely am not."

*Baba* stopped picking and turned to face me. "And just what is it that you think you're feeling?"

I paused, breathing deeply. "You once told me what it felt like when you met *Bibi*. You told me you felt the calling in your center and the itching around the left side of your chest where the bondmark appears. You told me you knew she was yours just as much as you were hers. I remembered every word you said. I've had the good fortune of witnessing the love you share with *Bibi*. Since I was a little faeling, I'd look around at the females—some of them beautiful beyond words—and analyze how my body reacted to theirs, beyond the usual attraction, of course. When I grew into a young male, there were hoards of females who would throw themselves at me, wanting to be with a tournament champion—wanting me despite them not knowing the *real* me. And I knew these females weren't my mate because they'd never made me feel like you had described.

"Until Asherah," I laughed under my breath, "my goodness. The feeling the first day she arrived at the gates of Atlantis. It was incredible, *Baba*. I thought the feeling would take me to my knees. I was embarrassed by how I felt. So vulnerable. I'd never felt like that before. In fact, at first, it made me a little angry; angry that she could make me feel that way."

I lifted my gaze. His expression had softened, giving me the encouragement to continue. "I know you've never been fond of my elemental mark. I've always understood why, even though I'll never understand why you cannot accept my fate—this wonderful path the goddess has chosen for me. But the journey of understanding is not my burden to bear. That is yours."

"*Guali*," he responded, his shoulders sagging. "I could never be disappointed in you. Atabey, forgive me if I've seemed ungrateful for the gift she has bestowed upon you. What I am is terrified. I'm terrified, Draevyn. Every day that the tension builds—and mind you, it is building fast—I worry that I may never see you again. And now you tell me you are to stand at the side of the very person the Akani seek to kill?"

"Over my dead body," I replied with a hint of menace. I couldn't bear that thought.

*Baba* threw up his hands. "Exactly, my *guali*. It will be over your dead body."

I pinched the bridge of my nose. "Sorry. Poor choice of words. I only meant it as a form of expression."

"But it's not just a form of expression, Draevyn. You're already in danger as her assigned Guardian. But as our King? Even more so. And I can't bear that. No parent should."

I placed a hand on his shoulder. "*Baba*, this is my calling. The goddess wants me to be by her side, and I do this gladly. Willingly. She is everything to me." The tears gathering in his eyes glimmered in the rising moonlight. "Please. Try to be happy for me. For us. She is an amazing female, and I don't say this because she is destined to rule this queendom. I say it because she has such a beautiful heart and soul if you just let her show you."

*Baba* sighed and threw the grapes he held into the bucket. "Do you love her?"

The question caught me off guard. I'd never formally told Asherah how I felt. My reply was one I'd never used regarding any other female in my life but my mother. "I do love her. With everything I have, with everything I am."

He grasped my hand at his shoulder. "Very well. I'll…I'll try to give all of this a chance."

"Whoa," I exclaimed, jerking back. "Did the great Zoriato Eliron actually concede?"

"Watch it, boy. I still remember how to check you."

"I wouldn't dare to forget," I said, placing an arm around his shoulders. "Come. Our females must be worried."

For the first time in a long time, I welcomed the camaraderie with my father. It'd been far too long since I had.

# Chapter 31

"And this is when he first learned how to plant the seeds in the garden with me. Look how little he was—such a sweet little faeling. Always clinging to my side," Samani recalled as she displayed the memory on the crystal tablet—the memory as bright as a movie on a screen. I couldn't get enough of the magicked videos. I could see Draevyn's tiny facial features, his semi-long dark hair beginning to grow past his tiny tipped ears, and the absolute naked glee of helping his mother in her garden. My heart squeezed at the idea that we might have a little faeling of our own.

Some day.

Not anytime soon, though.

We sat on a long loveseat on the patio, waiting for Draevyn and Zoriato to return. The dishes had been cleaned, tables cleared, and food put away. When Samani asked if I would like to see a few videos of Draevyn in his youth, I couldn't refuse. We filled our glasses and got comfortable before the outdoor fireplace. The heaviness from the dinner drifted away as Samani talked about Draevyn growing up. I tucked a few stories safely in my back pocket to tease him with later.

"Oh no. *Bibi*, please tell me you aren't showing her my faeling videos. You couldn't have saved those till at least the second visit?" Draevyn approached with an amused smile, taking in the scene before him. He leaned down and placed a gentle kiss on my head before sinking into the neighboring chair. I noted the gleam in his eyes and felt immediate relief.

Zoriato was slower to join our company. He padded to stand in front of us, observing us cautiously. I couldn't help but notice Samani's brow rising as she regarded him. His fists fidgeted at his side as he said, "Well, Princess. If you're going to be part of this family, you'll need to learn how to take care of the fields. At any rate, it'll make you a better Queen to understand how us farm folk operate."

Samani's gaze shifted back to me, and a smirk emerged on her face. I took that as his approval…and apology. And it was good enough for me. "Thank you. I'd love to learn more about farmers here in Sabana." I scrunched my brow. "Come to think of it, my knowledge of farming in the Above World is kind of limited. There's not much of it near The Keys, where I was raised."

Zoriato placed his hands on his hips. "Well, we'll just have to give you a crash course while you're here." He pointed at their nearly empty glasses. "You'll want to watch your intake for the rest of the night. We get up early around here."

"Real early," Draevyn complained.

"That's right, *guali*. There's no time like the morning to accomplish one's tasks with full strength and a fresh mind."

"Always trying to ruin the fun," Samani said, sighing.

Zoriato gave her a lovely grin, so at odds with the gruff male he'd been since we'd arrived. "Oh, come now, my love. I'm not always a bore." He wagged his dark eyebrows, causing a blush to spread across Samani's cheeks.

"You'll have to forgive them," Draevyn said to me. "They tend to delve into naughty talk regardless of who's present. And despite their *guali* wanting to gag every time it happens."

"Oh, stop." Samani threw a patio pillow in his direction, which he swiftly caught as he bellowed with laughter. "One of these days, when you have faelings of your own, you'll understand how hard it is to contain your love for your *nanichi* in front of them. It can't be helped."

My gaze slipped to Draevyn's, my cheeks heating.

Love.

That word hadn't passed through either of our lips, but I certainly felt that way about him. Only him. What I previously felt for any boy or man—John included—couldn't compare to the absolute rightness of…us.

Of our bond. Sitting. Waiting, just beneath the surface.

And after what was a shaky introduction into the family, I couldn't help but hope that maybe we'd finally come to a point where we could express that love to one another in words—three simple words that held so much significance, so much weight to them; three little words that stood on the tip of my tongue, dying to spill from my lips—dying for me to convey just how I felt about him.

"I think it's time to retire, *liani*. Leave the two love birds alone, yes?" Zoriato took Samani's hand and lifted her to stand, placing a chase kiss on her lips.

"Yes, I suppose. I'll need to prepare for tomorrow's gathering in honor of our special guest," she glanced over her shoulder and gave me a mischievous wink.

"Gathering?" I asked.

Samani lifted her slender shoulders in a casual shrug. "Just as soon as you arrived, we decided to organize a small gathering of the farming elementals to meet you. Nothing big. Just a small outdoor meal with friends."

The apprehension built in my stomach. With everything happening, I wasn't sure what kind of welcome I'd receive from the farming elementals, but a determination to win their favor sprouted from a little seed within.

Pun intended.

Plus, anything that Samani Eliron put together was sure to have a certain flare to it, given the skill with which she handled meals for the Guardians and dinner for us. Hospitality was clearly one of her talents. I had to wonder what Samani and Aurelio would do as a team. "That sounds wonderful. Can't wait," I said sincerely.

Zoriato and Samani departed arm and arm through the open doors, leaving us with nothing but the dying fire and the wind rustling the leaves upon the vines for company. Draevyn rose and slid into the vacant seat beside me, his strong arm pulling me into his side. I couldn't help but rest my head on his shoulder—the warmth of him providing a comfort I felt deep in my soul. I held my gaze on the dying flames in the fireplace, watching them twist and dance with the gentle breeze.

"So," he started.

"So."

"I'm sorry about my father," Draevyn murmured as his fingers glided up and down my bare arm—my scales fashioned in pop collar tunic style with sleeveless arms that Aurelio had taught me to do before we left Atlantis.

"No need to be sorry. He loves you. He wants what's best for you."

"That doesn't excuse him from treating you the way he did. He shouldn't have said the things he did about Cathan. That's not fair to him."

I didn't know the best way to breach the subject of his future as my King. There was no easy way to do it. So I forged ahead and said, "You know many Atlantians will have the same perspective as your father."

Draevyn went silent for a moment. "I understand."

"Being by my side won't be easy. You'll be ridiculed. There's a lot you'll be expected to give up. And you've worked too damn hard just to willingly let it go."

His fingers graced my chin, pulling it to the side to meet his intense gaze, robbing me of breath. "I want you to listen to me and listen to me carefully, *nanichi*. I understand what being by your side entails—as your mate, Atabey willing—but also as your Guardian. I understand the things weaker people will say about me and the dangers that may come our way. *Our way*. Not just *your* way, for you'll never have to worry about facing those dangers alone. I'll be by your side every step of the way. I'm not the type of male who flippantly decides his path. When I know something is right for me, I go for it. And you are right for me. You are my path. You have my heart. You have my soul. And love is such an inadequate word for how I feel about you, but you have it, too, nonetheless." He leaned down, his warm cheek sliding against mine as he brought his lips to the shell of my ear. "I love you, Asherah Delmar. I am madly, deeply, in love with you," he whispered.

Whatever pretty words I had died on my tongue as he brought his soft lips to mine, kissing me fervently, passionately, and with wild possession. My fingers slid into his hair, pulling him toward me, hungry. Seeking. This male, this absolutely wonderful, strong, beautiful male, just told me that he loves me.

Me.

The wallflower. The girl who was always just a friend. Nothing more. Chrissy's permanent wing-woman.

Me.

Draevyn loves me.

The revelation pinged around in my mind as I leaned back, breathing rapidly against his lips. "I love you, too."

He pulled back slightly. A flutter of vulnerability I was unused to seeing on him lay heavy in his stare. "You don't have to say it back. That's…that's not what I'd expected in return. I just needed to let you know that—"

I brought my pointer finger to his lips, silencing him. "I'm not the type of female who flippantly decides her path. When I know something is right for me, I go for it." The corner of his lips lifted with the use of his words. "I love you, Draevyn Eliron. With my whole heart and soul, I love you. Everything I am is yours."

Draevyn rested his forehead against mine. "Thank you."

"You do not have to thank me for loving you."

He chuckled lightly. "Perhaps it's not a thank you for loving me as much as it's a thank you for being so patient with my father today. That is something I *do* have to thank you for."

My shoulder lifted. "Eh, what family doesn't have their issues? Plenty of families like to act as if they're all smiles and happy times. That's a damn lie. All families have their challenges."

"Well, you rose to the challenge today." He sighed. "And I'm afraid you might have to continue rising to it tomorrow. It's going to be a very long day."

My brows dipped. "Just how early do we have to get up tomorrow?"

Draevyn groaned. "Early. Real early." With his water magic, he extinguished the fire—the steam hissing and rising into the evening air. He rose and held his hand out. "Come, my Queen. Let me show you to the royal chambers."

I tsked. "Royal chambers," I mimicked as we entered the home, closing the French doors behind us. "Don't act like a guest bed isn't good enough for me. I was a college kid, after all. I did couch surf," I remarked as we ascended the stairs leading to the second floor.

"You're not staying in a guest room. You're staying in mine."

My brow rose. "Your parents won't mind?"

He looked at me aghast. "You realize you're among the Fae now, yes? We aren't exactly known for our modesty." Right. That wasn't something I was used to. Talk about culture shock. "Besides," he continued, "I want you by my side. It's the best place I can protect you."

Draevyn led us to a large wooden door with intricate carvings. He pushed it open revealing a dark room with dim faelights flickering throughout. A large four-poster bed with a fluffy navy-blue comforter and puffy white pillows screamed in invitation. Suddenly, I yawned. It couldn't be helped. The adrenaline of the visit had finally subsided.

Draevyn led me to the bed and pulled back the sheets. I instantly dropped my scales, his Caribbean green eyes caressing my naked form, overriding my exhaustion and causing my thighs to clench.

"I want to bury myself inside you," he said in a sensual timbre tone, "but you need to rest."

My lower lip dipped in a pout, but I obeyed, scooting under the covers he held up for me. His bed was magicked. It had to be because sleep came for me the moment my head hit the pillow. The last thing I remembered was the warm feel of Draevyn's naked body sidling up behind mine, bringing my back to his chest. In the safety of his embrace, I drifted to sleep.

It turns out that staying up drinking faery wine was not the brightest idea when working in the fields the next day. Granted, I didn't have a hangover like the humans do—for that, I was grateful—but I did feel my body drag with every motion of my arms and step taken. As I worked on the next set of vines, I could hardly believe the amount of sweat that rolled off my face and scales. My amazement grew every time I turned my head and found the other workers moving at an unimaginable pace—their heads periodically twisting in my direction to catch a glimpse of the princess working alongside them. I didn't want to draw any attention, but I understood their curiosity. So far, they'd been very cordial. My hands picked up the pace in an effort to keep up with them. The last thing I wanted to do was be a burden or to seem weak in their eyes.

When we arrived at the barn earlier that morning before the sun had even risen, Zoriato had requested Draevyn's help in a different field filled with various types of vegetables, the labor far more intense in that field than in mine. I didn't know how that was possible as my hand swept across my forehead, drenched with sweat. The hot, crisp air was very different from the humid, tropical climate of The Keys, which felt more like a wet blanket. This level of heat held a certain intensity I was unused to.

"It's the magic," a woman called from the next row. "It's a beast, but it sets the grapes just right."

I peeked through the branches. A stout human woman with crow's feet that swept out around her eyes smiled at me—her dark hair with a few streaks of gray pulled tightly back in a bun. "It's the garden elementals. The temperature is unlike anywhere else in Atlantis," she said as she threw a few grapes in her bucket. "But oh, does it produce some of the best faery wine ever to hit your tastebuds."

"Yes, I seem to remember that from last night," I agreed with a wince. "Probably wasn't the best idea to indulge before coming out in the hot sun to work."

The woman's shoulders shook with laughter. "I suppose not. We humans don't exactly have the greatest tolerance for the stuff. Although some of us have certainly worked up our defenses." She leaned in between the branches. "It's in the name of science. Have to make sure the wine's just right," she winked.

I chuckled as I plucked a few more grapes from the vine. "Oh yes, we wouldn't want to mess with one's scientific methods."

"Certainly not." The woman hoisted her bucket, slowly trudging her way to the next cluster—the sounds of the grapes hitting the bucket echoing as she worked. *Pluck, pluck, pluck. Thump.* "I'm Bucoana, by the way."

"Asherah," I called.

"Oh, I know who you are, Your Highness. Half the damn town is beside themselves with awe that a Princess is actually in the outskirts of town." *Pluck, pluck, pluck. Thump. Pluck, pluck. Thump.* "When Zoriato announced to the crew that you'd be working with us today, we had to help Samani pick some of the crew's mouths up off the ground. They could hardly believe it. A royal getting dirty with the farming folk," *Pluck, pluck. Thump.*

I froze, a sense of unease spreading throughout my aching limbs. "Did…did my mother…Queen Neleah, I mean…not come out here often?"

*Pluck, pluck.*

A long period of silence ensued—the rustling of the vines from the surrounding rows emanating around us.

*Thump.* "I suppose you wouldn't know one way or another if she had visited, eh? Or any of the other folk high up there in the capital—you being in the Above World and all."

I nibbled on the inside of my cheek. "Right. Yes, I…I wouldn't know."

*Pluck, pluck, pluck. Thump.* "It's okay, dear. The way your parents hid you from the rest of the queendom? That did not settle well for some. Was she more concerned with the humans in the Above World than the very ones in her realm? No one will ever know. Save yourself, maybe. But since she never told you about Atlantis, it would've been hard for Queen Neleah to tell you her thoughts on the matter." *Pluck, pluck. Thump.* "I'm not blaming you or anything. It's just some of us felt a little forgotten. Sorry if that came out a bit harshly. I'm sure some would consider my comments outright disrespectful."

I resumed my plucking. "It's not disrespectful at all. Everyone is allowed to express their feelings. It's your experience, after all. You know the ins and outs of Atlantis, and you're entitled to your opinion. You feed mouths both here and in the capital and all the towns along the way. It's important that I hear your thoughts; it's important that they hear them, too. How else does the realm improve if we don't listen to our people? The council can't expect to make decisions that could potentially change the lives of everyone in the farming towns like Sabana without seeing how life is here on the ground. That's just ridiculous. You and everyone else in this field are welcome to speak freely with me. I don't mind one bit."

The vines next to me rustled. Bucoana's torso popped through the row of vines, her eyes giving me a once-over. "Huh. Interesting." The next moment, she backed away and returned to plucking. "You know what, Your Highness?" *Pluck, pluck, pluck. Thump.*

"Yes?"

"I think you're going to do just fine with the farm folk. You keep shining your shine. You'll surely win their favor."

My lips quirked. "I surely hope so."

My newfound respect grew for the farming country and the families within it. From what I'd observed, every worker in that field—both Fae and human—worked their tail off to provide for our people. And from what I gathered from Bucoana, there were hostilities directed toward Mom and the council because of their lack of involvement in the farming communities of Atlantis. A renewed sense of purpose emerged within me. I'd make sure they were taken care of and heard.

The temperature slowly dipped as the day progressed. Every bone in my body ached when Samani found me at the end of my row, her cheeks rosy—a warm smile flashing on her face. "There you are. How did everything go?"

I wiped the moisture off my forehead for the hundredth time that day. "Good. Just the workout I was looking for."

"Excellent," she beamed. "Why don't we head to the house so we can freshen up? Then you can help me get everything ready. The rest of the crew will be done shortly, and I could use the help."

"I'd be happy to," I said, following Samani down the row toward the house. I spared one last glance over my shoulder, hoping to catch a glimpse of Bucoana, but she was farther down, having worked much faster than me. I'd have to catch up with her later.

After quickly bathing in Draevyn's wonderfully warm shower—one I wished I could linger in longer after the hot day—we strode in the direction of the oak wood barn. The rich smell of smoked brisket permeated the air as we approached the picnic tables before it. My stomach grumbled in response, causing Samani to chuckle. "We'll be eating soon enough."

Checkered cloth table linens lay perfectly across several picnic tables, with napkins, utensils, and plates placed in even stacks each. The entire little area was prepared to perfection by the time the workers from the fields strolled in. While weariness hung heavy on the group, the smiles on their faces could be felt as they gathered up their plates and began serving themselves from the buffet that lined the wall of the barn. It was a feast unlike any other I'd witnessed, one that came from the work of their hands. For them, I was sure nothing could be more rewarding.

As I stood with the biggest cheesy smile on my face—soaking in the moment—I thought of Bucoana, her voice playing on repeat in my mind.

*I'm not blaming you or anything. It's just some of us felt a little forgotten.*

Bucoana wasn't blaming me, but I blamed myself

nonetheless. Perhaps it wasn't my fault that Mom and the council didn't pay much attention to the outskirts. But that was about to change. I would see to it.

A set of strong, muscular arms coiled around my waist from behind. I would have panicked if it weren't for the tingling sensation in my center. "Hello, *nanichi,*" he whispered in my ear.

The smell of sandalwood drifting from his skin from the shower he must have taken assaulted my senses. I twisted in Draevyn's arms, wrapping my arms around his neck. "Hello, my love."

The joy that spread across his face at my term of endearment could be felt in the next realm. He leaned in and kissed me slowly.

"Hey, you two," Zoriato called. "Quit your canoodling and get some food before there's none left."

We giggled as we pulled apart. When we turned, a good number of the crew had stopped to stare—their eyes pinging between us.

Draevyn cleared his throat and murmured, "They didn't...they don't know that we..."

"Oh. Right. That we're a thing."

His shoulder lifted as he slid his fingers through mine. "Or that I'm 'thinging' with any female at all. I've never brought a female home before. I'll likely never hear the end of it."

Sure enough, some of the male members of the crew began whooping and patting Draevyn on the back as our steps brought us closer to the buffet filled with tender meats, roasted vegetables, stark white rice, various white and deep yellow cheeses, and faery wine. Once our plates were filled to the brim, we scanned the area, looking for a place to enjoy our meal.

"Your Highness!" called a familiar voice. My gaze

drifted in the direction of the call till it settled on Bucoana—her short arms waving frantically in the air, nearly whacking the Fae male that sat next to her. I smiled as we made our way to the two empty spaces at their table.

"We saved a spot just for you all," Bucoana said enthusiastically.

"Thank you," I said as we laid our food on the table.

"Bucoana, Tenebuy. Nice to see you all again," Draevyn greeted.

"*Tau*, Draevyn," Tenebuy said, reaching out to shake Draevyn's hand. "How is everything in the capital?"

"Hmph. As to be expected."

Tenebuy shook his head. "That good, huh?" His gaze slid to me. "Pleasure to meet you, Your Highness."

"Please, call me Ash. The pleasure's all mine."

Bucoana playfully swatted his shoulder. "You hear that, Tenie? The future Queen said to call her *Ash*. We're moving up in the world."

Tenebuy's shoulders shook with laughter.

"Well, Asherah, you couldn't have found yourself in better company," Draevyn told me, "Tenebuy has been working as a garden elemental with us for decades. He's been the lead climate adjuster for the past three," he beamed before filling his mouth with a heaping forkful of food. He closed his eyes with a rumbling moan. "Just as good as I remembered it."

That sparked my interest—the climate adjusting, not the rumbling moan. Although, that equally held my interest. "So, you adjust the temperature?"

"Yup," he confirmed. "It's important for the growth of the crops. I've seen rookie elementals scorch entire fields if they didn't get it right." He shook his head. "It's disastrous when it happens."

"Don't act like it didn't happen to you," Bucoana

teased, hiding her smile behind her glass of wine.

"Now, I never claimed that it didn't happen to me. My heart hurts seeing all those crops go to waste. It's different for a garden elemental. We can *feel* the crops."

My brows lowered. "Wait, you can feel the crops?"

"Every day," he confirmed as I ate a bit of my food, stifling back a moan as the savory flavors assaulted my taste buds. "That's the beauty of a garden elemental," Tenebuy continued. "We can tell what they need, but some elementals just learning to communicate with their crops tend to get the messages wrong, hence the fields of crops that are ruined in the process. That's precisely why Samani and Zoriato have a rigorous internship program. Took me nearly four decades to gain my permanency."

"But we're all glad you did," Bucoana beamed with a certain gleam in her eye; she and Tenebuy shared a look before he cleared his throat and looked the other way, but not before a slight blush crept up from his neck to his cheeks. Bucoana masterfully moved on to safer topics, engaging with him again.

I observed them with intense curiosity—my gaze traveling between them as I ate my food. Clearly, Bucoana was a human, and he, a Fae. It wouldn't be impossible for them to be together. Reneah had informed me that relationships between humans and Fae were perfectly acceptable. I couldn't imagine what it would be like to let someone go after falling in love with them. If what I assumed was true between Bucoana and Tenebuy, I didn't know if I could bear it. Could I be with someone I was doomed to lose?

Could Draevyn?

I couldn't help but think of the risk we faced ahead, the risk Draevyn faced in being with me.

"If you think any harder, you may hurt yourself or

others. What in the realms are you thinking about," Draevyn asked, interrupting my musings.

I glanced down at my food, my cheeks burning. "It's nothing."

He pushed a strand of hair behind my ear. "You blush so prettily when you lie." He brought his mouth to my ear. "It makes me want to do very naughty things to you," he whispered, his breath tickling my neck. I nearly moaned out loud, thinking of all the delectable things that mouth could do.

"So, Draevyn," Tenebuy piped up, the teasing tone matching the knowing grin. "When do we start calling you 'Your Highness?'"

"You will do no such thing," he growled.

"But it's true," Bucoana implored. "You will be the King Consort."

Tenebuy's brow rose. "Or perhaps you all haven't had that conversation yet."

"Oh, I don't think they've had that conversation yet, Tenie. Just look at their faces."

"You may be right, Ana. I've never seen Draevyn blush that way before, and I've seen him in the fields red-cheeked to the brim."

"The poor souls."

"They can't even look at each other."

"Isn't that cute?"

"Endearing."

Draevyn winced in my periphery. "I forgot how well the two of you embarrass people with your banter."

Bucoana shrugged with innocent eyes. "Just putting things into perspective for you, boss."

Draevyn groaned, much to the pleasure of Bucoana and Tenebuy, who roared with laughter. I couldn't resist joining in.

Night had fallen, and everyone had had their fill. More stories and laughter were shared. It was only when a small group broke away and began playing instruments that had been stored within the barn that everyone began to dance. There wasn't a human or Fae who wasn't smiling, dancing, or both. When the band had ended their melody, I watched as a flood of people scurried into position—each pair taking a side and facing their partner. The flames from the bonfire flickered across the area, highlighting their movement.

"What are they dancing?" I inquired.

"Areito. It's a traditional Atlantian dance," Draevyn answered, his arms closing around me from behind. I leaned into him, his chin coming to rest on top of my head.

I watched the dancers in fascination as they moved in perfect unison—their intricate steps, the way that they matched the beat perfectly, and the utter joy on their faces. "It's beautiful."

"Would you like to learn?"

I turned in his arms, my hands drifting over his immaculately sculpted chest. "Perhaps there's a different type of dance we can do, one that requires just the two of us, one that we already know." I flicked my head toward the barn.

Draevyn smiled salaciously. "Does the lady want to play?"

My head dipped in a single nod as I bit my lip.

He took my hand in his. "This way, my Queen." With a quick glance around, we traveled into the depths of the darkened barn undetected—the dim glow of the faelights casting areas in shadow. The smell of fermenting wine immediately hit my nose as we strolled deeper into a dark corner littered with wine barrels. My heart kicked in my chest, my core aching in anticipation. He pivoted to me, lifting me on top of a wine barrel—his eyes hooded with desire. "I've wanted to bury myself inside you so badly, Asherah. It drove me mad not seeing you all day, not being able to taste you, feel you." He dove into my neck, sucking the skin just below my ear into his sensual mouth. "Just seeing you be the Queen I know you to be makes my cock hard. My beautiful, strong, delicious female." His breath, with hints of faery wine, coasted across my lips as he moved his mouth over mine. "I need to claim you."

"Then claim me."

Draevyn's mouth pressed down on mine. Possessing. Claiming. When I sucked his full bottom lip, Draevyn made a low noise in his throat that contributed to the ache between my thighs. "Are you wet for me, Asherah?" I obliged his curiosity and parted my scales at my slit. His hand breached the opening, finding it drenched with desire. His thick, deft fingers gathered my wetness. With his heated gaze never leaving mine, he brought his fingers to his mouth, moaning around them as he sucked them clean. I stifled a moan, melting into a puddle of liquid lust. "You are so ready for me." His big, powerful hands brushed over my curves. "Drop your scales, nani-chi. Let me see all of you."

One by one, each layer of my scales retreated, revealing my bare skin to his hungry gaze. Draevyn leaned down, taking my pert nipple in his warm mouth, the surface of his coarse tongue causing my legs to twitch. His fingers dipped inside of my heat, thrusting to the swirls of his tongue. I couldn't control my hips as they rode his hand, the soft pad of his palm rubbing against my sensitive clit. My need built as he took my other nipple in his awaiting mouth—his thrusting picking up pace. Just as my climax was about to break throughout my body, he dropped to his knees, and his mouth was on my pussy, his tongue swirling circles around my swollen bud. His deep groan sent vibrations throughout my core, becoming my undoing. My release ripped through me, my hips bucking against his mouth as he lapped up my juices like a man dying of thirst.

Grabbing the underside of my thighs, he pulled me to the edge of the barrel, the rim digging into my ass as Draevyn dropped his scales, positioning his hardened rock-hard length to my opening. I leaned back on my arms and watched as he slowly slid into me, my chest pumping with every thick inch that stretched my dripping wet entrance. He fixed his hungry eyes on me as he thrust all the way in, my mouth releasing a moan I couldn't contain and my eyes closing in response.

Draevyn gripped the base of my neck. "Open your eyes, nanichi. I want you to watch me as I take you." As if some hidden force had taken over my body, my eyes opened to the sight of us joined together, my desire glistening on his length as he slowly moved in and out of me. "Good girl."

And then, he showed me just how good I had been.

Draevyn fucked me with quick wild pumps of his hips, his cock hitting the back of my womb over and over till I felt my need rising once again. His hand gripped my ass, holding me tightly to him as the other played with my clit. The feel of him was maddening, and I found myself addicted to this particular brand of Draevyn.

"Drae, I'm going to—"

"Give it to me."

My body thrummed as I came around his cock. When his body began to shudder, my name left his lips as he came inside me.

With deep-satiated breaths, he brought his mouth to mine once again, the taste of my arousal still lingering on his lips. His tongue was slow and gentle.

"That is a dance I'll never forget," he whispered.

"I'm willing to be your dance partner anytime," I breathed against his lips.

We remained joined together in each other's arms for a long while until Draevyn delicately pulled out from me. He summoned water from the nearby well and cleaned me thoroughly before discarding the water on the ground. "Come. Let's go to bed."

My scales spread across my body as I let loose a satisfied sigh. "Won't they miss us?"

He laughed amusedly, wrapping an arm around my waist. "Not from the sounds of it."

We exited the back of the barn into the cool night, escaping the festivities like two thieves in the night.

With the early morning light streaming into the room, I rubbed the sleep from my eyes, stifling a yawn. My body instinctively gravitated toward Draevyn's warmth. I scooted into his side, my leg draped over his muscular thigh. My skin pebbled when his hand began drawing lazy circles across my back. The dozens of gleaming medals that hung on metal hooks on the walls just above the dozens of trophies proudly displayed provided a glimpse of a younger Draevyn. The thought had me smiling against his chest.

"I'm glad we came here," I confessed.

"I needed this," he admitted. "I needed you to see where I grew up, to meet the people of Sabana. They needed to see you here."

An uneasy feeling sunk in my gut. "I'm very disappointed in my mother."

His hand paused momentarily before he asked, "And why is that?"

"Because she didn't come out here often. Neither did the council."

"Ah. Bucoana," he said in understanding.

"Yes, she doesn't exactly hold back her feelings on that matter."

"Or any other matter," he murmured.

I chuckled against his chest. "I like that about her. How else would I have known that we need to do better at helping the people of Sabana and farming towns all over Atlantis? Just because they don't reside in the capital doesn't mean their voices shouldn't be heard."

"It's a very wise and diplomatic perspective. I'm proud of you for voicing it. If you become an advocate for our people, they will love you all the more."

The sounds of the breaking dawn fluttered through the open window—birds chirping, the low bustle of workers laboring in a distant field. It was quite a contrast from the sounds of the capital, the sounds that awaited me as soon as I left the safety of Draevyn's arms. I snuggled closer to him.

"I'm also glad you got a chance to meet my parents and that they got an opportunity to get to know the real you. I needed them to see the source of my happiness for themselves. My parents are very fond of you."

I groaned. "I don't know about that."

He turned fully toward me. "My father?"

I nodded.

"Believe it or not, that's about as joyful as Zoriato Eliron gets. Trust me. He likes you. It may take a while for him to come around to the idea of us bonding, but if Atabey gives us her blessing, there's not much anyone can say about it." He pulled me to him, his hard length pressing into my stomach. "So, let them talk. I truly don't care."

The tips of my fingers brushed against his chest. "And you…you're sure about this? You're okay being bonded to a Queen?"

He cupped my cheek. "Yes, Asherah. I'm more than okay. This feeling goes beyond what you might know of love in the Above World. Our kind, when we feel something for another, it's primal. A calling. It pulls deep within us. That's what lets us know our soul has a partner, someone to walk this life with. And I'm not talking about completing you. You do that all on your own without any help from me. The purpose of a mate is to complement each other wholly, as partners in this long life." He placed a flattened palm between my breasts. "Is the weird tingling sensation beginning to get stronger by the day?"

"It is," I breathed.

"And do you feel a certain restlessness when I'm away?"

"Yes," I admitted.

His eyes searched mine. "That's the bond, nanichi. And the way to fully enact it is to attend the bonding ceremony—to attend Guake'te—where before Atabey, our bond is affirmed by the Bohiti. That bond is sacred. And I choose that with you."

The tears welled in my eyes. "I choose it with you too. Thank you…for choosing me." I shrugged as a tiny smirk lifted my lips. "Even if you're a little overbearing during our training."

He smacked my backside playfully. "That, my dear, will never change."

And while the rest of the world waited for us beyond the blissful confines of Draevyn's childhood bedroom, he made love to me—long and slow, his body expressing exactly how he felt.

# Chapter 32

The days and weeks flew by in a flurry of events since our time in Sabana. Myles had returned to Atlantis and immediately began our lessons again, much to my relief. He all but guaranteed that Melysah wouldn't be an issue any longer, but the problem was that it wasn't exactly true. Her recent attempts at interfering in our lives had been of a subtle sort: sending Kane to spy on us, condescending comments in council meetings regarding my lack of knowledge, and the way she always appeared to be around. But nothing, absolutely nothing got under my skin more than how she outright flirted with Draevyn right in front of me—or tried to anyway, since that flirtation was a one-way street. I nearly knocked her teeth out when she mentioned the tryst between them that happened decades ago. While I trusted Draevyn implicitly, it still had me running hot with anger.

It didn't help that Draevyn was gone to conduct

another training. While I understood this would happen and often, given his position with the Guardians, it didn't ease the ache I felt in my chest when he was away. It seemed to be getting worse the closer we became.

I tried to distract myself from his absence by diving into an ancient tome on the long, wooden library table before me—the faelights hovering above the table providing the perfect amount of light in the otherwise darkened second floor of the library. Lux kept busy skimming his pile of books across from me, a worried crease on his forehead as I placed another book on the pile he'd already skimmed. He blew a raspberry. "This task is fucking daunting."

"That it is, my friend," I said, turning to another page of elemental symbols. "Although it's fascinating to see so many marks. Some of these are very beautiful. There are just so many. An element for just about everything."

Lux huffed, flipping a page. "The goddess is wise. She thought of everything. I'm surprised there isn't an element to sort through grains of sand."

"That would be a rather boring element to have," I said, smiling at him.

"Nah, Atabay's calling is like a siren song. It calls to the individual."

I glanced over at his wrist. "What elemental mark are you?"

He held up his wrist, twisting it this way and that. "A historical elemental. Analyzer and absorber of history."

"Ah, that explains a lot."

Lux shrugged. "Can't be helped. I love the stuff, hence why I wanted to help you in this mission."

"Well, then, I'm glad I have you on my side because it looks like this will be one hell of a task." My brow furrowed. "There's a dome astrologist elemental?"

Lux's face lit up. "Oh yes. That's one of my favorites. They work in tandem with the dome lighters. You see, the dome lighters are the elementals responsible for lighting the dome, dimming it to reflect the nighttime of the Above World. But what is fascinating is that the constellations change, and they do so on their own. The dome lighters are basically the vehicle for which the stars are presented to the Fae. It's up to the dome astrologist to determine the new map of stars and record them before the changing of the stars happens again. Once recorded, that's where the fun begins. They begin analyzing all the symbols held within the stars to see if any prophecies are held within. The astrologists are some of my favorite elementals to speak to." His smile slowly dropped. "Well, when I'm here. And when I'm permitted to speak with them."

My heart panged with empathy for him, and my admiration grew. Lux was a historical elemental through and through. His knowledge of Atlantis and its inner workings was proof of that. He should be averse to learning about the Water Fae, but he wasn't. "Is Corenathia that much different than Atlantis?"

Lux glared at me with fierce intensity. "Corenathia is unlike any of the other realms. It is ruled by a Queen who rarely cares about the Fire Fae within her realm and will end anyone who dares to challenge her. And humans are nothing more than collateral."

"So, you do have humans left in Corenathia."

Lux's deep brown eyes widened. "I've said too much."

"I won't say anything."

"You'd be a fool not to."

I broke off the intense stare-off and flipped a page. "Well, I'm a fool, I guess."

From my periphery, I saw him rake a hand through his fire-red hair before he continued, "The people of Corenathia tell tales of how Atabey herself blessed Queen Sessi, how Atabey came to Corenathia when she was a babe to declare Sessi the Forever Queen—whatever the fuck that means."

I noted how he didn't call her "mother" when speaking of Queen Sessi. It was on the tip of my tongue to ask, but I assumed it was a sensitive subject. However, I couldn't resist moving on to other topics that piqued my curiosity. "And your brothers and sisters?"

"Just one brother and one sister. How such an evil female was able to conceive multiple children is truly beyond my understanding." His arms went wide. "But here we are."

My forehead creased. "I thought the Fae had trouble conceiving?"

"You're correct. They do. The goddess only knows what kind of deal she made with Maboya to secure that kind of fertility."

"Maboya?"

Lux's face paled. "The Great Evil Spirit," he said, a quiver of fear in his tone. "He is the most evil entity who preys on those who thirst for power and those who long for things they shouldn't have. To make a deal with him is permanent. Those who are foolish enough to do so end up regretting it. I'm surprised you haven't heard of him."

A shiver crept up my spine. "We have something similar in the Above World."

Lux snorted. "The Devil? Maboya makes the Devil look like a child doing tricks for attention. Believe me when I tell you. Maboya? He's far worse."

"You speak as if you've met him."

"Not met him. Felt him—somewhere in the confines of Queen Sessi's palace. I'm certain of it." A beat of silence ensued, the eerie information settling within me like lead at the bottom of a bucket. Lux cleared his throat, his eyes returning to his newest tome to skim. "Anyway, all of this contributes to the notion that Queen Sessi is the prophesized Hekiti. She's just short of calling herself a goddess these days." He looked up from his tome. "I suppose you don't know about the Hekiti either?" When I shook my head, he continued, "The Hekiti is the goddess' chosen one. It is said that she will bring the realms together in peace during the next ice age. " My brow furrowed as I remembered Myles mentioning a prophecy. "So," Lux continued, drawing my attention back to his tale, "of course, Sessi took the prophecy and made it her own, and the Fire Fae lapped it up like it was valid. The rest of us who know better stay silent because we'll lose our heads for voicing anything against our dear Queen."

I reared back. "She would take her own son's life?"

"Spawn."

I blinked at him. "Pardon?"

He flipped another page. "Spawn. The correct terminology is spawn. At least, that is what she calls us." He lifted his brown eyes again. "And yes, she would kill us if we crossed her. I have two siblings *left*. She's taken the lives of my other two siblings, may Atabay carry their souls through the Veil."

I gaped. "That's horrific."

Lux let out a humorless laugh. "You're telling me. I'm the one who's had to live it." He inhaled deeply. "Let's pray to the goddess that you never have to step foot in that realm. No telling what might happen."

"Can't you just stay here?"

"Not unless you're willing to marry me." My lips rounded in an 'o' with that revelation. "And if my eyes have not deceived me," he continued with a mischievous grin, "it would seem that a certain Guardian has already taken your heart. Am I right?" I couldn't help the blush that crept up my cheeks. He smiled like the cat that caught the canary before flipping a page. "That's what I thought."

"That can't be the only way to stay here. Couldn't you seek asylum?"

"The rules of my queendom are absolute. No one may seek asylum in another realm. No one can leave without the express permission of the Queen herself. A petition for visitation could take years for approval. It just depends on how generous the Queen is feeling."

My brow furrowed as I flipped a page. "Isn't that something that your council would take care of?"

Lux bellowed with laughter, a shush coming from the librarian on the first floor who must have overheard him. "There is no council. Corenathia isn't a democracy. There are no representatives from its towns. There is only her rule. Always."

My ire began burning bright. "I really dislike your mother."

"She's my Queen. Not my mother," he seethed. "Mothers are supposed to be loving and nurturing. They're supposed to care for their children and want what's best for them. Mothers have a heart. Queen Sessi has no heart. She is incapable of feeling anything but love for herself."

I suddenly missed my own mother with a fierceness that I hadn't felt since her passing. Lux was right. Mothers were supposed to be loving and nurturing; mine had been, thankfully. I swallowed the grief that had stuck in my throat. "You are welcome to stay here." I sighed with a gentle smile. "When I become Queen, I'll find a way."

His cupid-bow lips lifted, returning my smile, and his face lit like it was the first time anyone had ever shown him empathy or understood his situation in Corenathia.

"Well, doesn't this look cozy," said a voice that instantly had my anger rising to a fever pitch. I twisted in my seat to meet the amused gaze of Melysah, who stood a few paces away, her pale blue eyes traveling between us. "And how wonderful, you all…bonding…over books. Perhaps Prince Lux will give you a good reason to pay attention to your studies," she said, shrugging. "Or perhaps he'll provide the perfect distraction to keep you from your studies so you'll fail the requirements to become Queen." She glanced down at her pearl-polished nails. "Either way, it seems like a win-win to me. I'm sure Draevyn would love to know you're flirting with the enemy."

I tried my best to express all the petty pity I could muster on my face. "Aw, that's so cute. You think I keep things from my lover? We tell each other everything. You know, like a bondmate should?" I let that implication sink in and knew it had hit its mark when Melysah's expression morphed into pure loathing.

"Draevyn would never present you at the bonding ceremony."

"Wanna bet?"

Melysah's chest pumped. "You barely even know what the Atlantian traditions are. In the eyes of the Atlantians, you're a simpleton."

I lifted a shoulder in a lazy shrug. "Simpleton or not, it'll never change what I am to him." My lips quirked. "And doesn't that just get under your scales?"

Melysah gave one last huff before she disappeared

through the stacks and out of the library if the telltale bang of the door against the stone was any indication.

"Way to stir the pot, Ash."

"Someone needs to put her in her place," I said as I flipped the page.

"That one does not play nice. That one...she likes to play with fire."

My eyes snapped to his with that comment, the warning evident. We spent the rest of the afternoon in silence, trying to find anything that could lead us to an explanation of my elemental mark, but to no avail.

A knock at my door pulled me from my very captivating read—the new vampire romance I picked up at Fae Flings on the way home from university. Oh, how I loathed when people knew just the right scene to interrupt. "Come in."

When the door swung open, and Draevyn walked through the door—a heart-melting smile on his gorgeous face—all thoughts of the book were forgotten. I all but leapt on him, his strong arms wrapping around me as he swung me around in a circle. His joyful laughter went straight to my heart.

He gently placed me on the floor. "Miss me, did you?"

I went on the tips of my webbed toes and brought my mouth to his, kissing him chastely. "Maybe a little bit."

"Mmmm, you've been busy though, yes?"

"Yes, there's a lot to tell you," I said when an idea instantly came to me, "but since this involves the dome constellations and the sun is setting, maybe I could bring you up to speed in the gardens?"

He leaned down, his soft lips kissing the area just below my ear. "Just what kind of…speed…will you be bringing me up to?"

I tapped his shoulder playfully. "The serious speed."

His lips peppered kisses across my jaw. "I am being serious."

"Please?"

He pulled back, a look of mischief cresting his features. "Well, when you beg like that, how can I say no?"

After grabbing a blanket and a few odds and ends to nibble on, we strolled through the palace toward the gardens. I filled him in on everything that he'd missed, from Lux's passion for history to the monstrous abuse he endured at the hands of his very own mother to the constellations—which was the primary reason for the trip to the gardens. I left out the part about running into Melysah because I was having a great day. Why ruin it?

"I figured since you've been here longer than me, you could help me understand what I'm looking at," I said as I held up my leather tote. "I even brought a book on the most recent constellation patterns."

Draevyn huffed a laugh. "I could practically teach a class on the constellation patterns. Mind you, I'm obviously not an astrology elemental, but the stars shine a little brighter out in Sabana than in Borike'n. As faelings, that's all we would do is look at the stars. Could practically walk home to their pattern if need be."

I threaded my arm through his as we meandered through the darkening gardens. "Well then, I have the perfect person to help me."

After winding the pathways to the outer part of the gardens, we reached the charming gazebo, and the memory of our last time there flashed through my mind—my cheeks heating. I settled the blanket in the grassy area before it, leaning back on my arms as I made myself comfortable. Draevyn dropped next to me, doing the same.

"I hate feeling any empathy toward a Fire Fae, but I can't help but pity Lux," Draevyn said. "Queen Sessi sounds like a nightmare of a mother."

"That's an understatement," I agreed.

"You always hope that even the evil ones have a good bone in their body." He shook his head, a long strand of his dark hair falling over his shoulder. "That one seems like she's allergic to good bones."

My brow furrowed. "I know I'm still learning of the Fae and cultural practices, customs, and all of that, but is it…normal for a Queen to kill her offspring like that?"

Draevyn sighed, laying flat on the blanket. "Unfortunately, the Fae can be ruthless from time to time. Of course, here in Atlantis, things are a little different." He tilted his head to glance my way. "That is on account of your lineage. Your ancestors have been some of the best in the Fae realms. The Fire Fae? They tend to lean toward their baser instincts."

"And the Air and Earth Fae?"

"The Air Fae are the most peaceful, to be sure. They don't enjoy conflict. If they can, they try to stay out of it. Their Queens have been known to marry for peace than for the bond."

The pulling sensation in my chest twinged at that. It would be hard to deny that calling. "Why would anyone do that?"

"Unfortunately, Queens have been known to marry for alliances. There have only been a handful in your line. Not many."

I thought of my conversation with Lux.

*'Can't you just stay here?'*

*'Not unless you're willing to marry me.'*

"Can Lux marry Queen Laenah?" I inquired.

"If she weren't already in negotiations to wed his older brother, I would suppose so."

"Oh." My shoulders slumped. "And Queen Ayi?"

"Very much a lesbian and very happily mated. It is said they have one of the greatest love stories of all time." His brow furrowed. "Why are you so concerned about who he marries?"

"Because it appears that's the only way he can get out. Until I think of something else, that is."

He reached behind my back, twirling a strand of hair. "You wouldn't marry him, would you?"

My mouth fell open. "That's insanity."

Draevyn shrugged. "I had to ask."

"That's a hard no, Drae. I'd hope you'd know that."

The smile that emerged on his face was one of happy relief. "Thank the goddess."

I came down to lie on the blanket. "So, where do you want to start?" I asked him.

"Hhmm, most of the stars from the last constellation change remained the same with a few distinct exceptions. The changes were exciting."

I nuzzled closer to his side, laying my head on his shoulder. "How so?"

"Well, for starters, when the changeover occurred, there were four new clusters of stars. The change occurred about a hundred years ago. It took a long time for the astrology & historical elementals to piece everything together." He pointed to my leather tote. "Why don't you get your book out?"

I did, returning to his side, sitting cross-legged and thumbing the book open to the map displaying the most recent change. "Okay, ready."

Draevyn perched himself on an elbow and summoned a dim faelight, guiding it to the area of the map with an oddly curved shape constellation. "This is what they call the Cobo."

I squinted. "It's a shell."

"That it is. The Cobo is a very sacred artifact, one that Atlantians have never discovered. Our earliest texts only mention its creation. None of them identify its existence." His finger moved to the cluster of stars next to the Cobo. "Interestingly enough, this is another artifact that ancient texts mention, but has never been discovered. It's called the Jujo, and they say it is a snake made of iron."

My forehead creased as I glanced at the dome, studying the Jujo constellation in the sky. "But we can't touch iron. How can a sacred Fae artifact be made of material none of us can touch?"

"That's the question many historical elementals have asked. It's theorized that the goddess herself made the Jujo." He pointed out the next cluster, this one in the shape of a bird. "This one is my absolute favorite of them all. That is the Guaraguao. It's a red-tailed hawk. This one took the longest for historians to figure out. The answer was found in a text dating back more than three millennia. The historians who studied the ancient book wore head-to-toe garments to avoid damaging it. They hate it when texts get ruined. When they discovered the meaning…goddess, the celebrations went on for a week straight.

"Anyhow, it is said that a red feather from the first red-tailed hawk held enormous power and lay in one of the realms undiscovered until the one called to summon it can find it."

My brow furrowed as I studied the cluster on the

dome. "Who will be called to summon it?"

"Patience. I'll get to that part in a moment." His finger moved to the final constellation. "And this is the Anacaona, otherwise known as the golden flower. The location of this artifact has been theorized to exist in Earthos. The Anacaona is a sacred symbol in their realm. Beyond the Earth Fae acknowledging the theory, no one dares to ask about it.

"But the most fascinating thing that connects all of the symbols? Our prophecies tell us that each of these sacred objects can only be retrieved by the Hekiti, the goddesses chosen one."

I perked up. "Lux mentioned that his mother thinks she's the Hekiti."

Draevyn snorted. "She wishes. The Hekiti is the most sacred. The prophecy tells us that she will bring peace to the realms. Queen Sessi is the furthest thing from peace. She's chaos personified."

With the clusters identified, I placed the book aside, laid back, and stared up at the stars. "Tell me more about the Hekiti."

"Hekiti means the One. It is reserved for the goddess' chosen. It's been theorized that the Hekiti is the goddess' daughter reincarnated. Others say the Hekiti will have a piece of the goddess's soul within her. They're all theories. However, the prophecy holds the most important clues to identify the Hekiti. It is said she will possess all the elements."

I turned my head toward him. "All the elements?"

"Yes, she will have water, fire, air, and earth. No Fae has ever had two elements, let alone all of them. It's unheard of."

"Oh yeah, I remember Myles mentioned that now," I told him as I pondered over that little tidbit of information while returning my gaze to the stars. "That kind of power in the wrong hands would be terrible."

"Right, which is why it could never be Queen Sessi. How can someone so evil want to save the Fae and humanity?"

Scooting into his side, we lay there in blissful silence—the soothing sounds of the Shingu River drifting by the only sound. It did nothing to calm my thoughts. Something about the constellations bothered me, but I couldn't place my thumb on it. The feeling stayed with me long into the night, even as I drifted off to sleep under the stars in Draevyn's arms.

# CHAPTER 33

"Again."

Dax had been taking me through my paces for what seemed like an eternity.

But it had only been a few hours.

The sweat dripped down my face and onto the surface of my scales, the ends of which were brought up to my collarbone and down the lengths of my arms. I gripped my trident tightly—a soft glow emanating through my hand. I twirled it into position, readying myself again—giving Dax a nod.

He wasted no time. His massive, muscular arms hoisted his trident over his head with ease and swept it down in the next second. In a move that even I was shocked by, I blocked his blow before swiftly twirling with my trident, landing my hit on his side. As it hit its mark, we paused.

Dax's face lit with pure delight. "You're getting much faster."

"Thanks," I said, willing heaps of air into my lungs.

"I want you to focus on the form in your twist. Grip higher on the trident stem. It will deliver a harder blow," he instructed, rubbing his ribcage. "Although, that last one was pretty hard."

I winced. "Sorry."

Dax fluttered his large hand. "Don't be. That's what I want you to do. I can take it." He gave me a reassuring wink. "You're doing great, Asherah. I wish half my Guardians had your focus and determination. It would do them a world of good."

His words had me beaming with pride. "Thank you."

A young male faeling ran through the open doors of the training facility with an envelope in his hand. "For you, General Lumeya."

He took the letter, his cobalt blue eyes scanning the parchment. Dax ran his fingers through the long strands of his blond hair and let out a deep sigh. "I need to go. The little council tyrant requested my presence."

My eyes narrowed. "Why does she want to meet with you?"

Dax shrugged. "Who knows? She's acting bitchier than usual. Even Roarvyn, who has a knack for letting things roll off his shoulder, is growing impatient. Something must have crawled up her ass."

I had an inkling of what that something might be— or who rather—but didn't voice it. No sense in doing so. Dax was already aware of Melysah's petty games. "I'll hang back and practice a bit."

"Sound plan." Dax planted his trident on his shoulder as he strode for the exit. "See you tomorrow."

The training facility was blissfully empty. I summoned water to quench my thirst, gulping the cool water with relief as it traveled down my throat. I splashed a bit more on my heated face, feeling instantly relieved. I wasted no time rolling through my practice swings with my trident, my mind zeroing out the world around me.

Left, down, turn, swing, twist up—

WACK!

I pitched forward, unable to breathe, my eyes wide, as my knees hit the ground. Immense pain spread out through my back, immobilizing me.

WACK!

The impact sent me flat to the ground. I couldn't think. My vision became clouded with stars.

I needed to move.

Fast.

With all the energy I had, I rolled to my back just as a glowing trident slammed on the floor next to my head. I gazed up at Melysah's sneering face.

"You really should watch your back, Princess." Melysah swung her trident over her head, aiming the tips at my torso. I hoisted myself in a crouch just in time, watching with sick satisfaction as the impact from Melysah's trident against the ground reverberated throughout her body.

"You really should learn to fight fairly," I bit back.

Melysah positioned herself in a fighting stance.

Oh, yeah. We were doing this.

I wasted no time. I thrust my trident into Melysah's torso, prompting her to bring her trident down for the block. I quickly twisted, landing a fierce blow into her side.

But Melysah, with her decades of training over my own, dropped into a well-practiced fighting stance— her gaze assessing her opponent and calculating her next move. And move she did. With a grace I had to admire, she swirled her trident, the blows landing with a clank against my stem and vibrating throughout my body. Her feet followed a careful dance as if she were recalling a warrior dance she'd practiced in the quiet confines of her room. I challenged each step and blocked each move she made around the room, her face held in fierce determination.

With my own determination building, I blocked another blow and immediately jabbed her in the stomach with the base of my stem, just as I'd practiced with Dax. He'd be proud.

Speaking of…

"Aren't you supposed to be meeting with Dax? Seems like that would be a better use of your time."

Melysah readied herself for another go. "Not the way I see it." An evil grin spread on her obnoxious face. "And to answer your question, I needed some way to get you alone." She came for me then, her trident swinging in a graceful flow. My body, already heavy with exhaustion, could barely keep up with the blocks. The impact on my scales would leave a mark tomorrow. That was for sure. I needed a way to end this. I dropped and swung my leg out, catching Melysah unaware, her body hitting the ground.

I rose from the ground and smirked down at her. "I truly appreciate you coming all this way to practice with me, but this session is over."

Melysah clenched her teeth. "Not yet, it's not." Her foot reared back, then pitched forward, catching me in the stomach. I bent over, trying to bring air into my lungs as Melysah rose from the ground.

"Perhaps we should do this like real females." She fashioned her scales to cover her breasts and left tiny shorts shaped on her lower body. Everything else was pale-colored skin. "Skins and tridents only. What do you say, Princess?"

I stood at full height, dropping my scales to match hers with a lift of my chin. "Challenge accepted."

And then we sparred.

I could feel the determination rise within my soul. Going against everything that I stood for, I wanted to beat Melysah within an inch of her life to teach her that she could no longer bully me and mine. When her trident swept at my knees, I leapt and twisted—my trident cutting through the air and smacking into her back. She jabbed at my heart, nearly nicking me with the tip of her trident, her sneer only growing when I blocked the hit. I pushed her back and jabbed the stem into her nose with a sickening crunch. As the blood leaked from her nose, she twirled her trident, her next move unreadable as she swung and whacked me in my side, taking the air from my lungs.

Blow after blow. Cut after cut. My limbs began to tire, and Melysah didn't look any better—her breathing became more erratic, and the hits she made felt like taps against my skin.

It was time to end this charade.

I swung the tip of my trident across Melysah's lower abdomen, the blood seeping down what little scales she displayed below. Melysah's hand flew to her open wound, her mouth hanging open as she stared at me in disbelief.

"That's for stalking me."

Before Melysah could recover, I twirled with all my strength, sending a blow into Melysah's stomach. Melysah crashed to the floor with a groan. "And that's for sending your lapdog after me."

I stepped to her side, Melysah's body trembling as her

furious gaze fixed on me.

Oh, how I wanted to pierce Melysah straight through her gut. I wouldn't, though. That's not who I am.

But I could act like I was about to.

I lifted the trident above my head, baring my teeth. "And this, this is for trying to come between me and Draevyn, like you mean anything to him."

Just before my motion brought the trident down in a mock stab, Melysah's fingers flicked. Pain in my stomach like I'd never felt stilled my breath. I glanced down at the three ice daggers sticking through my stomach. I dropped to my knees, the taste of iron filling my mouth. When she rose from the ground, I spat blood at her feet. My vision clouded with the effort to breathe.

Melysah stood over me—the stars in my vision peppering her satisfied smug. "For the record, I feared for my life. At least, that's what I'll tell them. And here I was, simply trying to teach you how to fight. Seems like a poor way to repay me." She crouched down as my head lolled to the side. "You know, Draevyn met me at Guake'te once," she said as she bit her lip, the corner of her mouth quirking. "Mmmm, there was nothing quite like it. I'll never forget the feel of him, the way his body moved against mine, or the look in his eyes." Despite my lack of oxygen, I could feel the anger rising in me like a tangible thing. Melysah stared in the distance. "There was something in his gaze that evening, something that let me know I was his despite his words," she recalled, her evil gaze shifting back to me. "I get your obsession, the desire to make him yours." Her hand snapped out and gripped my chin, her nails cutting into the skin of my cheeks. "But he is not yours to have. He never was. He never will be. So, I want to make myself very clear. You won't be attending the bonding ceremony. While the other Atlantians find their mates, you won't even sniff the air around the temple. You'll be safely within the confines of the palace—likely touching yourself with how potent the lust emanating from the bonding ceremony is—but you'll be nowhere near Draevyn. And do you know why?"

Melysah waited for an answer, but my voice failed me. I opted to spit in her face instead. I anticipated the slap that came across my face—almost reveled in it as my body listed to the side. Melysah rose and summoned water to clean her face, but it did very little to wash away the expression of righteous anger. "Do you know why, Asherah? Answer me!" she bellowed.

"No," I murmured through a gargle.

The smile that emerged on Melysah's face was one of pure delight. "Because I'm a true Atlantian. A true Water Fae. I've studied the council text. Scoured them. You don't want to find out the ways I'll retaliate. But above all, my plans for you don't include Draevyn because one day, he'll present me before the Bohiti as his chosen bondmate." I thought that was very unlikely. The room began to fade into darkness. "Draevyn is *my* mate. You have no place here. You are nothing but a little distraction, Asherah Delmar." I closed my eyes, but not before I winced when one final dagger pierced my middle, followed by Melysah's cackle. "Pathetic."

My eyes flew open one last time as Melysah ripped the daggers from my body—the hot flow of blood seeping out of my wounds. She turned toward the entrance. "Go find Dax. Let him know his little Princess has been injured in a training exercise."

It was the last thing I heard before the darkness claimed me.

A low murmur of voices broke into my consciousness—voices my mind slowly began to recognize, the fragments of their conversation piecing together even before I had the strength to open my eyes.

"She was supposed to be guarded by Belamo. He'd told me he had her while I went to see what was amiss with the grand council wench," Dax seethed in a low whisper.

"Yeah, well. He did as you asked. He just didn't know Kane had been banned from guarding Asherah when he came to relieve him," Dad said with a sigh. "Whatever the case, Myles will get to the bottom of it. I'm sure he's ripping her a new asshole as we speak, in the most Myles way possible, of course."

"Will that woman stop at nothing?" Reneah asked, appalled.

"Apparently not," Draevyn said. A small moment passed before he went on. "I can't help but feel responsible."

A chorus of 'no's' went up.

I mustered my very little strength and attempted to open my eyes. The faelight assailed my senses before the shapes began to take form. I blinked a few times to get rid of the dryness. The stone room of the infirmary was one place I hadn't expected to be. My gaze found Draevyn sitting in a small wooden chair with his face buried in his hands. "It wasn't your fault," I said, my voice cracking.

Four sets of eyes swung to me, the concern evident on their faces. Draevyn moved his chair, placing it by my side. "How are you feeling, *nanichi*?" he asked as he slid into his seat.

My gaze flew to Dad. He'd never heard Draevyn call me that. Cats out of the bag, I supposed. My gaze shifted back to Draevyn. "Like I lost a really good sparring match."

"Is that what really happened?" Dax asked, eyes begging for the truth.

I hated lying to the people I loved and cared for, and Dax fell into that category. Since arriving in Atlantis, he'd been my mentor and someone who looked after Dad with great honor. That's why when I replied, "That's what happened," an overwhelming sense of guilt came crashing down on my weary body. One look at Draevyn told me he didn't believe the lie that rolled off my tongue.

I tried to move up the bed, but the pain caused me to wince. Draevyn's arms reached under mine, gently pulling me to sit. "How long have I been out?" I asked.

"A day," Dad answered. He appraised me with narrowed eyes. "You know you can tell us anything, Sher? Did something happen in there that wasn't supposed to happen?"

Reneah handed me a cup of water and adjusted the pillow at my back. "Seems to me like the wench took a couple of cheap shots," she remarked coolly.

I huffed a humorless laugh. "She may have." My gaze snapped up to the group. "But we're not going to report her."

"Why the hell not?" Draevyn asked, his tone heavy with anger.

"Because we're not going to stoop to her level."

"But she violated you in the worst way," Dax insisted. "We've seen your wounds, Ash. We found you bleeding out on the floor. Had you not been Fae, you would have died. I counted four gaping wounds. That's not a sparring match. That's a death match."

I glanced down at the cup in my hands. "Yeah. Well. She didn't win, did she?" I shrugged.

"Sher." I met my father's worried gaze. "You don't have to be brave. Everyone in this room knows you already are. If she did something—anything—that is a violation of our laws, she deserves to be punished. She cannot do this to our Queen."

"But I'm not your Queen. To Melysah and the Water Fae who think like her, I'm barely even a Princess."

I couldn't help but notice the look of worry the group shared with each other.

Draevyn took the cup from my hands, placed it on the small nightstand beside my bed, and took my hands in his. "I want you to pay close attention to what I'm about to say. When you're dealing with a realm as big as Atlantis, you'll always have those who are narrow-minded. Those who don't support you, your decisions, and your leadership will always exist. Whether you asked for it or not, it's part of the role, *your* role, as the Queen of Atlantis. So, every time those who oppose your rule begin striving for attention, I want you to remember one thing and this one thing only. Other people's opinions of you are none of your business."

An eyebrow lifted to my hairline. "How are they none of my business?"

Draevyn shrugged. "They're none of your business. What you think of yourself is the only opinion that matters. That's it." He motioned around the room. "Not even the opinions of the people in this room matter."

"My opinion about her trident training matters," Dax murmured.

Draevyn shot him a look. "The point is," he continued, "you need to have thicker skin. It's about to get a whole hell of a lot worse."

I sighed, nodding in resolve. "You're right."

"That's our girl," Reneah beamed.

"So," Dad cut in, "with that all said, do we need to report Melysah?"

"That's what she wants." My determined gaze met Dad's. "And I won't give her the satisfaction." I couldn't help but glance at Draevyn, whose lips lifted in a smirk.

The room went quiet before Dax spoke. "She's like Teflon, that one."

Dad's brows furrowed. "How do you even know what Teflon is?"

Dax managed to look affronted. "I'm not a complete imbecile. I do keep up to date with new advancements, slang, and terminologies in the Above World...brah."

Draevyn snorted.

"Alright, you two bickering ninnies," Reneah cut in, motioning for the door. "Let's leave Ash to rest." She glanced my way. "I'll make sure the healer knows you've awakened. I'm sure you'll be more comfortable in your own bed while you heal. I'll see when we can get you moved."

"Thanks, Reneah."

With a gentle smile, she followed Dad and Dax out of the room, leaving Draevyn and me in silence. He scooted his chair closer to the bed, reaching up to tuck a stray strand of hair behind the tip of my ear. "I'm sorry."

I brought my hand to the back of his, holding it against my cheek, reveling in the warmth. "Please don't. It's not your fault."

"It is. This is because of me. And her obsession."

I smirked. "Not to break your ego, but this has to do with more than just you. She doesn't think I'm fit to be

Queen."

"Yes, but she's always contested your right to the throne. She only started to get violent when she saw us together."

My head tilted, kissing his palm. "True. But us being what we are to each other is not your fault. If anything, it's a burden we share together."

His gaze grew intense. "What did she say to you, Ash? And don't lie. Not to me."

I stayed silent for a beat before the confession fell from my lips. "She doesn't want us bonded."

"Fuck."

"She seems to think that the two of you are bond-mates and that I'm not worthy of being yours." I debated the following admission. I'd had other lovers in the Above World. None of them could ever compare Draevyn. I chose not to speak of them in front of him because it didn't matter. And who he'd been with before me didn't matter either. That was B.A.: Before Ash. But a part of me wondered why he'd sleep with Melysah when, from all past conversations about her, he seemed to detest her very existence. My curiosity won out. "She told me that you met her at Guake'te."

Draevyn's lips pressed together. "That is a lie."

"Not as she tells it."

"Asherah," his gaze grew serious, "have I ever lied to you?" I shook my head. "Then, do me the courtesy of letting me provide you with the truth. Please."

"I'm sorry. I wasn't trying to accuse you of anything."

"I know you weren't. It just angers me that she implied that I'd gone there with her. I hadn't, by the way. I'll not lie to you and say nothing happened between her and me. It did. I didn't regret it at the time because I didn't know who she truly was. She hadn't even been appointed to the council yet. Everyone knew she was trying to work herself up the ranks, as was I within the Guardians. Perhaps that's what made her appeal to me.

"But not even with all the energy the bonding ceremony brings, not even as I bedded her—and others—that evening, none of it compares to how I feel with you. None of it."

My heart warmed, but my curiosity continued to prod for more questions. "And you had no intention of presenting her to the Bohiti?"

"No, I swear it. I've been to the festival dozens of times over the centuries. I've never felt like presenting anyone. But I do feel like presenting myself now because I've known…"

I waited for him to elaborate. When he didn't, I asked. "You've known what?"

"Would you come with me somewhere? When you're feeling up to it."

I nodded.

He sighed with resolve. "Good. That's good." A small smile broke on his face. "It'll give me a better chance to explain."

I wondered what he was up to, but his answers gave me enough reassurance that Melysah's feelings were unrequited. He said it was me he wanted to take to the bonding ceremony. I wanted our bondmarks so badly, so we could move past this whole ordeal.

But Melysah's voice rang in my mind.

*'Draevyn is my mate. You have no place here. You are noth-ing, Asherah Delmar. Nothing but a little distraction.'*

A deep sense of worry festered in my gut. I had no idea what plans Melysah had, but we were sure to find out. Nothing and no one—even Melysah—would keep us from the bonding ceremony.

# CHAPTER 34

We swam through sparkling turquoise waters, rising toward the Above World. My heart kicked in my chest. I could almost smell the ocean breeze and feel the energy of the world above us. It had been too long since I'd been up here. I didn't want another natural disaster to be the only reason for a visit.

But the bigger question was...

What was Draevyn up to?

As if sensing my probing question, his head twisted back with a smile—the light from above reflecting off his bluish-green scales. *"Relax, Princess. We're almost there."* He twined his hand in mine. The light grew with each flick of our feet. The sun's rays wobbled across the ocean's surface, causing them to dance to and fro. I couldn't stop myself from smiling if I tried.

The ocean floor began to rise, and Draevyn slowed his pace.

*"We'll have to approach slowly and check for people. Otherwise, the scales will give them a bit of a shock."* A devilish grin emerged. *"Of course, we could always arrive naked."*

*"Heading to a nudist beach, are we?"*

Although I couldn't hear his chuckle, his shoulders shook with laughter.

The outline of tall, bright green trees rising just beyond a cream-colored sandy beach came into view. When our heads slowly breached the water, I immediately recognized the small island. It was part of the tiny slivers of land scattered all over The Keys—islands that were too remote to live on but provided a tropical backdrop to a thriving island living feel.

Draevyn slowly twirled around, his dark hair floating on the surface as he scanned the area. My gaze swept around, doubly ensuring no boats floated near the tiny island.

"Quickly. This way."

We trotted up the beach, my toes sifting through the coarse grains of sand. A trail leading into the trees came into view, the branches and overgrown bushes invading the space an indication that there hadn't been anyone here in some time. "Where are we?"

Draevyn's face radiated delight, the excitement emanating so strongly that it could be felt from a mile away. "My *secret* hideaway in the Above World.," he said as he easily pushed aside the overgrown bushes, guiding us up the path. "I've had it for a while."

My brows dipped. "Are you allowed to have a secret hideaway?"

"No. It's forbidden to come to the Above World without the express permission of the council or the guard."

I pushed aside a wayward branch, the sun's rays barely penetrating the canopy of trees high above us. "Well, consider your secret safe with me."

"I sure hope so," he said as we reached the end of the trail—his face lit with pure mischief. "Because you're the only one who knows about this."

"And what is this exactly?" I asked right before a gasp left me.

We emerged in a shallow clearing. One massive tree with branches reaching high into the air held a small wooden structure—its weathered wood hidden in the shadows. A rope ladder hung from the opening, dropping to the patchy grass below. I could just make out an opening at the top, the window cutouts visible beyond the entrance. "It's a tree house." I glanced at him with wide eyes. "You have a tree house in the Above World."

He chuckled. "Your face is priceless."

I strolled toward the structure, placing my hand across my brow to block out a wayward ray of light. "How did this survive the hurricane?"

"It's protected with the same magic as your home." His muscular shoulder lifted in a shrug. "And I may have checked on it while we were here last time."

"Is it safe to go up?" I asked as I continued gaping at the tiny structure nestled in the trees at least three stories high.

Draevyn's hand met the small of my back. "There's only one way to find out. I'll go first, just in case," he said in a child-like tone I'd never heard from him before. His excitement was infectious. Draevyn gave the rope ladder a sharp tug before ascending. I couldn't help but admire the firm curves of his ass through his scales on full display for my enjoyment. When he was halfway up, he turned, and a dark brow lifted. "Are you coming up?"

"Hhmm, I don't know. The view is rather nice from

down here."

His gaze turned heated as he let out a groan. "Come, you little vixen. I have plans for you."

I bit my lip and obeyed. The rope gritted against my palm, my abs and thighs burning with the effort to pull myself to the top. With each rung, my breathing labored. Draevyn knelt with anticipatory glee at the little doorway. When I finally reached the top, his hands came under my arms, lifting me through the opening. The little tree house was large enough for us to stand, but not much more than that. Five paces in either direction would take us to the other side. I approached one of the window cutouts, and what I saw took my breath away.

Above the treetops, the shoreline of The Keys emerged, revealing its beautiful sandy beaches and bright green palms swaying in the wind. The scene resembled a breathtaking watercolor painting, one I knew all too well. A pang of longing hit my heart. "It's my surf spot," the very same one I visited every morning.

I turned and found Draevyn rummaging through a large wooden chest on the other side of the treehouse, pulling out a large, red flannel blanket. "That it is," he said as he shook it out, the dust motes catching in the light as he placed it on the weathered, wooden floorboards.

I returned my gaze to the one spot that held so many beautiful memories. "How long has this been here, Draevyn?"

His arms coiled around my waist, pulling me to him. "A couple of decades."

My whole life.

He'd had a secret hideaway within spitting distance of my home my whole life. How many times had we been close to each other?

We stood in each other's arms, watching the sun glisten across the water—the warm, humid wind whipping around my face, causing the loose strands of hair to tickle my cheek. My home was but a spec in the distance. "I miss it."

"Miss living up here?" he asked, his breath tickling the tip of my ear.

"I think…I think I was so invested in getting out of here and seeing what the other coast had to offer that I forgot just how beautiful it was. I took it for granted."

His full lips peppered soft kisses down my neck. A long sigh left me, and I relaxed into his hold. "How could you have known what was to come?" he murmured against my skin. The lids of my eyes descended as his tongue snaked out between his lips, licking a sensual path all the way to my ear. A moan escaped me as his hand spread across my stomach. "Drop your scales, Asherah." I obeyed, revealing myself to him—my scales slowly retreating as his fingers glided to the apex of my thighs. When he parted my folds, the most delicious groan vibrated against my back as Draevyn found me wet and wanting. His finger wasted no time and moved in tantalizing circles around my swelling nub. I gently gripped his arm to steady myself.

"I'm going to tell you a little story, Asherah." His other hand brushed my hair over my shoulder. "It's a story of how this treehouse came to be." When my breath came in tiny pants, his fingers slowed their movement. "Once upon a time, a girl was born in the Above World on a warm day in April." He nibbled on my earlobe and slowly dipped two fingers into my center—his palm creating a tantalizing friction that had me slowly riding his hand. "On that day, a Fae male felt his chest pulse with awareness," he continued as I desperately tried to focus on his words. "It was unlike anything he'd ever felt before—a magical call from the Above World, a world he'd rarely been to and had no inclination to see." He reached for my breast, gently cupping it in his hand. He teased my tight nipple between his thumb and middle finger to the point of pleasure. "He decided to answer the call. So in the dead of night, he followed that pulse to a tiny canal littered with boats of all shapes and sizes." I froze, realization beginning to dawn. "The Fae male quietly pulled himself up on a dock at the back of a charming two-story beach house." My hand snapped out, stopping his movement. I turned to face him, my eyes wide, my breathing ragged. "He kept to the shadows as he climbed to the second story," he whispered, his fingers lightly brushing against my hips, "where he was sure to find the answer to his call. What he discovered would change his life forever." His intense eyes searched mine. "In the arms of his Fae Queen was a tiny faeling, one the entire realm of Atlantis knew nothing about. One the goddess herself had led him to."

"Draevyn," I breathed in astonishment.

His palms came up to cup my face. "He watched as her parents cloaked her in a veil of human skin, intent to raise her in the Above World, intent to raise her where he could not protect her. But that did not stop the male from trying, for he knew this was what he was called to do."

My vision blurred, and my throat closed up. I could scarcely believe what I was hearing. I didn't dare speak as a tear escaped down my cheek and onto his hands. "So, he swam around her little island and back to Atlantis so often that his family began to worry something was amiss—that he had gone mad. They weren't wrong. His worry for the veiled heir's safety drove him from all his goals and responsibilities. They hardly mattered anymore. It was then that he decided to find a little island of his own to seek refuge in so he could remain close and check in on her.

"And when she grew into the most beautiful woman—stunning even in her human veil—something other than his need to protect her started to develop, something he didn't want to admit to himself. For this female he'd guarded in secret his entire life caused him to feel things he'd never felt before.

"He would seek her out every morning just to watch her take to the waves with such incredible skill that he was unable to take his eyes off her. He wondered if she would ever grace the gates of Atlantis, wondered just how long it would take for the Queen of Atlantis to tell the realm. But he was willing to wait until she did.

"Then, one evening, word came to the Guardians of a security breach in the Above World. The Queen had been attacked, and the Fae male's heart seized. The guilt consumed him because his first thought hadn't been whether his Queen lived; it had been about the young female the Guardian had been protecting in secret his whole life. But the answer came through the gates of Atlantis that night, and in that moment, he knew he would never part from her."

The tears from his admission continued to flow. "You've known about me this whole time."

"I've known about you since the day you were born, Asherah. That is how I know unequivocally that you are mine just as much as I am yours. I don't care how many bonding ceremonies I've attended, or how many lovers you or I have had in the past. None of that fucking matters. There is no one else—no one in Atlantis or the other realms or the Above World—who will ever capture my heart the way you have. The call of the bond says so. Can you deny your own call, *nanichi*? The call to me? Your lifelong call to be in the ocean with the marine life? Embracing your true nature, yes, but answering a call of your own that burns in your chest?"

The words wouldn't form on my tongue. I knew the calling he spoke of. Growing up, I'd felt it every time I was out in the ocean. And now, I felt it every time we were together. I'd become more enthralled by it as time passed. "No," I rasped. "I can't deny it."

The relief in his eyes was palpable. "Come to the bonding ceremony with me, Asherah Delmar. Say you'll present yourself before the goddess as my bondmate so that we can finally honor that call. Say you'll be mine."

I gently gripped his wrists—a smirk lifting the corner of my lips. "I mean, are you asking or telling?"

Draevyn chuckled lightly. "You can't make this easy, can you?" He rested his forehead against mine—the tiny specks of blue amongst the green visible in his eyes. "Asherah, will you present yourself before the goddess as my bondmate?"

I brought my lips within an inch of his. "Yes."

Suddenly, my breath caught. The familiar pull at the center of my chest grew into something different, into something so fierce it brought my widened gaze to Draevyn's. His jaw slacked.

"Thank fuck."

His mouth crashed to mine with all-consuming need. I moaned into his mouth when I felt his scales dropping and the press of his erection into my belly. Love, passion, and desire all fused in his scintillating kiss. When he fell to one knee, placing my foot on the thigh of his bent leg, exposing the liquid heat between my thighs to him—my breath left me entirely. His hungry gaze remained fixed on me as his tongue licked through my soaking wet slit. I gripped his hair between my fingers as he swirled around the sensitive nub, his firm, powerful hands squeezing my ass and pulling me tighter to him. All thoughts left my mind as my hips rocked back and forth with desperate need. He hummed against my clit like a man who'd gone days without water and greedily sated his thirst. My release unraveled as I called out his name—pure ecstasy coursing through my body.

But Draevyn Eliron wasn't done.

He rose from the floor, his fingers digging into my thighs and lifting me until my legs were wrapped around him. When he slammed me up against the wall, the wood creaked at my back. With one hand, he held me up as he guided himself to my entrance. He took me in one quick thrust. The groan that left his lips nearly caused me to come again. His enormous cock stretched me impossibly wide. I could hardly breathe.

Draevyn licked a trail across my bottom lip. "You are meant for me, *nanichi*." He slowly pulled out to the tip and slammed back into me, my head hitting the wall behind me. "Every inch of you calls to me." He thrust hard into me again. "Consumes me." He brought his mouth to my ear. "Let me show you just how much I love you."

And then, Draevyn showed me. His hips pistoned into me harder and harder with each delicious thrust, another release building on the tail end of the other. I was a prisoner to his body, and I prayed to the goddess he'd never let me go.

"Goddess divine. You look so beautiful when your tight pussy squeezes my cock," he rasped in his timbre tone, eliciting the most sensual moan from my lips. "I want to feel you come again." His hand slipped to my clit, rubbing the tight bud feverishly. "Come for me, my mate."

Stars began to cloud my vision. I closed my eyes and threw my head back, my nerve endings firing as I came around him. Draevyn let out a thunderous grunt, bucking his hips into my heat as he slammed my body hard against the wall—his cock beginning to throb within me.

He thrust forward one final time with a primal roar of pure lust as his forehead, slick with sweat, came to rest in the crook of my neck. We were a pile of liquid limbs desperate to hold on to one another, his thighs shaking. Draevyn pulled his head back and gazed at me with wonder, the most delectable smile emerging on his face.

Without warning, the wall behind me gave way—the loud snapping of the wood was not likely something I'd ever forget. I toppled back, my legs dislodging from him in instinct to save him from falling over with me.

My arms flailed behind my head as my feet lifted from the treehouse floor.

Draevyn's eyes widened in panic. "Asherah!"

It dawned on me then. There was nothing to break my fall. Being this high up in the trees, this fall would be at my peril.

But midway to the ground, a massive gust of wind came at my back, holding me up mid-air. I chanced a look around, certain that an Air Fae must be nearby.

But we were alone on an island with no Fae or human around.

My brows knitted together in complete puzzlement. *It couldn't be.*

The wind was coming from…

On instinct, I steadied myself, determined to will the wind to lift me higher. When I began rising in the air, my wide eyes slid back to Draevyn—one single solitary word left his lips.

"Hekiti."

My toes gently scraped across the boards of the wooden treehouse floor, the wind at my back holding me steady as I reached for Draevyn's outstretched hand. I carefully placed my hand in his, afraid that if I even breathed the wrong way, the wind at my back would disappear, and I'd fall to my death. Dust and fallen leaves swirled around the tiny tree house, causing a whirlwind around us as my feet finally landed firmly on the floor.

The wind died then.

Draevyn stared at me with wide eyes gleaming with something akin to fascination or awe. I couldn't tell. I could barely breathe. Slowly, ever so slowly, Draevyn brushed his palms up and down my upper arms, his gaze traveling over me, checking for any cuts. "Are you alright?"

"I think so," I answered, but my shaking hands indicated otherwise.

Draevyn rushed to the blanket that the wind had swept away and now lay in a pile against the far wall. "Come sit down," he said, placing the blanket on the ground before us. He rushed by my side and guided me on shaky legs to sit in his lap. He cradled me in his arms, trying to calm my nerves. "Breathe, *nanichi*. Just breathe."

I inhaled, filling my lungs, and exhaled slowly through my mouth. With each pass, the thumps against my chest became less of a pound and more of a steady rhythm. Draevyn rubbed slow circles on my back as I asked, "What just happened?"

I'd never seen Draevyn smile the way he did then. "You're a marvelous, wonderous female. Something so special. That's what happened." He surveyed the gaping opening of the treehouse. "The Hekiti. This is remarkable. Two elements."

My forehead creased. "And you're sure there aren't others who have more than one, right?"

He lifted my head with a gentle grasp on my chin. "No, Asherah. It's unheard of. There is only one who has been prophesized, one who the goddess herself will choose." His hand slid to the back of my neck. "If you are who I believe you to be, you are extraordinary, a gift to Fae and humans alike. You remember what the Hekiti is?"

I nodded. "The one who can find all the objects."

"No, Asherah. It is so much more than the objects. It's an honor, the highest there has ever been and ever will be. It means you are the bringer of peace to the realms. It means the goddess has blessed you with an immense power—the power of all four elements. Someone like Queen Sessi would kill leagues of humans with that kind of power, but the goddess chose well. The goddess has chosen *you*."

I didn't know what to say, the words failing me. I cleared my throat. "What if there's an Air Fae on the island we didn't see? They could have conjured it."

Draevyn looked at me in stark disbelief. "Not even you believe that lie. And you know it." He sighed but froze, his gaze fixed on my wrist. His hand snapped out and held it up to my face. "Do you see this?" He pointed at the circle. "I believe we have an answer, Asherah. I believe it's been in front of us all along. The Hekiti. The circle that makes your mark different from the other Queens. You need to face the facts and not leap headfirst into denial. There's no time for it. The next ice age is upon us."

I shook my head. "It's not denial that I'm feeling." I went quiet for a long moment, the confession building on the tip of my tongue.

"What is it, *nanichi*?"

My hands began fidgeting. "It's just that…it's a lot. The pressure. The chance of failure. It's all just…so much. I was just finding my place in Atlantis as its future Queen. Now, I'm expected to bring peace to the realms? It's too much. It's way too much."

He placed his hands on mine, stilling them. "You are not alone. I'm here by your side. Your father, Dax, Myles, and even Aurelio and Reneah when you need to escape and let loose. Have a little fun." I dipped my chin to hide the small smile that emerged. His fingers came to my chin, lifting it to meet his beautiful aqua eyes, full of love and courage. "We'll all be here to help you, to guide you. And if you ever find yourself in a situation where you are alone, helpless," he placed his palm at the center of my chest, "I'm always here. We're in this together. Do not be afraid. The goddess gives her most important missions to the Fae who can bear the weight of them." He leaned forward, bringing his full lips to mine in a chaste kiss. "My beautiful warrior Queen," he whispered. He brought my wrist to his lips, kissing my elemental mark with a reverence that moved me. "We need to visit the Bohiti."

"Will she know more?"

He nodded. "She has tomes of her own that might confirm our theories." His gaze turned fierce. "You mustn't tell anyone what happened here. Not even your father. Not yet, at least. The Bohiti will let us know what we should do. Until then, not a soul can know. If anyone were to find out, your life would be in immediate danger."

"I promise I won't tell anyone."

He gave me one final lingering kiss. When I leaned back, I surveyed the damage our tryst left behind. "I'm sorry about your treehouse."

Draevyn laughed. "No need to apologize, *nanichi*. It was all worth it." He kissed my shoulder. "I'm not likely to forget it."

"It will be a great story to tell the grandkids."

He brushed the back of his hand across my cheek, his gaze heavy with a love that made my heart swell. "That it will." He sighed heavily. "But for now, we need to visit the temple."

When we rose from the floor, something caught my eye just out of the gaping hole in the treehouse. "Draevyn, look."

I'd seen a million sunsets just like the one before us, the dying light of the sun casting its final rays upon the islands. My vision blurred. I'd taken moments like this for granted. Hell, I'd taken *the sun* for granted. The dome light provided something similar, but nothing could beat the actual thing—the orange hues in various shades reflecting off fluffy clouds. I leaned back into Draevyn's chest, the both of us admiring the beauty before us in blissful silence until the sun dipped beneath the horizon.

# Chapter 35

My steps were light upon the stairs of the temple, my mind flashing images of the last two times I'd been here. It seemed so long ago since I'd met with the other Queens, since Mom's Wylemei and the disastrous events that followed. Would Mom be proud that she'd given birth to the Hekiti, the bringer of peace to the realms?

Had she known?

The possibilities raced through my mind as our steps carried us further into the temple, where one of the Bohiti's Priestesses greeted us—her stark white priestess garments flowing behind her. She bowed in reverence. "Welcome, Princess Asherah, Commander Eliron."

"Greetings, Priestess," Draevyn addressed. "We are here to see the Bohiti. It's a matter of grave importance."

Her gaze traveled between us. "I'll get her straight away. Please, be seated," she said, motioning to the settee along the neighboring wall. We slid onto it, my heel tapping repeatedly on the white marble floor while Draevyn's spine went ramrod straight.

Would the Bohiti believe me? Or would she think I'm a power-hungry Queen desperate to be important, like Queen Sessi? With Draevyn the only person who'd witnessed my air element, how would I even prove I was the Hekiti? I wiped my palms across my scaled thighs and blew out a breath.

It seemed like an eternity before the Priestess re-emerged from the depths of the temple to summon us. "This way." Draevyn took my hand in his as we followed the Priestess down the long, dark corridor that led to the Bohiti's quarters. My breath quickened with each step, a deep sense of unease causing my legs to shake.

Draevyn squeezed my hand. "Breathe. Just breathe."

I dipped my head in a nod and straightened my shoulders, trying my best to keep it together. We reached a tall wooden door with intricate carvings—vines twining beautifully toward the very top of the door. The Priestess knocked gently, and the door creaked open a moment later. Several faelights flickering beyond the doorway greeted us as we followed the Priestess into the room. The door clicked shut behind us, bathing the room further into darkness.

She stood before a heap of puffy crimson color floor cushions—a low mahogany table positioned at its center. "Please, take a seat. She'll be here momentarily."

With that, she turned and left the room—the click of the door shutting sounded like a cannon in the quiet room. As we sat side by side waiting for the Bohiti, I surveyed the darkened quarter with its beautiful tall ceiling, interesting trinkets decorating the wall-to-ceiling bookshelves, herbs hung from lines of cream-colored twine—

the smell infusing the room.

Silk-slippered padded steps reverberated off the hall-way walls. The Bohiti entered a moment later with her hands clasped at her middle.

"Princess Asherah, Commander Draevyn," she said, bowing. She sat gracefully upon the pillows on the other side of the table before asking, "To what do I owe this honor?"

I threw a side glance at Draevyn as he nodded in encouragement. The Bohiti, a look of concern on her face, tilting her head. "Whatever it is, you can tell me."

I tucked a strand of hair behind my ear. "We recently discovered something. About me."

"Oh?"

I cleared my throat, not quite believing what I was about to confess. "I…uh…well, I kind of summoned air."

The Bohiti's eyes went so wide that I thought they might pop out of their sockets. "I'm sorry, my dear. Did you say you summoned air?"

I nodded.

"Dearest goddess divine," she breathed. "Are you able to do it again?"

A thousand butterflies erupted in my stomach. "I don't know." I glanced at Draevyn.

"We were in the Above World when it happened," Draevyn explained. "She fell out of a treehouse. The wind came up at her back, saving her."

"Goddess," the Bohiti said, bringing her palm to her collarbone. "That sounds traumatizing." She shook her head. "What in the world were you doing in a treehouse in the Above World?"

"Eh…long story," I murmured. Draevyn tried to hold back a smile at the blush heating my face. "When the wall I was…um…leaning against gave way, I fell backward, and then came the wind."

The Bohiti gave us a knowing smirk before asking, "Very well. Do you think you can conjure it again, Princess?"

My shoulders lifted in a shrug. "I'm not sure."

She gave me a gentle smile. "Well, there's only one way to find out. Let's give it a try."

I breathed deeply, holding my palm up. My brows furrowed in concentration. For a few long seconds, nothing happened at all. But then, a mini-cyclone began forming in the cradle of my palm—the tiny dust moats that peppered the table whisking into the spout. I held it for a few seconds before it dissipated.

The Bohiti froze, her mouth agape. When she sprung from the floor, she nearly toppled over. Draevyn and I shared a look, both of us shrugging. She scampered to the back of the room and began pulling out several large books from the shelves that lined the back wall. All we could do was watch as she returned with her stack and dropped the books with a thud on the low table before us.

She selected a weathered book from the pile—her gaze lit with wonder as she sifted through the pages. "This is so exciting. So *very* exciting. To think, in my lifetime." Her long, silky black hair shifted as she shook her head. "My parents are never going to believe this. The Hekiti. In Atlantis."

"So, you do think I'm the Hekiti?" I ventured.

"Oh, to be certain. No one—and I mean no one—has ever had two elements. You are rare, Princess Asherah." Her gaze traveled to my wrist. "I'm such a bubble-head for not thinking of it sooner."

"The elemental mark?" Draevyn guessed.

The Bohiti nodded. She smiled up at me. "May I?"

I placed my wrist in the cradle of her palm. Her finger grazed the circle just below the symbol that marked me as the leader of my realm.

Or it *should* mark me as the leader of my realm.

Damn council politics.

"I remember seeing the dot during your elemental ceremony. I thought it odd. I should've investigated the symbol then." She released my wrist. "Nonetheless, the answer is an easy one to find."

I blew out a breath. "I've been looking everywhere for an answer," I told her.

"Ah, but you have to know *where* to look. The books in the library wouldn't hold information that sensitive. For its protection, information regarding any prophecy would be held here in the temple."

I sighed. "Why didn't I think of that?"

The Bohiti waved a delicate hand in the air. "Not to worry, my dear. You're here now. That's all that matters." She began flipping through the pages, her fingers working feverishly. She paused on a page and began scanning the text—her brows dipping. "Ah!" she said, jerking back. "Here it is." She swiveled the book around, and my breath caught. An exact replica of the elemental mark on my wrist was printed in deep black ink—the Queen's mark with a small circle toward the bottom. Just below the symbol, clear as day, it read 'Hekiti.'

My gaze snapped to the Bohiti, who was smiling like she had found the greatest treasure. "You're it, Asherah. You are the goddess' chosen, the one who is prophesied to bring peace to the realms."

The weight of her declaration pressed down on my chest and gripped my lungs in a vice. "What now?"

"Now, the journey begins." She flipped a few more

pages, scanning the text again—her finger pausing on a paragraph as she read. "Ah. Here's the prophecy: *A flower born from the soil, a snake molded from liquid fire, a feather lost in time and space, a shell once revered but long forgotten. The Goddess's sacred trove.*

"*When the ice age dawns, the Hekiti of might will rise. A daughter chosen by the Goddess and blessed with all elements will bring the great evil spirit to his knees. She will lift his harrowing weight from the human race and welcome them into the realms.*"

The Bohiti glanced up, beaming, before she continued to read. "Scholars say the Hekiti must fulfill the goddess' call. The bringer of peace must retrieve the Goddess' trove, sacred objects left by Atabey in each of the four realms: the Cobo of Atlantis, the Jujo of Corenathia, the Guaraguao of Airelandia, and the Anacaona of Earthos. The only one with the power to retrieve the objects is the Hekiti, the Goddess' chosen. When the Hekiti possesses all four objects, the power of the Goddess shall be hers. "

Draevyn squeezed my hand. "The constellations we saw the other day," he reminded me.

The Bohiti nodded in agreement. "The change in the constellations caused quite the buzz in the temples. We held our theories. This just confirms it." She returned her attention to the passage. "Alongside the Guardian of the Realms, she will lead her army against the power of Maboya and save the humans in the Above World and the realms. The Hekiti will hold the key and the gift to change humanity."

"Guardian of the Realms?" Draevyn's brows dipped. "I don't recall ever hearing about a Guardian of the Realms. What exactly is that?"

The Bohiti's smile grew. "It's the other part of the prophecy, my dear." She returned her attention to the prophecy. *"A powerful warrior will be called to reign by the Hekiti's side. Her bondmate and protector. The Guardian of the Realms. Only he can be strengthened by her power in the Goddess's quest for peace.*

*"With the might of the Goddess's trove and the warrior's blessed trident, the Hekiti will turn the key of fate."*

The Bohiti regarded a paling Draevyn with great elation. "The Guardian of the Realms is the Guardian called to protect her for eternity. The Guardian of the Realms is the Hekiti's bondmate."

# Draevyn

# Chapter 36

Y ENTIRE BODY LOCKED UP. MY TONGUE felt heavy in my mouth—the Bohiti's words racing through my mind. "The Hekiti's bondmate?"

The Bohiti nodded again with pure excitement, my barely-held panic flying over her head. "Yes, The Guardian of the Realms. It's a vital part of the prophecy." She flipped a few more pages, stopping when she found her next passage. "The Guardian of the Realms is a bondmate unlike any before it. On the day of the Hekiti's birth, an inexplicable force will call the Guardian of the Realms to the Hekiti, a call to protect the faeling. When faeling becomes Fae, this call will evolve into a bond."

I chanced a glance at Asherah. She kept her head down, her hands fidgeting in her lap.

"The Guardian of the Realms will serve as the Hekiti's bondmate, protector, and mentor. Their bond is sacred and infinite, for the goddess will grant both the Hekiti and the Guardian of the Realms powers to overcome the challenges of the forthcoming ice age. He will lead her armies against the Maboya and help the Hekiti usher in a new era for humans and the Fae.

"Beware, the Guardian of the Realms cannot fully answer the call if he or she is not properly bonded to the Hekiti, leaving the prophecy unfulfilled."

Asherah exhaled loudly, drawing my attention—her gaze fixed on the ceiling. I reached out and stroked her cheek. "What's wrong, *nanichi*?"

She looked at me then, and I froze when I saw tears welling in her eyes. "You didn't ask for this."

My hand dropped. "You didn't either. We're both called to this."

She shook her head and went silent as she wiped away her tears.

"Could you please give us a moment, Priestess?" I asked the Bohiti.

She nodded and rose from the floor with her book. "I'll gather the tomes to help us understand the objects."

"Thank you."

She gave me an empathetic smile before her strides carried her to the back of the room.

Asherah's sniffling filled the silence, and my heart squeezed. I inched closer to her, my arm draping around her shoulder. "Please don't cry, *nanichi*. You're breaking my heart."

"I'm sorry. It's just…this isn't what you asked for, Drae. You've already sacrificed so much as my Guardian. You should be given a choice." She shook her head. "This is wrong."

The tips of my fingers came to the bottom of her chin, tipping it up to meet my gaze. "Asherah, nothing changes. Nothing. I've already made my choice. This just gives a title to my rightful place by your side. What did I tell you? I'll be there for you. Always. So what about my part in the prophecy changes anything between us?"

I watched as the understanding slowly dawned on her face. "But…you could choose not to attend the bonding ceremony with me."

"There is no choice. We're going."

"But you could say no."

"And risk the fulfillment of the prophecy?" I shook my head. "Absolutely not."

"And you're sure?"

"I'm more sure in this moment than I was back in the treehouse." I cupped her face. "This isn't just about us anymore. This is about what both you and I are called to do together. The goddess has blessed us with the chance to achieve something great. I can feel it, Asherah. This ice age is different from the last. Something big calls us to embrace our greatest selves. Do you not feel that?"

Her hand rested on mine. "I do. I just…I…I love you so very much. I understand your calling to protect me. But then, who protects you?"

I let loose a sigh. "My brave, beautiful mate. You already know the answer to that question. Firstly, the armies, my Guardian brothers and sisters who are dear to me, will protect me." My thumb swiped over her delectable bottom lip. "And you, my Queen, have the most important item to guard, more important than any of the goddess' objects. You'll protect my heart, for that is entirely yours and yours alone." I leaned in, bringing my mouth to hers—the salty taste of her tears mixing with the sweet taste of her lips. It will take several lifetimes of gratitude to the goddess for gifting me such a magnificent mate. I planned on giving my thanks every day of my very long life.

The sound of The Bohiti clearing her throat broke us apart. She approached with several large books and a wide smile. "I think I may have found something." The table groaned as she placed the heavy tomes before us. "I should have figured it out sooner. I don't think I'll ever forgive myself." She flipped through with one hand and waved the other around. "But no matter. The best place to start is with the obvious. The Cobo. This object will heighten the Hekiti's Water Fae abilities and enhance new powers—the power to part the seas and the power to become water itself, the latter of which can be transferred to the Guardian of the Realms upon their union at Guake'te." She glanced up from the book, wagging her eyebrows.

A sense of excitement rushed through my body. "We'll be able to turn into the water?"

The Bohiti shrugged. "That's what the book says."

Asherah and I glanced at each other with our mouths practically on the ground.

"But how do we find it," Asherah asked.

The Bohiti's shoulders sagged. "That's the issue, isn't it? The object hasn't been seen since the scribes first wrote of it. The text only tells us that the Hekiti will be called to the Cobo."

Asherah's disappointing sigh reached my ears. "And the other objects?"

"Right, let's see." She turned toward the end of the book. "We have the Jujo. Scary little thing. It states that it's a serpent made of iron that rests somewhere in Corenathia. There's no telling how you'll get the Jujo out of that realm. But again, it states that the goddess will guide you."

"Doesn't seem very helpful," I remarked.

She slowly blinked her obsidian eyes. "I don't write the prophecies. I just read them." The Bohiti continued reading. "The only one who can retrieve or handle the Jujo is the Hekiti. Not even the Queen herself knows where it is. Fascinating."

"And what happens when I retrieve the Jujo?" Asherah asked.

"Like the Cobo, the Jujo will strengthen your Fire Fae abilities and introduce new powers. However, this power cannot transfer to the Guardian. The Guardian of the Realms can only take on qualities from the Hekiti's original element. That would be water."

"Just when I was beginning to feel special," I teased. Asherah's answering chuckle brought a smile to my face.

The Bohiti turned the page. "Next, we have the Guaraguao. This is the red-tail feather. I fear this one will be the hardest to identify. There are likely a gazillion feathers in Airelandia. How you'll find a single solitary red one is beyond me."

When I noticed Asherah's immediate unease, I cleared my throat. "With the help of the goddess."

"Very true, wise Guardian," the Bohiti agreed. "And, of course, we have the last one: the Anacaona, otherwise known as the golden flower. The exact details are very limited given Earthos' tightly guarded realm, but the text states that it's more than likely a flower made of gold." The Bohiti's brow furrowed. "None of us really know what goes on in that realm. Even the Priestesses are tight-lipped."

The Bohiti looked at Asherah, her gaze heavy with warning. "I don't know how you'll find all the objects, Princess. But it would be best if you started looking now. Once your other elements begin to emerge, your power will call to Maboya, alerting him to your presence."

My eyebrow lifted to my hairline. "A part of the prophecy you failed to mention?"

The Bohiti blinked. "Did I not mention that? Goodness, I'm really scatterbrained today, aren't I?" She shook her head. "No matter. I'll keep looking through the texts for more clues. That should be enough to start your journey." She reached forward, placing her hand upon Asherah's. "You are magnificent, Princess—a true gift. Whatever may come, you have the entire support of all the priestesses here in the temple. We'll scour every text for any information that may help you in your quest. In the meantime, it's important to tell no one of this."

An expression of unease crept across Asherah's beautiful features. "Not even my father?"

The Bohiti shook her head. "Not even him. This information can have disastrous consequences despite someone's good or bad intentions. Those with the best intentions will want to celebrate the coming of the Hekiti. And those with bad intentions—"

"Will want to end her life," I finished.

The Bohiti winced. "Yes, I'm afraid so."

My hand clenched in a fist. "They'll have to get through me first."

"Of that, I have no doubt. Regardless, it's crucial that you all keep this between yourselves and the priestesses. We are sworn to the goddess and to keep her secrets. You won't need to worry about one of us divulging anything." We rose from the floor when it was clear the Bohiti was through interpreting her tome. She gave us a reassuring smile. "I believe I'll see you all at Guake'te in a few days?"

I glanced at Asherah as we turned for the door, a blush spreading across her cheeks. "Yes, we'll be at the bonding ceremony," she answered.

"Wonderful!" the Bohiti beamed.

As we strode down the hallway for the temple entrance in near silence, our steps echoed off the walls as I said, "We'll need to bring Cathan to Sabana."

Asherah froze. "Why?"

I tucked a strand of hair behind the tip of her ear. "Because I'd like my parents to meet your father before Guake'te. Might as well get the first meeting over with."

Asherah let out the cutest little groan, bringing a smile to my face. "Don't we have enough going on already?"

My laughter peeled through the empty temple as my arm coiled around her waist. "Relax, *nanichi*. It's customary to announce the union to the family. We can also invite anyone you'd like. Dax, Reneah, Myles, and Aurelio. I'm sure they'd enjoy the outskirts," I mused as we descended the temple steps. "Besides, it'll be nice to have some time away before we begin your quest."

The weariness grew in her gaze, and I couldn't completely dismiss it. I felt it in every fiber of my being. After the bonding ceremony, my life would change forever.

# Chapter 37

MY NERVES WERE LIKE BEES BUZZING IN MY veins as we approached the beautiful Eliron home—the canoa listing from side to side as it rolled up the driveway. Dad sat ramrod straight on one side of me—his fingers drumming against his knee—while Draevyn sat on my other side, his leg jiggling against the floorboards. We remained safely within the confines of the cabin—tiny glimpses of Sabana peeking through the cabin door along the way. Bright orange, pink, and yellow begonias grew in plethora, spilling out of window flower boxes. My nose detected a whiff of rosemary beneath the smell of freshly baked bread. Myles, Aurelio, Dax, and Reneah opted to sit in the open air. I kind of wish I had as well. If Dad understood what this trip was about, he hadn't let on. He'd simply agreed to the invitation Draevyn sent on his parents' behalf. But Dad wasn't a fool.

He'd seen how Draevyn was with me and vice

versa. Having already been a mated male—formally mated—it was impossible for him not to know.

When we came to an abrupt stop, Draevyn rose from his seat, helping me to stand. His smile was genuine, but his gaze held a hint of nervousness. "Ready?" he asked.

I squeezed his hand. "As ready as I'll ever be."

The group descended the steps of the canoa. I couldn't help but notice the special attention Dad gave Reneah, his hand lingering a little longer in hers. Something seemed to pass between them, his eyes searching.

*How curious.*

Just then, Samani and Zoriato emerged from their home; Samani's wide and infectious smile was like a calm aura settling over the group. She made a beeline for me, wrapping me in a fierce hug. I giggled as she squeezed. "Miss me?"

Samani leaned back, surveying me with a smile. "Of course I did." She shifted her attention over my shoulder. "Welcome, everyone! I hope you all had a nice swim up the Shingu." When her gaze found Dad, she instantly dipped in a low curtsy. "Your Highness. My name is Samani." She gestured to Zoriato, who stood stoically behind her. "This is my mate, Zoriato."

In Zoriato fashion, he stiffly bowed at the waist. "Your Highness."

"It's a pleasure to meet you," Samani continued—her dark hair tied tightly at the back of her head, causing her cheekbones to stand out prominently. "Asherah has had nothing but wonderful things to say about you."

Dad smiled warmly and gave a nod. "The pleasure is all mine. And may I commend you on raising such a wonderful son. Draevyn's been an excellent addition to the Guard and a brilliant mentor to my daughter. You must be very proud of him."

"Don't compliment him too much," Dax cut in with a smirk, his arms crossed. "His head's already big enough as it is."

Draevyn rolled his eyes. "You're one to talk."

"I'll take that compliment," Samani said proudly. "Thank you."

"Well, let's not daddle out here. There's plenty of drink and food inside," Zoriato motioned to the entryway. "Come along."

A flurry of glasses filled to the brim with wine, savory snacks, and casual conversation ensued. I naturally migrated to the patio, sliding into my favorite spot by the outdoor fireplace. The fading light of day painted the sky in shades of deep orange and yellow as a subtle chill spread across the patio. I shivered in response, which hadn't escaped Draevyn's notice. He began loading wood in the fireplace, starting a fire that grew from small to roaring within seconds. I let the cushions envelop me as I sipped on my faery wine. "Perfect."

Draevyn chuckled, his body providing more warmth as he sat beside me. The telltale sign of shuffling feet and growing conversations reached our ears as the rest of the group gathered outside with drinks in their hands and heaping trays of food. Dad stood at the edge of the patio gazing out at the grape vines planted in perfect rows— Zoriato joining him to admire the view. "This is stunning," Dad proclaimed.

"Thank you."

"And the wine is fantastic, too. You must have centuries of experience for the taste to be this extraordinary," Dad complimented.

There was an absolute look of pride on Zoriato's face. Dad was always the charmer, even when faced with someone as grumpy as Zoriato. He pointed at my father's glass. "That's one of our most prestigious. It's an award-winner three decades running. Every harvest, the neighboring wineries attempt to take the top spot. They can't figure out our methods, and my crew remains loyal to our family. They'll never sell my secrets."

That brought a laugh out of Dad. "Then, I strongly suggest you do everything possible to keep them. It's tough to find a dependable crew. It took me centuries to find a team of Guardians I could trust." That was news to me. Dad gestured to the closest row of vines. "Care to show me a bit?"

"I'd be honored. Now, these here are the oldest on the entire estate. My great-great-grandfather planted..." Their voices faded into murmurs as they slunk their way down the row.

"It's not polite to eavesdrop."

I twisted to Draevyn, his mischievous grin making me smile. I shrugged. "Couldn't help it. I wasn't sure how your father would react to mine."

Draevyn's line of sight went over my head, his eyes narrowing. "Cathan can get just about anyone to have a conversation with him. It's impressive."

I lifted my wine glass. "Something he didn't pass on to me."

Draevyn pushed my hair behind my shoulder. "You have other extraordinary qualities, ones that I'm very, very fond of."

"Ugh, the cuteness overload is real!" Aurelio exclaimed as he plopped in the seat across from us—his face positively gleaming with delight.

"And nauseating," Dax murmured around the rim of his glass.

"I disagree," Reneah said, popping a grape in her mouth. "It's like watching one of my romance novels come to life."

Aurelio feigned fake outrage. "Oh my, Rennie. I've read some of the books in your room. That is quite the… *intense* compliment."

Reneah tsked, throwing a grape at him, which he deftly caught. "Don't act innocent."

Aurelio brought his perfectly manicured hand to his collarbone. "I would never."

The group burst into laughter. I couldn't think of anything more perfect than this: my friends and my father here with my future bondmate's family, everyone enjoying each other's company. It felt like my found family, something I didn't even know I was missing. It was more than I could ever ask for.

I had to wonder when the bottom would give out. I'd been doing my best not to think about the objects, the Hekiti, or the bonding ceremony and just…be in the moment.

When everyone's voices rose an octave higher than usual, it became obvious it was time to eat—everyone having had little to eat since we departed the Capital that morning. With little in my stomach, I could already feel the effects of the faery wine, my head a little light.

"*Guali*, why don't you fetch your father and Cathan?" Samani asked as Myles helped her set up the outdoor dining area. "It'll be time to eat soon."

Draevyn placed a chaste kiss on my cheek and rose into a long stretch. "I'm on it."

"Do you want company?" I asked him.

He briefly stared in the distance. "No, that's okay, *nanichi*. I think I'll have a chat with Cathan while I'm out there," he said with a wink.

My knowing smile followed him as he disappeared between the vines.

"I spy with my little eye someone who's planning on going to a bonding ceremony," Aurelio teased.

I shifted my attention to Aurelio, who was smiling behind the rim of his glass. Reneah covered up her laugh with a hand.

I gave an ungraceful flutter of the hand. "Oh hush, you two."

Reneah held her palms up. "I'm not saying anything. I think it's wonderful." She sighed wistfully. "Makes me wish I could go, too."

Aurelio tsked. "Oh, stop, little human. You know you'll still have fun. The energy of the ceremony can be felt throughout Atlantis." Aurelio wagged his eyebrows.

I tilted my head. "Why can't you go to the ceremony?"

"The ceremony's only for the Fae, sweet Asherah," Aurelio answered, his lips lifting in a grin. "The humans can still feed off the energy of the ceremony, and they do. But they're strongly advised to keep to the confines of their quarters for their safety."

I jerked back. "Why is that?"

"The Fae," Reneah began, her tone heavy, "they can get a little wild during the bonding ceremony. It isn't safe for humans to be anywhere near the festivities. Boundaries exist because the humans…well…we don't have the power to resist the call, and the Fae have been known to take advantage of us." She stared in the distance. "That kind of power brings you to your knees."

"Quite literally," Dax murmured. Reneah sent him an incredulous look.

I pursed my lips in thought. "So, if the humans have to stay in their quarters and the Fae are at Guake'te, who's protecting Atlantis?"

"Every Guake'te, the Guardians rotate assignments,"

Dax informed, taking a sip from his glass before he continued. "The priestess provides them with a potion to lessen the effects of the ceremony. It's a wild, wild night. We Fae embrace our primal instincts. It would be challenging for anyone with nefarious intent to try anything anyway. The power from the bonding ceremony is too strong. And those of us without mates? The urge to feel, the urge to embrace desire from everyone is a real, real thing." A devilish grin emerged. "I was on duty last year. Which means this year? I'm indulging. I plan to stay at the temple festival until dawn."

"Once the ceremony begins, my door stays firmly locked, and Myles stays safely within my confines. I have some wicked plans this year." Aurelio tapped his lip. "Which reminds me, I'll need to make a stop at Fae Flings for some provisions."

"Did I hear my name?" Myles inquired from behind us, where he assisted Samani with the silverware.

My face flashed hot as Aurelio erupted with laughter. "Nothing, darling. Just telling everyone how wonderful you are."

"Hmph. Somehow, I don't believe that."

We moved on to safer topics, but my mind drifted to Dax's remarks about the bonding ceremony—a nagging desire began heating my core as I thought of losing myself with Draevyn.

"There's nothing to be nervous about," Dax said, cutting into my thoughts with a Cheshire cat smile. "You don't have to be shy about it, either," he continued when he saw my obvious discomfort. "It's only natural. You're bondmates, after all."

My finger traced the rim of my glass. "Not yet."

"It doesn't take the Bohiti's ritual to see that the two of you are bonded. I've never seen him like this with anyone. Being a Guardian had been his only passion until you." His gaze softened. "Relax, Asherah. The ceremony is a happy event. Don't fear it. Enjoy it."

I smiled. And just like that, my worry turned into anticipation.

# Draevyn

# CHAPTER 38

I'D BEEN IN SEVERAL SITUATIONS WHERE MY nerves should've shot through the roof, but they never did. I had a particular talent for keeping calm under moments of high stress. As a Commander, it was expected. Which is why I knew the conversation I was about to have with my Regent was one of the most important of my life. Every single one of my nerves fired with each step I took down the pathway between the vines, my breath quickening. I heard the low murmur of voices before I found them next to the oldest vine in the vineyard, Baba's arms moving animatedly, as he often did when he discussed our family's vineyard.

"Hello there," I called out to them.

"Oy. *Guali*. I was just telling Cathan about the Eliron vine."

*I know*, I wanted to tell him. I tried and failed to

hold back my grin. "Bibi is summoning you all. Dinner is nearly ready."

"Wonderful. My stomach was beginning to riot," *Baba* said, rubbing circles on his stomach.

I cleared my throat. "Uh, Cathan. I wondered if I might have a word with you privately?" I could feel the heat crawling up my neck and thanked the goddess for the darkening evening sky above us. The look the two shared and the smirks didn't help my cause.

"Of course," said Cathan.

"I'll leave you all to it then," Zorito said, giving me a firm squeeze on the shoulder as he passed me by.

"Winning people over, as usual, I see," I marveled.

Cathan shrugged cheerfully. "If the man is about to become part of my family, I figured I'd better warm him up a bit."

"Ah, so you already know what this is about then?"

"How could I not? I don't think I've ever seen my daughter so happy." He sighed. "And you forget, I was once a bonded male as well. I can see the signs. Truthfully, anyone with eyes can see what's happening between the two of you."

I threaded a hand through my hair. "You should know that I believe Asherah is extraordinary."

Cathan nodded. "That she is."

"And I have grown to respect and love her."

I could just make out the severity of his gaze. "I hope you do. Respect and love are essential, but so is knowing what's to come, what's at stake," Cathan said in a tone that left no room for anything but the seriousness surrounding her troublesome future. "So, before you tell me of your intentions to present yourself with my daughter before the Bohiti, I have a few things of my own to tell you. Because being the bondmate of a Queen will come with its own set of challenges, ones I know first-hand." Cathan picked a hanging leaf from a vine. "Do you know how long I was bonded to Neleah before her death?"

I rubbed a hand down my face. "Over five hundred years?"

"Five hundred thirty-seven years, two hundred twelve days, and seven hours, give or take. Every moment of that time was spent loving her, protecting her. But it was also spent answering to her. If she needed me in the Above World at her side, I was there. If she needed me at Queens Council, I was there. I was there if she needed me to look after Asherah while she handled matters in Atlantis or with the human delegation. When she asked me to keep Asherah a secret, I vehemently disagreed. Yet, I folded because, as Queen, her decisions superseded mine."

I let that information sink in for a moment. I'd never considered that Asherah would have complete power over our decisions, but I also didn't think she'd ever override a life-impacting decision like hiding a faeling. But becoming the Guardian of the Realms meant there were severe decisions we'd have to make. It meant being able to work as a team as we both set out to answer the goddess' call.

"I can see I've struck a cord."

I shook my head. "It's just that," I sighed, knowing I couldn't divulge what we had discovered, "without being in the situation, it's hard to determine what she'd do. Asherah…she's…I'd like to think she's different from her mother, but in truth, you're the only one who'd know that. So I ask you, do you feel your daughter would act the same as Neleah did with you?"

"She might," he said, crossing his arms. "And you'll need to decide how you'd react if she did. I agree. Asherah is a different person from Neleah. I'd like to think I had something to do with it, but only the goddess knows. I hope the two of you continue learning how to grow together and communicate beyond whispered words of love and lust. Those two things can only take a relationship so far. You'll need something more if you're expected to go through whatever the goddess has in store for the both of you."

*Did he know?* It certainly sounded to me like he did.

"I loved Neleah. The goddess chose my bondmate well, without question. But I must confess, we had moments in our relationship that were incredibly frustrating, moments that Asherah is completely unaware of. I have never and will never speak ill of her mother in front of her. I never wanted her to feel the tension that had built between Neleah and me from time to time. That wouldn't have been fair to her. But the emotional pain I felt was a genuine thing, and there were quiet moments when I questioned whether I could continue on the way we were. But there was no way out. Once the bond is set, there's no erasing it. It's there for the rest of your lives. And it will let you know when it's unpleased that you are away from your bondmate—like a sentient being within you. Your need for her will scream inside you, and if she is off doing her duty? There'll be nothing you can do to ease the ache."

"I don't plan to leave her side."

Cathan scoffed, shaking his head. "You may not plan to, but it will happen. Of that, you can be certain. Can you handle that?"

"If I must. I'll do whatever it takes," I declared fiercely.

"And are you prepared to put yourself second?"

My brows furrowed. "If you ask if I'm ready to put

my Queen and bondmate first, the answer is unequivocally yes."

The corner of Cathan's mouth twitched as he gave a nod. He closed the distance between us and placed a hand on my shoulder. "Then you are ready, *guali*."

My heart squeezed, and I swallowed the knot that formed in my throat. "Thank you," I croaked.

"Come. Let's get back to the others. I suspect you have an announcement to make," he said with a wink.

# Chapter 39

The scales against my belly felt tight as I leaned back against my chair in the most delightful food coma. Music drifted from the tablet in the middle of the table. At one end, Zoriato and Dax talked intensely to themselves. To no one's shock, Aurelio and Samani chatted like two long-lost friends. They hadn't even come up for air as their hands dramatically flourished in the air every minute or so. Dad and Reneah were having a very different kind of conversation altogether, one that I noted brought a blush to her face on occasion. And it would seem Draevyn had one too many glasses of faery wine based on his very public display of affection that included him pulling me closer to him and placing sweet kisses just below my ear. With the faery wine coursing through my veins, I hardly had the will to push him away.

It was only when Draevyn rose from his seat that the public display of affection stopped. Or so

I thought.

He drummed a knife against his wine glass several times, encouraging the rowdy group to quiet down. "If I can have everyone's attention, please," he said over the low hum of dying conversations—everyone's attention shifting to him. His delicious dimple emerged as he began speaking. "I'm sure it's no surprise that those of you who are dear to Asherah and me are here today." He reached down, taking my hand and pulling me up to stand—his strong arm looping around my waist. "It was important to have all of you here to bear witness to my oath." Dax whistled, and Reneah shushed him before returning her doe-eyed gaze to the both of us. "This beautiful, smart, warrior female swept into my life and helped me to see the world through her eyes, a different world with so much hope. As much as I tried to resist the call, I couldn't. It was damn near impossible," he said, with his gaze locked on mine. My throat began to tighten.

"It is why, before all of you, it is my honor to announce our intent to present ourselves to the Bohiti at Guake'te."

Cheers and whistles erupted around the table as Draevyn's mouth crashed to mine, my laughter pressed against his lips. Our joy was so potent, so tangible it could almost be seen. I had never been so happy. I never dared to dream of it.

"This calls for some dancing!" Samani called over the table.

"To Asherah and Draevyn. May their bond live for eternity," Dad bellowed.

Clanks from the wine glasses sounded as Samani raised the music on the tablet. Draevyn brisked me onto the open area Samani had miraculously cleared for dancing—pulling me into his body and swaying to the up-beat tempo. He leaned down, bringing his lips an inch of mine. "I love you, *nanichi*," he whispered.

"And I love you, my mate." The corners of my mouth lifted in a smile as we kissed, interrupted by more whistles and clapping around us. Draevyn's deep timbre laugh warmed my soul.

By the time all the wine had been drunk and every-one had their second helping as a midnight snack, my cheeks hurt from all the endless smiling. Eventually, the patio emptied as everyone succumbed to their exhaus-tion, heading to the second-floor guest rooms.

And as the sun's first rays began filtering into the room with Draevyn snoring softly in my ear, I final-ly drifted to sleep, knowing no matter what tomorrow held, I'd have my mate at my side.

# Chapter 40

Reneah moved around my room on a mission. She'd laid out golden bangles and a golden circlet—the beautiful long lilac fabric attached to it flowed across the bed. She'd informed me that it was customary for the Fae males and females who were bonded or planned to be during Guake'te to wear ceremonial garments. The anticipation had been a low hum in my stomach all day, increasing as the hours ticked by. Only a little time remained before the ceremony, and Reneah didn't want to be anywhere near the palace during Guake'te. She worked feverishly through the scores of sandals in the closet to find a matching pair. "It's a good thing the Fae don't like to dress up often. Makes my job easier," she called from inside the closet, her voice muffled. She emerged a moment later with a pair of golden sandals, the long straps dragging across the floor. "But your closet could do with a bit of re-organizing, so when you do dress up, I'll be able to tell where I put things. I'll add that to my list of to-do's." She placed the sandals on the ground at the foot of the bed.

"I wouldn't worry about it. I'm in my scales more often than not these days."

Reneah's lips lifted in a grin as she gave the rouge on my face one last inspection. "Look at you. You've come a long way from the girl who first breached the gates of Atlantis in your *Instant Mermaid Just Add Water* tanktop."

I shook my head. "Isn't that the truth?"

"And about to be mated," she said, her voice croaking slightly. "It's enough to make a woman cry." She fanned her big, brown eyes.

The corners of my lips tipped up. "Oh, stop, you mother hen."

"Can't help it. I'm just so happy for you."

"Thank you."

Reneah let out a breath to gather herself. "Alright. I'll go check on your father and make sure he has everything he needs. I think *you* have everything you need. You'll be okay dressing yourself?"

"I dressed myself for twenty-three years before you came along. I think I'll be okay."

Reneah nodded. "Very well. I'll leave you to it. Enjoy every minute, Asherah. Despite the…you know… intensity of the ritual, it's a special moment in a Fae's life. Cherish it."

"I will."

With one last pensive look, she turned and exited the room, leaving me to stew in my nerves and thoughts.

Bonded.

*I will be soon.*

My hands started fidgeting. Draevyn's note I'd received earlier in the day advised that Aurelio would escort me and that I should meet him at the steps before the temple just beyond the tents of the Guake'te festival.

Where things were said to get a little…wild.

I glanced at the wall clock; it had barely moved. I let out a sigh, not sure what to do with myself. Maybe some reading time would help calm my nerves. I sank into the cushions of my reading chair, grabbed my book from the table, and began reading.

As I'd done with most of the books I've read, I'd barely come up for air. It wasn't until a knock sounded at the door that I lifted my gaze to the clock on the wall. "Shit!" I threw my book on the side table and rushed to the door, throwing it open.

There stood Aurelio, looking spectacular with his hair perfectly styled and his ceremonial bangles on his biceps. His pointer finger traveled from my head to my toes. "These don't look like the garments you should be wearing to bond your mate."

My brows dropped. "These are my scales."

"Precisely. And we'll be late to the festival if you don't get dressed in five minutes."

"I thought you'd be holed up in your room with Myles all evening?" I asked, closing the door behind him.

"And miss the Guake'te festival? I wouldn't dream of it. Myles will wait in our quarters until I return. Now, shoo. Hurry up and get dressed."

I didn't hesitate. Delicately placing the bangles over my wrists and positioning the draped fabric that hung from the golden circlet on my head, I gave myself one last perusal in my floor-length mirror. It was odd seeing so much of my skin. I felt…exposed. A slit carried from my ankle to my upper thigh, complimenting the flowy long skirt. The sheer material rose from my hips and wrapped around my neck to cover my breasts, the cool air cresting across my bare back.

"Marvelous," Aurelio said from behind me. "If Draevyn doesn't faint at the sight of you, I'll be sorely disappointed." He turned for the door. "Let's get out of here."

The current of the Shingu carried us to the entrance of the temple park in no time. My heart beat so fast, I thought it would pop out of my chest. As we came to the head of the pathway leading up to the temple, my eyes went impossibly wide.

"Welcome to Guake'te, Princess," Aurelio said, shooting me a roguish grin. He sashayed expertly through the crowd of festivalgoers. A sea of beautiful ceremonial garments of every color and blueish scales glinting against the warm faelights blanketed the park—the most sensual and erotic music filling the space. Everyone swayed to the drumbeats that thrummed through the crowd. Kissing. Touching. Feeling. It was all so…

Infectious.

A low buzz built in my core as my hips swayed of their own volition—the beat coursing through my body. A hand wrapped around mine. My eyes, which I hadn't noticed were closed, snapped open to Aurelio's face lit with amusement. He guided me further down the path. Large bright, white tents lay in perfect rows and reached two stories high. The flaps on most of them were drawn back to reveal the revelry inside. The low faelights cast light on the futons within, the bodies melding into one another. Skin to skin. Heads thrown back in various states of pleasure.

I couldn't take my eyes off of them.

"And the ceremony hasn't even begun yet," Aurelio yelled above the hum of music and murmur of the crowd. "Come. Follow me. We have the tent closest to the temple."

"We?" I asked, shifting my attention to him.

"Draevyn, Dax, Myles, and Cathan insisted on having a few Guardians present for your safety."

*Of course, they did.* "Won't the Guardians…you know," I motioned around me, "be a little too distracted to protect me?"

"Not if they followed orders and drank the potion our very talented priestesses concocted for them. It suppresses their innermost desires. I'd bet my shoe collection that Draevyn watched as they drank it."

I didn't doubt that either.

Aurelio pulled back the flap of the tent erected closest to the temple. Inside, nearly two dozen Fae milled about eating, drinking, or sucking someone's tongue down their throat. I spotted the Guardians assigned to me this evening, each in their corner with a look of pure boredom on their faces. I leaned toward Aurelio. "I thought it was just going to be you and Myles?"

His gaze snapped to mine. "Of course, it's just going to be me and Myles." I bit my inner cheek as he sideglanced, understanding finally dawning on his face. "Oh, you mean, are we open?"

I motioned around the room. "Fair question, given that we're in your tent, and there's a lot of…skin."

He spared another glance around the room, his devilish smirk returning. "There is a lot of skin. But Myles and I are exclusive. Not that there's anything wrong with being *inclusive.* It's just that once mates bond, other partners don't hold any sexual appeal." His heady stare followed the very nice ass of a male who had nearly dropped *all* his scales. "But we can certainly watch and appreciate. Goddess. He must work out for hours."

I couldn't help but ogle. "Goddess, indeed."

Aurelio broke his attention from the male and took my hand. "Let's get a refreshment. I'm suddenly very parched."

We ventured through the small crowd, coming to a long table against the side panel of the tent with cheeses, bread, wine, and other items to nibble on. I grabbed a cracker and tucked it into the shadows of the quiet area by the tent wall, Aurelio coming to my side. The debauchery unfolding around us was overwhelming. I didn't consider myself a prude by any stretch, but I'd never found myself in such a provocative place.

Deliciously provocative, much to my surprise.

"So, how long do the festivities last?" I asked him, my attention drifting to a couple in the middle of the tent who'd just dropped the upper part of their scales. The male leaned down, taking her pert nipple in his mouth, and she threw her head back with obvious pleasure. A few people gathered around them with hungry eyes. I could feel the heat rise to my cheeks. My gaze remained glued on all their movements.

"Well," Aurelio began, his gaze fixed on the couple, "for those of us who are mated, we leave when the priestesses thrum the bell. It signals the beginning of the ceremony. Oh…this is about to get very interesting."

Another male settled behind the female, the bottom portion of his scales dropping as he pressed into her backside and licked a pathway up her neck. His hand snaked around her hips and wrapped around the other male's hardened length. My eyes widened as I clenched my thighs. "Well, then."

Aurelio chuckled lightly. "Welcome to Guake'te, little Princess."

I tore my gaze away. "Who are all these people?"

"These guests here have been hand-selected for our tent. Vetted to the highest degree." He gestured with his wine glass around the room. "Everyone you see here is a supporter of yours through and through." He brought his glass to mine with a clang. "It's almost time. My male awaits me at home." He drained his cup, setting it on the table beside me. "Relax and enjoy. When you hear the bell, Draevyn will be waiting for you at the stairs." He gave my arm a firm squeeze and exited through the tent flaps.

Despite knowing everyone in the tent had been vetted, I remained on the side of the room. My gaze landed on one of the three Guardians assigned to my tent. It mustn't have been a very strong potion if the female riding his lap were any indication. I found the other two guards in similar states of pleasure in the throughs with a male and female.

How had the potion worn off so quickly?

I let out a wince when I felt a small prick in my foot. My gaze snapped to the floor just as a hand pulled back from outside the tent. My brows furrowed. "What the fuck?"

But the room began to spin before I could analyze who or what that was. The bell from the temple tolled, and everyone donning ceremonial garments filed for the exit.

But I couldn't move.

I couldn't keep myself standing.

My knees dropped to the floor. Not a single person paid any attention when a rustling sounded from behind me, the tent's tarping lifting. A cloth came around my mouth and nose. I could do nothing to fend them off, my body completely immobile as the whole world began to fade.

"Sleep now, Princess," I heard my assailant say before I drifted off to unconsciousness.

# Draevyn

# Chapter 41

I ADJUSTED THE CEREMONIAL BANGLES wrapped around my biceps for the millionth time as the sound of the bell tolled across the park, magicked to overpower any sounds in town—a signal to all of Atlantis that the ceremony would soon begin.

It was time.

My heart kicked so hard that I glanced down to make sure it didn't beat through my chest. My gaze stayed there. The bondmark I'd never wanted before—never thought I would have—would soon appear across my chest, a sign to the world that Asherah was my eternal mate.

*Mine.*

I shook my head in pure disbelief and couldn't help the smile curving my lips. I watched the dozens of couples silently filing in before the temple steps to present themselves before the Bohiti.

Their eyes held firm to the large bowl that hung from chains at the center of the entrance as they waited for the priestess to light the oil within.

*So much has changed.*

I never thought I'd feel more passionate about anything else but being a Guardian, and while my role as Commander was still important, I knew being Asherah's mate would be the most important role in my life. My gaze drifted to the top of the pathway that led to the tents, observing anyone with long dark hair and blue eyes, but none were Asherah.

*She'll be here.*

Movement at the top of the steps stole my attention. A priestess emerged from the darkness of the temple; a long pole lit like a match reached for the bowl way above her. The oil caught fire, and the temple drums began a steady rhythm—the potent energy from the temple cascading over the crowd as collective gasps and moans met my ears. The energy hit me hard, my eyes closing with its intensity and the center of my chest humming a call only my mate could hear.

*Where is my mate?*

I sighed with relief when I felt her fingers brushing down my back, her lips pressing softly on the crease between my shoulder blades, making my cock stir beneath my scales. Her arms came around my waist. It wasn't until my arms rested on hers that a strong sense of wrongness took over. I opened my eyes, looking down upon the pale skin and long pearl-polished nails of someone who wasn't Asherah. I broke through the ceremonial fog. As I turned out of the embrace, I was met by Melysah's deep brown eyes—her body clad in pale peach ceremonial garments. "Draevyn," she whispered wantonly.

My anger overrode every sensation. "What are you

doing here?"

Her forehead creased. "I'm here to present myself to the Bohiti. With you." She rushed forward, attempting to wrap herself around me again.

I placed my hands on her arms, stilling her forward momentum—the heady power of the ceremony urging me to embrace the skin-to-skin contact. I groaned with lust and the effort to push away from her. "You know damn well I'm not here for you."

Yet, Melysah remained determined. She shook off the rejection and licked her lips. "But you are. Can't you feel it, my love? I know you do." Her eyes became lustfully hooded. "You want me."

"I am not your love, and that is the power of the ritual. You know it."

"It's the call," she insisted, bringing her hand to her chest. "It's right here, Draevyn. Present me, and you will see we are bondmates."

"I will not present you." A deep, lustful groan laced with anger escaped my lips as I fought hard through the wave emanating from the first bondmate union. The potent desire and the urge to mate had my cock aching in a way I'd never felt before. I breathed through the moment, desperate to calm the feeling as I watched the next couple ascend the steps to present themselves.

Melysah's hand came to my chest, her determined gaze searching mine. "This is us."

I brushed her hands off. "This is *not* us," I hissed through clenched teeth. "There will never be an "us," Melysah. I'm Asherah's mate. Hers and hers alone. Why can't you get that through your head?" I leaned down to her eye level. "I want you to hear me loud and clear. What you and I had? It was a tryst while in the throws of Guake'te—something every Atlantian enjoys during the ceremonies. Nothing more. I'll never present myself to the Bohiti with you. I've never wanted or felt called to present myself to the Bohiti with you. I. Do. Not. Want. You."

And then I saw it: the realization that broke through her lustful haze, her face flushing as my jaw clenched tightly. Her eyes shifted beyond me, her head dipping in a single nod.

The small pinch between my shoulder blades, coupled with the next wave that crested from the temple, brought me unwillingly to my knees. When Melysah casually strolled forward, almost to the beat of the tribal drums echoing against the temple walls, my eyes widened in a deep sense of panic. The realization that something was very, very wrong outweighed the power of the ritual. I struggled to move, but my limbs wouldn't listen. Darkness had fallen over the park; festival goers passed right by without paying any attention—their need to feel and fuck overriding everything else. I could do nothing when Melysah bent down softly placing her lips against mine. Her fingers threaded through my hair at the nape of my neck and tugged painfully, forcing me to meet her fiery gaze. "If I cannot have you, Asherah never will."

"What have you done?" I managed to croak.

The evil smile that spread across her pale face sent a shiver down my immobile spine. "I did what I must."

A meaty palm holding a white linen cloth came into my line of sight, covering my mouth and nose—the pungent and sweet scent overwhelming. I fought for consciousness, fought to catch anyone's attention, but it was hopeless with the power from the ceremony affecting everyone around me. I could do nothing but watch Melysah's retreating form before everything faded to black.

# Chapter 42

THE POUNDING AT MY TEMPLES WAS THE FIRST unwelcome feeling that stirred me from unconsciousness. The second feeling caused my eyelids to fly open; the painfully strong, deep sense of desire I needed to immediately satisfy. The craving to answer the call humming in my chest grew with the distant beat of a tribal drum. It coursed through my body, imploring me to find my bondmate. It superseded the ability to identify my surroundings, the bed that was both familiar and somehow not. I wondered why my arms were spread over my head and why my legs matched them, pulling my limbs spread eagle toward the bottom of the bed. As I tried to rise, my question was answered.

I glanced up and found large iron shackles around my wrists—thick chains tied taut to the bedframe jingling as I attempted to move. The overwhelming panic brought bile to my throat, but as a wave of something so potent and indescribable settled over the room and brought a moan to my lips, it faded away. A new desire to relieve the growing ache between my legs emerged. I gripped the iron chains as the feeling assaulted me, my back arcing of its own accord.

"My goddess, you're simply intoxicating when heightened with pleasure," a familiar male voice said from the dark corner of the room. "It's making it impossible not to stroke my dick right now, Asherah."

My eyes snapped open, the panic growing anew through the wave of lust enveloping the room. I wasn't prepared for who emerged from the shadows while I lay completely helpless and chained to a bed.

Kane Ruema.

*Fuck.*

"Of course, my mistress wouldn't be pleased if I smelled of you when I returned to her," he said as he casually strolled to the bedside.

My breath came in quick succession as I felt the telltale signs of my release building from the energy surrounding me. The ache was unbearable. And when Kane's fingers skimmed the scales of my legs, I was mortified by the moan that escaped my lips unbidden, mortified that my ceremonial garments now lay on the floor beside the bed.

I watched as Kane bit on his lip. "Look at you. So incredibly horny. I bet if I took these chains off right now, you'd ride it. Wouldn't you?" His hand traveled higher up on my thigh; the feelings of lust, shame, and terror fought for dominance within me. But it was lust that had me arcing into his touch. I gripped my iron chains tighter, trying to fight against the sensation and how good it felt.

"I won't, of course. The mistress' directions were very clear. You're to stay here till someone finds you tomorrow morning." Another wave from the ceremony crested through the room. Kane grabbed the noticeable bulge between his legs, stroking himself over his scales. "Fuck. Even with this potion, I can sense it." He laughed. "I can't even imagine what you must be feeling right now."

"Fuck off."

"Oh, I plan to." Kane's hand snapped out and cupped my center, and it took every ounce of remaining will to keep my scales firmly in place. "But I'm saving myself for my Queen." A deep sense of mortification outweighed all other feelings warring within me. "Don't worry, Princess. I'm not talking about you. I'm talking about the true Queen of Atlantis. My true mate." The meat of his palm pressed against the scales above my throbbing nub, and the level of shame was overwhelming when I moved my hips to meet him. The tears began to well in my eyes with the effort to stop my traitorous body. "You fucking sick asshole!" I voiced ahead of a moan I couldn't control.

"That's it, little Princess. I'm taking what is Draevyn's while he's taking what is mine. Seems only fair, doesn't it?" Another wave came, and I finally broke. The chains warmed under my palms as I thrashed against them, but my attempts to avoid pumping against his hand were of no use. The constant waves of pleasure from the ritual had me in complete submission. "My goddess. You are divine when you come. No wonder Draevyn is hooked."

"I hope he fucking kills you," I hissed through clenched teeth.

"I'll be too locked behind the brig if he tries to come for me. That's where I'll be when I confess to your kidnapping and tell them it was my idea and mine alone." Kane shrugged. "We must do what we can to ensure the proper Queen is on the throne." His hand slowly moved up my torso, cupping my breast, the scales holding him back from pinching what he wanted. "Certain sacrifices must be made." He sighed like he wasn't blatantly violating me.

To my utter penitence, another release began to build behind the last. A knowing grin spread across his face. "It's infuriating, isn't it? I'm afraid it won't stop until the morning." He released my breast, and the guilt from the longing I felt for his touch hit me hard. "I'm saving myself for my Queen, though. So, I need to be careful, or else my own willpower will snap." The bed dipped with his weight, his mouth coming mere inches from mine. "And I'm so fucking close to snapping," he breathed against my lips. I had enough presence of mind to turn my head, my tears falling to the pillow. But that proved to be a bad idea when his tongue coasted up my neck. I squirmed in both pleasure and shame. "Mmm, if your neck tastes this intoxicating, there's no telling what you taste like between those beautiful legs of yours."

"Stop," I rasped.

"Stop?" he murmured against my skin. "But your body isn't telling me to stop, is it?"

"Just stop! Please!"

"Well, since you asked so nicely." He sighed and pulled back, my body sagging in both relief and disappointment. "I guess I'll go and wipe the tears from my mistress's face. She's bound to have returned to her quarters by now. She'll be so distraught when Draevyn rejects her again," he sneered.

Another wave came through, and I moaned with the onslaught. "Rejects her?" I managed to ask.

"One way or another, my Queen is about to discover that Draevyn Eliron is not her bondmate as she has claimed for centuries. Either he agrees to present himself with her before the Bohiti to prove to her that he isn't her mate—as I have told her repeatedly—or he refuses, leaving me to pick up the pieces of her broken heart once again." He stared off in the corner of the room. "One of these days, she'll realize that her mate has been in front of her this whole time."

Melysah's mate wouldn't be in this realm much longer if I had anything to do with it, but I didn't think saying that while chained to the bed at his mercy was a good idea. "You think she's your bondmate?"

His head snapped to me. "I know she is." He rose from the bed and stood over me. "And I'll let you in on a little secret. I plan to be right at her side when she takes over Atlantis. It will be me who will be King, not Draevyn fucking Eliron." He placed clenched fists on the edge of the bed and leaned in closer. "So, again. I'll take the fall for kidnapping you both. My Queen will set me free when she takes the throne."

I froze. "Both?"

He rose with a smug expression on his face. "Did I not tell you the best part? How could I forget? Should Draevyn refuse her—which he will—we plan to remove him from the realm. Melysah's quite viscous when she doesn't get her way. Makes things so much hotter in the bedroom." He reached down and grabbed his crotch.

*Gross.*

"We'll take him somewhere no one can find him and leave him to die. So, the real loser in this? It's you. You're not sitting a single pretty little ass cheek on that throne. You're not getting your bondmate. And the real Queen will ascend. It's perfection."

Sheer panic coursed through my body but was immediately extinguished by another wave. "I'll kill you myself."

The bastard laughed.

He laughed.

"You can try." He tapped his finger to his chin. "But something tells me you won't be in this world long either." He casually stepped back, heading for the bedroom door. "Enjoy the rest of the evening, *Your Highness*. It may very well be the last bit of…pleasure…you feel for a long time."

He turned and left the room.

The sweat dripped slowly down my forehead onto the pillow, joining the endless tears that had fallen throughout the evening. A deep sense of hopelessness replaced the endless waves of pleasure that had died down, with the sky beginning to lighten outside. With the fog of lust lifting, I began to think of ways I could get out of these chains. From what I understood, iron rendered a Fae's power useless. But I wasn't just any Fae. I was the Hekiti. There had to be a way. I had to warn the others about Melysah and Kane's plans and Draevyn's kidnapping. I wouldn't stop until I found him. Of that, I was one thousand percent certain.

My gaze drifted to the chains above my head, my brow furrowing when something clicked in my head. Through the haze of the dramatic evening, I seemed to remember the chains heating in my grip at some point.

Did I…

I wrapped my hands around the chain and focused with all the strength I could muster, and felt the chains begin to warm.

Those chains would have to get a whole hell of a lot hotter than that.

I remembered how my air element emerged. It was a moment of panic. I thought I was going to die. And yet, it was Draevyn's life in danger now. My bondmate had been kidnapped. I paused when a deep sadness swept through me. Draevyn wasn't my bondmate, at least not officially. We'd have to wait another turn around the sun before we'd have a chance to present ourselves before the Bohiti again.

And didn't that just piss me off?

In fact, it pissed me off so much that the chains began burning bright orange. I channeled that single irritating fact through the palms of my hands and watched with utter satisfaction as the chains began to melt and drip onto the bed.

The bedding began to sizzle.

"Shit."

I summoned water to douse the tiny fire by my head. I'd need to work quickly, then. I let loose a determined groan and watched as one of the links finally broke free on my right, followed by the other. A pained cry escaped my lips as my arms dropped—the muscles in my shoulders burning like hellfire. Within minutes, my ankles were freed. I wrapped a palm around each shackle, melting them, and my eyes went wide when I realized that my scales below the shackle burned like fire.

Lit like a Fire Fae.

I didn't have time to ponder over that little fact as I did the same to the rest of the shackles, finally freeing myself from the nightmare I'd been thrust into the night before. With my limbs aching, I ran from the room toward my father's quarters, my feet pounding against the stone floor and my chest pumping for air as my muscles protested. When his door came into view, I wept with relief.

But when it opened and Reneah exited the dark room beyond the door—I stopped short, my mouth dropping to the floor in open shock. Her hair was slightly disheveled, and her very human red silk pajamas hung slightly askew beneath her floor-length cotton cardigan. When Reneah closed the door behind her and finally met my very confused gaze, her eyes went wide as she wrapped her cardigan tighter around her body.

We simply stared at each other.

Reneah was supposed to be safely away from the palace, away with the humans in the human quarters. She wasn't supposed to be anywhere near the palace until the morning, and the sun had just risen, which meant she'd been in Dad's room all night.

The sound of pounding footsteps coming from the stairwell broke our stare off, Dax and Myles emerging through the entryway, heaving for breath. They stopped short when they took in the scene before them.

"Oh shit," Dax and Myles exclaimed at the same time.

I pointed to Reneah. "I take it you all knew about this?"

Dad's bedroom swung open, his head peeking through the opening with blurry eyes. Those eyes whipped into saucers as he realized who was in the hallway. "Oh shit."

Myles and Dax exchanged a glance before Myles stepped forward. "I'm afraid explanations will have to wait. Draevyn has been kidnapped."

"We were both kidnapped. Separately."

Four sets of eyes swung in my direction, but it was Dad's furious gaze that held my attention. "Who did this?"

"Melysah and Kane."

My arms remained crossed as my gaze pinged between Reneah and Dad—the former looking anywhere but in my direction. Myles sat beside me in the deadly quiet living area, his foot tapping a mile a minute. And Dax chewed his nails in the corner of the room, monitoring everyone like we might implode. The ticking of the clock echoed across the room, heightening the anxiety taking residence in my body.

*Tick. Tick. Tick. Tick.*

I read a book like this once. You know…the one where one friend starts dating the other friend's father. In fact, I actually adored reading this trope. However, now that I was living it, my feelings about the trope had drastically changed. I made a mental note to avoid that particular section at Fae Flings. So many questions ran through my head.

So many.

But all of them would have to wait.

I cleared my throat. "Okay. We need to figure out where Draevyn is."

The entire room breathed a collective sigh of relief.

"Melysah claims she had nothing to do with the kidnapping," Dax informed. "She's already telling the council that Kane did this alone."

I could feel the heat rise to my face. "Lies. All of it." After the things that Kane said and did, I could hardly compose myself enough to say, "That motherfucker said he'd tell everyone it was his idea when he held me captive." I could still feel the ick of his touch against my skin. It's a much different memory without the effects of the ceremony encouraging me to let go of myself.

I felt…gross. Dirty even. I hated feeling that way. Hated still recalling his touch on my most intimate of places. I swallowed past the lump in my throat.

"Sher," Dad started, his gaze empathetic, "did he… are you—"

"I don't want to talk about it," I cut in, shaking my head. "I can't. Right now, I need to focus on rescuing my bondm…" I sighed, "Draevyn."

"He's still your bondmate, Asherah," Dax reassured me, his tone every bit the gentle giant that he is. "Just because you weren't formally bonded doesn't mean he's not. In fact, I'm willing to bet that the key to finding his location is within you. The call from the ceremony is so fresh, you'll likely be able to let the bond guide you."

I sat up straighter. "I can do that?"

"Of course," Myles confirmed. Dark circles blanketed the area under his eyes, a clear sign that Aurelio's night had gone as planned. "Why don't you take a few deep breaths and see if you can find the tether? Close your eyes."

My lids came down, and I inhaled deeply. I was met with nothing but darkness.

"Exhale," Myles guided me.

I let out a slow stream of air followed by a slow inhale.

"You may start to see a faint string of light coming from your chest," I heard Myles say. "Try and lock in on it and follow it to the end."

I steadied myself and let my body relax. As my breathing steadied, the rest of the room fell away, and I found the faint light floating before me—the bright, faint blue rope tethered to something—someone—in the distance. Carefully, I followed it to the end. My brow dipped in a furrow when the tether brought me into a dark cavern, the faint light of the moon streaming through an opening at the top. It was a moon I'd witnessed a million times before in the Above World. It cast its light on a male form, his head hanging forward as he hung from two iron chains embedded into the cavern ceiling. The beautiful face I'd kissed so tenderly now displayed deep, bloody gashes—the blood slowly trickling down his face. I gasped as my eyes flung wide open. "He's in the Above World. They have him captive in some sort of cavern." I leapt from my chair. "I'm going after him."

"We'll go with you," Dad said, rising from his chair.

"I'll find Aurelio," Reneah murmured.

I swiveled to her, her gaze cautious. On the one hand, I didn't enjoy the idea of…whatever was happening between them. On the other hand, Reneah was the first friend I'd made in Atlantis, and that meant something to me. "We'll talk when all of this is over, okay?"

A mixture of relief and hope sparked in Reneah's eyes. She gave me a solemn nod before I turned my attention to Dad, who was looking at us with equal caution.

My spine straightened. "I'd like to talk with you as well."

His Adam's apple bobbed on a swallow. "Of course, Sher."

I wheeled around and hurried out of the room and down the stairwell—Dax, Myles, and Dad trailing me. My mind was in a frenzy of panic. The image of Draevyn hanging in the cavern brought bile up from my stomach.

"We need to speak with Tibu," I said to the others as we strode across the palace bailey—the portcullis rising with our approach.

"Oh, right," Dax said as he kept pace beside me. "I'd forgotten how you can speak with sea creatures."

Our steps quickened when the mote came into view. "I'm sure you've seen my mother do that a million times."

"Actually, no," Dad countered, stopping me in my tracks. I turned to him, meeting the amused look on his face. "Your mother never had that ability."

"She didn't?"

"No. That's a Sher thing."

My brows furrowed. "Huh." I'd have to ponder over that one later. Without wasting another minute, I dove into the water, following the current to the open sea.

It didn't take long for Tibu to hear my call. He met me in the murky water lit only by faelight. I could feel his concern as he reached our group, circling slowly around us.

"*Asherah Delmar. You're in distress.*"

"*Hello, Tibu. We need your help.*"

"*Name it, and it is yours, my Queen.*"

The others kept their gazes glued to the massive shark. Dax swam a little closer to my side when Tibu swiveled in the opposite direction. "*My…mate was kidnapped before we were properly bonded. I don't know where he is exactly, but I can see a cavern through the bond.*"

"*Hmm, that's most alarming.*"

"*Do you know of any caverns in the Above World? Ones that may be close to Atlantis?*"

A pause. "*I can think of a few places, but it will take some time to search them all.*" A few smaller sharks arrived behind Tibu, and Dad froze beside me. I could feel Myles closing in at my back. "*These are my brethren. They'll assist you in finding your mate. With several places to search, I think it wise to split up so we can cover more area."*

*"Thank you, Tibu."*

*"You're welcome, my Queen. We are skilled at tracking. I'm confident we will find him. Perhaps, if the villains are still with your mate, you'd be kind enough to provide us with a… snack."*

The fuckers who kidnapped and tortured Draevyn getting torn apart by sharks seemed like a small mercy, but it would have to do. *"You have yourself a deal, shark."*

I relayed every word Tibu had spoken to Dad, Dax, and Myles. I'd search the waters with Tibu. Dax and Myles would pair up with part of Tibu's brethren while Dad would search with the other half. We set out on our way.

Seven caverns. We'd searched seven caverns so far, and I was beginning to lose hope. The bond was starting to fade with the passing day. The sun's rays coasted across the ocean's surface like a drape of light floating in the wind. Draevyn had been hanging from those iron chains for several hours now—several hours of him lost to me. I could only imagine the pain he must be feeling.

*"Do not worry, my Queen. There are only two more caverns left to search. We will find him,"* Tibu said confidently.

Tibu slowed as he approached a sea wall littered with plankton and algae. Strips of seaweed drifted across the surface as we entered the underwater cave—the darkness immediately enveloping us.

Suddenly, something within me lit like a beacon. *"I think he's here,"* I told Tibu.

*"Go. I will send the call to the others and stand guard in the water. You have my protection."*

My tail whipped through the water as the bond went from dim to bright. I swam past Tibu and followed the call till it brought me to a shallow pool, the sun's rays filtering through the opening at its center. My heart beat heavily in my chest as my fin peeled into scaled legs. I breached the surface.

And there hanging as he had been in my vision was my friend, my lover.

My mate.

Draevyn was scaled from the hips down, the 'v' at his lower abdomen visible. Even with the evident signs of exhaustion, he still looked like a fallen god.

And my fallen god wasn't alone.

Sitting at the bottom of the rock that Draevyn hung over was a Fae clad in brown trousers and a dirty tunic—picking his nails with a dagger, utterly unaware of my presence. Next to him was a Water Fae—casually leaning back on his arms as he stared at a spot on the cavern wall—the pure picture of boredom. His chest was bare and wholly exposed, like a threat didn't lurk anywhere near him.

I could hear the blood rushing to my head at the sight of them looking so casual as my mate hung near death just a few feet away. I channeled all the anger of the past twenty-four hours into a wave that formed beneath my feet, the water churning with an angry roar as it lifted me high in the air. I unleashed my trident, the two males jumping from the floor with staggered steps and wide eyes. I chanced a glance back at the shallow pool, witnessing the fin slinking lazily back and forth.

It was time to feed.

I returned my attention to the seething males as I said, "You dared to touch my mate," my voice echoing in the darkest tone I'd ever heard from my lips.

The Fire Fae male conjured fire in his palm. "Look what we have here. The wannabe Queen. It seems you've picked up some skills since last I saw you."

It hit me then who this male was: one of the Fire Fae from The Blue Fin, one who was responsible for my mother's death. My hand tightened around the stem of my trident.

An evil grin spread across his face. "Ah, you do remember. Good."

"Yes, it is good. Your death will be that much more satisfying."

He let loose a sinister laugh. "Little fishies can burn, Princess. Are you sure you want to play?"

I tilted my head and let him see the upper half of my scales burn like molten lava, let him see the trident in my hand—its light reflecting off the wave carrying me. The Fae froze, eyes wide, struggling to comprehend. "Are you sure *you* want to play?"

I didn't give him an opportunity to answer.

I leapt from the wave, landing before the Fire Fae while the Water Fae attempted to escape on the other side of the rock and into the water. I watched with sick satisfaction as he scrambled back when rows of gleaming white teeth breached the surface. It distracted me enough to miss the fireball hitting my chest. I glanced down at the scales that lit a little brighter than the others. My head snapped to the Fire Fae, who glared at my burning scales with his mouth hung open. I tilted my head. "Aw, you didn't think that would hurt me, did you?"

The Fire Fae dropped into a fighting stance, baring his teeth as he said, "I may be just one Akani, but you can't defeat us all. Our Queen will rise!"

"The fuck she will." My trident whirled through the air, the stem catching the male in the side—a grunt resounding before he wheeled around with his blade, the tip nicking my throat. Blood dripped from the cut and sizzled as it touched my fiery scales.

"You're nothing but a faeling with a glowing, golden toy," he spat.

I dipped into my fighting stance. "Well, you're about to meet your end from the tip of my toy, asshole."

With a loud roar, he lunged forward with his dagger above his head, my trident clanking against it as it came down on me. I pushed it away and jabbed his nose with my stem. I relished in his cries of pain as he gripped his nose, the blood seeping through his dirty fingers.

Taking advantage of his moment of pain, I wheeled around and whacked his head with my trident. Before he hit the ground, I impaled him in the stomach with the tip—the blood squirting from the opening.

But I'd barely had a moment to revel in his pained and anguish scream. The foolish Water Fae wrapped an arm around my neck from behind, cutting off my air supply. "You will never be my Queen," he breathed into my ear. My trident dropped to the floor as I wrestled against his grip. As I struggled for air, the Fire Fae crawled across the rock, reaching for my trident. His hand scratched across the bare rock as I dispelled it—a curse of defeat and pain leaving his lips. When stars began blanketing my vision, I clawed at the Water Fae's arm. My gaze shifted to Draevyn, and the sight of my mate hanging from those chains a few feet away gave me everything I needed to rally through. I reached back for his face, sending all my fire magic to my palms—the sickening smell of burning flesh invading my nostrils on a deep inhale as he released his hold. His wail echoed loudly against the jagged cavern walls, and Draevyn's drooping head lifted slightly.

He was *alive*.

I summoned my trident and whirled around as I lunged forward and pierced the scales at the Water Fae's thigh. He fell back on the rock, the blisters already forming on his panicked face. Before he could register his last moments on this earth, I raised my trident in the air and slammed it down, piercing his chest. He wailed in pain as I dislodged my trident. His cries were cut off when I lodged the tips into his throat. I ignored the gurgling; I ignored the sick snap of his neck as I twisted my trident. I ignored the blood splattering on my scales as I cut his head loose.

But you'd best believe I paused and watched as his head sailed through the air with a swat of my trident, landing firmly in the jaws of the awaiting shark. That, I couldn't ignore.

Draevyn's wail of pain sounded behind me, dragging my attention. The Fire Fae gritted his teeth as he sent tiny fireballs into Draevyn's bare back. He stabbed that nasty dagger into Draevyn's lower back. I ran at full speed, shooting ice daggers into each of his eyes with perfect precision. I'd like to think the years of playing darts at The Blue Fin helped with that particular skill.

With one final stab of my trident through the male's heart, his body gave a final jerk before going limp. I conjured air, lifting his body on a frenzied whirlwind. "Game over, dickhead." His body dropped into the water with a deafening splash, the rest of Tibu's brethren tearing his body apart. I watched with a satisfied grin. What did that say about me? I didn't really care.

"*Nanichi.*"

I wheeled around to Draevyn, his head giving a slight bob. "Draevyn!"

My muscles burned as I climbed to the top of the rock, my nails digging as I reached him. Flakes of blood trickled to the ground below as I gently cupped his face. "My love. Wake up. Please." I kissed him softly on the lips—the salt from my tears mingled with the coppery tang of his blood.

A pained groan left his lips as he lifted his head an inch. The swollen, narrow slits of his eyes landed on me. "*Nanichi,*" he croaked. "*Nanichi.*"

The tears flowed like the Shingu down my cheeks. "I'm here. I'm here."

Water splashed behind me, drawing my attention. "Sher!" Dad called. The others had arrived, their eyes wide as they beheld Draevyn's state as he hung limply.

I returned my attention to his iron chains and followed its path to the cavern ceiling. I gave the chain a sharp tug, testing the strength of it. My biceps protested in pain, and I finally relented, holding back a sob.

"No. Use." Draevyn murmured. "Tried that."

Right. Because that would be the first thing he would do. I understood what must be done. I knew it meant exposing what I was to Dad, Dax, and Myles, who stood a few feet behind me.

But Draevyn was worth the risk.

I brought my hands to the chain at his left arm, carefully avoiding his scales or skin. "I'm going to get you out, but you have to remain very still." I thought I heard him chuckle.

"Sher, what are you doing?" Dad asked.

I didn't turn when I answered him. "Trust me." I channeled all my anger into a single link in the chain. I thought of Melysah touching what was mine. I forced myself to think of Kane taking what wasn't his. I thought of the Akani who'd tried to abduct my mate. I thought about waiting another year to complete the bond with my lover.

Mine.

My teeth gritted with the force of the power that flew to my palm and lit in a low glow. The metal began to drip on the rocky ground. When a few accidentally dropped on his hand, my heart skipped as he hissed in pain. "I'm so sorry. So sorry, love."

"Goddess divine. Is she doing what I think she's doing?" I heard Dax ask.

"Yes, Dax. I believe she is," Dad replied.

Despite how heavily I concentrated, I didn't miss the point of pride in his voice. Finally, the link gave way. Draevyn bellowed in pain as I caught the brunt of his weight under his arm. "Hold on, Drae."

I glanced over at Dax, Cathan, and Myles, their faces arrested in shock.

"Can…uh…one of you hold him up? Please?"

Dax snapped out of his trance and rushed up the rock, taking my place under Draevyn's arm. I immediately got to work on the other chain, gripping another link in my palm. My mouth fell open. The shades of my scales were completely different—burnt orange mingled with a lighter shade of peach. With no time to think about that particular change, I began funneling the last remnants of my power into the chain link.

A few more drops landed on Draevyn, his grunts of pain muffled by Dax's shoulder. "It's okay, Drae. You got this, brother. Be strong. She's nearly there," I heard Dax encourage.

"I can't believe what I'm seeing," Myles exclaimed.

After what seemed like an eternity, the link finally broke, and Draevyn grunted as his knees hit the ground. Dax stepped back as I knelt in front of Draevyn, cradling his head matted with dry blood on my shoulder. "You're free. You're free." I gently swept his hair off his face.

"I'm so…sorry. Should…have been…there," he wheezed.

I brought my warm palms to cup his bruised cheeks

and kissed him softly—his chapped lips gritting against my smooth ones. "There's nothing you could've done differently. And none of this shit is your fault."

His eyes began to droop. "So tired."

"It will be my honor to carry him to Atlantis, Princess," Dax said from behind me.

I twisted around and jerked back. Dax, Myles, and Dad knelt on a knee at the shoreline with their heads bowed. "What are you all doing?"

Dad lifted his head, the tears spilling from his eyes as he uttered one single word.

"Hekiti."

# Chapter 43

A few days had passed since Draevyn's rescue, yet he remained in a deep sleep in the infirmary. There was little I could do; the healer kept reminding me, but I refused to return to my quarters. I just couldn't. Not with the memory of what happened coming to mind every time I walked in the door. Despite the tension between us, I'd sent a note asking Reneah to move my things to different quarters. Hopefully, the change would help the nightmares plaguing my dreams. In the meantime, I remained by Draevyn's bedside, sleeping in the comfy recliner whenever possible.

A soft padding of footsteps sounded from the hallway. When Reneah popped into the doorway, a deep sense of apprehension grew. She held up my note. "I got your letter." Her gaze drifted to Draevyn. "How's he doing?"

I felt the tension across my brow as I turned and observed my mate. "He's woken up a couple of times. The healer thinks it's better if he's unconscious for a bit longer to give his body more time to heal." I winced, turning my attention back to Reneah. "Apparently, those assholes gave him a potion to slow his healing."

Reneah shook her head. "Fucking Akani. They're a completely blasphemous group of beings. I hope they find the rest of them."

I sighed. "Me too."

Reneah smoothed out her dress shirt. "I…uh…primarily came to ask if you wanted your things moved to the Queen's quarters? We…your father, I mean. He's relocated as well. Wanted a new start."

Well, that was news. I cleared my throat. "Um. No, don't do that. The people might see it as presumptuous. I'll move into the Queen's quarters when officially crowned."

Reneah nodded. "Okay. Right. That makes sense. Smart."

An uncomfortable silence grew between us. I fidgeted with my fingers in my lap. "Is there another reason you came?"

Reneah blew out a breath. "Yes." She pointed to the chair just next to mine. "May I?"

I nodded, knowing I would dread the next few minutes.

Reneah slid into the chair and pivoted her body toward me; her dirty blonde hair shifted with her movement. "So, I need to speak with you about Cathan."

"You mean *my father?* That Cathan?" I tried and failed to keep the bite out of my tone.

"Yes," Reneah murmured, glancing down at her lap. "I know you're angry with me."

"With the both of you, actually." When Dad stopped by the infirmary to check on Draevyn, he tried to breach the subject of his relationship with Reneah, but I immediately stopped that attempt. I just wasn't ready to go there with him.

But with Reneah, who'd been my closest friend before this debacle? Yes, I would have that convo. Reneah was still my friend despite the drama.

And I wanted to know...

"How did this happen?"

Reneah shook her head. When she lifted her brown-eyed gaze to mine, tears gathered in her eyes. "I didn't mean for it to happen. Truly. I just..." Reneah huffed out a breath. "You know how deeply I cared for your mother, yes?"

"I do."

"Well, she was very dear to me, and losing her has been so hard. I'd been working by her side since I was a teenager. The honor was so tremendous. The position has been held by one of my family members for centuries. Neleah and Cathan treated us like family. And after her passing, I felt it was my duty to not only serve you, my new Queen, but also to look after Cathan. He needed someone to talk to, someone who understood the pressures he was under while trying to navigate the challenges of your return to Atlantis. It hasn't been easy for him."

"I know it hasn't." I hadn't meant to sound defensive, but he was my father, after all.

Reneah grimaced. "Of course you do. I didn't mean to imply that you didn't." She blew out another breath. "Anyway, since Neleah's passing, we just began to lean on each other, and a friendship formed." Reneah's shoulders lifted. "And then something...more formed. I don't know how to explain it, but I just found myself checking in on him more or finding excuses to be in his quarters. We would talk until long into the evening, long after my duty called for."

"And then Cathan began summoning me more. We just…flowed. We understood each other's grief over Neleah." She blew out a long breath. "I know better than to fall for a Fae, let alone the King. It's expressly forbidden for any of the palace staff to have any type of relationship with the royal family. Even my friendship with you has been questioned, but he insisted that I was something more to not only you but to…him. We decided to move forward with…whatever this is…in secret." She shook her head. "Nothing good can come of relationships between a Fae and a human—let alone a Fae who's my friend's father. But when I received Cathan's letter asking me to join him at the palace for Guake'te, something came over me. I'd blame it on the energy of the ritual, but I had already made my decision before the ceremony started." Her eyes held mine, imploring me to understand. "I did try to resist for all those reasons. Of that, I can assure you."

So, Dad sent her a letter. Interesting. I tucked that away for later. I appraised her. "So, this wasn't happening when my mother was alive?"

Reneah jerked back. "Oh, my goddess. Of course not, Asherah. How could you think that?"

"It's just so close to her passing. It's been less than a year."

"Yes, but…you have to know I'd never do anything like that. I would hope by now you'd know me well enough to know that that's not who I am."

I let loose a sigh. "Sorry. Yes. You're right. I didn't mean to imply anything was going on before my mother had passed. I just…" I paused, trying to find the words. "I'd never expected my father to be with anyone else. I've always known him to be my mother's."

"Yes, I know. And I'm honestly not the person to talk to you about why he chose to act on his feelings for me. That's a conversation best suited for both of you, one I encourage you to have. He's desperate to talk to you."

Guilt immediately consumed me, and my shoulders sagged. "I know. This situation with Draevyn has been…overwhelming."

"I don't mean to overwhelm you further. I just wanted to speak to my friend," Reneah said, the warmth radiating from her smile.

I couldn't help but return it. I reached across the armrests and grabbed her hand. "We'll be okay." I watched as Reneah's shoulders dropped. "It may take some time to…adjust. And please reserve the freaky conversations about my father for Aurelio. I don't want to hear it."

Reneah laughed through the tears. "You got it, Your Highness." She stood from her chair and held out her arms, beaming. "May I have a hug?"

I couldn't deny her. I rose and wrapped Reneah's small form in a fierce hug. When she pulled back, the corners of her mouth dropped as she wiped away her tears. "Whenever you're ready to talk about what happened in your quarters—"

I shook my head fiercely. "I can't," I said as my throat closed.

Reneah placed her hand on my arm and gripped it gently. "It's okay. We don't have to go there. Just know I'm here if you need someone to talk to." Reneah dropped her hand on an exhale. "Well, I'm off. I'll take care of everything. We'll have you moved into your new quarters by nightfall."

"Thank you."

She turned for the exit with a relieved smile. "If you need me, you know how to find me," Reneah called over her shoulder.

"In my father's quarters?" I called after her.

"Ouch," I heard Reneah say from beyond the door.

"Why in the realms would Reneah be in your father's quarters?" I heard Draevyn rasp. I wheeled around, his eyes barely open but fuming. "And what the fuck happened in your quarters during Guake'te?"

It had been a long afternoon, one that tested my patience. On the one hand, I wanted to tell Draevyn every detail. On the other, I knew that the infirmary was not the place for that discussion. So, I pulled the Princess card and demanded that they move him to my new quarters where we could both be comfortable. I felt terrible pulling rank to make it happen, but there was no one in the world I could talk to except Draevyn, no one I felt more at ease with as I became my most vulnerable.

One of the greatest lessons I learned from my parents growing up is to always be honest with each other. Dad told me long ago that the key to a lasting relationship was to have open and honest conversations and to never keep secrets from your partner. *'That's the sign of a strong relationship,'* I could hear him say in my mind.

But as I watched Draevyn soak in the details of what occurred in my bedroom the evening of Guake'te, I wasn't so sure that advice was solid. His eyelids no longer drooped with exhaustion. They had gone wide midway through my story. The good news? Color had returned to his face, which had been ashen since the tragedy.

The bad news?

His face was burning red. "I'll fucking kill him."

"I did tell him you would, which is why he told me that he'd confess to everything so he'd be safely in the brig."

"I'll tear up the fucking brig," Draevyn seethed.

"You won't."

"I most definitely will."

"Let me rephrase that. You can't."

Draevyn pulled himself up on the bed, wincing from the strain of doing so. "And why can't I?"

My knuckles turned white. Everything in me wanted Draevyn to march over there and pound Kane's face in until he no longer breathed, but I knew how delicate everything was in Atlantis. I had many enemies, and because the goddess called me to be her Hekiti, I would need Draevyn. There'd be swift penalization if he took Kane's life. I swallowed the lump forming in my throat. "You can't because I need you," I whispered.

"And you have me," he protested.

"Not if you're held accountable for Kane's death. There are laws we must follow."

Draevyn's expression grew stormy. "Fuck the laws, Asherah. He violated you. Am I to understand you want me to sit by and let that asshole get away with it?"

I bit my lip to hold back the sob threatening to emerge.

"*Nanichi*, what is it? Whatever it is that you're thinking or feeling, I want to know."

I shook my head, unable to form words.

Draevyn patted the side of the bed. "Come here. Please."

I rose from my seat on unsteady feet and perched

on the side of the bed. Pure, unfiltered terror began to spread as all the revelations from the evening of Guake'te began to form on the tip of my tongue. Draevyn's hand snuck into mine, and I squeezed my eyes shut.

*Would he still want me after this?*

"I…" my body began to shake as I sobbed, "I am so ashamed."

The warmth and safety of his strong arms, still weak and healing, wrapped around me as Draevyn pulled me into his lap and rocked me gently. "You have nothing to be ashamed of."

"But I…didn't…stop him. My traitorous fucking body *wanted* him," I shouted through my tears. "It's so vile! I wanted to feel. I wanted him to do everything that he did to me. And I'm ashamed because I couldn't control it."

Draevyn leaned back and placed my head between his palms. "Listen to me. What you felt during Guake'te? That has nothing to do with him, Asherah. Nothing," he seethed through gritted teeth, his thumbs wiping away the waterfall of tears flowing down my cheeks. "That has to do with *us*. It has to do with our call to one another and the call of so many other bondmates who participated in the ceremony that evening. It's a feeling born of love. He distorted that feeling, made it something it wasn't supposed to be. He held you chained. This is not on you. That is on him. Do not let him rob you of the love born during the ceremony. Do not let him win."

"But how can…how can you still want me?" I questioned before sobbing yet again.

"*Nanichi*. How could I *not* want you? He doesn't get to take what I feel for you away. To hell with that." He brought his mouth to mine, kissing me fiercely—the salty taste of my tears pressing into my mouth as he swirled his tongue with mine. He broke our kiss, breathing against my lips. His eyes held so much love and awe I didn't feel worthy of. "You are my mate, Asherah. I don't need a ceremony to tell me that. And when you find your mate, you stick by them, even when something terrible happens. You stand by their side to remind them daily of how special they are and how much you love them. And I do love you. I've never loved anyone this intensely in all my life. And no one is taking me away from you. Not some fucked up weak male who takes what isn't his, not some delusional entitled female who doesn't deserve to breathe the same air as you do. You are mine. I am yours. Nothing is going to change that."

As I brought my palm to his face, his stubble roughly brushed against my skin. "Make love to me, Draevyn."

His entire body stilled. "I'm…I'm not sure that's a good idea."

"Please, Draevyn," I whimpered through a low sob.

He brushed the hair back from my face. "Asherah, you've been through something most females need lots of time to process. It's okay to take that time. We don't need to rush it."

"I don't want to take that time. What I need is you. Please. I want *your* touch. I need to feel *you*. Us."

Draevyn's gaze searched mine for any lingering signs that I might not want to do this before his head dipped in a solemn nod.

"I love you, Draevyn," I whispered against his lips.

And then there were no more words. There was only feeling, reverent touches that spoke a language only lovers knew. Draevyn pressed me down on top of him—my legs straddling his hips. His growing erection rubbed against my core, spiking my need. I wanted to feel him in my mind and in my soul. I wanted to erase the disgust that hung heavy on me from the foul memories of Guake'te. I wanted to feel what I should've felt that night with my mate.

His strong hand coasted up and down my back as we explored each other with lazy, sensual kisses. Draevyn grabbed my backside, and I gasped with pleasure as his cock pushed against the scales at my aching center. "You're in control here, *nanichi*. Tell me what you need."

I couldn't think past the heightened pleasure as I rocked my hips against his hardening length. "I want…I want to replace the memory of it."

As if sensing my needs, he gripped my ass tighter—encouraging me to move against him. I closed my eyes as I began rocking faster, my need building. An image of Kane above me flashed in my mind, and I grimaced.

"Open your eyes, Asherah." My eyelids flew open on his demand. "Look at me. I'm the one you're using to bring yourself pleasure. Take me." I leaned forward and placed my hands on the firm dips of his chest to anchor myself to him—my eyes fixed on his heated gaze. "That's it. Take your pleasure. Feel who it is beneath you." I bit my lip to stifle the moan that his words caused. The muscles began to tighten in my core as I succumbed to my release—my eyes remaining on my mate as my nerve endings fired.

"Who does your body belong to, my Queen?" he asked as his hips slowly rolled against my clit, extending my desire.

"It's yours."

Draevyn gripped my hips hard, stilling me. "Wrong." He lifted his back off the bed, bringing his face within inches of mine. "Your heart and soul are mine just as my heart and soul are yours, but your body doesn't belong to anyone. It's no one's right to take it." His words stole my breath as my gaze drifted from one eye to the other. "Your body belongs to you and you alone. Who you choose to share it with is a decision made by you and you alone. Your body is a divine gift meant to be cherished, a gift I promise to honor all the days of my eternal life." His hips rolled as he pressed me firmly to him. My head hung back in ecstasy as my need began building again. Draevyn took the opening, sucking the space between my shoulder and neck, shattering all the memories of my nightmare. It was his hair I was threading through my fingers. It was *his* warm tongue devouring my neck. "Will you gift yourself to me, *nanichi*? Will you let me give my body to you in return?" he murmured against my skin.

I instantly dropped my scales. "Yes, I…I need you to take me. Please."

All the pent-up passion and desire came crashing down with his kiss—all the anticipation of the ceremony that should have been ours to share. Scales gave way to skin as he bared himself to my wet, throbbing center. He reached between us, wasting no more time lining his tip to my entrance. His other hand threaded through the hair at the nape of my neck and pulled gently. "Eyes on me as you take my cock into you." I reveled in the stretch as I sunk onto his hard length, his mouth catching my moan as I began to move.

Draevyn lay back against the bed, content to watch me as I rode him, the need in his gaze growing in intensity. The slapping of my hips against his echoed against the walls. Draevyn's breaths became shorter as he looked up at me with pure love. I'd never tire of the way he looked at me. He took my tight nipples between his fingers—my breath catching as he rolled them. "Who rules your body?"

I thought about who had tried to take what was not his, and in my mind, I slammed the door to that nightmare shut. "I do," I breathed.

"That's right, my warrior Queen. Now, come for your mate." He pressed his thumb onto my swollen nub, rubbing circles till I could take no more. I shuddered around him as he thrust hard into me once, twice. "Fuck. Asherah," he called out as he came, his cock pulsing inside me.

With my breaths coming in quick succession, I collapsed on top of him, blissfully spent. I savored the feel of his damp skin against my breasts, knowing that this was my rightful place. No one would ever take that away from me.

Ever.

# CHAPTER 44

THE DAYS HAD PASSED BY IN A SLOW PROCES-
sion of visitors checking on both me and Draevyn.
News had arrived about Melysah's suspension
from the council until they could conduct a deeper
investigation regarding her involvement with the
kidnappings. That didn't stop me from doubting
whether something would finally stick to her.

With everyone I cared deeply about sitting in
the living room of my new quarters—quarters that
had been beautifully decorated in a different style
by Aurelio and Reneah—I had bigger things to
worry about.

"But...how?" asked Dax for the millionth time.

It was the question none of us had the answer
to.

"There's no reason for Asherah to enter the
realm," Myles asserted as he rested his chin in the

cradle of his palm. "With Airelandia? It's not a problem. Gaining access to that realm is a simple request to my counterparts, but Corenathia? Earthos? It's a much bigger challenge. There are only a handful of diplomatic missions that are acceptable."

"Such as?" Draevyn asked.

"Trade, pilgrimages, peaceful missionary," Myles answered.

"Well, the trade option is out for Corenathia," Dad stated defeatedly. "We haven't traded with them in a millennia."

"But could we possibly start?" I inquired. "That would give us reason to open negotiations."

"I'm afraid that's out of the question," Myles said, followed by a long sigh. "Queen Sessi isn't open to trade with Atlantis. Our goods are outlawed there. If anyone finds even one fruit from our outskirts, it's an automatic ten-year sentence."

I jerked back. "Seems excessive."

"Seems cruel, is what it is," Reneah said from where she sat beside Dad, a look of deep contemplation on her face. If Dax, Myles, and Dad knew about me being the Hekiti, then I refused to keep it from Reneah and Aurelio. I wanted their feedback just as much as the others. "For the sake of her people, I pray that they at least trade with Earthos. Otherwise, I'm not sure how they could sustain the realm with little to no soil to maintain crops. The garden elementals can only do so much."

The group murmured in collective agreement.

"What about a soiree?" Aurelio suggested with a gleam in his eyes. "Who doesn't love a good excuse to get dressed up and show off?" Aurelio ignored the hand of every male rising in the air—except Myles, of course. "It could be the party of this century. I can see it now," he said, his hand arcing through the air. "A night of burning passion and union."

"I don't know if passion will be the only thing burning if we lock ourselves in Corenathia with a bunch of Fire Fae who would want nothing more than to bring Atlantians to their knees," Dax said.

"It's a nice thought, my dear," Myles said encouragingly. "Perhaps a bit premature for the current state of affairs."

Aurelio's shoulders slumped in defeat as he sank back into his chair.

"You mentioned pilgrimage," Dad said, his arm draped around the back of the sofa he shared with Reneah—his posture incredibly at ease around her. We hadn't spoken. Not with everything that had happened. I still wasn't ready.

Myles winced, drawing me from my observations. "That's only if someone is escaping a realm and seeking refuge."

The group murmured in disappointment.

"And peaceful missionary?" Reneah asked with hope in her voice.

Myles glanced at her with empathy. "I'm afraid that is reserved for the priestesses. It's an effort to exchange information with the High Priestesses of their realm. It's more of a spiritual mission only for them."

"So, that's it then? There's no other way?" I asked.

Myles' gaze swung to Draevyn and back, his entire body tensing. "The only other way is through a marriage with one of the Princes of Corenathia, but seeing as how you are all but mated, I'm afraid it's not an option."

My mind flashed back to my time with Lux in the library.

*'Can't you just stay here?'*

*'Not unless you're willing to marry me.'*

My spine went straight as I gasped. All heads turned in my direction as a smile grew on my face. "I have an idea."

The bell above the door to Fae Flings Bookstore chimed as we entered—the rich scent of freshly brewed coffee entered my nostrils on an inhale. I glanced around the room, noting that the store was thankfully free of people, plus or minus a few in the front room. Those who perused the cowboy romances froze, gaping at us.

"So, this is the infamous Fae Flings," Dax said, observing the books on the shelves in passing.

I glanced at a few of the titles in passing, unable to help myself. "It is." My brow lifted as I smirked. "Perhaps you might find something to please the ladies within the pages of these books."

Dax huffed. "I know plenty to please the ladies, thank you very much."

I giggled as we reached the counter. Ezra's head lifted from her latest read, and her eyes flared. "Your Highness."

"Hey, Ezra." I pointed to the back room. "He there?"

Ezra's mouth morphed into a tight line, and I held up my palms. "I don't mean him any harm. And you're not in any trouble. We just need to speak with him."

Ezra's shoulders dipped as she flicked her head toward the back room. "He's there. Anything I can get you all while you're here?"

"Does that say *Spankuccino*?" Dad asked, the crease between his brows appearing.

"Those are my favorite," Reneah said. Her cheeks flamed when Dad smirked at her.

Nope. Still not used to it.

"Ezra, was it?" Dad asked.

Ezra dipped her head. "Yes, Your Highness."

"We'll take one Spankuccino."

"Coming right up."

I strolled to the back and parted the curtain covering the backroom entryway. I immediately sighed in relief. The chair across from Lux was blissfully empty. I padded across the room and sank into it. Lux's gaze snapped up from his book, a smile spreading on his face. "Asherah. Here for a little reading?"

A dark shadow blocked out the light, spreading across the table. Lux's smile fell as he took in Draevyn's imposing form standing beside the table—Dax, Dad, Myles, and Reneah standing just behind him. "Oh, shit."

"You're not in trouble," I said quickly, Lux's narrowed eyes fixing on me. "Promise."

He set his book on the table. "All right, then. To what do I owe this incredibly unique pleasure?"

"I need a favor."

His red eyebrow rose. "I'm listening."

"You want to stay here in Atlantis, don't you?"

"I think we've already established that it's impossible for me to stay here permanently."

"But if it were possible, you'd want to stay here, yes?"

"Of course, you know I'd do anything not to return under my mother's thumb."

"Marry me."

Lux's mouth dropped fully open.

The sound of china crashing to the floor by the doorway garnered our attention. Ezra's wide eyes were held on me and Lux. "Sorry. Didn't hear a damn thing.

Nothing. I'll…just…grab another Spunkuccino."

"Oh. It was a Spankuccino," Reneah corrected politely.

Ezra nodded. "Right, right. Spank, not spunk." She dashed from the room.

Lux nearly climbed out of his seat as he received Draevyn's piercing gaze. "You'd have me risk my life? Your bondmate will fucking kill me if I so much as graze a hair on your head." His gaze dropped to the area where my bondmark should've been; my scales fashioned low enough to reveal the markless skin. "You're not bonded."

A low growl came from Draevyn.

I speared him with a glare before returning my attention to Lux. "Not yet. It's an incredibly long story I don't have time to explain right now," I said. I let out a long sigh. "Marry me."

"Are you insane?"

I shook my head. "Not marry me for real."

He sank back down into his chair. "Well, thank the goddess for small miracles. Do you mind telling me what's going on?"

I blew out a breath. "I found out what my elemental mark means."

He smiled so brightly. "That's wonderful news." When I didn't speak, he fluttered his hand. "Well, don't keep me in suspense over here. What does it mean?"

"Perhaps it's better to show you." I held up my palm, calling a sphere of water into its center. Lux looked incredibly bored when I froze the sphere. I kept my eyes on him as my palm began to heat. A slow trickle of water fell to the table below as I melted the sphere—my entire hand burning as bright as molten lava.

Lux drew in a shaky gasp. "Holy shit. You're—"

The tip of Draevyn's trident appeared at Lux's neck. "Don't finish that sentence. Not in public."

He nodded. "Right. Sorry. It's just…" Draevyn lowered his trident, Lux's brow furrowing for a moment before the realization sunk in. "You'll need to get into Corenathia to get the Jujo."

"Correct."

"And you want to fake a marriage so that I can present you as my future wife before my mother," he stated as fact.

I smiled. "I knew you'd figure it out."

"But how in the realms will that help me stay in Atlantis?"

I wrinkled my nose. "That's the trickier part. Since I'm not bonded yet, it will be easier to convince your mother that we are, in fact, planning to be married. We'll return here as soon as we've found the Jujo." I spared Draevyn a glance. "Draevyn and I will attend the next bonding ceremony in secret. You and I will stay betrothed for as long as it takes to find the four objects. You'll be safe here."

"That's *if* you find the four objects. There's no guarantee that you will. That means there's no guarantee that I can stay. Or that I'll live if my mother finds out the truth."

I placed my forearms on the table, leaning in. "You said marrying me was the only way. I'm trying to help you here."

"I never said I *wasn't* going to do it," he said, his nostrils flaring on an exhale. "You're the…" he waved a hand around, "you know…almighty. I don't think I could face Atabey beyond the veil if I said no. Yet despite that, I want you to know that I'm not saying yes because of what you are to the realms." The corners of his mouth lifted. "I'm saying yes because you're my friend."

I jumped out of my seat with a squeal and wrapped my arms around my friend, squeezing him as he *oofed.* "Thank you, thank you, thank you."

Lux reluctantly returned my hug at first, no doubt sensing the tension coming from my bondmate. "Don't thank me yet."

I leaned away. "Why?"

His face turned serious. "The Jujo has only been recorded in our texts. No one has discovered it, not even my mother. We'll need to do our homework first; find out where it is."

"I can help with that," Myles chimed in. "I've been doing some preliminary research. My mate is gathering a few more texts as we speak."

Lux gave a wince. "While I appreciate it, I'm afraid your texts in Atlantis might not have what we need," he said defeatedly. "This may take a long time to find, perhaps even beyond the next Guake'te."

His veiled warning caused my heart to skip a beat.

Before I could spiral into panic, a firm hand landed on my shoulder. I turned, meeting the comforting gaze of my bondmate. "You'll do what you must, *nanichi.* This is for the realms. It's bigger than us. Besides," he pointed his trident at Lux, "it seems your betrothed over here is a bit of a brainiac. The two of you together may find the answers to the location in no time."

"Forgive me," Lux cut in, "I don't want to give anyone false hope. Just wanted to make sure you both understand what you're getting into."

"We do," I said. "And we can come up with a plan before we leave. I just wanted to make sure you were committed."

Lux dipped his head in a nod. "I'm on board. Let's

get married."

"Oh, count Atabey's blessings!" Ezra exclaimed from the doorway. Reneah grabbed the Spankuccino from Ezra before she dropped yet another drink. Ezra suddenly noticed everyone's eyes on her with a brutal warning. She made a zip across her lips. "This is a safe space. I know nothing. I see nothing." She looked between Lux and me with a wink.

Well, at least someone was elated.

"We'll need to present this information before the council. They gather in an hour," Dad advised.

Instant dread grew in the pit of my stomach. "Will Melysah be present?"

"She's been banned from the council until further notice," Myles said, the dread easing. "You don't have to worry about running into her."

"Then, let's not waste any more time," said Draevyn. "I want Asherah in and out of Corenathia as quickly as possible. The sooner we can retrieve the Jujo, the better."

"I sincerely hope it'll be quick," Lux said, his tone heavy with warning. "My mother doesn't like to be deceived. If she finds out about this, it will be really, really bad. And there won't be anyone there to protect her. Corenathia would freeze over before she'd let an Atlantian Guardian into the realm." His gaze traveled around the room. "As long as you all are prepared to take the risk, I'll do everything in my power to help."

"I don't have a choice," I said, rising from my chair. "The goddess marked me for a reason."

Lux nodded in understanding, but it was the realization that Draevyn wouldn't be by my side that stirred my helplessness as we fled Fae Flings.

My heel tapped repeatedly against the stone floor of the council chambers. Dad reached under the table, steadying my leg with a raised brow. I cleared my throat, dispelling the frog that had lodged itself there. After this, there'd be no turning back. Roarvyn sat across from me, the perfect epitome of boredom, with his elbow propped on the armrest and his chin in the bed of his palm. "You gonna tell us what this is about, Princess? Or do we have to guess?"

I opened my mouth to speak, but the sudden crash of the chamber doors slamming into the walls had everyone's attention. Every muscle in my body went rigid. Melysah raced into the room, stomping her way to the top of the council table. She slammed the tome she'd anchored in the crook of her arm on the table. Leaning forward on her arms, she glared at each and every member before fixing her gaze on me, her anger palpable. "You cannot ban me from the council."

Dad returned her glare. "I believe attempted kidnapping—"

"Alleged kidnapping!"

"—disqualified you from the council whether you like it or not," he finished.

She leaned in further. "You. Can. Not. Ban. Me. From. The. Council." Reaching for the bookmark squeezed between the pages of the tome, she flipped open the book and read aloud. "The second in line to the throne must be present for every council meeting called. For the sake of Atlantis, she must stay informed of all information and bylaws that govern the realm in the event that she is called to rule."

"Well, maybe when you organized our abduction, you should've remembered the bylaw that states that kidnapping is a crime," I quipped.

"Alleged," Melysah said between gritted teeth.

I glanced at Roarvyn. "Is this true?"

Roarvyn let out a breath. "I'm afraid so. Banning her was a long shot. It was only a matter of time—"

"Before I figured out how to take my rightful place?" Melysah said with a scathing smile.

Roarvyn rolled his eyes in dramatic fashion. "Then would you please take your rightful place and sit your ass in your seat? This session is nearly done, and Princess Asherah has an announcement to make."

Melysah plopped down in her seat, giving me her undivided, furious attention. "By all means, Princess," she said, flourishing her hand. "The floor is yours."

I shifted my attention to the rest of the council, Shaegana nodding in encouragement.

"Lux Zarlonia Nacan has asked for my hand in marriage."

An audible gasp sounded across the room.

"No. No. No." Roarvyn murmured, muffling his protests with his hand.

I cleared my throat. "I believe this union is best for the peace of the realms. I've accepted his offer."

"That's such a lovely sacrifice," Shaegana said. Her gaze drifted over my shoulder to Draevyn, who stood behind me against the wall. "To do this for the good of the realms."

"It's entirely unheard of," said another council member at the other end of the table. "A true sacrifice for the good of the people."

"Excellent." The cheery tone of Melysah's voice

drew my gaze to her. I'd never seen her smile so wide. "Is that it then? No other news to report?"

I arched an eyebrow. "No?"

"Wonderful. This council meeting is adjourned." Melysah's chair scraped against the floor as she leapt from her chair in a hurry for the door. All the council members slowly trickled out in her wake.

All but Roarvyn.

He sat in his chair, pinching the bridge of his nose.

"Are you going to tell us why you're silently freaking out over there?" Dad asked. Myles and Draevyn came to stand behind us, looking equally perplexed.

Roarvyn dropped his hand, glaring at us all like children. "Do you have any idea what you just did?"

"Agreed to marry the Fire Fae Prince?" I ventured.

Roarvyn scoffed. "You agreed to do a whole hell of a lot more than that, Princess. You all but handed the throne to her. You're supposed to take your examinations to formally be named Queen." Roarvyn's gaze cut into my soul, and panic sliced through me. "You just withdrew your right to the throne of Atlantis."

TO BE CONTINUED...

Want to read the post-throne room attack "Draevyn's Distraction" *spicy* scene from Asherah's perspective? Scan the QR code to sign up for my newsletter and receive your FREE bonus scene!

Looking for more from the world of Atlantis?
Reneah and Cathan's novella
Coming November 2024

Jump into the world of this Pirates of the Caribbean-inspired steamy historical romance that many argue is not a myth but a legend.

# The Legend of Gasparilla

# Author's Note

Thank you for reading The Veiled Heir and letting me share this world with you. While the Florida Keys doesn't have the best surf spots in Florida, I took some artistic liberties when creating Asherah's "surf spot." So, if you really want to take up surfing, visit Cocoa Beach or New Smyrna Beach.

Many of the terms used in The Veiled Heir come from the Taínos, the indigenous culture of many islands in the Caribbean. However, I took artistic liberties when creating this book, so while similar, there might be slight differences to the actual Taíno terminology.

Despite the devastating impact of Spanish colonization, the spirit of the Taíno people and their language has not been extinguished. Their descendants, through sheer determination and resilience, have managed to keep their language and stories alive, a testament to the strength of their culture.

Whether we are direct descendants of the survivors or those who caused the genocide, we all share a responsibility. It is our duty to illuminate the remaining aspects of the Taíno community and to support the organizations that champion their cause. By incorporating their culture and language into my stories, I hope to contribute to this effort. It's high time the Taíno community receives the recognition and support they deserve.

To learn more about the Taíno culture and their spoken language or to find out how you can help, please scan the QR code below:

The Modern Taíno Dictionary       Higuayagua: Taíno of the Caribbean

# Acknowledgments

This book would not be possible without the support of my husband, Brian. Being my mate isn't easy, but the goddess stuck you with me, and you're doing a great job! I'm grateful to have you by my side as we venture into this new world together.

To Brittany and Megan, you are the most fantastic duo. You enthusiastically help me through all of my creative thoughts and bookish ideas. I couldn't have asked for more incredible friends, and I consider myself fortunate to have you in my life. You're my secret sauce! To my alpha reader, Katie. Thank you so much for the incredible feedback. It meant so much to me. To Kelsey, thank you for jumping in and organizing my ARC & Street Teams. To Hayley, thank you for taking the baton and shining!

To all my friends and family who continue to support me, it means so much to me. Thank you for your encouragement.

To my editor, Ramona, thank you for your insight and attention to detail. Your skills are spot on, and I'm truly grateful to you. To Joan and the Krafigs Design team, thank you for your patience while working on the cover design. I'm super excited to share the other designs with the world.

To all my fabulous readers, thank you so much for all the love and support. I literally couldn't do this without you.

# ABOUT THE AUTHOR

S.T. Fernandez (a.k.a. Stephanie) is a Latinx author originally from Orlando, Florida. She lives in the beautiful small beach town of Ventura, California, with her husband and two wiener dogs. Stephanie graduated with a Bachelor's in English Literature from Saint Leo University outside Tampa, Florida.

An avid reader of all things romance, Stephanie mostly reads books in the fantasy and paranormal romance genres. She enjoys creating stories that readers can disappear into just as much as she enjoys disappearing into a good book. When she's not writing or marketing like a mad woman, she's likely out on her patio soaking up the California sun with a book in one hand and a nice glass of red wine in the other.

Instagram: @stfernandezwrites
TikTok: @stfernandezwrites
X: @stfernandez

www.ingramcontent.com/pod-product-compliance
Lightning Source LLC
Chambersburg PA
CBHW032059310726
48972CB00001B/25